MW00942685

Alex Sapegin

THE DRAGON INSIDE

Book four

Crown of Horns

Translated by Elizabeth Kulikov
Cover design by Marat Gabdrkhmanov

ISBN: 9781980565765

Litworld, 2018

A brief note from Alex:

The adventure is almost over so please enjoy.

Contents:

Part 1. Dashed Hopes.

Russia. N-ville. One day after Andy's disappearance...

A caustic blue-gray cigarette smoke, intermingling in its white turbidity with the smell of coffee, hung in several layers in the air of the small room. A tall young man with short spiky light hair and intelligent eyes on his strong-willed face pulled the second to last cigarette from the almost empty pack. The gas lighter sparked. The smoker sucked till his lungs were full and blew a thick stream of smoke out at the ceiling. The gray layers, hanging in a multi-tiered cloud over the floor, started to move, their whirls and twirls creating strange, fantastical shadows on the wall. The image on the screen changed and made the thin computer monitor, its coolers buzzing, give off a pale green glow. The man's face, bathed in green through the smoke, became sharper and took on a predatory character.

The man took another drag and forcibly extinguished the half-smoked cigarette on the edge of the overflowing ashtray.

"Enough. I gotta drink some coffee." The wheels of his chair squeaked. He pushed his legs against the floor and rolled over to a second table where an expensive coffee machine proudly stood. As a result of his clumsy movements, a thick folder fell off the desk which had previously been lying there peacefully. Photos spattered to the floor from under a layer of sheets of paper, squeezed together by a plastic cover.

"Butterfingers...."

Pressing the button on the device, which smelled of coffee grinds, he stood up in an easy, fluid motion and picked up the rectangular color photographs that had flown all over the room.

"Mother Nature never stops amazing me with her imagination," the young man said, looking at the boy in a photo.

"A chip off the old block of that brainless muscleman. Go figure. It's so very… very…."

"Very what?" a short, stout elderly man silently appeared in the doorway. He was strikingly different from the young man in the room. He had dark, combed-back hair, touched with gray at the temples, and a high forehead. His round face and belly, bulging under a light shirt and tight belt, witnessed to the fact that he wasn't a fan of athletics. What he had in common with the guy in the room was his smart, persistent, penetrating gaze, poise, not characteristic of your average Joe, and plasticity of movements.

The dark-haired guest noticed the photograph. "Stop smoking like a chimney! You could cut this fog with a knife. You can die from carbon monoxide poisoning, you know!" He said, coughing from the fumes, and tapped at the keyboard of one of the dozens of breakers installed on the wall near the door. The smoke started flowing towards one of the vents. "That's better, let's air it out. Now, where was I?"

"It's all there. I'm rereading it. I can't get it into my head…."

"Break it into little pieces so it'll fit between your ears, and then all of a sudden you'll get it."

The young man smiled at his old colleague's tirade:

"When I was a kid, I read so many books about parallel worlds, it's incomprehensible! I never thought I'd have to deal with it in real life."

"Get used to it. In our work, even without parallel worlds, there are surprises out the wazoo. Sometimes it happens. Something so out-of-nowhere and unexpected, it knocks you off your feet. Want to know something?"

"Yeah."

"You're being removed from observation."

"What!?" The young man's surprise level was off the charts. "Um, m-m-major!"

The "m-m-major," fully enjoying the effect of his announcement, walked over to a small couch in the corner, sat down and crossed his legs.

"No whining!" The major looked at his employee, assessing him. He clicked his tongue and shook his head, as if thinking whether or not to say something, but the command's orders aren't open for discussion. "Calm down. You're going to be heading a separate group. Osadchuk's people are going to be working under you. You've got two days to take over. Don't let me down, senior."

"Are they organizing just one group?"

"No, idiot, I just said you'd be heading a SEPARATE group. Osadchuk will be heading the command operations center."

The young officer snickered.

"Is command launching the 'Shadow'?"

Standing up, the major walked to the exit, stopped just before the door, and turned around:

"Command has sanctioned the first phase of operation 'Squid,' but within the framework of the 'Shadow,' get ready for some counter-intelligence." And, seeing the young man's uncomprehending expression, he added: "the counterintelligence guys are more experienced at weeding out 'frenemies' abroad, along with their Russian henchmen. Ah, if only we could attract the old guys from OBKhSS[1]. They'd untangle Bratulev's economic ties...."

Russia. Moscow. Eight and a half months later.

"One more time?" Yaroslav Kopilov, an old schoolmate of Kerimov's, waited for a nod and stretched his hand towards the Dictaphone. Obeying the slight touch to the sensor button, the device came to life. A child's voice resonated from the speaker, saying something in a sing-songy foreign language.

Yaroslav Kopilov, like his friend, went into science after finishing high school. He chose the social science of linguistics. Both he and his heavyweight wrestling champion friend were drawn to English, but Yaroslav, unlike Kerimov, who loved physics best of all the subjects, decided to dedicate his life to the study of languages. No one was surprised that Kopilov moved to Moscow, where the prestigious Bauman University Faculty of Linguists opened its doors wide before him. The other scholar got into Moscow State University (Russia's equivalent of Harvard), and at that, the two friends' paths diverged for over twenty years.

As it turned out, the knowledge of an all-around Indo-European scholar allowed him to earn more than just bread and butter: a little caviar on top, too. The main thing was to know where and how to push and then use the knowledge you've earned of several languages. Kopilov was a very smart man, successfully uniting commercial exploits with academics. In twenty years, he had traveled almost the entire Earth as part of his scientific studies and manufacturing and commercial activities. Suffice it to say, he'd done well. His life was a success. Yaroslav was still single, but a personable, charismatic man, who toiled for two hours in the gym daily, was not deprived of feminine attention. Truth be told, schools of the arts were always populated by more female students than male. Indeed, in reality a handsome man, wealthy in every sense, attracted ladies.

When the phone rang late at night in his bachelor pad, it was a real surprise. The person on the other end of the line was someone he did not at all expect to hear from. There was no small talk. Kerimov took the bull by the horns from the very first moment. He could do that–take it by the horns or, if needs be, smack it in the face. In school, he was a "nerd" who slackers and hooligans didn't dare talk to.

"I've got something going on," he said over the phone after a brief greeting. "Yary," Kerimov remembered his school nickname. "I need your help. A consultation."

"Hm," Kopilov coughed, dumbfounded by the pressure. "I guess I'm free tomorrow. Come on over, we'll sit down, have a chat and a consultation...."

"I don't have time. Tomorrow I fly out. I want to meet with you today." Yaroslav looked at the clock. *Damn, what poor timing, Masha was supposed to come over in half an hour....*

"Iliya," Yaroslav began carefully.

"Your girlfriend can wait," his former school friend interrupted him rudely. "I'm standing near the entrance. Come on, open the door, please. The intercom doesn't work."

Yaroslav swore and went to the entryway.

"Fourth floor, apartment seventeen," he said into the microphone, pressing the button.

"I know."

"Of course you do," the linguist thought, "if you've managed to find my number and butt in at the most inopportune time."

In twenty-something years, Iliya hadn't changed a bit. He was just as big and noisy. The spacious apartment seemed to shrink as soon as he stepped inside. The friends hugged briefly. Yary invited his old friend into the living room.

"So what brings you here?" the host asked when they had each consumed a glass of cognac. The guests took a digital Dictaphone from his inner jacket pocket.

"I need your opinion as a linguistic expert," he said and pushed the button. Three minutes later, Yaroslav had completely forgotten about his date....

The woman who showed up pushed the button on the intercom in vain and tried to reach her date by phone. He didn't hear his phone, which he'd left in the entryway. The door of the entryway was awarded a loogey, and the "old goat" earned more than one curse....

Listening to the recording once more, the linguist rubbed his nose.

"If you were trying to surprise me, it worked. I can guess what it is you're going to ask. Yes, it is a language, but it's not a member of any linguistic group I know of, although the syntax, structure, and pronunciation are closest to English. What the girl's saying in the recording isn't gibberish. There are a clear system and structure to the utterance. As an old phoneticist, I can say I heard about a dozen consonant sounds and at least five vowels sounds, both of which follow established patterns. Can you leave me the recording? I'd like to dig in a little deeper, see what some specialists I know have to say about it."

Kerimov scoffed: "I can offer you a job—you and your specialists. But be aware that you'd take total and complete responsibility for anyone you bring in to the project. And I mean—" He ran his finger across his throat.

"Oh! Wow, top secret, huh?"

"Strictly, but it's worth it. You'll be compensated accordingly.

You'll have your work cut out for you."

"I get the feeling you're trying to get me to defect to your side!" Yaroslav laughed out loud and then choked on his laughter when he saw the serious look on Iliya's face.

"I'm not trying to seduce you, for God's sake! Hard work, good pay. But I warn you, if you decide not to work under me, you can't divulge one word or even a hint of what you've heard here tonight. I'm not mixed up in any spy games, believe me, but I can get my hide tanned for sharing secret information."

"That bad?"

"Yes, Yary, that bad. Think about it, reflect, meditate. You can make a list of crazy linguists who are prepared to sell out their own mothers for the sake of new knowledge, and send it to me." Iliya Evgenevich slapped his knees, scooped the Dictaphone up off the coffee table and stood up. "Well, I've probably worn out my welcome! Time to get a move on."

"How can I get in touch with you?"

"My number should be on your phone from when I called."

The host patted his pockets.

"Aw, damn...," swearing, he ran to the entryway.

A few seconds later, the guest heard the kind of foul language that can only be realized by the Great Russian Language. His schoolmate was right to become a linguist! His specialized education gave him real pearls of expressions.

"What, old dog, lady problems?" Iliya Evgenevich teased the Casanova.

"Haha," he said sardonically.

"Bye-bye," Iliya shook his friend's hand.

"You take care of yourself."

Yaroslav, through the window, watched the massive figure of his uninvited guest walk away until he went through an arc and out of sight. His phone suddenly began to rattle on the table.

"Yes?" Kopilov barked into the phone.

"Good evening, Yaroslav Anatolevich. You can speak a little more quietly; I'm not deaf." The man called by his first name and patronymic experienced astonishment coupled with fear. It was the voice of an acquaintance from "the Company.[2]" *May he be three times cursed; can't forget about him, even over two decades later! Oh, Iliya! Not mixed up in spy games, you say? I'm having some*

sort of premonition that my problems are just beginning....
"Yaroslav Anatolevich," the voice went on.

"Yes?"

"We heartily recommend accepting your schoolmate's offer."

"I'll think about it...."

"No thinking necessary. Please take our recommendations with the utmost gravity."

He hung up. Kopilov looked at the blank screen for a minute. His opponent's phone number was not there. Wasn't that just like the sins of his youth, to come back and haunt him. The phone crashed into the couch in one sound fling. A part flew off and dolefully clanked against the leg of the coffee table.

The linguist again employed some choice words....

* * *

Leaving his friend's house, Iliya got a taxi. He called to the driver:

"The hotel 'Izmailovo.'"

"Fifteen hundred roubles," the taxi driver said, his gold tooth sparkling.

"Are you crazy? It's not far from here!"

"I won't do it for less than a grand. If you don't like it, walk to the metro."

"Drive." Kerimov got into the car, bracing from the cold.

"So, a language unknown to science," Kerimov thought, situating himself on the back seat. *So many surprises. How could Olga know an unknown language? Well, if we toss logic out the window, there's only the theory that her knowledge is somehow coming from Andy. Some sort of mystics. On the other hand, who knows. We've been shown there's magic there, more than once. Maybe a magical connection has somehow come about between the two of them? They are brother and sister, after all. I can't think of any other way to explain the changes that have taken place in our Olga.*

11

The changes that had taken place in their younger daughter scared Iliya Evgenevich and Elena Petrovna out of their minds. It wasn't just that over the last few months she had gone from a happy, carefree child to an exact copy of her older brother after he'd been struck by lightning. The color of her eyes, the iris and the white, had begun to change. In the last two months, an abundance of bright yellow dots had appeared around the pupils. The whites had become light blue. In order to hide the changes, he went to an optics store with his daughter and obtained small contact lenses of a light green color and sunglasses. Olga often did not want to wear the contacts, but she never forgot to wear the children's sunglasses.

After the New Year's vacations were over, Olga began frequently talking in her sleep. It would have been one thing if it were in Russian. But it was in an unknown, as Kerimov was now finding out, completely unheard of tongue. The next morning, his daughter did not remember a thing, or at least that's what she said. It was possible.

The pair made a striking impression: a girl and a huge canine. Bon followed his mistress everywhere. Again, some sort of mystical connection came about between the child and the dog. Bon obeyed Olga, even if she didn't say a word. There were no commands such as "sit," "down," or "come." She used gestures or looks instead. As soon as Olga looked at a corner, the dog would occupy the spot. While waiting for his mistress after her classes, a slight movement of the girl's hand, and Bon was off to fetch her knapsack, grabbing the strap by the teeth. The children were jealous. The teachers whispered that she was a witch. And Olga didn't stop being an excellent student and making the grade. Her report card was full of "A's," but just one look at the girl was enough to tell that she was not of this world.

A remarkable incident occurred on February 23rd. This is a Russian holiday dedicated to the Defenders of the Fatherland. It is also unofficially known as "men's day," where women often give small gifts to their husbands, boyfriends, fathers, sons, and male co-workers. The Kerimovs had decided to celebrate the day by eating out in a restaurant. In honor of the holiday, Iliya Evgenevich allowed Irina, whose line of suitors was so long, Iliya had stopped counting after the first ten, to bring her new young man along to the lunch. It was a nice time. Even Olga was constantly smiling, but no one was quite sure exactly why. It was either the general atmosphere at the restaurant, or the funny scenes being acted out on a stage by the invited actors. An elderly gypsy woman approached Elena as they were leaving. Her husband was busy helping Olga get her coat and hat on. What it was that made her go outside, she couldn't say.

"Want me to tell your fortune, my pretty one? I'll tell the whole truth!" the black-eyed woman said. Elena Petrovna stood, frozen to the spot like a rabbit in front of a boa. The dark eyes' gaze seemed to fix her in place.

"Would you like me to tell your fortune?" a child's voice said from behind the old woman. The gypsy spun around and locked eyes with the light-haired girl. Olga removed her sunglasses, which she previously always wore while outside, and smiled. Her smile looked predatory, foreboding to the old lady. She made the sign of the cross several times and started running in the other direction, shouting something in her language. Olga put her glasses back on.

"That lady's aura was yucky, sprinkled with blackness," she said. Iliya and his wife glanced at one another. They never heard another word out of her about auras and such, but the incident was firmly fixed in their memories.

After that day in the restaurant, Mr. Kerimov began regularly recording Olga's night time babbling on the Dictaphone. If it were possible to solve the problem of energy consumption to maintain a portal, the recordings could later be useful in deciphering the language of the world where Andy was transported.

How was he? The regular searches they conducted through the apparatus, although short, were not yielding any results, but the head of the institute was one hundred percent sure his son was alive, and he wasn't just relying on his own feelings or blind hope. He was believing in what his child told him. Once when he and the wife were yelling at each other for the nth time (unfortunately, fights had become a common occurrence in their home. You'd think Andy's disappearance would bring them together—they shared the grief, after all! But no, their relationship had taken a bad turn), Olga walked in. The spouses fell silent. The girl stood in the doorway for a few minutes, casting a strict glare at her parents.

"Andy wouldn't like this, your fighting," she said after the pause. "He's having a hard time as it is, and here you are, going at it!"

"How do you know how Andy's doing?" Elena asked cautiously. She was aware of her husband's latest research.

"I feel it," she answered curtly and went to her room. Bon's claws clanked on the floor as he followed her.

Elena Petrovna collapsed into a chair and began to sob.

"Iliya, I can't go on like this...."

And he could? What about him? Did his wife think he was made of steel? As if there wasn't enough turmoil around him at work! An incomprehensible carousel was constantly spinning around the institute. Bratulev, who promised to send a new security service boss and show up himself, had yet to fulfill any of his promises. It was good that the finances kept flowing. It would have been a sin to complain. The golden rain shower showed no signs of stopping. But all attempts to contact the oligarch failed. He had to get by on his own and wind up his employees, which did not provide any spiritual consolation. Screw work, but on top of that, Lena was constantly deriding him... what was with her? What was she hoping to accomplish? She can't go on? As if he were having an easy time? When did he ever keep any pills with him? Now they were in his pocket at all times. His heart seemed to have been acting up lately....

Work, his wife, his daughter, Andy, and again his daughter, more specifically, the younger one. Mr. Kerimov thought long and hard before letting anyone hear his recordings. But, once he got to Moscow, he decided to find, since he had the opportunity, his school friend. Once he had finished his business about the institute's problems, he got on the Internet. Experience had shown that you could find anyone but God himself on the web. And yes, googling his name yielded a multitude of links, three of which related to the object in question. Two of those listed his friend's place of work. After that, it was just a question of applying his knowledge. Champagne and a big box of chocolates.... Yary was a ladies' man then; he still was.

In his words, Kopilov indirectly confirmed the idea about a connection between Andy and Olga. If only he could think of how to take advantage of this connection while he was in charge of the institute and could use their administrative resources.

Taking his Personal Digital Assistant out of his pocket, Iliya began to sketch a diagram and the configuration of the apparatus. The driver, busy keeping his eyes on the road, did not interfere with his passenger. There was something incomplete about the diagram Iliya's young colleagues had presented. For over two months now, Kerimov, who was used to and adept at seeing the big picture, couldn't for the life of him isolate the "speck" interfering with his perception and complete the configuration. The colleagues were doing something unnecessary. To the quiet hum of "Retro FM," the outlines of yet another vector diagram materialized on the screen.

Setting the PDA aside, Iliya put his head back against the high, firm headrest and observed the dank spring drizzle hitting the car's roof and windows.

Andy, baby, you've really set quite a task before me. Iliya Evgenevich's gaze slid across the little computer's screen, which had gone dark to save energy. *It would be nice if we could bring back the past, but it's too bad, that's not possible. Hold on....* It seemed the pocket computer was jumping into its owner's hands of its own accord. *Why are we using the opposite vector direction for time in our calculations? The vector of direction, essentially, can go in the opposite direction from ours. How can we keep track? There's the snag, there's the mistake. Time can't be negative! The calculations and counting should not be conducted from negative values, but from positive ones.*

Somewhere on the edge of his consciousness flickered the taxi driver's foul language as he cursed the people who'd gotten into a crash and caused the traffic jam. Abandoning the world around him, Kerimov drew diagrams interspersed with formulas.

It was a tumultuous night, full of feverish frenzy and no rest. Iliya used up all the minutes on his phone and twice went downstairs to the lobby to add funds. Not being able to sleep, he didn't allow the others to, either. His new ideas needed to be sent to the personnel post-haste. Awoken from his sound sleep, Alex asked for an explanation and swore at his boss for not taking his computer with him. The PDA flatly refused to email the diagrams outlined by the Kerimov.

Russia. N-ville.

The minutes before the Boeing 777 airplane landed in his home airport seemed to go on forever. As soon as the plane's landing gear touched the ground, Kerimov turned on his cell. He found a charging station and discovered a whole series of text messages and missed calls. Interrupting the stream of messages as they came through one by one with little chimes, his wife's face lit up the phone's screen.

"Yes, honey."

"Iliya, where are you?" His wife sounded like she was panicking. Something serious had happened.

"I just flew in. Still on the plane."

"Iliya," she sobbed through the phone. He could hear Bon whining. "Come right home."

"What happened?"

"There's something wrong with Olga!"

* * *

"Seventeen New Bauman Street!" Kerimov cried, jumping into the first taxi and swatting a hundred dollar bill at the driver. "Step on it!"

"Are you gonna talk to the cops?" the taxi driver asked phlegmatically.

"Screw the cops!" He took two hundred more dollars from his wallet. "Go!"

"Money talks," the driver chimed and slammed on the gas.

The car took off.

"Iliya!" His wife, her face stained with tears, grabbed him by the arm and pulled him to the kids' room. Bon, whining, jumped to his feet.

Olga was laying on the floor in the fetal pose, ...glowing with a ghostly light. She looked like a bioluminescent mushroom at night. The room smelled distinctly like ozone. Kerimov senior's hair stood on end. An electrical discharge ran between the arch of his glasses and his right temple.

"OH, my!" he exhaled and darted out of the room. "Lena, bring the wire from the pantry. We'll try grounding Olga to the heating system."

"No need," Olga stretched her legs out. "No need," their daughter repeated quietly, getting up onto her knees. "It's all over. I'll just sleep a little."

The girl leaned to one side. In one leap, Kerimov was beside her and picked his daughter up in his arms:

"Honey, what's happened to you?"

"The guy said it's all..."

"What guy?"

"I don't know. He said Andy didn't mean to do this. He's still learning. I didn't understand all of it."

"Honey, what guy did you talk to?"

"I don't know, he was here," Olga, not opening her eyes, touched her head. "He said that Kerr shouldn't be here.... I'm gonna sleep."

"Who's Kerr, Olga, baby, what's this Kerr you're talking about?"

"That's what the guy called Andy." Olga opened her eyes for a second. Iliya Evgenevich almost dropped his daughter from the ring of his arms. A chill ran down his spine like he'd never felt before. For a split second, he thought she had vertical pupils, like a cat's. No, he was seeing things. He set his daughter down in bed and covered her with the blanket.

His phone vibrated on his belt.

"Hello?" he answered, exhausted.

"Mr. Kerimov," Alex's cheerful voice grated his nerves

something awful. "Where have you disappeared to? We're all waiting for you."

"Go on without me," he said, tucking her in and patting Bon on the head.

"What about the apparatus?" Alex asked, discouraged.

"Do what you want. I can't be there. The apparatus' configuration is at your disposal." He hung up and set the phone down on the child's desk in the room.

"Iliya…,"

Kerimov turned towards his wife, who was standing in the doorway.

"Not today, Lena," he said, taking two steps towards the door and slamming it in her face. "Sleep, sweety," he said, sitting down on the floor and resting his back up against the bed. The large man, not used to retreating when fate dealt a blow, silently cried.

"Dad, I'm hungry."

"What?" Iliya rubbed his eyes. Had he fallen asleep? Yes, it was dark outside, and the little clock on the wall said 10:55.

"I'm hungry, Dad," Olga tugged at his collar.

"Yes, yes, one second. Do you want pelmeni?" he asked his daughter, moving his legs, which had fallen asleep along with him from the uncomfortable position.

"Yes please."

"Let's go see what's in the fridge."

"I don't want to walk." She jumped onto his back.

"Let's go, rider cowgirl."

Elena wasn't home. Perhaps it was for the best. She'd probably gone to her mother's while Iliya and Olga were sleeping. Where Irina was, God only knew. Iliya Evgenevich sat at the table and watched Olga gulp down her pelmeni, burning her lips on the hot noodles, practically not even chewing. She washed them down with orange juice.

"More, please," the baby girl said, finishing her first helping. She was feeling like a bottomless pit.

"Wow! You're not going to pop?"

The second helping was finished almost as quickly as the first. The small child had acquired a simply beastly appetite. Looking at his daughter, Kerimov couldn't get rid of one nagging thought.

"Honey, do you think you could tell me how Andy's doing?" He tested the waters.

Olga stopped eating and closed her eyes. Her father got another shiver running down his spine.

"He's alive."

"Honey, do you think you could help find him? Daddy's got a special searching apparatus at work...," he said, wading in deeper. Olga shrugged.

"You want to take me to work with you? Wow, awesome! I won't have to go to school on Monday. But how can I help look for Andy? I don't know."

"That's okay. Maybe we'll think of something as we go along."

The thought that had been tormenting him all yesterday evening and today had finally taken on substance and then action.

* * *

"Alex, are you sure you did the math right?"

"Definitely, Denis. I've told you a thousand times. I'm not an imbecile!"

"Alright, sorry, don't take it personally. You surprise me, Alex. You're like a little lamb. Do you really trust the boss that much? That oddball Paul Chuiko," (who was in the room working with them, a fourth member of the Bandar-log gang) "as soon as he saw the new calculations, we couldn't tear him away from the computer for half a day. Now we're building the blocks according to his diagram. He's a science freak, can't sit still, as it were. But you—you're a mathematician!"

Oleg Maksimov stepped out from behind the accumulator block:

"Stop mouthing off! Are you going to help us or what?" He poked his finger into the polarizer mounted on the cart. "Remember, in the transition chamber you'll have to figure things out for yourselves, and the small blocks will have to be carried on your own backs. I still have the point of focus to adjust."

"We're coming, we're coming," Denis said, waving his hand dismissively.

"Tell me, Bandar-log face," Alex said to Denis, pushing the heavy cart. "Before you started working at this shady establishment, had you ever heard of Heim's theory? What are you staring at me for? So you hadn't. But the boss enlightened me on that physicist." Remezov nodded. "Uh-huh. And did you know that Walter Dröscher and Jochem Häuser, who, like our unforgettable boss, paid attention to Burkhard Heim's theory,... their work is still at the theoretical research stage?"

"Yes, I know. You can work while you talk, you know." Denis responded, snapping the cable connectors.

"Yeah yeah. A lot of solid physicists are convinced that modern technology is not at all capable of giving off the tension in the field and creating other conditions necessary for a 'puncture' through space, that is, they can't give Heim's theory a practical application. All their efforts to attract the Z machine from the Americans' Sandia National Lab[3] have amounted to squat. Those Yankees won't let anyone near their machine without mucho dinero."

"Hey, banana-eater, what's the point?"

"The point is, you dipstick, that the boss began his work back in the eighties. He's piggy-backing off the work of our most esteemed colleague Heim. Get it? In the West, they're still scribbling on paper, and in Russia here, we are doing the test in the field, the roots of which were put down during Soviet times! And you and I are the ones doing them, not Joe Shmoe. I read Dröscher's work. It's about as far from Kerimov's as here to the moon. So, don't you touch my oddball. He's taking us straight to a Nobel Prize! But hey, who am I talking to? Mr. Nuclear, are you even listening to what I'm saying?"

"Alex, you're a mathematician, right?"

"With you, dunces, I've become a physicist whether I like it or not. I'm prepared to argue that the power consumption will decrease, and the system of double feeding the circuit will allow the 'window' to stay open for several hours. What do ya wanna bet?"

"Loser gets a noogie!"

"A noogie's not enough!" Oleg entered the conversation after rolling up another block. "Alex gets to give you a noogie every day all next week, and Paul and I get to slap you in the back of the head if it works. Why are we busting our balls here all weekend? Work should be fun."

"And what if Alex is wrong about the math?" the leader of the Bandar-logs didn't give up.

"Then you get to slap each of us on the back of the head," said Oleg.

"Strange math. You want to give me two slaps and one painful noogie every day, so that's three acts of violence against my person, but I only get to give you one each?" the main jungle resident said, plugging the second block into the power supply system.

"If you wanna back down, just say so," Alex, leaning over the framework that contained the control devices, egged his friend on.

"Alright you baboons, you're on!"

"Oleg and Paul, you're witnesses!"

Five hours later, their work on setting up the apparatus was finished. Paul Chuiko conducted the first adjustment of the installation.

"What the heck, let's go ahead and launch the blocks under pressure," Denis suggested, "and fire it up in different modes."

* * *

"How are things in the jungle? What can the great Bandar-log people tell me?" Kerimov asked the group of young men, who were sitting in the break room drinking coffee.

Alex, the genius with numbers and mind-boggling formulas, smiled mysteriously, adjusting his glasses. Oleg pretended not to have heard the question since he was busy examining the bits of tea at the bottom of his mug. He was the only one of the gang who didn't abuse coffee.

"Well?" Iliya looked gravely at Denis Remezov. "Or do you want me to dance Kaa's death dance? Come clean, you blockheads! What have you done!?"

"It's always the same," Denis said sadly. "I told you that a prophet's never accepted in his homeland, and no one will value you on merit. You could fall into an open manhole, and no one would notice. What, Paul, do you think our wild boss will give you a bonus for solving the problem of the accumulators consuming energy? Or you, Alex, will he give you some new glasses to help you keep pineapples and bananas straight? And what can I expect? I changed the apparatus' configuration, AGAIN, without permission. Who cares if we can now keep the 'window' to a certain interesting parallel world open in observation mode for an hour and a half, and open for transport for two minutes. That's neither here nor there. Our fate is to die in the stomach of an old boa with an unquenchable appetite...."

"How long?" the old "boa" asked in surprise.

"An hour and a half in observation mode. We thought of a new scheme and tried it out yesterday," Remezov clarified.

Kerimov stepped forward and awkwardly hugged Denis.

"Boss, I'm not one of those," he began.

"You can start shopping for new glasses for Alex. I'll shower you with pineapples and bananas!" Iliya Evgenevich slapped Paul on the back of the forehead as well and then quickly changed his tone. "I'll give you two days to finish off the scheme and get the apparatus in order. On Wednesday, he'll be here *in person!*" He pointed somewhere in the middle of the ceiling with his big finger that looked more like a sausage. "Don't embarrass me, guys."

"We won't!" Denis barked. The rest of them nodded enthusiastically in agreement with their "leader."

"In ten minutes, I'll be expecting you in the operator's room. Show me what rabbit you pulled out of the hat over the weekend." Mr. Kerimov said, and left the room, slamming the door behind him.

Three pairs of eyes stared at the main Bandar-log. Remezov, sighing gloomily, lowered his head. Slap-slap. His head flinched from two slaps from Oleg and Paul. Alex gave him a hearty noogie.

"God forbid I ever again make a bet with some crazy mathematicians," he whispered, rubbing his noggin.

"Dad, when are we going to look for Andy?" they all suddenly heard the girl's melodious voice coming from the operating room.

"Sweetheart, just wait a bit. The Ban... uh, scientists are finishing their lunch." The scientists stared at one another in stunned silence.

"Let's go," Paul Chuiko summed up their common thought. He couldn't wait to see the new arrival.

Russia. N-ville. Two days later...

Iliya Kerimov positioned himself near the turnstiles at the arrivals room. The A-330 flight he was expecting had landed some time ago, the passengers had deboarded, but the high-level guest was not among them. *Perhaps, our sky-high higher-ups decided to change plans last minute? But why wouldn't they have let me know? Or has Mr. Bratulev decided to come in his private jet? It's entirely possible; it's happened more than once.*

"Iliya Kerimov?" he heard a voice behind him. Kerimov turned around. His eyes met those of a tall, athletic man wearing a conservative business suit and shiny black shoes pointed at the toe. "Come with me. Mr. Bratulev is waiting for you in the car," he explained, and gestured to Iliya to follow him. "Don't worry about your car. A driver has already been instructed to pick it up and will be waiting for you on site."

Iliya Evgenevich glanced at the exit and noticed two more "aides." This made sense. The resident of the sky had planned out his visit beforehand and taken the necessary security measures, including seeing to the timely cover of his own butt. The new chief of security he'd been promised hadn't yet arrived. On the other hand, it was possible that the leadership had decided not to force things by inviting competitors and secret service officers to create an unhealthy fuss about one particular scientific "racket." Proceeding to the exit, Kerimov nodded to one of the "aides." He quietly gave an order into the microphone attached to his lapel. The other pair of "men in black" covered Kerimov from possible interference from the direction of the street.

"Hello, Mr. Bratulev. How was your flight?" Kerimov said politely once he was inside the boss' armored Land Cruiser. It was air-conditioned and chilly inside. The armored car emitted a small black cloud of pollution from its pipe and took off. Security vehicles drove ahead and behind them, making up a motorcade. In addition, several different, simpler types of cars left the parking lot along with them, which differed from other cars of the same brands in their fancy interiors.

"Hello," the "racket" owner answered and shook the scientist's hand. The oligarch had a strong handshake, very masculine. "Although it's still evening back there, but now I'm in Russia. Let's get down to business. Iliya, my time's too important for small talk. Please, for starters, give me the overview of what happened there, and we'll take a look at the details on site. What was it you wanted to tell me?" Mr. Bratulev asked. "You can speak freely. I trust my people."

Kerimov took his laptop out of his bag.

"It's simpler to show you and then answer questions." He removed a flat device from his computer used for destroying the hard drive, entered a long password and, pulling up an image on the screen, turned the monitor towards his guest Mr. Big Stuff.

"What is the meaning of this?" the oligarch asked, looking at landscapes depicting tropical scenes or sub-tropical islands. While he was still speaking, the image changed. Now the screen showed mountains overgrown with forests.

"It's a planet, actually a parallel world, to be more precise. It's located fifteen minutes from the Earth time axis of coordinates which we accepted as 'point zero.' The planet is a lot like Earth, except for the fact that there is no intelligent life on it."

"Well well." The guest drummed his fingers on the seat.

The director of the institute looked at his employer while a feverish thought process was going on in his head. There was something strange about Bratulev's behavior. Most certainly he was acting strange. Previously, the guest from highest heaven would be laid-back when he visited N-ville. Sometimes he was even too uninhibited, not shying away from patting one of the science guys on the back. In general, he liked playing the role of Santa Claus with his shiny bags of bonuses. It often occurred to Iliya that the oligarch was pretending to be a strict but fair parent or deity who didn't mind lowering himself to their level and listening to the needs of the simple mortals. Now he wasn't like that. Was it just that they were alone, and he did not see the need to throw dust in the eyes of the public or play any roles at all? A completely different man was sitting in front of Iliya Kerimov. He was deathly tired, weighed down by a mountain of problems, as downtrodden by life as Iliya himself.

Bratulev was nervous and did not try to hide it. There was no trace of his previous laid-back demeanor.

"I won't believe for a minute that you've limited yourselves to just one world," he broke the silence.

"I can't believe for a minute that they haven't reported to you about our discoveries," Kerimov responded. Bratulev coughed, but let the little impudence slide.

"They reported to me. A daily summary of the institute's progress was put on my desk, but don't you think, Iliya, that you're taking a few liberties through your professional position?"

"You mean in searching for my son?" the scientist's eyes flashed an icy glow from under his knit brows. "It was my searching that led me to all these worlds. If you're interested, we've clearly determined and recorded the coordinates of two dozen worlds. Half of them do not contain intelligent life. These worlds can bring you such fabulous profit, that the gold of Fort-Knox will seem a trifle."

The oligarch laughed a strained laugh:

"Iliya, why aren't you telling me that the day before yesterday your guys made a successful attempt to open a spatial portal to Kamchatka?"

"I wanted to surprise you."

"Naive soul." Bratulev handed Kerimov a thin black leather folder. "I have a surprise for you too. Read this."

The folder contained three A-4 sheets of paper with

typewritten text. Kerimov shot the oligarch a puzzled look.

"Read it, read."

"It turns out...," Iliya mumbled in shock after reading the last line. When it rains, it pours. Just what he'd been afraid of. Kerimov had long-since felt wary of this happening, but he decided to feign surprise and play a role. *Hm, I might make a nice career for myself in the theater.* His surprise seemed quite natural, and Bratulev didn't notice anything. Now it became clear why Mr. Big Stuff was not his usual child-like self.

"It turns out," Bratulev echoed sardonically. "Get ready for a change in leadership. You think 'Bratulev doesn't care about the institute?' After all, your institution is my offspring, too, and I did not at all like its being taken away from me!" The oligarch cracked his fist against the armrest with all his might. "Damn it, and there's nothing I can do about it, absolutely nothing! I was surrounded like a wolf, and they're preparing to sick all the dogs! What gold and wealth of Eldorado, Kerimov? What profits are you talking about if because of your little mickey-mouse outfit I might lose everything?"

"Why did you come to Russia? You could have sat there in the States and not give a crap?"

"To make a deal, Kerimov, to make a deal. My business is in Russia. Someone's obviously controlling the people and representatives of cunning government agencies that have taken my business into a hard turn, and that someone gives the impression of being fully competent. You read the papers. The institute is under a tight lid. They won't let me to the table, but they might let me lick up the crumbs that fall from it, which is nothing to sneeze at. Or maybe they won't. I don't understand why the KGB kooks haven't taken over yet?" The oligarch turned to the window and watched the scenery for a few minutes.

Iliya Evgenevich decided not to break the silence. *You're in for tough luck, Mr. Oligarch, but hope springs eternal, so go ahead and hope.... The government's not stupid. They won't let a sure-fire secret weapon of steel against the evil Americans out of their hands. And you haven't yet learned to lie, Konstantin Ivanovich. Something else brought you back to the homeland. The crumbs from the table are total rubbish. Now a certain Kerimov is of much more interest to the government, that unknown man, ...*

well, only known in narrow circles. I'm more important to them than Bratulev, who can be easily written off and no one will notice the loss. That's what you're here to negotiate. Anyone the Russian state perceives as a threat, it expels from the country, or worse. And with a secret like that, I don't think banishment is the mercy you can look forward to. The secret service has such a long reach.... And here I was thinking they'd take over on Monday already, but they didn't. The successful opening of the portal to Kamchatka was a death sentence to nuclear equation: rockets, planes, and other carriers of nuclear weapons can be thrown into the landfill....

People from "the Company" were probably already well aware that when you open a galaxy of other worlds, there are bound to be one or two that are high-tech and more advanced than old lady Earth by about a hundred years. Opening a "window" and the observation regime allow us to contact them and... to steal. Highly developed technologies in exchange for rare earth elements and natural elements dug up from the "empty" worlds. Who could refuse a deal like that? Moreover, you could have guessed it from the very beginning. The probability of what was happening now was determined by scientists two years ago. Yes, he reached his goal, but at what price? Andy! Kerimov turned away from the oligarch and looked out the window. *Andy, it would have been better if Olga hadn't found you.*

It seemed his hopes of getting his son back were not fated to be realized. He'd been fooling himself all these months. He'd dreamed of a family and a career, but now his ambitions had been sent down the toilet. His drop of vanity, which all creative people have to one extent or another, withered to the root. For almost nine months, he stubbornly pursued one goal. He kept going, deep in his soul knowing that he and his baby were being closely watched. He was never a fool, and he learned to read between the lines in his research career back in his youth as a college student. All these months, he'd been deceiving himself, cherishing the hope that if they could just get a little farther, just a little more—and Andy would be there. He hoped that it would be before the competent authorities took over the institution, but as to the fact that this would happen sooner or later, not a single sensible employee doubted. Too an ambiguous a discovery was made within its walls. Kerimov, with the methodicality of a heavy asphalt paver, paved ahead, hoping the oligarch's money would hold off the state for some time, but his billions were powerless before the thoughtful attack of the secret services. The secret operation generals struck at the most painful place for anybody with deep pockets—at the wallet! To be precise, the schemes of financial transactions and the dirtiest (they're the most profitable) earnings were uncovered. Three sheets of typewritten text did not reflect the above picture; however, conclusions could also be drawn on the basis of the dry numbers printed on the sheets. They'd grabbed the institute owner by the throat and slowly squeezed. He understood the smutty hint and decided to earn an indulgence. Billions of little green papers on one side of the scales, the notorious scientific center on the other. You don't have to be a seer to guess which of the two bowls will outweigh the other. *My God, how hard it is in my heart to find my son and then lose him again. Dashed hopes....*

Bratulev's voice sounded like thunder from a clear blue sky:

"Iliya, what were the experiments involving your daughter you conducted on Monday?"

There was a cloud click inside the car. The scientist-husband looked with surprise at the elbow rest he'd ripped out of its place on the seat. The "aide" sitting in front scoffed and cast a careful glance from the "violator" to the oligarch. Bratulev carefully took the now useless car part from the director of the institute and set it on the floor.

"You don't have to answer that."

"I was looking for Andy," Iliya wheezed.

"And you found him, I know."

Kerimov threw the black folder onto the floor:

"...And, it seems, I lost him again...," he looked at the sheets of paper protruding from the folder. "The government security agencies probably won't allow me to conduct any personal matters there now...."

Bratulev wanted to ask the scientist one more provocative question regarding his youngest daughter, but, seeing his reaction to the last one, decided against it.

Iliya Evgenevich once again turned to the window. His nerves together with the stress of the last few days would probably give him a heart attack. Olga said not to worry. But how could he not worry if there were terrible things happening in that awful magical world? Kerimov clenched his fists till his knuckles turned white. He wasn't expecting to see Andy like *that*, no one was. Except, perhaps, Olga…

Russia. N-ville. Two days previously…

"Let's go." Paul Chuiko, practically jumping up and down from impatience, booked it out of the cafeteria. The door clapped shut behind him, muffling the sound of his friends' loud laughter. "Those jerks," he said into the emptiness.

"Dad, why do you have such a big TV here?"

"It's the main screen."

"Like what astronauts have?"

"Yes, Olga, that's right."

"Cool!"

The boss' head popped out from behind the server shelves. Chuiko plopped himself into the chair of the second operator's workstation. As soon as his butt had squished the leather seat, Olga, running ahead of her father, ran into the operator's portion of the room.

She looks just like her older sister! It's too bad I can't see her eyes behind those children's sunglasses. Paul involuntarily swallowed and looked back at the guys leaving the cafeteria: *the scoundrels.* The evenings were filled with innumerable quips and comebacks. Raising one eyebrow, Denis stopped halfway there and stared at the boss' daughter and Chuiko, frozen in the chair. He called Alex over and whispered something in his ear. Alex tried to glance around—and got a light slap to the back of the head. Listening to the "chief," Alex nodded and grinned. Those scheming skunks—they've already thought of something.

Chuiko looked askance at the monitor, where in the black

flatness of the dead screen, he could see the reflection of Olga and the boss. He heaved a sigh. What demon had possessed him to blab to Remezov that he was interested in Irina Kerimov? They'd had a few too many at the Christmas party while celebrating the holidays and the successful launch of the apparatus. Paul was quite candid, as he usually is in that state. Denis listened to his friend and played along with a wise look. When he heard the titbit about the boss' older daughter, he hiccuped and asked, interested, with the stupidest look on his face, "Where did a hero-lover meet a lady with such good prospects?" Never met her? Why the romantic feelings then? Saw a photo of her? Denis again hiccuped. And where, it would be interesting to know, do they give out photos of the beauties of N-ville? Paul explained that in the boss' office half his desk was strewn with family photos. Remezov stopped hiccuping. He scratched his butt and nodded in agreement, as if to say yes, true, the boss' office is full of photos.... So, that means his friend fell in love with a photograph? At twenty-eight years old? "Well, yeah!" Chuiko answered and took another swig of beer. At that moment, he wasn't capable of noticing the small malignant fires he'd kindled behind Denis' eyes. Today only the boss himself remained unaware of a certain promising employee's unrequited love for his eldest child. Although, Iliya was pretty keen and kept abreast of the latest office gossip. It was possible he had heard this rumor too, but if so, he wasn't letting on. Fickle Irina had no shortage of suitors and could have easily instigated any one of them to go against Chuiko. He needed clear-headed employees, well able to think. Ah, youth!

"Are you ready, brother rabbits?" Kerimov asked the main Bandar-log.

Denis stood at attention and barked at the top of his lungs: "Definitely!"

Their leader's lips turned up into a sad grin:

"The response is 'always ready.'[4] But what am I talking about? The Pepsi generation's not familiar with the pioneers. How are the final preparations coming?"

"We can start in thirty minutes."

A new player came onto the scene:

"Greetings to the whole honest company."

"Hello, Mr. Gennady," Olga was the first to greet the newcomer.

"Hello, Petrovich." Iliya shook the bony hand of the head of the internal guard of the institute, a colleague and old friend of his. They'd started working together back in the eighties and whom he invited to their projects, when, unexpectedly and all of a sudden, big business took an interest in the topic in the person of Bratulev. How the oligarch found out about their secret research wasn't important. The main thing was, he gave them money to keep them going. "What's the cause of the delay?"

The old guard looked sternly at the young people, who began to shuffle their legs and lower their eyes.

"Our eagles frittered away all the oil for the diesel engines over the weekend." Petrovich eyed Denis, calling him out. Denis looked like he had several excuses on the tip of his tongue. "As soon as they're finished filling up the tank from the fuel tanker, and then we can get started."

"We recorded every expense in the log," Remezov just had to put a word in his defense.

"I'd put you down as our greatest expense...." Petrovich snapped. "I'd give you a piece of my mind, but there are children present." Denis winked at Olga and made a funny face. The girl laughed. "Instead of making faces, why don't you get to work on the preparations. Mr. Kerimov, a minute." He and Kerimov stepped aside.

"Why did you bring Olga here?" Petrovich asked the boss from the doorway of Iliya's office. When it was just the two of them, they could be a lot less formal with one another. Kerimov was a little hesitant to answer. He moved his lips but said nothing. But his colleague and old friend's sincere expression did not give him a choice. He needed an answer.

"Gennady, you don't have to believe me if you don't want to. But Olga has acquired some extrasensory abilities. I want to use them to search for Andy."

"Yeah... apparently, you've been deeply wounded."

Petrovich looked at his friend with compassion. "Do *you* believe it?"

Kerimov scoffed:

"Absolutely, Petrovich!" His friend looked truly astonished. "Unfortunately...," Kerimov added quietly. "Let's drop it for now—you'll get the chance to see for yourself. But I only ask you one thing: what happens in the room stays in the room. Instruct our monkeys and the old guys."

"Alright, we'll see what comes of your little quest," Petrovich said, and quickly darted back to his post. Bon, whom Olga had left in her father's office, quietly walked up to the man from behind and poked his nose into his right palm. Petrovich, not expecting to see an enormous dog behind him, jumped back ten feet. Iliya chuckled. "You're a fool, and your stunts are even more foolish, geeze," the "old guard" said from behind the half-closed door of the boss' office and retreated from the room faster than a fly.

Bon wagged his tail guiltily and went to the corner where his mistress had sent him. Kerimov stood up, walked over to the pup and pet him on the head.

"What do you think, old boy? Will it work?" he asked the dog. Instead of answering, Bon licked his chin and beat the floor with his tail a couple of times. "Thanks for the support."

A disciplined bustle reigned in the room. The operators finished the preliminary testing and awaited the command to launch. Iliya Evgenevich's eyes went to his daughter. Olga was sitting in his chair and looking with interest at the work of her father's subordinates. The scientists, upon seeing their leader, ran to their places in accordance with the rules. Remezov gave the usual tired old report on the state of the preparations. Kerimov pulled another chair up to his desk and sat down next to Olga.

"Launch."

"Launch!" Denis parroted the command.

The lights blinked as usual, and the walls shook. Olga looked at her father, frightened.

"Don't be afraid," he smiled at her.

"I'm not."

"That's good."

The shaking slowly died down. The diesel power stations went into design mode. An exchange began:

"Turn on the visual of the external electromagnetic circuit."

"Yes, sir."

"Apply voltage to peripheral devices."

"Applied, sir. The field is activated."

"Internal circuit at fifty percent!"

"The accumulators have gone into start-up mode."

"Flip the polarizers, launch the magnetic set," Denis commanded.

"They're flipped. The electromagnetic-blocks have been activated." People were typing on their keyboards importantly and monitoring the parameters of the controlled stations.

"Turn on the impulse generators and the quantum installation."

"They're on, sir. The quantum installation is on." The walls once again started to shake. Latticed structures mounted on the platform, were covered with a narrow-meshed grid of electrical discharges. Metal bars fell on the windows.

"Begin synchronization…"

"Synchronization at ten percent… Twenty… Twenty-five… Forty percent… Sixty…"

"Establish the exit point."

"Exit point established."

"Synchronization at seventy percent… Seventy-five…"

"We have focus."

"Synchronization of the temporary stream is at ninety percent. Ninety-five… Ninety-nine…" There was a loud click. Olga flinched. Her small palm covered her father's hand. A virgin taiga appeared on the screen. It was night-time there.

"The apparatus is in observation mode," Denis reported.

"Good," Kerimov answered. "Olga?"

Olga, removing her glasses, jumped down from the high seat and walked up to the main screen. The girl was mesmerized by the giant light-blue disk heavily raising its round body over the horizon. It poured silver light onto the treetops. The far-away mountaintops sparkled in the night. The ground was covered in dark shadows.

"What's with the sound?" Iliya managed to tear his eyes off the epic scenery and ask Oleg.

"A couple of minutes...," he mumbled, focused on his adjustments. "The 'window' is in observation mode. The temporal flows along the internal circuit aren't completely synchronized. There's a gap of about one-thousandth of a percent, otherwise they'd be able to see us. But as it is, we're kind of 'out of bounds,' so the sound is coming through with a bit of distortion. I'm adjusting the settings of the filter program... one sec." His fingers beat at the keyboard with insane speed.

Emitting an embarrassing sound, the speakers came to life. Everyone in the room froze, afraid to breathe and thereby disturb the harmony of the idyllic night-time scene. The sounds coming from the other world flooded the operator's room. They heard the loud chirps of insects, probably analogs of Earth's crickets or cicadas. There were the cries and whoops of predators. Something made a "who" sound like an owl. The tree branches rustled in the wind. They could see and even hear pine cones falling to the ground from the high treetops.

"Andy's here," Olga said, touching the screen with her hand. "I feel it!" Dozens of eyes glanced at the institute director all at once, then fell on the girl. Iliya instantly sensed their gaze on him and his daughter.

Olga stood in front of the enormous screen. The light pouring out of it enveloped the girl from all sides. Her long light hair seemed to be glowing of its own accord. This created an ethereal impression, as if a fairy from a fairy tale were hanging in the air against the backdrop of the silver tips of the forest giants and steep round edge of the planet.

"Well I never...," Denis mumbled from behind his clenched teeth.

Someone's small involuntary sound broke the all-encompassing awe. People squeaked their chairs; a rumble of whispers rolled through the room.

"Olga."

"Yes Dad," she turned from her concentration on the other-worldly image to her father. Her yellow pupils flashed under her long bangs.

"Iliya? What the...," Petrovich wasn't the only one in shock and finding some choice profanity to express it. Half the room put forth some sort of expletive upon seeing the girl's face clearly.

Kerimov ignored the general hum of shock and addressed his daughter:

"Honey, can you feel where Andy might be?"

"I don't know—where he is," she said.

"Denis, can we work on the external focus? What observation radius can you get me?"

Alex answered instead of Denis:

"About three thousand miles. Once you go beyond the specified range, the energy requirement gets significantly larger, and it overloads the system. That'll close the 'window.'"

"Alright, three thousand then. Denis, give me sequential displacement from the exit point in all directions for five hundred miles."

The image zoomed to the right. Rivers and lakes could be seen on the bottom of the screen. Olga stood near the screen and closed her eyes. She completely abandoned the world around her.

"Not that way..." Upon hearing the quiet voice, Denis changed the application load vector, sending the "window" westward. A shiver suddenly ran over the girl's face, and then, it looked like wind was playing with her hair. They jerked and moved by themselves. "Mr. Denis, keep going."

"Okay," he responded, moving the "window" even further westward. Petrovich shook his head behind Remezov. His friend's idea no longer seemed ludicrous...

"Two thousand miles. Careful, Denis, slow down," Chuiko said.

"Farther," Olga still hadn't opened her eyes. Her hair was fluttering from an otherworldly wind. From contemplating such a picture, buckets of cold shivers ran down the onlookers' spines. The employees of the institute looked with admiration and horror, first at the director of the institution, then at his daughter, and which there was more of in these stares, even the Most High himself couldn't say.

Through the "window," cultivated fields flickered as dark rectangles in the night. They could begin to make out small and large populated areas. The tops of the hills, overgrown with age-old forests, remained in the background. The silver ribbons of rivers shone like so many slithering snakes. Denis lowered the tension. The distance from point zero grew to two and a half thousand miles. Stretching it any further was dangerous. On Sunday they'd run experiments a few times with the "search window." The border of their maximum viewing range, determined by point zero, never exceeded three thousand miles. Why this was remained to be determined, but as they crossed the invisible border, the electrical energy requirements shot up, the apparatus went into overdrive, and there was an emergency shut down. Olga let them know by a wave of her hand that they should stop moving west. For a few minutes, she turned around in place, still not opening her eyes, swayed from side to side and suddenly jerked her arms.

"That way!" Her thin finger pointed in the direction of the staircase. It was like in that joke about the drunk who got into a taxi and said, "Turn right!" Then, "Where are you going?" "To the right!" "I don't know where your right is, but follow where I'm pointing!"

Denis shrugged, glanced at the boss and, counting on his intuition, moved the "window" to the south. The image zig-zagged here and there, back and forth for another ten minutes until a city appeared on screen, located at the edge of a wide river and encircled by fortress walls.

Olga froze.

"Here, that's where Andy is. He's nearby. I can't...," she whispered and collapsed to the floor. In one fell bound the boss leaped over the computer desk and picked his daughter up in his arms. "I'll lie down for a while, Dad. Don't take me away," she protested when her father started to head for his office. He had to obey and let her stay in the operator's room.

The city Olga had indicated was on fire. The red glow of flames was visible from afar. Denis carefully moved the "window" towards the city walls. The institute employees got up from their seats and crowded around the main screen.

"What's going on there?"

"Who knows!"

A drumming rumble came from the speakers. Denis switched

the angle of observation: in the northern part of the city, against a background of columns of black smoke, they could see bright flashes.

"Den, zoom in on the explosions," Chuiko expressed everyone's thoughts.

"Look what's happening!" one of the employees muttered.

A frenzied massacre was going on in the narrow streets. They couldn't make out who was fighting against whom.

"Oleg, wake up!"

"One second," Maksimov sang, adjusting the image for clarity. "How's that?"

"It'll do."

"Oh my...!" People turned their faces from the screen in horror.

Archers on the roofs let out a few arrows into the crowd that was blocking a street. The effect of their shooting was unexpected and shocking for scientists unaccustomed to blood. Most of the arrows produced bright lights upon striking, which lit up strange translucent domes. Two arrows exploded at the very edge of a line of soldiers with white armbands. The first exploded, tearing three shield-bearers to shreds. Bloody scraps, smoking and spinning, flew towards the "window." Olga turned away. Alex covered his mouth with his hand and ran out of the room, but didn't make it all the way to the bathroom. Two others followed him; they made it.

The second arrow hit the wall of a building. A shower of crushed brick flew in all directions. People screamed heartrendingly. A whole host of cracks quickly spread through the wall; the upper part of the wall collapsed onto the crowd. The noise of the battle could not drown out the crackling of bones and the dying screams of those who were crushed under the main piece of the collapsed building wall. Olga buried her face in her father's chest.

"Don't look." His wide palm covered his child's eyes.

Vera, the commercial director's secretary, actually fainted. "What in the world was she doing here?" Kerimov thought. Paul Chuiko got sick in the corner of the room.

A little closer to the "window," a two-story house collapsed like a house of cards. Several guys in full-length robes had launched strange globes at it that arose from nowhere. The street was covered with dust.

"Magicians, may they be cursed," Denis expressed the common opinion.

Through the dusty air they could perceive the outline of a tall man with swords in both hands. The swordsman punctured the translucent dome over the mages with his body and went on a killing spree. The employees of the institute went pale as "Snow White" and watched slack-jawed as the unfortunate mages' heads were separated from their shoulders and fell to the ground.

The battle picked up with renewed force. Bearded men in horned helmets appeared from behind the barricades and obstacles blocking the paths to a large building, similar to a barracks.

"Woah, Vikings! I'm sure of it! Those look like Vikings!" Vasily Lukyanenko cried, the senior technician and a big history buff.

The position of the men with the white armbands worsened, but then something happened at the beginning of the street. The fighting crowd swayed to one side. A few swordsmen, denoted by the rags on their arms, hacked the defensive barrier down and ran towards the scorched ruins from the other side of the city. The rest of the fighters, who broke through the encirclement, came rushing after them.

Denis sent the "window" after the people who were retreating. He had already forgotten the goal of today's search, and he wasn't the only one. The whole crowd of institute employees was glued to the screen, however painful it was to look, waiting to see how the battle would end.

The road was clear. Not a single person stood in the retreating crowd's way. The inhabitants of the city were huddled in secluded nooks; pale shadows of faces flashed several times in the windows.

The armed crowd moved towards a small fortress near which a dozen singed houses were emitting hot flames. Some of the houses were destroyed down to their foundations. Piles of bricks were the only thing remaining to tell the world that a house once stood here. Corpses lay on the pavement in motionless black blotches. The closer you got to the fortress, the more of them there were.

"The accumulators of the external circuit are running low on power," Maksimov checked the indicators and announced, "We have about ten or fifteen minutes left."

"Don't interrupt!" Petrovich scolded him.

When the retreating people were about two hundred and fifty yards from the fortress, a lone warrior stepped onto their path, dressed in plain clothing, a leather vest and a helmet that half hid his face.

"Yeck, another magician! They're as plentiful as dirt there," one of the "old guys" spat, when a bow and quiver materialized in the guy's hands.

Denis carefully moved the "window" towards the new mage and fit him in the screen in such a way that they could see both him and the crowd that approached him. The mage fitted his bowstring on the bow and prepared to fire.

Thud, thud, thud, the bowstring sang, its song intermingling with its loud clicks against the bone wrist guard on the guy's left hand. Two people were struck and fell under the feet of the crowd running behind them. A swordsman who was running ahead of the others knocked all the arrows fired at him to the side.

"Tanavidau Targ," the mage said quietly, then followed it with some foul language—in their native tongue. Kerimov broke into a cold sweat. "Targ," the warrior added, when the swordsman repulsed two more arrows. The rest of his shots were aimed at others. Three more people fell under the tromping feet of the living wave. His bow disappeared, and he grabbed a sword from thin air.

"Andy!!!" Olga yelled. "Dad—that's Andy!"

"WHAT?!" a few people, including Kerimov, cried at once.

"Denis, give me visual on him—zoom in as much as possible!" Kerimov said, jumping up from his seat.

"I can't, it won't go any closer!"

"Darn!" Kerimov hugged Olga tightly.

It can't be. This cold-blooded killer can't be my Andy. But his voice.... And the natives probably don't know how to swear in Russian. In just a second, his son dealt with the swordsman by chopping off his legs. The crowd rushed at him. A short bolt of lightning shot from Andy's left hand. The guy with a white armband who fell victim to the bolt shrieked and fell to the ground to be trampled by the crowd.

Andy moved backwards. He'd lost one sword. The blade got stuck in a thick wooden shield. The bolts of lightning his son gave off beat down even the most eager opponents.

"Put the 'window' behind him—we have to give the impulse to open the portal—quick!!!" Kerimov shouted at Remezov. "All operators take your places according to the regulations. Begin."

"Boss, we've never done that before!"

"Quickly!" the director of the institute became livid.

Arrows with luminous tips flashed over Andy's head. Fiery pillars swelled in the crowd of people who pounced on the lonely warrior. The grim reaper harvested another few souls. The new death-dealing treats blew a second row of soldiers to bits. Remezov hadn't yet positioned the "window" behind Andy's back when the aforementioned bearded men in horned helmets began to jump out of the alley at the people beaten down by magical arrows. The white armbands started throwing their swords on the ground.

"Denis!" Kerimov dashed to the main operator's work station.

"I'm ready. Send the impulse to the internal circuit!"

There was no response to the command. The lights went out.

Darkness fell on the learned company, mitigated only by the light of the monitors, still running on battery power. The back-up power generators kicked in with a strained squeak.

"Why'd it shut down?" Denis said awkwardly.

"Lukyanenko, check the electrical control room," Iliya Evgenevich ordered in a calm and somewhat lifeless voice. The senior technician galloped off to the electrical panel. Petrovich turned on the emergency lighting. Four dim lamps flickered on beneath the ceiling in explosion-proof cases. "What luck...."

There was no need to explain to anyone present the sarcasm of his phrase. Denis and the others guiltily avoided eye contact with Kerimov. He was a scary sight just then. It seemed that the boss had put on a white mask instead of a face and had drawn dark circles around his eyes; his gray bloodless lips whispered something inaudibly. Olga put on her glasses, jumped off her chair and went to her father. Kerimov pressed his daughter to him:

"It'll be okay..."

"I know," the girl answered.

"You know, don't you," the scientist smiled through his tears. "You little smarty. Don't tell mom, okay?"

"I won't tell anyone."

"Good girl."

"That's all for today." The senior technician walked in. He smelled strongly of fused insulation and singed wool. The burnt body of a large rat fell to the ground. "It chewed on the divider, the brute. Just look what it's done. We'll have to change the cable funnel of the six-cable, and maybe the cable itself; there's no reserve, and the main machine in the switchgear is zero four kilovolts. Well and so on."

"Do you need help?" Iliya asked. Olga grabbed her father around the waist.

"I need money. I'm going to the grid." Lukyanenko kicked at the charred rat corpse and called one of his junior workers over: "get rid of this." The poor guy carefully picked up the rat by the tail and hurried to the hall. Vasily turned to their leader and continued their choppy conversation: "I've got a pretty good idea of some of the figures. It'll cost about ten grand to fix it, maybe fifteen."

"Vera," Kerimov addressed the commercial director's secretary, who was pale as a sheet after watching the epic "historical film." "Write Vasily an expense allowance for twenty thousand. Will that do?"

"Yes," the senior technician nodded. "Can I take a company car?"

"Take the field vehicle. When will you get it up and working again?"

"By this evening," Vasily answered and left.

"Let's go home, hon. Wait, wait a minute honey," Iliya stopped next to Denis. "This is what I've thought of, Den. Oleg warned that you quantized the internal circuit with a tiny pause in the temporal flow...," Remezov nodded. "You and Alex, calculate the possibility of working with the opposite flow. That is, the puncture will be backwards, as I see it, that calculation will be relevant for simple spatial portals within our old woman-Earth.

The visual 'window' will be easier to open, and then, as in a lighthouse, we penetrate the subspace transition. Petrovich?"

"I'm here," Petrovich spoke up.

"I'm going home. You're in charge. The guys should whip it into shape. We'll run a test of the apparatus tomorrow. Come to me…," Kerimov picked up Olga in his arms and followed John out the door.

The institute employees silently watched the director's powerful figure retreat. He was a dark silhouette covering the light from the window at the end of the long corridor. The gang couldn't shake the feeling that the ash from his burnt soul had settled on them all. Oleg Chuiko stared at the blackness of the screen, unseeing. He wasn't the only one to notice the change that took place in his boss. The boss' temples, just two hours ago only slightly gray, were completely white.

Russia. N-ville. Two days later…

"Iliya, Iliya!"

"Huh? What?" Kerimov snapped out of his memories and looked at Bratulev. "Sorry, I was lost in thought."

"I can see that," the oligarch smiled. "Let's drive over there. Tell me, did you step up security on site?"

"No, no one increased the staffing schedule of the security service."

The train of vehicles bypassed the security stop and, driving up to the main building of the institute, stopped.

"Strange," the "aide" said from the front seat when he saw people coming out to meet them.

"What?" the oligarch caught his bodyguard's worry.

"Now they've done it… if my senses serve me correctly, the site is no longer yours. Guards don't carry submachine guns."

A smart-looking young man approached the Jeep. Behind him stood another greeter: an elderly man with a handsome dark face, a serious gaze, and an air of authority. These two men were not institute or security employees. Kerimov saw how Bratulev tensed up. He noticed a flash of recognition in his eyes. Bratulev opened the door himself and stepped out of the car.

"Hello, Mr. Bratulev," the elderly man greeted him.

"Hello, Major General." The oligarch seemed to be deflating like an air mattress.

"Mr. Kerimov," the general addressed the scientist. "This concerns you too. What are you looking at? Take us to your office."

"What do you need me for?" Kerimov played the fool. The general wasn't playing along for a split second and only shook his head judgmentally.

"Mr. Kerimov, we'll have a separate conversation with your *former* employer somewhere else, in a more private setting. But with you, I'd like to discuss the conditions under which you can continue your work…"

Kerimov walked along the corridor trying not to pay attention to the smart young men and women filling his colleagues' offices. The uninvited guests were printing papers and packing archives and computers into numbered boxes. Living statues in bullet-proof armor holding short automatic weapons stood on every corner. He felt extremely uneasy. The general's mentioning that it would be possible to continue his work inspired hope, but what was the catch?

Bratulev was not allowed into the building itself. The other secret serviceman who had approached Bratulev and his bodyguards asked Konstantin Ivanovich to follow him to a guest house, where … was waiting for him…. Iliya didn't hear the last name of who it was that was expecting Bratulev in the guest house. But judging by the businessman's reaction and that of his "aide," he ascertained that it was someone Bratulev knew. The "aide" adjusted his tie and tugged at his suit coat. Bratulev glanced about as if he were being hunted down. Emitting a blue solar exhaust, three heavy-duty trucks and a Kamatsu truck crane drove into the Institute. The loaders had come.

"Hello, Nastya," entering the reception room, the former director greeted his former secretary, who, sure enough, was still at work.

Kerimov rarely visited his personal reception room. He preferred to work in his office, which was located next to the operator's room. Nastya, who was more often than not left to her own devices, had created a kingdom of flowers in the room. She had a real talent as a florist. For all the abundance of greenery, she did not thoughtlessly fill up vacant places, but distributed beautiful thematic compositions to the offices. Truth be told, the scientists came here to admire the flowers and relax. Iliya had brought the secret service General here with a specific goal in mind: the room so pleasantly refined by the secretary put people in the mood for light conversation, not forced bargaining. The General appreciated Iliya's subtle move but didn't let on.

"Nastya, could you make us some coffee, like you do, with the herbs," Kerimov asked her. "Please," he opened the door for the tall guest. "Don't let anyone in to disturb us." Iliya looked at the broad-shouldered guy standing near the reception room door. Nastya smiled slightly. "And don't forget, two coffees only. Don't make any for our young gentleman—he's on duty!"

Nastya snickered into her fist. She too felt uneasy about the new arrivals, but she was more confident now, following her boss' lead. Iliya Evgenevich closed the door. The young secret serviceman would get a cup or two of the aromatic beverage, no doubt.

"What kind of conditions are we talking about?" Kerimov took the initiative in the conversation, sitting down in a wide armchair. The general was seated comfortably on a small leather sofa. He smiled with just the corners of his lips, tapped a folder he'd brought, loosened his tie, and responded:

"Mr. Kerimov, I'd like to clarify the priorities right away. I don't want there to be any misunderstandings between us—nothing left unsaid. I can tell you we're most extremely interested in continuing the research."

"Hm, your words give hope, but you mentioned conditions, so that means there's a catch. Just your interest isn't enough to keep the research going. We need a team for that, that knows what it's doing. We need scientists united in mind, equipment and a whole staff of specialists to maintain this equipment and, something that's also important, we need these scientists to actually want to work. So, you have to keep them interested somehow. If you don't have any questions regarding the equipment, please take it away quietly. You know, working with people requires a lack of inhibitions during the thought process. It's not 1937, you know[5]."

The general shot the scientist a piquant look.

"It would be a lot simpler if it was," he said. "Can you even imagine what this discovery means?"

"I can," Kerimov answered.

"You can't imagine anything!"

There was a cautious knock on the door.

"Come in," Kerimov allowed. Nastya walked in carrying a tray with two cups of coffee, a coffee pot, and a small basket of sugar cookies. The room was filled with a delicious aroma. The general's nostrils fluttered.

"Thank you so much." Nastya smiled at the general and slid out the door, not forgetting to close it firmly behind her.

"How nice," the general said, swallowing. "Hm, back to business," Leonid Vladimirovich Sanin again took on a serious tone. "What were we talking about?"

"About realities."

"Exactly, about realities. And today they are such that we can get into an unpleasant tangle of global proportions. Your discovery, Mr. Kerimov, disturbs the entire system of political counterbalances in the world."

"Which one? Major General, you said you did not want any misunderstandings between us, so I'll ask you to clarify—which of my discoveries? Don't think me stupider than I look. I'm not a system analyst, but I can analyze. Your agency remained completely invisible to us until just recently; therefore, you're interested in the result we achieved in building passageways within the borders of Mother Earth. But as far as interworld portals, you're prepared to let that go for now... I just have to clarify which exactly you're prepared to sacrifice and why. Regarding the first scenario, I agree with you completely. The Earth portals are a bomb, much more frightening than any nuclear weapon..."

The general smiled a child-like smile at the scientist's naive words.

"And all the same you've decided not to disarm the portal mine but to continue research in this field. Why?"

The representative of the competent authorities ceased his smiling. General Sanin carefully set his empty cup down on the coffee table. He looked at Kerimov, elbows resting on his knees, hands folded.

"You do know how to steer a conversation, Mr. Kerimov. Not everyone can go from the circumstances of collaboration to the cause and effect in two sentences. Well, it's even more interesting that way. You, you're old school. You won't try to dissect my every word into the smallest details. Please don't interrupt." Leonid Vladimirovich stood up and, folding his hands behind his back, started to pace around the room. Kerimov waited patiently.

"Let me say again: the state, represented by us, is extremely interested in continuing this research, and it will go on, here. With or without you, but better with. Now I'll go over the 'what,' 'why,' and 'how.' What can the new worlds offer Russia? It's a question with a wide range of answers: from free territory, fossils, farmland in zones, let's say, of not risky agriculture, to new technology, new markets, and a solution to the problem with our demographics. That's one. The possibility of evading international tension. That's two. New allies, devil take it, that's a possibility too. That's three. Clean worlds, unspoiled by civilization, will be a beautiful bargaining chip in our negotiations with the rest of the world and with those high-tech civilizations you've discovered. That's four. Don't judge. Why should Russia deal in worlds? Because the nice folks at Langley know all about your experiments, and so do some other interesting bureaus, they don't think that their organizations are the only ones in the know about what the Russians are up to. They kept a keen eye on your former boss and on the institute. Western secret services immediately record all those who purchase and place orders for the manufacture of high-tech and special equipment. From the very beginning, the institute left a powerful mark, and the checking wasn't just organized only by lazy people. Smart people got interested: who needs these devices, and what for? It's amazing that they didn't take you, you personally, seriously." The General scoffed. "Although, for the last year and a half, N-ville's been so full of 'frenemies,' you run into them more often than not. We had to really break a sweat to keep them away from the fact of your results."

"You know, I didn't notice your work at all."

"I thought I asked you not to interrupt." Iliya showed his palms as if to admit his own guilt and invite the general to go on. "The fact that you didn't notice our work is not due to your lack of attention, but to the mastery of our agents and colleagues from the adjoined services who went all out so as to, how should I put it, not allow it. I have to give Bratulev his due—he hired a former employee of our little 'racket' to help him protect his own activities, and this man, Smith, was able to keep the secret, and to what extent he couldn't, he issued so many rumors that in the fog of gossip there's no seeing straight. No way to tell what's what. The main disadvantage was the fact that the Americans intercepted telephone conversations and internet traffic from the very start, but we were powerless to do anything about that. They were playing from their territory. We, for our part, spent significant resources and efforts concealing the institute's work, and in the intelligence game we were able to beat our foreign opponents. The latest breakthrough has been kept confidential. Our 'friends,' so to speak, only know about your ability to open a passageway to one or two parallel worlds. It's not a lot, but it's enough to set a political carousel in motion unlike anything you've ever dreamed of, even during the fall of the Soviet Union. They'll ask Russia to share this discovery, they'll ask at the highest level. If we refuse, then so many forces and funds will be used that Russian politicians will be wiped out completely. The existing global system (the US and the West) won't allow a monopolized control of the gates. Don't worry—we'll come up with some sort of ironclad excuse for not letting the 'primitive Russians' alone control a discovery for 'the whole of civilization,' and then nukes, aircraft carriers, an invisible planes will get involved, and in short, you've got world war three. The dumbocracy won't give up its conquests.... So, let's switch to the next question. Why are we going to deal in worlds? Because Russia alone can't bear that load. In this country at this time, there simply aren't enough resources to enact programs for exploring and utilizing the new worlds. For now there's been no mention of quickly establishing direct contact with the new civilizations, and time is running out—the clock is ticking. I won't try to hide the fact that, if we announce to people the possibility of leaving this fragile world of ours and going somewhere far, far away, somewhere there's not even a simple toilet, a lot of folks will head for the unknown, and do we need that? The process should be controlled. Once we announce the discovery, we knock the ground out from under the feet of many hawks and enlist the support of such states as India and China. Our neighbors are experiencing such extreme overpopulation that their problems with resources simply pale in comparison. We need to weaken the flow of Chinese pressing on our Easter borders. I think both countries will grab on to the opportunity to solve their problems painlessly with both hands, both feet, and a full set of teeth. Which would, by the way, solve ours, too. Billions in foreign currency would be provided to Russia for the construction of interworld portals. And here, we gently turn to the strictly economic issue, which is, given the current realities, at the head of the political shake-up we've initiated. Without disclosing the technology of opening portals, we'll invite Western companies and states to cooperate and create the appropriate infrastructure. We can also offer joint mining of useful minerals. I need to specify right away: it should appear that there are no more than two or three worlds. That way the number of birds killed by one stone will be beyond our wildest dreams. We can safely say that, once we begin expansion beyond the border, we'll be pushing the global economic crisis further and further away. Firms and corporations that specialize in building cheap housing will perk up. The need for electric power enterprises, goods and services will increase; the mining industry will come to life. There simply aren't enough fingers and toes to list everything. The money involved will be measured with so many zeros that no sensible politician will dare to go to war against his industrialists, and they will not be interested in a war with Russia for the reasons described above. We'll give it all to them of our own accord— here, take it, I don't want it. Naturally, the tricky Americans and Europeans will want to know the methods and technologies for building portals, and here we can tell them where to go. Official secrets are so much easier to protect from the political point of view. In response to any movement to discover the secret, we can raise a howl to the heavens and excommunicate the offenders from the feeding bowl, or threaten them with excommunication. No matter how you spin it, to my great regret, the modern world is ruled by money, but now that's working in Russia's favor. The last question remains: 'How?' How can we hide our research on populated worlds and subspace portals from the attention of foreign secret services and industrial spies? Tell me, Mr. Kerimov, where's the best place to hide a flame?" And the general answered his own question, "Inside a fire." Undercover studies are most easily hidden under the official veil. And for this last secret, Russia will fight using all possible and impossible means. Your work has provided the country with more than twenty years of advancement over its closest competitors, but we still can't let our hair down and just rely on this advancement. In fact, we have to work from the assumption that we have just five or seven years head start. During this time we, that is, you, not only have to create this entire industry and organize the manufacturing, but also to develop ways to counter and protect against unauthorized opening of portals on our territory. I hope I do not need to explain to you the military and strategic importance of your discovery? A separate center will be set up to conduct work on the study of inhabited worlds."

"You speak very well, sir. You've got it all figured out, but will what you say actually happen?"

"Yes, and I'm not the only one who's convinced of it. Our system analysts are, too. Of course, everything that I told you is just an outline of the predicted events. It's impossible to take all the underwater stones, reefs, and human stupidity into account. Let me tell you something you're not supposed to know about. Our opponents believe with every fiber of their beings that we'll do everything in our power to hide information on passageways to parallel worlds, and we've tried hard to convince them of that."

"And in fact?"

"In fact, tomorrow there'll be a meeting of the Shanghai Cooperation Organisation countries, and if the doors are closed, our 'guarantor' will get the news to the right countries. Prime Minister of India's going to be there, which adds piquancy to the situation. The president of Japan is on the list of invited guests. One problem—they 'forgot' about the Americans. In military tactics, this is called a proactive strike. Now the program of the visit and bilateral meetings is being rewritten anew. The new race is starting at the highest level."

"Major General, how exactly do you plan on keeping the secret of subspace traveling and the work on that? I have an efficient suggestion for you."

"Interesting. Let's hear it."

"Set up a research center in some empty world where time flows faster than it does here. If you do that, we can make full use of the head start and hide the secret laboratories from prying eyes. We can send a string of cars, for example, to Minute—that's what we called one very beautiful planet or world. We're not sure about how to classify them yet. Anyway, it won't be difficult."

"Mr. Kerimov, don't rush, I'm not going to argue with you. It's a very useful suggestion, but let's not forget about the microbiological factor. In many worlds, there is no intelligent life, which is a definite plus, but robots and automatic devices must be the first to step into strange worlds. We can't even begin to discuss excursions until we've conducted the necessary set of analyses and developed immunomodulating vaccines."

"Alright, just an idea. You're in charge."

"Mr. Kerimov, let's not twist the facts."

"Alright, I won't. Let's go back to the beginning of the conversation. What are your conditions?" Kerimov copied the general's body language. He put his elbows on his knees, folded his hands, set his chin on them, and looked straight at his guest. The general stopped in the middle of the room, said nothing for ten seconds, as if collecting his thoughts, and when the scientist's patience came to an end, said:

"The institute is changing bases. The current conditions do not meet the safety and security requirements. We'll have to divide your collective into three groups, which will occupy various positions and pursue different directions. You personally will take up the role of lead coordinator. You'll head the first group directly and will act on behalf of Russian Research on all levels. The second group will work on subspace portals; the third will work on the inhabitants of the other worlds. Think long and hard who you want heading the other groups. Please also give me a detailed list of missing equipment, and I'll hurry to assure you: seven months ago, we placed orders for the manufacture of the main components of the apparatus. Two weeks ago, containers with a triple set of equipment crossed the Russian border. You really must forgive us for taking advantage of the, ahem, stolen specifications." The general spread his hands guiltily. "In a separate list, please indicate all the scientists you would like to see in your institute. The corresponding work will be carried out for all candidates. Sorry, but you and your employees are now restricted from crossing the border. From now on, going abroad will be only with state permission for all those involved. Disclosure of information, ahem, as you understand, will lead to sad consequences. You and your people will have to give an incredible amount of signatures, written pledges of allegiance and confidentiality. I hope you realize that goes without saying. The wages of the employees will not be affected at all; on the contrary, the command decided to increase the level of material compensation. Since you are all becoming bearers of state secrets, you'll be provided with round-the-clock outdoor surveillance; your documentation and letters will be opened and read; sorry, it's a must. I repeat, the groups leading the developments that are not related to the official part will be relocated to a specially protected scientific center, communications with them are carried out through the latest satellites of the Ministry of Defense and can not be intercepted by a probable adversary. As for you personally, Mr. Kerimov, I can't say that I am extremely uncomfortable with you, but this is one of the unpleasant aspects of the profession. I ask you to pay attention to your eldest daughter and have a conversation with her. Hmm, I wouldn't want anyone to use her as leverage against you. Irina's inability to choose friends could cost us dearly. Understand, if you do not solve this issue within the family, then it…, um, I hope that Irina will not cause trouble. That's all from me for now. Questions?"

"I don't have any questions, but I have two conditions."

"Go ahead. I can guess what they are."

Kerimov cocked his head to the left and looked

questioningly at the general.

"Doubtless, you'll get a chance to search for your son. I want to say that this point will be one of the priorities for the third group."

"What arguments are you basing that on?" The chair squeaked plaintively. Iliya stood up from behind the table. Three steps forward, and he was standing across from the general. The two men stared at one another. They were so alike and so different. Both were used to giving commands and not backing down when fate threw challenges at them. Both had enormous responsibilities resting on their shoulders, and if one of them was prepared to place his country, himself, and hundreds of lives on the altar, the other was not prepared to sacrifice himself. He had hard work ahead of him and gaining his son to look forward to, whom he'd already lost twice. His deceased hope came to life again. The staring contest didn't go on for long. Kerimov was the first to take his gaze to the side. It was hard to look into the eyes of a person who had taken the responsibility for people's lives upon himself, and was aware of this responsibility. In that moment the scientist believed the secret service leader's words—the Major General wasn't lying. He believed in that what he was saying was true. Iliya could sense a strong iron rod in the general's character. With a will like that, you could move mountains. Apparently, that's why they hired him. He obviously laid the cards on the table, and that was hardest of all.

"Magic, Mr. Kerimov, MAGIC! It's possible. It might be that in the unknown worlds, it will be possible there too, and maybe even in ours, who knows? Command has no prejudice against this possibility, and we need to know what to expect. Extrasensory perception and shamans—it's not nonsense. It's proven and documented. You've probably read various articles in the tabloids, hm, they're actually right about a lot of things. We didn't find Atlantis, but we made enough progress. Magic. What can it give us? And what can it give the masses? Someone from our world could learn it, that's for sure. No one doubts that. The world your son disappeared to will be studied very carefully. We've hired linguists, academics, historians, specialists in middle-ages weaponry and fencing. We're preparing those who will make the first contact. From what we've gathered, we know that that world is fairly harsh; the battle in the streets you witness spelled that out for you very clearly. If I were in your shoes, I would be jumping for joy that Andy was able to assimilate himself into the local society and that he is able to defend himself. To hold back a crowd like that... and what quick reaction time he had... Our fencing expert watched the whole thing with her mouth wide open. I'm sorry, but I don't understand your reaction to seeing your son kill people."

"You couldn't understand!"

"Stop it, I do understand!" The general stepped closer to the scientist. His eyes flashed with anger. "My children serve, both of them! They've both come under gunfire, so I know very well what it's like—losing a little bit of your soul every day. Be happy, Iliya, that Andy's alive. He really showed what he could do, and what he can do is amazing. We will use that ace. We just have to get him back to Earth."

"What do you need him for?"

"Do you want me to list everything? Okay, here we go. Your son somehow managed to meld into the society of that planet." The general held up his thumb to count "one" the way Russians do. "The picture you saw of the battle shows that he is fighting on the side of some group, which means that he can render invaluable help in assessing local realities and the political situation." His pointer finger joined his thumb: "Two." "The fight you witnessed showed very clearly that things with our 'neighbors' are not so simple, and apart from swords and bows, we may be facing things that go well beyond the bounds of ordinary perception. What follows from this? The result is that the role of Andy, who is a magician, increases many times. Or maybe we shouldn't go into that world at all? In addition, it would be foolish not to use a person who knows the language." He held up his middle finger: "Three." "Is that enough for you?"

"He's just a boy!"

"Really? Tell me, how does time pass in that world?" Kerimov didn't answer. "As far as I know, over two years have gone by there, and Andy is now almost nineteen. He's perfectly capable of killing in cold blood. I don't think it's accurate to call that warrior a boy. What was your other condition?"

Kerimov, after being rebuffed like that, looked like a dog that's been kicked. But the fire of tenacity in his eyes had not gone out, but burned even stronger. The scientist reminded of the same opinion on most things. He understood in his head that his son was already not the boy he had been eight months ago, and that the general was right about a lot of things. But… in his heart, Iliya Evgenevich could not accept the idea that his son had grown up.

The general broke the extended silence:

"I do believe that the second condition's name is Olga?"

"Don't you dare touch her!" Kerimov's clenched fists cracked.

"I feel sorry for you, Kerimov. Really, as a fellow human being, very sorry. Tell me, what made you bring your daughter to the institute? Well, why don't you answer? Tell me this, then. How are you planning on searching for Andy? Unfortunately, we cannot ignore that fact. As our analysts suspect, the changes taking place in Olga are a result of Andy's influence. The mutual influence between the two worlds has already begun, and your family is the first to experience it. The girl has undergone visible physiological changes that glasses and contact lenses can't hide. Our specialists have observed your daughter using certain instrumental methods, albeit from a distance. But certain facts tell us that stopping the research would be extremely ill-advised. I'd like you to take a look at a few things for me," he said, taking a folder from the couch and extracting a few photos and papers from it. "Please." He put the materials on Kerimov's desk.

"I don't understand what these photos are of?"

"I'll gladly explain." Major General Leonid Vladimirovich stood up behind the scientist and pointed to the first photo. "The photographs show human auras. The scale is the same on all of them. Don't look at me like that. I'm not joking or kidding in the least. I'm not trying to pull the wool over your eyes. The first photo shows an ordinary human aura. Images number two and three show the auras of people who have demonstrated extrasensory abilities. This has been proven using the scientific method. The fourth photo shows an indigo aura…," the general fell silent.

"And the fifth?" Iliya asked, examining the last one. If what the general had said was true, that all the photos were to the same scale, the last aura was about three times bigger than that of the people who had E.S.P. and almost four times bigger than the ordinary person. Kerimov guessed whose aura it was before the general spoke.

"The last aura belongs to Olga. Notice how saturated with color it is, and how thick the external energy envelope is. The sixth photo shows her aura at the beginning of our observation. See how strong the changes are. Maybe you'll be relieved to know this; maybe it'll make things harder on you; I don't know…."

"Just tell me."

"Our in-house personnel, whose auras you saw on the second and third photos, flatly refused to work with your daughter and didn't care to explain why."

"What's on the paper?"

"It's the experts' conclusions on the DNA analysis we did of Andy and Olga. Samples of your son's tissues we got in the hospital where he was treated after a lightning strike. We also obtained a few hairs from the training suit left by his archery teacher. Similarly with Olga. In December, she caught a cold, and your wife took her to a clinic, a couple of drops of blood from the laboratory's analysis was enough for us."

"What do they say?"

"Without a doubt, they're siblings."

"Haha."

"Yes, it's funny, if you consider the fact that only identical twins yield identical DNA analyses. Don't look so shocked. Calm down, please. Your children's DNA is almost as alike as that of identical twins. Isn't that interesting? Draw your own conclusions."

"And Irina?"

"With her it's simpler. The analysis showed that she is their sibling, and that's all. Nothing out of the ordinary with your eldest daughter. Except, perhaps, being a bit wishy-washy, but I hope you'll see to that."

Iliya Kerimov carefully set the photographs on the edge of the desk, walked around it, and sat down heavily in his chair. His head was spinning. The major general had outplayed him on every level. Apparently, the secret service had long since been preparing for this conversation. In order to create the necessary effect, they had complied psychological profiles and calculated every possible reaction. They had the time. The former director got an idea:

"Did you send Bratulev the materials on the work we did back in the late eighties?"

"Why would we just send it? The secret was sold for a nice sum."

"Understood," Iliya said tiredly, leaning back in his chair. "I'll work. You've counted on that from the very beginning and weren't expecting any other answer from me. But don't go near Olga. If anyone comes near her, I'll kill him with my own bare hands. Enough long-distance observation."

"I'm glad we've come to an agreement. We can see about this last issue again later on, in a year or two."

"Don't count on it."

Time will tell, the general thought, collecting the photos and the results of the DNA analyses into the folder. *He's a strong man, and he knows how to roll with the punches. We're in business.*

"On that note, allow me to take my leave. Volodya, the young man in the reception room, is from now on the commander of the people we've provided for you. Starting now, you don't take a single step without a bodyguard. Until next time."

"Goodbye."

* * *

It was quiet in the apartment. His wife hadn't yet come back from work. Irina, as always, would be back with the rising of the stars. Iliya walked into the children's room on tip-toe. Olga was drawing. In the middle of the room, on a big piece of white poster paper, she'd drawn a dragon. Kerimov, not bothering his daughter, sat down on the edge of the bed and watched Olga color the mythical beast, her tongue slightly protruding out of concentration. The drawing looked phenomenal. You couldn't tell it was drawn by a 9-year-old. Bon got up from his dog bed and, his claws clicking against the floor, walked over to Iliya. The dog's heavy, hairy head laid on Iliya's knees. The scientist's right hand was covered in his thick fur as he patted Bon's neck. The dog heaved a sigh and closed his eyes, enjoying the massage.

"Like that, boy?" Bon gave a loud "pufff" in response. Scratch me, it meant, don't stop. Kerimov smiled sadly.

Olga set her crayons aside and turned to her father. He saw a puzzled look on her face, then an understanding one. She got up off the floor, sat down beside her dad on the bed and covered his hand with her small palm.

"It'll be okay, Dad." His daughter's warmth and understanding made him feel better.

The door downstairs slammed; they heard keys hit the shelf. Not taking her shoes off, Irina went straight to her room. Never a moment of down time for that girl.

"Go on, keep coloring, my dear," Iliya said to Olga. "It looks great."

"Where are you going?"

"Don't worry, not to work. I'm going to talk to Irina."

Irina was sitting in front of the mirror, giving herself what seemed like a total makeover.

It was a familiar sight: clothes strewn all over the bed and the floor, a lace bra hanging from the dresser knob, makeup, books, and other objects in every corner and on every surface. It looked like a small tornado had gone through the bedroom.

"Did you need something, dad?" Irina asked, putting on eyeliner.

"We need to have a serious talk."

"Dad, how 'bout not right now. My friends are waiting for me."

"Let them wait. They won't break."

"Dad!" Irina jumped up.

"Sit down," Iliya said calmly and a little annoyed. Irina obediently sank down on the chair. Her father's heavy glance and tone of voice made it crystal clear that there was no room for antics and did not promise anything good if she disobeyed....

Russia. Somewhere not far from N-ville. Two weeks later…

Two hours dragged on like Monday after a busy weekend. The minibus, with its thick curtains and a driver that was separated from the passengers by an opaque divider, gently swayed from side to side over the potholes, its engine roaring from time to time. Olga hadn't yet finished watching her cartoons when she fell asleep on her father's lap. Iliya closed his laptop, carefully folded his coat and slid it under his daughter's head. Volodya, sitting across from the Kerimovs, smiled warmly. "Will we be there soon?" Iliya asked him silently, just by tapping his watch. The bodyguard shrugged. He was never on site.

Two weeks, unlike the last two hours, had flown by unnoticed. The day after his memorable conversation with the General, Iliya Evgenevich was immersed in the hustle and bustle of re-structuring the institute and forming the research groups. Besides everything else, he still had the responsibility of placement of equipment in the new center, where the first and, on paper, only group was officially registered. Dozens of technicians were once again monitoring the apparatus and the control center. There was plenty of work to do. The next launch was possible no sooner than two or three weeks, weather permitting. Unlike his group, the third group had things already well underway. It was decided to conduct the first major launch onto the planet where Andy was living. Kerimov had handed today's hustle and bustle over to someone else in order to attend.

Fifteen minutes later, the wait was over. Under the wheels of the bus, the joints of the reinforced concrete slabs knocked. The engine gave a final roar, and the vehicle stopped. Behind the thick curtains, Kerimov could see the shadows of people approaching the bus. A moment later, the side door opened.

"Please exit the vehicle," a man said.

Iliya took Olga by the hand.

"Volodya, my laptop…." The bodyguard nodded. "Bon, come on."

The dog got off the bus too. He circled his owner a few

times and lifted his hind leg over the front wheel of the stuffy, smelly bus. The guards did not expect to see the dog. A pair of sentries immediately pointed short machine guns on the dog, who was watering the wheel.

"As you were," a voice said to the guards from the guardhouse. The major general was coming to greet them.

"Hello, Mr. Kerimov," he said quietly.

"Hello, major general."

"Let's go. I hope we haven't offended you with such a 'happy' welcome?"

"No."

"Excellent. We have a few security checks to get through first; warn your daughter. Then we'll get down to business."

* * *

The elevator creaked as it got lower and lower. With a quiet rustle, staircases swept past.

"We're going way down," Iliya said to no one in particular. The general shrugged indifferently. A "ding" announced the end of the journey. The doors opened to either side. "Wow!"

The scientist was duly impressed. He had been expecting to see a narrow hallway, not a large room with a twenty-foot-high ceiling. Olga corrected her glasses. She was silent the whole way. Numerous security checkpoints seemed unable to shake her equanimity. The general motioned for them to follow him.

Iliya observed the many people working behind the glass walls. An ideal cleanliness reigned. The floor, ceiling, and walls seemed to have been treated with dust- and dirt-repellent chemicals.

"We're almost there." The general passed a card through the reader of the electromagnetic lock of the next door.

"Oh wow!" The view behind the glass broke through Olga's wall of equanimity. Kerimov remained silent, because he could only express himself with interjections.

An enormous cave, filled with the lighting of powerful projectors, hung over the little people-ants. Fifty yards from the

59

glass gallery, they could see the blocks installed of the teleportation apparatus. Dozens of technicians in pure white overalls were buzzing around the "barrels" which were the accumulators.

"They're assembling phase two," the general explained. "They launched the first one three days ago, after fine-tuning." Kerimov nodded. They'd completed the task 24 hours ahead of the deadline.

"Where did you put the transition chambers?"

"Lower, at the optimal focus point. The transition chambers technically belong to Rudin."

"Who's that?"

"You wouldn't recognize his name. It's a completely different domain. Let's just say his employees used to work for Biotab. Most of the personnel from the biological defense sector have been sent here on assignment out of Obolensk." Iliya nodded in understanding.

"Do they come from the Petersburg Research Institute of especially pure products and Lyubuchany?"

"Plenty of everyone. There are quite a few more biologists and microbiologists here than physicists. Crazy people. I'm sick of them already. They shake tubes and canisters of formaldehyde, yell at me for not letting them into the other worlds, and always need something. They'd only just assembled the apparatus when they started to creep around me like eels already. Some of them promised to be the first to take this center by storm. I had to threaten to shoot them before they finally calmed down. You've got it good; they've sent the most experienced microbiologists and bacteriologists to the first group. Although, I really can't complain. We're here." The general opened the last door.

"Well hello, you apes!" Iliya hugged Alex and patted Paul on the shoulder. Olga stepped to the side and watched the happy young men greeting her father, smiling, saying something. Several of them just waved.

Today's launch was carried out using two teams. The second team only assembled the apparatus, and the people worked together with Chuiko's group, which was deemed the main group for work on the "aliens" (people from the other worlds). The Bandar-logs were on cloud nine: Remezov became the assistant director of the second group while Oleg became one of Samoi's leading specialists! Only Alex was needed everywhere. His mathematical mind was necessary on all fronts. As a result, he got the list of commanding personnel at the base. This immediately made him the target of all sorts of jokes. Just because you're now a higher-up doesn't mean you get respect!

The new operator's room was three times larger than the original. The main screen was a compilation of dozens of plasma panels. It took up half the wall. The secret service spared no expense when it came to technical equipment. The brand new servers and computers were a pleasant sight for everyone to see.

"Wow, you've really outdone yourselves," Iliya joked caustically. "Who's overseeing the launch?"

"Chuiko is the senior-level staff member on it," Remezov answered, glancing at the major general.

"He's moving up in the world, that Paul Chuiko! How long till we begin?"

"Twenty minutes. Will you help us, fairy girl?" Denis asked Olga. The nickname stuck.

"Tell the operators to take their stations. Let's get ready, people," Paul's voice blasted over the loud speakers.

* * *

Iliya and Olga were standing in front of the main screen. Olga squinted at the giant disk of the light-blue planet emerging from behind the mountains. There was a different exit point this time. Instead of a Sequoia forest, the spectators saw a wide, sparkling river.

"He's not here," Olga said.

"What do you mean? Where's Andy?" Iliya said in surprise. The operators and the technicians all looked at Olga questioningly.

"There!" The blue planet shining on the world disappeared behind a large cloud. "He's there," she repeated, pointing to the planet that had disappeared behind the cloud.

Nelita. Andy...

Bright stars above his head and cold, cruel, intense cold penetrating throughout his whole body. Not a drop of heat. The amulet had sucked up everything, up to the very last drop. Andy struggled to crawl ashore. Where had he been thrown this time?

Clinging to the thin branches of shrubs that resembled Earth's purple osier and slipping over the moist clay, he pulled his disobedient body to the dry leaves that covered the ground on a small hillock. Targ! His teeth chattered. The wings of some nocturnal bird rustled overhead. He heard a gurgling sound coming from the right, about five yards away. It sounded like large bubbles bubbling up out of something. *Bul, bu-bu-bulp.* His numb muscles tightened; his trembling subsided for a while. A strange creature came into view, sitting right on very edge of the water where it met the clay shore. It looked like a cross between a toad and a fish. If based on the hind part of the creature, you thought it was an amphibian, the wide fishtail and small scales beginning immediately behind its webbed feet, which raised the toothy mouth upwards, would teach you otherwise. The "foad" (fish-toad) puffed up its throat sac, making another loud bubbling sound. The call of the ringleaders was picked up by a whole regiment of the throaty beasts; the song the foads rang through the night.

The tension that held Andy subsided. He laid down on the leaf-covered ground and turned over. *Again! I've made ANOTHER unexpected leap! Who could have guessed it would turn out like that? The stupid hunk of metal!* His right fist beat his chest.

"Hrr-r-r, aaah." Pain like a bright flash pierced the interworld traveler from head to toe. It was so intense he curled up in the fetal position. A red-hot volcano flared up in his chest. "Ah, hr-hr," Andy tried to catch his breath.

Hearing the sounds he was making, the foads fell silent for a while. A few minutes later, the "bulp"-gurgling sounds came back from somewhere far off. The water was lapping onto the shore softly, and the many voices of the choir broke the silence once more.

After waiting for the flame of pain to go out, Andy cautiously raised himself on his elbows and examined himself. He seemed okay, except for the fact that his chest and stomach were covered in some dried mud. A moment later, it became clear that it was not mud, but dried blood. Where could he have gotten wounded? Memory refused to suggest anything. Between the moment when he was literally sucked into the funnel of the portal and the moment he woke up on an icy hummock at the very edge of some strange lake, or a swamp, there was a gap. *Interesting: how many carcasses of self-taught magic artisans are lying in the ice and slippery mud? And where did the ice come from? You gotta look hard to find and get into a block of ice in the middle of a warm summer. Although, the ice could have appeared as a residual phenomenon from the transfer spell. That's probably it.*

But still, I don't get where the blood came from? I woke up on my back....

He carefully laid down again on his back. His chest ached. The pain came in waves. Andy listened to his body attentively. He got the impression that he wasn't himself, but just a small part of the former were-dragon. The lion's share of his "I," that energy, his attitude and understanding of the world around him, that he was used to and melded with while in dragon form, was left behind. He felt these were all left in his "pocket" in "the reverse side," where he used to keep money, weapons, and important objects. His soul strove to recover the losses, but all attempts to find what he'd lost hit a wall.

The wall that separated him from the lost half of his "I" stood firmly. In order to break the barrier to his consciousness, he had to break through to the astral, but in the state he was in, he could only dream of great feats. His fist hit the ground. The movement was rewarded with a new serving of pain. He felt as if someone had poured boiling water on his chest. How long would it last? How much could he endure? The decision to dull the sensation capabilities of his nerve endings made itself. As soon as he thought of it, it was done. As much as possible, he relaxed and dove into settage. In a flash, he fell out of it again.

A few seconds was enough to go into shock from what he saw, use up all his current powers of concentration, and remember a few details of the recent past. It was a sight to see. His internal store of magical reserves was empty. Not a drop of mana was left. Not a single drop! He felt as if he'd been sucked dry and then dried off with a blow dryer to boot. Compared to this discovery, the black sun-shaped scar on his chest where the amulet had ripped itself to freedom seemed like just a detail. The walls of oblivion cracked, opening the way to scrappy memories.

...The runes, arranged in strict order, looked like the facets of a crystal changed from raw crystallized carbon into a stunning diamond. As an experiment, he activated the first rune. The power nodules lit up with a blue flash, the facets began to twinkle...

In the center of his chest, just like a volcano erupting, the medallion with the red stone tore its way to the surface, breaking his skin.

Where is that stupid thing now? Andy once again dove into settage. The "stupid thing" was there. The yellow piece of crap had messed things up real good and then spread all over his ribs in a lifeless blotch. Strange, he couldn't sense any magic in the medallion. The red stone that had grown into his body where there was now a mark like a sun with rays, looked like a bony knob, not a magical artifact pulsing with endless power. So that was it.... but where did that leave him, exactly? Andy tried feeling the external energy sources and almost fell out of his trance again.

The world was full of energy. The magical field was bursting with mana. The measly streams that he fed on in Ilanta could not compare with the deep-water rivers flowing here. Only the astral could give more, but it wasn't possible to scoop it out of the "river." Mana didn't want to be "handled." It seemed to move away from Andy, slipping out of his grasp like water between his fingers.

Neither his second nor third attempts yielded results. The sources of magic did not want to feed him. What should he do? Without mana, it was impossible to change hypostasis. Andy rendered himself into his true essence...

His cry, full of pain and despair, made the swamp's chorus fall silent. The foads deftly vanished into the protection of the lake's depths. The animals that had come to the watering hole, invisible because of the mist, decided to wait to quench their thirst. The pitter-patter of feet and paws and the crackling of broken bushes testified to their hasty flight from an unknown danger. The yellowish-silvery light of the night-time luminary, better known to Andy as Helita, flooded the small clearing on the shore of the lake with its bright rays. The Eye of the goddess of death tried with curiosity to examine this strange being, something like a human. The creature differed from members of the bipedal race by two short stumps protruding from its back, an elongated neck on which it tried to hold its massive head, and large scales that cut through the skin on its arms and legs. Falling to the ground, the creature sobbed and gradually took the form of an ordinary person. The goddess' Eye moved along the dome of the sky in its eternal path, while the man remained to lie on the ground in an awkward position. The deep furrows of the earth, tilled with sharp claws, preserved the memories of the chimera that visited the shore of the lake.

The lake surface near the very cut off went rippling, and a wrinkled face appeared on the surface of the water. The round froggy eyes looked from side to side for a minute. Then, not identifying any danger, the first member of the foad race crept up onto the shore. Hundreds of fellow foads followed. They invaded the moist clay bank. The concert continued. Thirsty animals returned to the watering hole like so many silent shadows. The human figure didn't budge when set upon by a host of blood-sucking insects. But the blood they drank did not nourish the little beasts; they parted from the still body and fell down dead.

The morning freshness and the first rays of the sun beat the featherbed covering the mountain terrace and a small lake of dense fog, the milky cloud of which, yielding to the dawn, gradually thinned, broke into shreds, and slid from the slopes. The daylight, rising upwards, made the snow caps of an enormous mountain sparkle, along the gentle slope of which, like giant steps, dozens of forested terraces descended downward.

Andy woke up from the morning freshness which covered the motionless body in a plump layer of dew. The uncomfortable pose his body had been in for the last few hours left his hands and feet numb and his back like a wooden plank. His neck was completely disinclined to turn to the left or the right. Immersing himself in settage helped. Cracking like an old man, Andy stood up.

"I'm lucky, actually. All those who've made that trip before me and drowned ought to be envious!" He mumbled, glancing around. "Suck it!"

Andy didn't know whether the goddesses were on his side or not—but he wasn't planning on giving up. *Listen, Fate: you're barking up the wrong tree! I didn't live through the pain of the Incarnation and lose my loved ones to just throw up my hands now! The world is full of mana. Therefore, there's gotta be a way to get my wings and my magic back.... It could be worse.*

What do I know about Nelita? It's a very apt time to recall everything Jagirra told me. So what if it's been three thousand years since she left her homeland. The main facts ought to be still current. Under these skies there are a few intelligent races living side by side, and the dragons play the first violin. Who else? Elves, and I know humans and orcs, were brought over from Ilanta; there's also some miurs and sogots. Mom mentioned these races, but she didn't think it was important to expand on how exactly they differ from elves or humans. What the rest of the locals look like and whether they're tasty—I'll have to find out as I go along. Yep, that's it, alright—unless of course I get eaten first.

Jagirra said she studied at the university, which means there are cities and states on this planet. Educational institutions can't be associated with anything else. Most likely, the two worlds aren't that different. Andy scoffed—he would really have to rely on this assumption. His lack of knowledge of the basic rules and customs could turn out a proper mess, often a bloody one, which Andy was basing on his own sad experience. He didn't want to keep stepping on the same rakes over and over...

He picked some herbs and collected something like bast from them. He waded into the warm water up to his knees, then began furiously rubbing and scrubbing from his skin all the dirt and dried blood. When he was done with most of his bathing, Andy rinsed his face and, waiting for the ripples to subside, carefully examined his reflection in the dark water. His eyes hadn't changed, but that couldn't be said for the rest of him. He was skin and bones. His nocturnal attempt to change hypostasis had stripped him of a good ten or twelve pounds. The energy for the transformation was taken directly from the muscle tissue. It was a bad idea. Andy looked at his reflection and thought about his elvish hypostasis. Should he try it? After standing there motionless for a few minutes, he decided not to tempt fate. First, he'd better get something to eat (hopefully something plentiful) and accumulate some mana. Once he rubbed the green grassy stains off his arms, his tattoo became very noticeable. The golden dragon had lost all its charm and color. A pale blotch remained; there was nothing left of the image that had been drawn by the Lady of the Sky. You could barely tell it was a dragon; the runes had disappeared completely. How interesting. As it turned out, he wasn't the only one beaten down by life right now. If his sudden conjectures were correct, Jagirra had poured a hefty portion of mana into the tattoo and created a magical connection to the adornment's owner. The "bearer's" lack of mana and his losing the ability to do magic immediately took its toll on his "rider." It was a good indicator of his state/mana levels, by the way. He would use that in the future. Without mana, his chances of surviving in a foreign world had plummeted. It was hard to imagine himself as the victor over tough circumstances when his unforeseeable events had stripped him of all he had.

But what did he have? Was anything left? Nothing except his hands, feet, and head, which contained some gray matter. If he had a little more of it, he would have thought twice—thrice—about experimenting with portal magic.

There was nothing else to boast of. His last voyage from Earth to Ilanta had been luckier than this one. Then, he at least had some clothes on his back and a penknife. This time he was buck-naked, although bragging about his rear end would have been a bit inappropriate. He had no magic. When his abilities would come back, or if they would at all, he couldn't say. No money, no weapons. The only thing he still did have was true vision, but what use was that?

What should his next steps be? First of all, he had to get something heavy, preferably a club. Then find humans, and then go from there…

The dark smooth surface of the lake became covered with thousands of reflective sparkles, but no one was there to admire the play of light on the water. Snapping out of his reverie, the young man quenched his thirst, finished cleaning the blood and dirt off himself, and left the inhospitable shore. Having figured out his first priorities, Andy set out to find some suitable material for a club.

* * *

"Oh, come on!" A stone with a sharp edge cracked and split into two unequal pieces. "Targ!" Andy swore.

It was the third boulder to break to pieces in the last twenty minutes. Andy sat down on the edge of an uprooted tree, from which he had for a good hour now been trying to extract a length of the root, but the dead tree turned out to be stronger than stone. The root, which looked something like a club or a flanged mace, attracted him with its coarseness and sharp protrusions. It was a sin to pass by an accidental miracle of nature. Sin or not, the dead tree stubbornly refused to part with even a small part of itself. It seemed that nothing could be simpler: break off a chunk and stamp it, but the fallen tree begged to differ with Andy's initial assessment, showing him that such mistakes are punishable by hard labor. Andy, proving to the forest the difference between a naked man and a naked monkey, with perseverance worthy of a woodpecker, continued to hammer on the piece of wood. After all, what's the main difference between the first person and the last monkey? You can talk a lot about this topic, but the first difference is a stick clenched in a tight fist. You can even further rant that the stick was the first tool of labor, but one thing is certain: it was one of the first tools of murder.

The "little rod" Andy was interested in would hardly have suited for loosening the earth in search of grubs, but you could use it to give someone a good thump on the head. What else could he do? His karma was such that he ended up in the woods. Wandering through the wild thickets in Adam's garb was not quite comme il faut. Who knew what the local animals were like? He'd had more than enough encounters with hungry kitties in the past. He had no desire to sit, hugging his knees, under the hot rays of the sun and wait to become food for the mrowns or griffins. What if here too the carnivorous creatures had an irresistible gastronomic interest in bipedal inhabitants? The broken truncheon wouldn't add any rags around his waist and couldn't warm him on cold nights, but it warmed the soul. The main thing is that the club not be too heavy.

If he could trust his senses, the average Earthling or citizen of Ilanta should be a bit stronger than the average native Nelitan. He was basing that guess on how easy it was to move. Gravity must be of lesser force here than on the planet he'd left due to his own stupidity. It was a subtle difference, but enough to allow him to draw certain conclusions. It was entirely possible that this was exactly why the dragons did not colonize their cosmic neighbor. Flying under one's own skies was easier; they were lighter, and he could fly faster. Andy looked in the sky and clenched his jaw. What an evil twist of fate, to give him wings and then take them away...

"I guess this'll do." He picked up another cobblestone and tossed it in his hand. "Third time is a charm," thought Andy, hitting the root. The sun climbed to the zenith, knocking a profuse sweat from the portal jumper. Streams of sweat ran down his broad back. *If only I could plunge into the morning coolness...*

Crack—the third stone broke. Crack—the root broke off, unable to withstand the beating. Andy, planted one foot on the trunk above the stone-beaten fibers, grabbed below the wide crack with both hands, and pulled the lower part to himself with all his might. The tree could not withstand the last jerk. A dry click and the stubborn club that remained in the man's hands announced the victory of reason and perseverance over nature. However, the victory did not prevent him falling on his rear end as he went flying back when the root gave way and getting few splinters.

The club was pleasantly heavy in his hand. Andy turned the "instrument" side to side. *Wish I could burn the filamented end, but it'll work just as is, too. Let's hope I find people sooner than I have to use this thing! Although, could be....* Andy looked at the primitive weapon carefully. *I might need this to defend myself from humans or other intelligent creatures. They're a bit more threatening than predators. My own sad experience has shown...*

* * *

Walking around barefoot in the woods isn't the nicest way to pass one's time. Andy wasn't afraid of sharp stones or sticks; his heightened regeneration took great care of small wounds and cuts, but how would it deal with getting bitten by some poisonous beast? Springing over fallen trees and logs or pushing overgrown large-leaf plants away with his chest, he stepped on large insects a couple times. Thank the Twins, none of the ones he happened to crush turned out to be poisonous. A few times he caught a glimpse of brightly colored two-tailed snakes. Their creeping bodies split into two about two-thirds of the way down.

The woods were unusual—to put it lightly. His surroundings were more like tropics. There were huge fern-like plants, creepers, wide burdock in several tiers, tall trees of three or four arm-lengths around with multicolored foliage, moss hanging from branches like long beards, and the spicy smell of thousands of flowering plants. The bright colors everywhere were striking. The roar of strange insects, the screeching of birds in the sky, the shrill cries of unseen animals, the crackling, grunting, and flatulence. The forest lived an active life. It was indifferent to a small bipedal bug such as himself.

Something white appeared ahead. Andy clenched the club more comfortably. Hmmm. Either he'd met the first intelligent creature, or he missed something. What beast would hang a white veil between the trees? On the right, there was a muffled snapping—a bad sound, alarming. It seemed he really made a mistake in his evaluation of the situation. Now the clicks, accompanied by quiet footsteps, were heard from the left side. This was not good, not at all good. Ten yards ahead of Andy, the thick burdock-like leaves started swinging. He heard more clicks. The answer did not take long to present itself. A quiet tapping and the patter of paws now came from all sides.

Now you've done it, walked right into their trap like a rabbit in a snare. Someone decided to bite him, not even bothering to ask permission from the naked natural scientist. The "snack," stepping carefully, backed up against a fat tree. At least that way they couldn't come at him from behind.

No matter how much Andy prepared for the attack, he still almost missed the spider jumping at him out of the green carpet. It wouldn't be appropriate to call the monster a simple insect. The miracle of nature was the size of a bull terrier. It had six powerful hairy legs instead of the usual eight, and two eyes on thick stems. Otherwise, the "spider" wasn't fundamentally different from its earthly counterparts.

Time slowed down. Obeying his intuition, Andy fell to the ground. In the same instant, the five jumping beasts appeared over the bushes. Long bundles of cobwebs flew over the "game's" head. The first monster, legs drawn in close to its body, landed five feet from Andy. The evil creature clicked its pincers. Only a quick reaction saved the were-dragon from its spitting cobwebs into his face. *Take that!* A blow with the club sent the spitter flying to the ground. Stinking slimy guts splashed out from its crushed belly in all directions. The spider jerked its limbs a couple of times and fell still. An invisible spring threw Andy upwards. Just in time! The spot where he stood a couple of moments ago was covered with arachnid spittle.

Targ! It felt like a lash had struck him on the back. The six-legged scoundrel that had climbed the tree trunk had a better aim than his fellows. *A-a-ah!* He'd become a human target for the spiders' expectorating contest. Contorting his lips in pain, he turned around in the air. The tip of the club broke the spider's two front paws and tore off one of its eyes. The wounded creature fell to the ground and went into convulsions. A second blow, on the return swing, sent it to its forefathers.

Landing, Andy immediately jumped back behind the tree trunk for cover. A few cobweb-loogies hit the bark, but he didn't quite make it in time to avoid them all. The tip of the searing spider web lashed across his left cheek. It immediately swelled up, along with his left eye, as from an allergic reaction to a bee sting. The spiders did not think of letting the quick prey go so easily. Several six-legged beasts charged toward the tree. Despite the pain in his back and his swollen left eye, Andy jumped out from behind the trunk and cracked the hunter on the head, landing in the center of a fern-like plant. Fire burned his right leg. A thin whitish band in a snap wound around his ankle and shin. The spitting creature, lifting its front paws and rising on its hind legs, prepared a second portion of the poisonous web, but it apparently did not expect the biped to move so quickly. In memory of its fellows, the monster remained with raised front legs, because its rear end was beaten into the ground. Half the cephalothorax, with lifeless dangling eye-stems, was all that remained on the surface, along with raised front legs, like a surrendering soldier. Letting another batch of the poisonous spittle pass overhead, Andy fell to the ground, then got up, still very much in the game despite his injuries. A spider-shaped jumper rose up above the bushes. One powerful blow with the club sent it flying. Having lost one more companion, the spiders decided that the prey was not worth the effort and retreated towards the white veil, which in fact was a snare net for small birds.

Finally left alone, drained of all strength, the were-dragon plopped to the ground. He was extremely lucky that the poisonous web had not affected him the way the six-legged hunters were counting on; otherwise, he would have long-since been a white cocoon, swaddled arms, legs and all. His left eye was numb, his cheek swollen as from a cruel insect bite, and his leg and back burned with a hellish flame. The spiders had won, essentially. The battle was theirs. Only a few peculiarities of the loser's physiognomy allowed him to leave the battlefield in one piece, not in the spiders' stomachs. The dragon's blood flowing through his veins gave him immunity to lots of poisons. If only it could make him immune to the pain…

It was time to book it out of there. Please Twins, don't let the beasts challenge him to a re-match or go get backup. Who knew? Maybe that was one of their behaviors. Andy was not inclined to conduct an experiment, with his own neck on the line. All the less so since he had never heard of insects hunting as a pack… not counting ants, of course. *Ants… ooh! It would be funny if on Nelita they're as big as these brutes!*

* * *

He was hungry. His empty stomach began to look carnivorously at his spine, especially since it had been sticking to it for a long time. After his encounter with the spiders, no local and preferably edible creatures were found within reach. Birds preferred to stay closer to the crowns of trees; the other creatures supported the birds with all their hearts. Animals similar to koalas, running from branch to branch in the middle tier of the forest, upon seeing the stranger, immediately started to squeal, emptied their bowels of their contents and hid in the dense foliage. What the "koalas" fed on was a mystery, but the stuff they defecated out of themselves stank unmercifully. The spiders' guts seemed to give off the aroma of pink petals by comparison. It would have been one thing if the "bears" were just pooping. But with their shouts, they warned the rest of the forest inhabitants about the danger. A couple of times, Andy saw fleecy herds of small deer—maybe not deer, but something similar. Once he heard something big trample through the bushes not far off. Judging by the tracks they left, the size of the creatures' claws could compete with dragons' claws. By the way, about that—several times, Andy caught a glimpse of characteristic silhouettes in the sky.

Judging by his internal clock, this was already the seventh hour of walking on foot. Andy made his way past two natural "terraces." There was a convenient descent from the first; the second was overcome by a strong and rather long vine. He never found a single trace of a person or other intelligent being. No path, no road, no abandoned fireplace. It was virgin territory, unburdened by civilization.

Andy stopped near a little spring which flowed from between the roots of a tree with a reddish-brown bark and long blade-like leaves. He drank with pleasure. His teeth hurt from the cold, but nothing in the world can match the taste of the purest spring water. Springs always smell of life. The water somewhat calmed his stomach. It detached itself from his spine, but promised to return. The owner of the body carefully examined the trees: no fruits worthy of attention or any that might, despite the risk of diarrhea, satisfy his hunger. *What a pity! My stomach returned to my spine quicker than I walked away from that spring!*

Having quenched his thirst, the traveler grabbed the club with both hands and headed towards a wide gap in the "fence" of forest giants. A few minutes later, he was standing on the edge of a wide clearing. Despite his fatigue, injuries, and the situation which did not encompass any beauty to admire, Andy was amazed at the view that opened before him. The glade was strewn with huge flowers with blossoms of the size of a dinner plate. Thousands of butterflies of all shapes, sizes, and colors circled over the open buds. Andy got the impression of a living carpet, individual elements of which broke away from the general composition and sought to occupy another place they thought was due to them.

Andy wasn't able to admire the beauty for long. A light breeze carried the smell of a dog to his olfactory organs. Andy spun on the spot; a second whiff confirmed that his nose was not mistaken. A gloomy premonition played unpleasantly on his nerves. Everything would have been fine, except that the canine scent came from the direction he'd come from. They were tracking him! In a couple of seconds, he heard the yelping of more than one creature from the direction of the spring.

Is it Cerberus, come for my soul? Oh, legs, come on legs, get my butt out of here, fast! Andy ran towards a third "terrace."

He didn't make it. A pair of animals, similar to a cross between a wolverine and a porcupine, jumped out of the bushes across from him. For the most part, the beasts looked like wolverines. But they had bundles of long needles that grew between their shoulder blades. Their sleek paws, adapted to fast running, were another difference between the local fauna and the terrestrial beasts. The first animal, closest to Andy, stopped short and jerked its neck.

"Targ!" he yelled, when dozens of needles shot from the creatures and flew over his shoulder, literally a few centimeters from his nose as he turned his head to look back while fleeing. No need for a fortune teller—the needles were poisonous. The second animal barked loudly and tried to bite his heel. The club, crashing down on the base of the animal's skull, guaranteed no further such attempts. The dead do not bite.

Three more wild beasts sprang out of the bushes. Fate did not let Andy escape from the fan of needles fired at him. His naked buttocks were soon decorated with some unusual ornaments. His head clouded. These animals were more dangerous than spiders. And what had he ever done to them? With a movement of his left hand, he tore out the needles; in the next instant, he flew up into the air with a mighty leap, club in hand, and landed next to the first beast that attacked him. The club broke its spine. The buzzing in Andy's head was growing stronger and stronger; time was playing against him. Five more needles struck him in the right side. Andy's vision began to cloud, along with the noise in his head. He ran with all possible speed away from the terrible enemies. "I should have scrammed right away when I had the chance," he thought.

Where the giant bird came from, he didn't see—his dull reactions and failing vision really did him a bad turn. A jolt from the powerful beak sent Andy flying several yards back. He flew through the air half way and plowed the earth with his behind the second half. The bird took three broad steps and squeezed Andy with its foot. After a couple of seconds the wild beasts came running and, furiously yowling, circled around.

"Oh Targ," Andy hissed, when he was able to make out black collars on the animals' necks. He realized that the person he saw on the bird's back wasn't an illusion or a fluke. The wolverines' poison finally took its effect, sending the were-dragon into oblivion.

Nelita. Principality of Ora. Astal Ruigara. The catchers…

Farid jumped down off Guger. The trox, cawing loudly, released the fugitive from his paw. Behind him came the sound of Mirda's heavy footsteps. She was Iriel's trox, and Iriel and Farid were partners. The half-elf dismounted from the bird's back, along with the mage assigned to this search group. The catcher squinted at the wizard. *Ugh, have they really assigned this nonentity to me?* The mage pounded his bottom with his fists for a long while, stepping around bow-legged in a circle. *Interesting: what sins brought this upon me? What have I done to be sent to the Borderzone? Is this because of my handsome mug?* Iriel, catching his friend's look and grinning conspiratorially, pointed at the mage and made a naughty face. Farid returned the smile. The reason for the city-boy smart-alec's strange gait became clear: prickly burrs under the saddle pillow would make anyone uncomfortable.

Farid extended his hand. The half-elf high-fived him. He should be glad that male troxes were smaller than females, and he could, therefore, ride Guger alone. Fitting two saddles on Guger's back would have been problematic. The catcher glanced at the birds. Iriel's female craned her neck playfully and very lightly pecked Farid's trox. In a fiver, Mirda wouldn't be able to carry the guards on duty. The feathers on her crest were red, which meant soon it would be mating time, and she would lay an egg. That's why she'd been flirting with Guger half the fiver. She would guard her eggs for eight fivers, until the little chick or chicks hatch (troxes rarely lay more than two eggs at a time). It was unfortunate. During this time, Farid would have to work in another team or hole up in the village at the dugaria (transformation prison), and thereby cut costs. It would be great luck if Mirda chose Guger while in heat; then the catcher would get a third of the value of the hatch. *Ugh, I hope Manyfaces doesn't turn her gaze away from this humble border guard and his trox. I'm already sick of being a fugitive catcher...*

"Not one of ours," Iriel said, squatting. "He's disgustingly thin."

"He doesn't look like a dugar. Their bodies grow quite thick in the cocoons, and their expressions are like that of dumb babies," the mage butted into the conversation. The catcher frowned. Was it their place to discuss fundamental truths? "Look, does he have marks on his skin from the respiratory and waste tubes? He does have scars on his chest from the main concress, so, logically, there should be traces of the tubes."

"Teg Zidon, you're a mage; you're holding all the cards. And we're merely humble workers of the outskirts; we don't dare infringe upon your domain." Letting the mage go ahead, Farid stepped aside. For some reason, he had no desire to examine the prisoner's crotch and anal areas. Iriel got out some vegetable gelatin from the bag strapped to Mirda's right side and tied up the prisoner's hands and feet. He poured with guava juice on the vegetable gelatin, which instantly hardened, cuffing the prisoner more securely than some shackles. "Be careful—what if he's a mage?"

"It seems you may be right, Iriel, sir. This shkas isn't our client," the mage drawled, finishing his examination. "There are no marks from the tubes. Strange... I don't sense any magic in him, so your suspicions are in vain."

"You called him a shkas?" Farid said in surprise.

"Look at his eyes," the mage answered.

"A freak." Farid lifted up the prisoner's right eyelid. "Anything else strange about him?"

"That tattoo. Imperialists from the special guard get tattoos like that."

Iriel looked at teg Zidon skeptically. Pushing him aside, he leaned over the prisoner.

"You're mistaken, teg Zidon, sir," he turned to the mage. "The guards' tattoos have a different shape of wings. But it does resemble the coat of arms of the Imperial line to some degree. It's possible the shkas is one of the servants, and he stole something, which is why he was sent to the converter, plus, he's sure tall enough for a human guard. But he's too skinny. The Emperor doesn't take featherweight humans into the special guard. Our friend here would need to gain some weight, fat and muscle. What are we going to do with him? The guy escaped from the converter. I can't even imagine how he managed to get through the miurs' woods? How far is it from here to the Empire?"

"Far, Iriel. We'll hand the fugitive over to the prison warden."

"There you have it." Iriel looked at the wolverines. The half-elf's gaze searched for the three animals. "Farid, did you send Drax and Riga after him?"

"No, the rixes chased him straight to Guger. All five should be here somewhere."

"They're not. My heart tells me that this freak sent them to Manyfaces." Iriel got into his bird's saddle. "Let's look a bit."

"Careful, should you chance upon escaped dugars. Manyfaces only knows where these imbeciles can get to," the mage said.

"You're singing to the choir," the half-elf said. "Hai-ah, let's go, baby."

Farid made his prancer get down on the ground. He too saddled up and took the reigns. Zidon used a levitation spell to set the naked man on the trox's back. Passing the rope through the rings of the harness, the catcher secured his two-legged prey. Five minutes later, Iriel returned from his reconnaissance mission. Two dead rixes fell to the ground in front of his partner's trox.

"That cur!" Farid's fist hit the animal killer's cheek at full force. Andy gave a barely audible moan. "Take that!" He hit him a second time.

"Careful!" The mage intercepted the fist that was ready for a third blow. "I don't know about you, but I'd like to get compensated for delivering a LIVE criminal, not fined for delivering a corpse."

The catcher looked angrily at the city dweller and spat.

"Don't butt in, Zidon—it's none of your business. These rixes cost two golden pounds each. The fee for a corpse is one!"

"You're forgetting yourself, Farid!" The mage constructed some sort of interweave. A defensive shield grew up around him as he prepared to attack.

"Friend, it's not worth it," Iriel jumped down off of Mirda. "This scum will still get what's coming to him," the half-elf lightly kicked the shkas. "Let's go home."

* * *

"Who is this?" Teg Viged, warden at the border post and boss of the dugaria, examined the shkas caught by the catchers. "What are you looking at? It's a freak. You'll get ten jangs for this two-legged worm. And where, may I ask, are the three that got away? Who was it you were sent to retrieve, after all?"

"They're not there. The dugars could have headed south. They haven't lost their memories, right?" Iriel asked.

"No, plague take them!"

"They aren't complete idiots. They wouldn't head towards the miur mountains, even after the transformation. You need to send a couple of search regiments south and east."

"You think you're so smart—I've sent them already," the warden said. "Where did you say you found this thing?" Teg Viged squeezed the thin shkas' muscles.

"Half a crossing away from the miur territory."

"This Imperialist is far from home."

"Mr. warden, sir," teg Zidon stood up. "May I say something?"

"Go ahead." The warden turned to his colleague.

"I've checked this one," Zidon glanced at the prisoner. "Allow me to share my observations. First of all, he doesn't understand or speak our language, which is very strange, considering the fact that I can't find evidence of tampering with his mind." Iriel and Farid grinned. They remembered how hard they tried to get into the prisoner's mind. "I didn't sense any magic in the prisoner, but he is able to defend his thoughts most skillfully. Someone's taught him control. I can't understand what for? What else... when we intercepted him, I counted about ten marks on his back where the rixes' needles pierced him. After such a huge dose of poison, he should have been unconscious for more than a day, but the shkas came to about five hours later."

"What do you make of it?" The warden wanted the mage to get to the point.

"Someone has specially removed his knowledge of the language. It's not at all possible to do that in the dugaria. I think it's some sort of cunning set up."

"Zidon, you're making this way too complicated. Wonders like that happen, if the transformation process, once begun, was suddenly interrupted. With the breakdown of the neural connections of the temporal lobe and the central nervous system of the person, such muck is formed in the brain that even Manyfaces couldn't sort it out. It's a wonder the freak even kept his wits. However, his wits won't help him."

"You want to put him in a cocoon?"

"Yes. Let's finish what the Imperialists started."

"You're not even going to try to find out how he managed to cross the cat people's lands?"

"Zidon, how would I? You said yourself he doesn't understand a word. Should I look for a sharp wit and teach him to speak? Is that even possible? The freak has such gunk in his head right now we'd have to heal the sharp wit later. All your attempts to pierce the defensive wall are the consequence of this. There's nothing there—it's empty. Understand? I don't know what this shkas has been sentenced to the cocoon for, and I don't want to know. But I have no desire to contact the 'dark' princes. It would not be worth disturbing them for no reason, not by a long shot. So the cocoon will be the most logical option." Teg Viged snapped his fingers. Two strong creatures with hummocks of rolling muscles, sloping foreheads and a lack of any sign of intelligence on their faces stepped forward from a small nook in the wall. "Carry him to the reception platform," the warden commanded the dugars. Zidon shook his head in disapproval. Bad form. The warden was making a big mistake. He was an excellent administrator, but a mediocre mage—even a poor one. A lot of personal experience can't replace academic knowledge and intuition. "Let's go," the warden invited the three catchers to follow him.

The dugars dragged the desperately resisting shkas from the room. The freak turned out to be very strong indeed. The powerful dunces could barely manage the task of handling their future colleague.

"Who's THAT?" Farid asked, pointing to a beautiful woman coming out of a cocoon. Some mages were wiping the mucus off her.

"That's Farx Trigiv. Caught in the act of attempted rape. His intended victim was Madam Latirra's protege. They sentenced him to three years as a woman, sold to a bordello. After three years, his memory will return, and so will his natural form. This is it. Mark, please take our client." The warden patted the mage on the shoulder. Mark ran the "reception room."

Mark nodded to his boss and closed his eyes. One of the branches of a gigantic tree with dozens of cocoons hanging from its branches lowered to the platform. One could see glimpses of the silhouettes of the people inside them. The nearest cocoon opened....

Andy quit struggling. It was pointless. The gorillas were holding him tightly. Better save his strength. If intuition served him right, he would need it. They carried him outside. The group of three human men and one elf was chatting about something as they moved towards an enormous tree with green shells hanging from its branches. At least, that's what it seemed like from afar. The gorillas followed their masters silently. The closer they got to the tree, the stronger the shivers ran down Andy's spine. That tree imbued him with an irrational fear.

"Almighty Twins!" his disobedient lips muttered. There were people in the shells! Andy craned his neck—his eyes weren't deceiving him. About ten yards away from their group, the gorillas and a pair of mages retrieved a woman from one of the "shells" and wiped some sort of snot off her. There was a lifeless and obedient expression behind her eyes. A fat man in a red frock laughed deafeningly. The others didn't. Apparently, the joke was known to him alone. In ten steps, the gorillas reached a small platform that led to the horrifying giant. The lowest branch bent down and touched the ground. Guessing what would happen next, Andy began to struggle even worse than before. The gorillas swung their arms and threw him at the open shell.

"Noooooooo!" Andy screamed at the top of his lungs.

Some disgusting green feelers protruded from the open shell to meet its prey. They wound around their victim's arms and legs. As soon as the slime touched them, his fetters disintegrated. Andy tried to get out, but the feelers squeezed him tighter, pressing his arms to his body. The shell opened wider with a foul squirting sound. The feeler began to drag him to the slime-drenched leaves. When he was a foot away from the "shell," a few more feelers came out of it. The end of the thickest feeler divided into several parts, forming something like a flower with eight petals. The edge of each "petal" was covered in small hooks, and in the center coiled hundreds of whitish flagella. The "flower" struck him in the center of the chest. The hooks dug deep into his skin. Jerking with all his might, Andy managed to free his right hand. He couldn't think of anything better than pulling the "flower" feeler towards his face with his free hand and biting into it. White mucus flowed from the shell. The feelers holding Andy went straight and released their victim. Andy tumbled onto the platform from a height of sixteen feet. (The tree branch had climbed back up). He did not have time to catch his breath before the gorillas piled on him…

* * *

"Hm." The warden said, looking at the shkas being held by the dugars. "I wanted to make the best of the situation. We've got to get rid of him. Dugaria doesn't take scum twice, and it would be too much trouble to take this freak somewhere else. I don't have a stationary portal here. This is the outskirts, Tma take it."

"Maybe we should just…?" Farid suggested, running his finger across his throat. "Problem solved."

"Don't even think about it!" Teg Viged stopped him. "Ruigar arrives this evening, and the first thing he'll do is scan everyone, and if he detects the fluids of intention to kill, the cocoons aren't far off. Even thinking about it is forbidden! The dragon said only he can execute anyone here. But why am I taking such pains for your sakes? You know the sovereign's thing as well as I do: checking the memories of everyone who smells like death. Tma, it all started out so well. I would have written him down as a captured escapee; still identical idiots come out of the cocoons. And now what do we do? As soon as he starts reading our thoughts, several things will come to light, and this shkas along with them."

"Put a collar of obedience on him and give him to the free settlements," Zidon advised the warden. "Or throw him back where you got him."

"Hey, there's a thought! Farid, Iriel, pack up!"

* * *

"It's hot," Farid wiped the sweat off his brow.

"You can say that again." Iriel took a handkerchief out of his pocket.

"Aren't you just the aristocrat!" Farid laughed, watching the half-elf put the hanky back. "Tma, only half way. Let's take a rest at Yellow Creek."

"Okay."

Fifteen minutes later, their troxes perked up and started going faster. The birds could sense water nearby.

A couple of turns in the forest trail and the guards could see the shore of a wide creek that was named for the yellow sand washed into it from the mountains.

The catchers led their troxes to the bivouac built by the residents of a free settlement near the shady backwaters.

"We ought to give that thing a drink too," Farid said, nodding towards the tied-up shkas. The freak was lying on Mirda's back like a sack of potatoes, stripped of his will. The collar saw to that.

The half-elf poked the "cargo:"

"Hey, you, want a drink?" The shkas didn't move. Iriel removed his left foot from the stirrups and kicked the prisoner in the butt. "Drink. Do you want to? Why so quiet?" No reaction. "Our friend isn't speaking to us. I guess he doesn't want to drink."

"Check him out. Maybe he's passed out from the sun."

"Why do I have to do all the dirty work?" the half-elf mumbled. "Now I have to take care of shkases."

Iriel jumped down off his trox, grabbed the prisoner by the chin and waved his hand in front of his face.

"Tma!" he swore, seeing the freak's glassy, lifeless eyes. "Farid!"

"What?" Farid called back, undoing the straps of the saddlebags.

"I have to tell you something..."

"Out with it. Geez, these things are heavy," he said, pulling the bags off and setting them on the ground.

"The shkas is dead."

"Whaddaya mean, dead?"

"He's dead."

"Yeah, right."

"I'm not kidding! He's cold!"

"Tma of all the gods!" Farid ran over to the half-elf. "Coming, coming." He unbuttoned his cloak, retrieved a needle from his pocket, and slid it under the slave's thumbnail. The shkas didn't move. A drop of dark blood appeared under the nail. "Do you have a mirror?"

"Yeah."

"Give it here!" The mirror put under the prisoner's nose did not think of revealing any signs of breath. "Unload him, quick!"

"Where should I put him? He's dead!"

The border guards undid the knots of the fastening belts and lowered the limp body to the ground. Farid took an amulet from the saddlebag and ran it over the prostrate body for a few seconds, then pressed his right ear to the prisoner's chest.

"The scanner shows nothing. His heart's not beating. The brute! Even in death, he's inconveniencing me. What a fiver!" The guard jumped to his feet and wanted to kick the corpse, but Iriel blocked him with his body.

"Don't, you'll just bring shame on yourself. The dead deserve some sort of respect, and this one's earned it. Not everyone can escape from two dugarias."

"Respect this dung? Just try to add up how much he's cost us!"

"Yes, it's a pity about the rixes," Iriel agreed. "We'll save up for some new ones. Mirda will lay an egg soon, and I'll buy you a pair of pups. Maybe your dogs in the kennel are now grooming a female. A quarter of that litter will be yours too."

"Alright, I'm calm," Farid spit on the sand. "Iriel, do you have any amulets or spell capsules?"

"It won't help, Farid. If he were just wounded, that would be different. But the standard set of amulets can't raise the dead. Or do you just want to singe him with a combat capsule and bury the ashes?"

"There you go! The beasts will bury him!" the catcher answered, pulling the collar and shackles off the shkas. "Let's drag him over to the shade. Tma knows when he died. I wouldn't want him to start stinking and spoil my appetite. Let's have something to eat, then take him to the woods. What do you think: will Lord Ruigar grab us by the ba…?"

"I don't think so. The shkas died of his own accord. Let him scan our memories. We didn't kill him."

The border guards dragged the body far away from the rest stop and went back to the bivouac. While Farid prepared a simple lunch, Iriel got undressed and led the birds into the creek. The troxes plopped into the water happily and let the half-elf rub their feathers where the saddles go with a special balm to prevent chafing and parasites.

"Lunch is ready!" Farid cried from the shore.

"One minute," Iriel said. "You didn't touch my boots, did you?"

"No, what do I care?"

"Farid, did you cast a 'watchdog' spell?" The half-elf activated the defense and combat amulets hanging around his neck and leaned over the blurry print of a bare foot right where he'd left his shoes and outer clothes.

"You're offending me! Of course, I cast the spell, even with a double contour. Why?"

"Did you set it to exit mode too?"

"Iri, you've boiled your brains in the sun. What happened?" Farid activated his combat amulets, grabbed a short spear, and walked over to his friend.

"I get the feeling we've been had, real bad."

"THE SHKASSSS!" the guard hissed, jumping towards the sashes with swords. Iriel dove like a little fish to the saddlebags and in one well-practiced motion grabbed his fire-starter from the side pocket. Swords were good, but a chucker with fire spells in the capsule was better. He didn't care that one shot would cover a circle six yards in diameter and vaporize everything in that area. That's why he'd paid twenty weighty pounds for the little "toy." "The scanner!" Farid cried. The half-elf grabbed it from the bag and tossed it to his partner. "Relax," Farid said, thirty seconds later. "He's not here, at least not in a radius of a hundred yards around."

Iriel gripped the chucker more comfortably and scanned the edge of the woods with his eyes.

"Far, check to see what else is missing besides my clothes and boots."

"Tma!" Farid saw a gutted bag. "I'll find you—I'll kill you! That creature stole my old so-and-so!"

"Good luck with that," Iriel barked, getting out his extra set of clothes.

"What??"

"Tonight we have to go back, which means right now we can't make any search efforts. And tomorrow it'll be pointless to try to find him. Neither the rixes nor the mages will catch a traces of him. Say goodbye to your iron."

"There was a belt for it there too."

"And your belt... I just broke those boots in... may your toes be callused by them!" Iriel shouted in the direction of the woods and laughed out loud.

"What's wrong with you?" Farid said.

"Quiet, Far. Better be quiet," the half-elf said, catching his breath. "As far as everyone else is concerned, that shkas died. If they find out in the village that we were given a run for our money, they won't let us live it down for a century. He made complete fools of us. I can hear it now: we're washed up, too slack, haven't been chased by miurs in way too long...."

"But how did he do it? He was deader than dead!"

"Have you ever heard of settage?" Farid shook his head. "I have, and I was forced to think about it! What's more, Far, next time make sure you set the watchdog spell to exit mode. Ah, I can't believe he took my boots!"

* * *

Andy went down from terrace to terrace. For the second day now, he'd been making his way through the endless wood that covered the slopes of a gigantic mountain with its branches. The shirt he took off from the half-elf, on the second day, fell into disrepair because he took it into his head to go straight through the prickly thicket of some low-growing trees. As a result, the shirt got hundreds of small holes in it. The boots and thin leather pants suffered less. The half-blood definitely understood the point of footwear—there were soft, comfortable, and, as luck would have it, fit the little thief just right.

Not bad, not bad at all. My settage plan worked better than

I had hoped. It was a risk, of course, the danger of the hunters wouldn't be fooled, or would believe his ruse and decide to bury him, cremate him, or do any other ungodly things with the supposed corpse, but it worked out fine. And for a minute, there I was afraid of going into the trance too soon, and then the whole plan would have gone to Targ. If I'd had to play dead for five more minutes, the pretend corpse could have become a real one! Thank the Twins, my "death" was discovered right on time, and those men acted just as I predicted.

As for the borrowed clothing and short sword, I need them more than they do, and that'll be a lesson for the hunters. Let the stolen goods be considered payback for the needle under my nail. After Andy had stolen the sword from the bag and the half-elf's clothes, he crawled to a bend in the creek located downstream and quietly entered the water. For about fifty minutes, he waded along the bed of the creek, then went ashore, and got dressed. The pants and boots were a good fit; the shirt was a little wide. But that was okay—he would put some meat back on his bones. The sword, to be honest, was a piece of crap, no other way to put it. Andy sadly remembered his blades, but no sense fretting over spilled milk. Now, if only he could get his magic back. The stolen sword was made from poor-quality steel. Clicking his finger against the blade produced a short ringing sound, not a long melodious song. What can you do? Beggars can't be choosy.

Andy couldn't say how many leagues he crossed that first day. Trying to increase the space between himself and his possible hunters, he strove onward like a moose in heat. The sun, finally giving up, sank down behind the horizon. Helita came out, and he kept putting the leagues behind him, step by step. He once again offered up a grateful prayer to Jagirra and Karegar for giving him true vision, which also functioned as night vision. The expedition ended at the shore of a forest lake, which he dove into three hours after sunset. Here luck for the second time in such a long day smiled at him.

As soon as Andy got settled on a wide branch of a huge tree that grew right on the beach by the lake, the dark shadows crawling from the water onto the shore caught his attention. Helita, which had climbed higher than the treetops, illuminated the large turtles. They were ordinary turtles, just like on Earth. Andy almost fell off his branch. His stomach, which had once again started clinging to his spine, woke up and screamed, "FOOD!" Raw turtle meat didn't sound so bad to the starving guy. He mercifully clubbed a couple of them on the head with his chunk of iron called a sword and feasted. The next morning there was enough leftover for breakfast.

Perhaps because he'd reached his limit of "fun" adventures, the woods and the powers that be decided to leave the were-dragon alone for once and give him a calm day. That day, he didn't encounter a single jumping, spitting spider or other hungry predator that wasn't too picky about the menu. Also noticeably absent were humans, elves, half-bloods, or other intelligent beings, and Targ take them!

Evening came. Soon the sun would set. It was time to find somewhere where he, too, could lay down his head; his legs were aching. He was still getting over yesterday's incredible feat. Andy jumped over a narrow stream and froze on the spot. *Sooo, ... that's the footprint of some sort of intelligent creature, right under my feet! A path's been beaten. People, some sort of people, or... something.*

The loud, despairing cry of an adult and a child's scream interrupted Andy's thought process and settled the question of what direction the beings who made this path might live in. Without a second's hesitation, he grabbed his blade from the sheath and threw himself towards the child's cries. "Idiot!" the belated thought flashed in his mind.

Literally five seconds later, he heard the sounds of yapping.

"Targ!" The image of a wolverine formed in his brain. *Where is he going? Idiot!*

Andy leaped over a fallen tree and jumped abruptly. Poisonous needles flew under his feet. In an instant, he glimpsed a man lying on the ground with a dozen needles in his right side in one direction, and a large wicker basket that two wolverines were rolling along the clearing in another. The child's cries seemed to be coming from inside the basket. Another, smaller basket was laying near the man. Apparently, he'd noticed the beasts and managed to hide his child inside the container. Two more predators turned towards the biped dodger who'd intervened in their feast. Andy landed next to the man, grabbed the small box and hurled it at the nearest beast with all his might. The predator was not expecting anything of the sort and was sent careening back along the ground. The other beast jumped aside so as to avoid the box and craned its neck, preparing to fire in that direction, but Andy was no longer there. In the split second, after he hurled the box, he jumped after it to attack. His blade became bathed in bright red blood. Black needles stabbed into a nearby tree. One of the other two, counting on its poison and aim, decided to meet the enemy with needles. Andy jumped straight up as usual letting the "ammunition" fly under him, and then attacked the shooter. It ran to meet him—and with a pathetic cry fell to the ground from a crushing kick to the jaw. Now the one that had been sent packing by the box recovered and came at him, practically at the same time. The pressure of danger squeezed the home-grown superman to the ground. Another batch of needles swept over him as he hugged the ground. Andy then jumped to his feet once more and dashed behind the thick trunk of a tree, which was immediately struck by several long "gifts." A slant to the side, a quick glance at the beast, and his sword flashed white. The fourth predator's skull was decorated with an unforeseen ornament. The animal died not having realized that the hunt was over. Left alone with such a dreaded biped, the fourth wolverine decided to make its exit. With its tail between its legs, it disappeared into the thick bushes. Andy came out from behind the tree and pulled the blade out of the dead creature's body. The whole skirmish lasted no more than half a minute, but it drained his strength as if it were a two-hour battle.

Andy wiped the blood off his sword on the fur of the last beast he'd killed. He then attended to the man, who turned out to be a pure-blooded elf. The savior carefully pulled the needles out and felt the victim's pulse. He was alive. True vision confirmed this. The elf's spark of life still shone, dimly, but it wasn't about to go out. Some sort of magical amulet shone red around the neck of the son of the Forest. A white-haired girl crawled out of the box, looked at the dead beasts with her wide sapphire eyes and wanted to crawl back in, but then she saw Andy pulling the last needle out of her father's body.

She immediately forgot all about the box and the dead wolverines and threw herself at her father:

"Nana, Nana!" She looked at their rescuer with eyes full of tears. "Namiru pata Nana. Pata, namiru vayiti ma!"

"I'll help you if I can," Andy picked the elf up and put him over his shoulder like a sack of potatoes. "Strange language," he thought to himself. "It sounds a bit like Edda." "Lead the way! Iv tary vei!" he said in dragon Edda, hoping the girl would understand. She did.

"Come with me," she answered with a strange accent and ran along the path.

***

Nelita. Principality of Ora. Astal Ruigara. Border-crossing post.

Teg Viged was trembling. The warden of the border post was afraid to look at the sovereign Ruigar. His legs couldn't take it anymore; he needed to sit down, but the dragon's piercing gaze made him stand at attention and pull his tummy in.

"Warden, tell me: how many mages do we have at the post?" Ruigar hovered over the man, who was sweating with fear. The dragon didn't express his dissatisfaction at all, but subjects of the astal, the sovereign Ruigar, knew to fear not loud yelling and tongues of fire, but rather a calm, almost affectionate tone...

"F-f-forty one, s-sovereign," teg Viged managed to spit out, his teeth chattering.

"Including you?"

"Y-yes."

"And how many are at the dugaria at any given time?"

"Fifteen," teg Viged's head sank into his shoulders.

"And you're telling me that fifteen verified mages didn't notice anything?" The dragon opened his mouth. The yellow-white daggers of his teeth were visible.

"N-n-no."

"It's a shame. I'm beginning to doubt the professionalism of the border guards."

"My dear," an emerald dragoness who had flown in with Ruigar said in high Edda. The sovereign turned his eyes away from his guilty subject, who grabbed a handkerchief from his pocket and wiped his brow. "The scent is very old, and the guest could have been covered in defensive veils. I don't think it is possible to be noticed if you do not want to be."

"Old? I was here yesterday and did not smell a thing."

"You are scaring this poor man. May I speak with him?" Ruigar lifted his wings and stepped aside, indifferent. The dragoness walked up to the warden and changed hypostasis.

As scared as teg Viged might have been, the sight of the tall, handsome, golden-haired elf in a tunic made of spider silk made him forget his fear for a moment.

The woman, smiling enchantingly, extended her hand and grabbed him by the chin. Her sharp nails made him look up and stand tippy-toe.

"Look me in the eye!" Trying to jerk his head was useless; the dragon was holding it firmly. The man's mind shields were removed in a moment by the power of her will. "Hm, it is empty. Not a single memory to bring up..." The sharp-nailed hand relaxed. The man, free from the grip, fell to the ground. "You do not have to worry about this one. He does not have the hallmark of betrayal unless you count a couple of petty crimes treason. But we can look the other way about that. It is entirely possible that the guest was incognito here, or we are dealing with someone who has been given a gift of blood, but the ritual has not been done on him."

The warden sent a mental prayer to Manyfaces for not letting the dragoness dig too deep into his brain, and that she wasn't interested in that cursed imperial shkas.

Ruigar lay down. A translucent membrane covered his eyes. The emerald female didn't turn back to her true form. Instead she climbed up and settled nicely into the curve of the red giant's front paw. Teg Viged backed away. He snapped his fingers and a boy servant came to him from around the corner.

"Quickly bring some cold beverages and fruit. Tell Pron to bring a little table."

The boy ran off instantly. In a few minutes, a whole procession came forth from behind the corner. People brought wicker chairs and a table; fresh fruit smelled nice in baskets. Carefully, so as not to spill it, Pron brought in a large bucket full of ice, out of which peeked the necks of bottles of sparkling wine. The dragoness accepted the offering favorably. She moved from her beau's front paws to one of the chairs, sat down comfortably and pointed to a bottle of wine with her exquisite finger. Viged drove away the servants with a wave of his hand, himself remaining to play the role of waiter. Wise in experience, he knew that a well-fed dragon was a kind dragon. Judging by their behavior, the beautiful woman sitting in front of him had considerable influence on the astal. It would be useful to gain even a tiny fraction of her good will, so the warden sucked up to his master's girlfriend like a leach.

The cork popped and the sparkling wine flowed into the tall wine glass. The dragoness took the glass with the amber beverage and held it up to Ruigar's nose. The sovereign removed the film from his eyes and looked at his partner.

"It would not hurt you to relax a bit," Goldilocks said, smiling. "It is getting cloudy in here from your heavy thoughts."

The dragon snorted and swung his head from side to side. In one instant, the scarlet-scaled monster turned into a tall elf of athletic build. He was dressed in the latest fashion in the capital. The warden stopped in his tracks. He couldn't remember ever seeing the sovereign change his form, and now he was trying to remember the elf's facial features. The dragon cast an imposing figure even in elf form, emanating power. He had an even oval face, a strong jaw, a high, open forehead, and long, jet black hair gathered into a ponytail. His powerful mind was obvious from his brown eyes.

"Relax, you say?"

The woman nodded. The warden stepped away and tried to become invisible, or as close as possible, so the dragons, conversing in High Edda, wouldn't think he was eavesdropping.

"What is bothering you? Should we brainstorm together?" The

sovereign filled a second glass and sat down in an empty chair. The shadow of thoughts flashed across his face.

"It is that smell. Ilirra, if the guy did not want us to know about him, he would not have left a trace, that is for sure. I can not understand the point of his actions. What for? It is as if someone tried to leave us a trail, but to what? And why would a dragon be in a dugaria in the first place?"

"So you think it was a dragon? Have you considered that it might be a human who received the gift of blood?"

"You smelled it yourself. Humans do not smell like that." The elf closed her eyes in acquiesce. "What is interesting is that the tracks led to the bird barns. The scent is strongest there. The 'guest' hid on one of the birds, and no one saw a thing!"

"And what is the point of all this?"

"The empire." The sovereign fell silent. "Our observers are noting activation at the foot of the Celestial palace. I'm afraid the empire has 'digested' its conquest of the eastern coast and is now casting its gaze to the south."

"Are you going to organize a search?" The dragon chuckled.

"I think it is painfully clear that searching would be pointless."

Ruigar, finishing his wine, called the warden over.

"Tomorrow I will send an extra squadron of border rangers to your territory. I will give you one day to get the old barracks in order. Twelve mages will arrive with the rangers, and if something like today's incident happens again, you will envy the fate of the dugars!"

To the warden's good fortune, he was standing far-ish from Ruigar and couldn't hear the dragons' conversation. He probably couldn't have remained calm if he'd heard where the foreign man's scent led the sovereign. Only two birds left the bird barn today... carrying Farid, Iriel, and the shkas. But the prince's governor and right-hand man was mistaken as well—the empire wasn't even thinking about annexing the far-away territory—yet. The whirlpools of the political currents around the throne of the Celestial empire had a different subcurrent. He was also unaware that the time for "yet" was ticking away rapidly...

Nelita. Celestial Empire. The Celestial palace...

The vaults of the huge hall were lost somewhere in the heights. The impeccable illusion gave the impression of an endless space; even the most experienced and picky magician could not tell where the dome ended and the real sky began. The columns, stylized to resemble the Mellornys, extended branches of stone trees to non-existent clouds. Light gusts and drafts of wind that roamed the room moved artificial leaves, creating an indescribable play of light on the tiny mirrors inserted into each leaf. The real grass growing in the flower beds around the columns somehow naturally gave way to the polished green tile lining the floor. Small sunbursts, reflected from the mirror inserts on the leaves, rushed back and forth across the hall and fell on the walls and floor, creating a sense of celebration. Several huge mirrors, hidden behind the heavenly illusion, caught the sunlight and redirected it to a high surface at the far wall of the hall. If any observers were to enter the hall, they would see a picture of parted clouds and the sun peeking out from behind them, sending a broad beam to the throne area. The observers would also see a dragon lying on the floor in front of the throne platform.

The mammoth of a brownish hue, wings spread wide and horned head glued to the tile, was looking intensely at the person standing in front of him. The man, dressed in plain clothes, who looked more like a simple warrior than the owner of the majestic apartments, was not in the least afraid of the threatening monster. His noble face did not express a single emotion; only the corners of his plump, sensitive lips twitched from time to time. His gray eyes held the embers of a restrained wrath and rage. The man ran his wide palm over his short blonde hair and poked the dragon:

"Katgar, tell me what that word means to you."

"I try not to throw words around meaninglessly," the dragon answered.

"Even so? That's wise. But your oath?" The dragon said nothing. "Did you not take an oath of fidelity to me and give your word to serve with faith and truth? What prompted you to? Were those meaningless words?"

"No."

"How then am I to understand your tricks with the Circle of the Twelve? Have you decided that I've sat on the throne too long? Answer me!"

"I have nothing to say in my defense."

"Katgar, I don't recognize you. I can't believe that YOU aren't saying anything to defend yourself. Has my slippery dignitary been caught in the net of his own clever plans? It's a shame; I expected more from you. Was it a revelation to you that I was aware of your games? It's so careless to rely on dirty human beings! Where would I be if I did not know how to calculate my actions? But do you want to know who gave you away?" The man took a step toward the dragon and whispered the name. The tips of the dragon's wings jerked nervously; his tail hit the floor.

"I don't believe you!"

"Too bad. He gave his word. And kept it! It turns out that for some people, giving their word means something. Ah, Katgar, Katgar. Your faith has ruined you."

"You're a monster."

"I'm a monster? Shall I remind you of the oath you gave? Yes?" The man struck the dragon in the snout. The giant monster closed his eyes and, although it seemed impossible, pressed his head to the floor even harder. "Why have you come running to ask for mercy from a monster? Is it because you've realized the futility of the Circle of the Twelve's attempts to bring down the Celestial throne? Let me assure you: I've always been aware of everything that goes on there." The dragon's face expressed real surprise. The man scoffed. "Your secret society isn't so secret, is it? What do you think—who founded it?"

"It can't be?!"

"You ought to believe me. It's an excellent way to separate the grain from the chaff. Legends and songs of minstrels that told of the great secret about the fierce fighters of the invisible opposition.... I put a lot of effort into creating the image of the Circle of the Twelve, and I really didn't like that inside it someone was trying to form a closed caste. You *did* understand, didn't you, that there was something wrong with the conspirators, and decided to cover your tracks, and when it didn't work out, you ran to me. Remember the oath?"

"What will happen to me?"

"Nothing, you're just going to repeat the words of your oath, in blood."

"If I do that, you'll be able to control my clan."

"You should have thought of that before. I can do what I like with your clan as it is. The clan of a perjurer is ostracized. And that's fine if you just expand its scope a bit. Maybe it's worth spreading rumors about the connection between the Circle's latest failure and a certain imperial dignitary and the head of the Hekjar clan? Imagine, just IMAGINE what will happen! Not even the memory of your clan will survive. You see how it's all turned around? I'll be straight with you: you're alive because I need you, but the blood oath will allow me to guard my back from any further ill-advised actions by a certain dragon. I like your mind, resourcefulness, and ability to squeeze benefit from hopeless situations. As long as you are faithful to me, your loved ones are safe. Shall I give you time to think about it?"

"I'm not going to turn my nose up at second chances. I agree."

"You've made the right decision. I hope neither you nor I will regret it. If you said no, my 'fangs,'" he pointed to four dragons standing perfectly still between the Mellorny columns with gunners in their front paws "would have put you to an abrupt end, and I really don't like doing that. After they've done their work, it takes a very long time to get the place all cleaned up again. Enough cowering like a worm." The dragon folded his wings on his back and lifted his upper body off the floor. "Let's talk business."

The man rose to the dais and walked around the throne, tapping his fingers on the symbol of power. Having made some decision, he waved his hand. Obeying his slight gesture, an illusion of a map of the empire and the surrounding states flashed to the dragon's left. The pardoned dragon glanced at the presented illusory layout. The emperor occupied the throne.

"What are those flashing dots?" he asked.

"Portals. Interplanetary portals sealed three thousand years ago."

"As I understand it, something out of the ordinary happened, to make you pay attention."

"You understand correctly. Two days ago, the seals disappeared from the portals. Something's happening there." Katgar didn't need any explanation as to where "there" was. "But you know what? Without the keys and the passwords, we cannot open the portals, so, we still cannot get answers, and we cannot leave it all up to chance, either."

"I do not understand why the southern mark is circled twice?"

"The portal is located on the territory of the Principality of Ora. Your task will be to make either the portal or the lands—mine."

"War?"

"It's possible, but then in order to commence military action, we'll need a variety of excuses. Arranging these excuses will be another one of your tasks. Be careful, I don't need a conflict with the Miur. We're already stepping on the Great Mother's tail. And another thing, Katgar. You've lost the right to address me without using my title. You'll have to earn it again."

"Yes, your majesty. I will."

"Go on, think. I'll be expecting you the day after tomorrow."

The dragon lowered his head right down to the floor. The emperor waved his hand indifferently. The "fangs" standing off to Katgar's side accompanied their fellow dragon out of the throne room.

"Strange, very strange." The emperor stood up from his throne and went out to a wide balcony. Far below, he could see the city blocks of the capital. "Who removed the seals, and why? Was it a fluke, or someone's deliberate action? I need to send academics from the university to the portals. Two of you, follow me," he said to his silent dragon bodyguards, jumping onto the high stone railing and throwing himself down. The small cross-shaped shadow of the man with outstretched arms on the palace wall suddenly grew and sprouted wings...

Russia. Somewhere not far from N-ville...

"How are things?"

"We're observing, Mr. Chuiko," the operator answered the leader of the third group.

Chuiko pushed his glasses up on his nose and looked inquisitively at the main screen.

"I see what you're doing. It's an epic sight, like from some war movie."

A few of the young people agreed with the boss. The older operators said nothing.

The view on the screen was strikingly reminiscent of film scenes from the epics about the World War II, with thousands of people digging anti-tank ditches and putting up field fortifications. Something similar was happening in the magical world.

Thousands of toe-headed elves, simple humans, and what seemed like short people, but with glowing hair, were using magic to raise up banks and dig deep ditches on the approaches to a large mountain fortress. On level platforms far out in front of the ramparts, large round cobblestones were being buried in the ground with great care. On the slopes of the mountains, the forest was being chopped down and stakes were made from it, which were dug into the ground in front of the ramparts, forming respectable palisades. Hundreds of shorties with luminous hair erected stone towers about thirteen feet high behind the ramparts. The work was carried out in great haste, not stopping day or night. Paul went to his workplace and displayed the image on his personal monitor. The world Kerimov's son had fallen into was preparing for war. The boy got caught in a sticky situation, although what kind of a "boy" was he anymore? The boy cut off heads. It seems like he'd be a better fit for the army or the secret service than to be the object of pity. Paul shrugged. He'd been living on that planet for a long time already.

With permission from the command, the third group led a free search every night. What else could they do when the rest of the time their schedule was literally down to the minute? The population of the underground scientific center had grown by more than a thousand people over the past two weeks. All kinds of people—from biologists to philologists. You couldn't spit in any direction without hitting a PhD or a professor. Iliya Evgenevich had really stirred up some chaos, probably more than he could handle.

"Look, the pointy-ears are bringing mirrors from the fortress," Tessa Osin said, a young, talented girl who joined the third group straight out of college and still had a couple of months to go to give her final defense of her thesis. Her employer promised to help with that.

The elves really had brought five large parabolic mirrors on wheelbarrows. Each was about six feet in diameter. Now the short people with the glowing hair were mounting one of them on the upper platform of the first tower. Fifteen minutes later, all the mirrors were installed on revolving frames.

A dozen riders set off from the towers to the people working at the banks. Soon the working platform was cleared; not a single person remained in front of the towers. A dozen sheep were driven down the slope in the field.

"I get the feeling those elves haven't brought the mirrors in for nothing," Tessa again chimed in.

"Tessa, no need for commentary," one of the schedulers barked.

Tessa's sixth sense was right, but even it could not have predicted what happened next.

Climbing up to the platform towers, the elves turned the mirrors in the direction of the field and inserted into little notches in the back of the frames one sparkling crystal for each mirror.

Obeying some common feeling, all the operators in the

room froze along with the natives on the other side of the screen.

"Baaah, baaah," bleated a ram from through the speakers.

The bleating acted like a trigger. The mirrors became shrouded in bright radiance and shot forth a wide beam. The sheep turned into a cloud of steam in an instant; the earth turned black where magical lasers touched it. The forest hit by the beams was instantly burning brightly. The jaws of everyone in the operators' room dropped to their chests.

"OH MY...!" someone whispered.

"Did you record that?" Chuiko jumped up from his seat.

"We got it," Tessa answered. "Boss, don't stress. Everything's being recorded automatically. I wouldn't want to be one of their enemies! I wonder who they are?"

"That's exactly what I want you to find out. Let's begin a concentric search."

Part 2. All Clan Secrets.

Nelita. Freelands. Mellorny campground. Andy...

"Come with me," the elf girl said and ran up the path.

Andy, carrying the heavy body over his shoulder, followed.

"Faster, navi alamai."

"Girl, don't run. I'm not a horse," Andy snapped. The elf was heavy and awkward to carry.

"Please!" she pleaded. "Father may wake up not!"

"Not wake up?"

"Yes, I bad speak High."

"Terrific!" Andy thought, plopping the elf's body up higher as it had slid down. The elf moaned.

The girl stopped for a second, looked at the tired rescuer and waved her hand encouragingly as if to say "follow me." Andy had no choice; they walked on. Suddenly, it got incredibly hot. Sweat streamed down his back and poured over his face. The elf grew heavier with each step. The girl's heels, by which he had to navigate so as not to get lost, flashed about five yards ahead of him. After about ten minutes, Andy realized that if he did not get rid of the burden, the girl would have to save two limp bodies. A large insect buzzed past his ear.

"Na vamii ma!" the elf girl cried. Andy looked up from contemplating the girl's hem and raised his head. Help had come; he ought to be pleased, but the amount of iron staring him in the face did not inspire joy and optimism. Without straining his brains, two explicit conclusions could be drawn: one—they were not happy to make his acquaintance, and two—he wouldn't be able to run away. The insect, which turned out to be a feathered arrow, vibrated slightly in the trunk of a nearby tree.

A dozen long-eared Aborigines in light green cloaks kept him in their sights. Three of the pointy-ears showed off their bows with drawn strings and loaded arrows. The semicircle of their tribesmen pressed impressive arbalests with short thick bolts to their shoulders. *Very nice.* The elf girl jumped in front of the stern armed men and waved her hands like a windmill and tried to explain something to them. The man on his back was hanging like a sack of potatoes. The surrounding situation was far from understanding. The aborigines listened attentively to the incoherent speech, but they kept their eyes on the stranger. Silently walking on the low grass, three more Forest people came to Andy. One of them was clearly a mage. Obeying an imperative gesture, Andy carefully put the rescued elf on the ground. The wizard waved his hand. Targ! Invisible bonds tied the volunteer savior from head to toe. Unable to restrain himself, he fell flat to the ground, smashing his face and bloodying it. The archers removed the arrows from their bows and ran to the fallen man; they immediately rolled him up in a wide cut of cloth. A bag of sand dropped over his head, knocking him out. Hello, stars and darkness.

Consciousness came back on as from a light switch—click, and the lights were on. He felt a dull pain in the nape of his neck and a slight nausea. He was not bound. Having come to himself, Andy looked around. It wasn't a mansion, more like the office of an ascetic: floor, ceiling, wide bench and that was all. Oh yes, the scene was complemented by a strong old man in a light linen shirt and faded linen pants. The old elf occupied a wide log near the door that was hung with a curtain. He sat and looked at Andy. He was an old man of breeding, similar to Miduel. What conclusion could Andy draw from this? If he was similar to the ancient Rauu not only externally, he'd best be on his guard. Old guys like that resemble dandelions only in appearance. In reality, they were more dangerous than snakes. Let your guard down for a second, and you're theirs.

Andy, swinging his drooping arms and legs, got up and sat down on the bench facing the old man. The elf was silent; the guest did not know where to start the conversation, and so he forfeited the right to the first word to the master of the house. Why hurry? Judging by the lack of windows in the walls of this place, he would be here for a long time.

The pause went on for a while. The "woodsman" grunted. His thick eyebrows executed a short, intricate dance. Not a single muscle twitched on Andy's face. After waiting for another ten seconds, the elf spoke up, then, noticing the boy's complete lack of understanding, he broke off the conversation. It wasn't working.

"Maybe you are speaking High?" the elf switched to Edda.

"A little. This language is called High?"

"As far as I know, the language of the dragons always is called such. You did not know?" The old elf bowed his head to one side. His voice and intonation had a distinctly provocative character. Here it was: the old man turned out to be similar to Miduel not only in appearance. How to proceed? There was nothing he could do.

"Maybe I did." Andy shrugged indifferently. "Maybe not. I do not know. I have such a mess in my head right now, you wouldn't wish it on your enemies. I am surprised that I even remember my name." It was a short step away from the possible direct attack on the topic "who are you and where did you come from." Let's give the old elf a tasty little snack in the form of amnesia. Would he buy it?

He bought it. The elf nodded understandingly.

"After the dugar worse happens."

Stop: what was a "dugar?" The elf comprehended the guest's unspoken question.

"Do not tell me you do not know about dugars and the dugaria?"

"No," Andy laid his cards on the table.

"Unlikely. The scars on your chest tell the other story. You had a very close acquaintance with the dugaria."

Andy realized what he was talking about.

"That snotty tree with feelers and toothy shells?"

"It can be called that," the elf smiled. "A precise wording. A man escaped from a cocoon has every right to call the tree snotty. How long did you spend in the cocoon?"

"I do not know," the amnesia game continued.

"Hmm, and why did they sentence you to it?"

An indifferent shrug of the shoulders and gesture of the

chin from side to side.

"I do not remember my past."

"A rash claim for a shkas who killed three dangerous beasts with his bare hands." *Ugh, what a horrible word, "shkas." Leaves a bad taste in my mouth.* "I do not consider your poor blade a weapon. You have not forgotten how to battle."

"An art practiced to the level of reflexes is difficult to forget."

"Exactly."

"I know how to pick up a blade, but where this knowledge came from—I do not have the faintest idea."

"You have forgotten the events of your past, but you speak High splendidly. You must have some kind of selective amnesia." The old man got up from the log. "Who are you trying to fool?"

"You know, maybe it sounds provocative on my part, but I really do not remember anything from my past. All my memories start from the shores of the forest lake in two days' walk from the clearing where I killed the rixes!"

Andy flared up, expressing indignation at the lack of trust with all his being. He played perfectly. If the elves want, let them go and check. The turtle shells would serve as evidence of staying on the shores forgotten by the gods.

"I do not remember and do not know the general events. I do not remember how old I am or why they put me in the cocoon."

"And your name? You remember your name?"

"Kerrovitarr."

The elf coughed.

"That is a bad joke."

"I am not joking."

"I believe only a fool would joke about dragons' names. Do not even think about saying that to anyone else. Manyfaces save you from using that name in front of the dragons. They will tear you to pieces without a second thought. Perhaps, your parents gave you another name?"

"Andy."

"It means strong. An unusual name, but still better than Kerrovitarr."

"It is a fine name. May I ask a question?"

"You may."

"How does, eh, that man feel?"

"You were just in time. Atrael feels fine." The old elf realized who Andy was talking about and decided to help: "Please excuse me for the cold reception. If it were not for Lilly, we could have killed you. Strangers with good intentions do not walk about in our woods."

"I understand."

"That is the answer to that question. What requests do you have? I am in your debt. Atrael is my son. Lilliel is my granddaughter."

"I need this old man as a debtor like I need a hole in the head!" Andy thought to himself, and said:

"Will I be allowed to stay in your village for a while, learn the language and some customs?"

"The council will consider your request. I cannot promise anything. The fact that you are alive is already a miracle."

"When will I know the council's decision?"

"In the morning," the elf answered, heading towards the curtain. "You will be brought food in an hour. I hope you will not do anything stupid. As for satisfying all your natural needs, if you have never visited a tiv or don't recall, you may use white moss to clean up after yourself." The elf pulled the curtain aside and walked out.

What did he mean by "something stupid?" What possibilities are there? Andy would be as good as gold. Where would he go—without knowing the language, customs, or norms of behavior here? The old elf just didn't know what he'd almost gotten himself into. Now Andy just had to cross the invisible border of "almost."

In exactly an hour, he was brought a simple dinner. Andy lazily took a couple of bites of something like meat and returned the ceramic plate to the guard.

After dinner, a large cat came to visit him. The animal's short coat was a light brown color with broad black stripes. The length of the master's favorite pet was no less than a yard. Judging by her eyes alone her weight, she must be thirty pounds.

The cat yawned wide and stoically approached the intruder. Andy reached out and gingerly stroked the beautiful animal. The petting was accepted with all the dignity of a proud and independent animal. Following the cat's lead, he yawned too and stretched his whole body. Fatigue took its toll. He wanted to sleep. On the wide bench, there was enough room for him and for the tailed mistress, in whose spot, it seemed, he'd been assigned to sleep. Andy blissfully stretched out to his full height. The cat jumped on his chest, slightly trampled its paws and lay down, cracking like a tractor. Stroking the kitty, he did not know that her good disposition towards him decided his fate.

The council, consisting of the most respected residents of the settlement, debated how to proceed for a long time. Some hotheads offered not to even bother and strip the stranger of his head. Maybe he was specially sent by the enemy, and the rixes were not wild. Magic can do many things, including changing shape and color. Others, bearing in mind that he saved two of their relatives from imminent death by destroying wild rixes that penetrated to the village by some unknown circumstance, were for expelling the stranger. You did a good deed—thank you, and now get out and pray to Manyfaces to take you far from here. The eldest elf, listening to the speeches of the parties, frowned. Evael did not hide his emotions. He did not like the first or second options. Andy had asked them to help him remember the language, which was not such a big request. Did no one realize that the soldiers of the village could now receive substantial reinforcement in the form of the stranger?

In the midst of the dispute, Lilliel glanced into the hall of the council. She could not find Mimiv, her favorite pet anywhere. Evael stepped outside with Lilly. Three minutes later, the missing animal found in the guarded "guest's quarters."

"The stranger will remain in the village," Evael said, returning to the council.

"Bring forth at least one argument," Vadel, the commander of the squad of sorcerers, turned to him.

"You all know that Mimiv would not let a bad person near her."

"What has Mimiv to do with your decision to leave a stranger in the valley?" Vadel piped up.

"The cat came to him and is now lying curled up at his headboard. The stranger has no evil intentions, let him stay."

"You've decided to trust the instinct of the beast?"

"I have. Animals are not mistaken."

* * *

"Mimiv, up you go!" Andy carefully removed the front half and head of the rather big cat from his shoulder. The tawny striped favorite of the hostess opened her yellow eyes, yawned wide, and jumped off the couch. Moving away from the place of lodging for a couple of feet, she gracefully bent down and stretched her back and paws. Bayuk, who wanted to enter under the mat, got a pawful of claws in the muzzle, squeaked in protest and ran away to complain to Lilly. "Mimiv," Andy stroked the fighter, "why did you hurt Bayuk?"

The cat sniffed scornfully and lay down on the threshold. As if to say, this is my territory, and no arachno-like creatures ought to dare enter here.

"Will you come with me?" This question, which had become a ritual for the past month, as always, went unanswered. The cat's yellow eyes sparkled. Cats are independent creatures. Besides, soon Lilly would summon her for her morning bowl of milk, and swimming in ice water did not fit with breakfast or with a cat's nature. "I need to wash with my tongue," she seemed to say and, without delaying the matter any further, Mimiv started hygienic procedures. "You go where you please. Don't interfere with my licking."

"Some cats eat mice, you know." Picking up a piece of thick cloth which he used instead of a towel, and a belt with a sword, Andy left his "apartment."

"Mrrr, moir-r," the jaws chomped loudly.

Gently, the mat woven from thin vines dropped into place. Andy mechanically stroked the wall of the living house with his hand. The wide, thick leaves that formed its base creaked. It seemed that the temporary housing didn't want to let the lodger go.

Between the quaintly interwoven roots of Mellorny Atrael appeared. In the settlement they get up early; the local residents do not approve of laziness.

"Easy trails," he greeted Andy.

"Straight roads," he replied.

"Andy, wait." The elf put a small box at his feet. Judging by the way the straps were stretching, it weighed a lot. "I, uh," he said, embarrassed, "made you some bracelets and a belt."

"Thank you, Atrael!" Andy was delighted with the gift. "May I?"

"Sure." He smiled warmly. "Let me help you."

Atrael pulled out from the box shoulder pads and a few wide cloth bracelets for feet and hands on a leather backing with fabric-stitched lead plates.

"Move your arms, all right. Now jump. Do they rub on you?" fixing the metal, asked the elf. "Do not rush. Let us try on the belt."

That was better. Now Andy could train in his usual training equipment. The bracelets and belt were what he'd been missing this past month. When he worked at the half-orc's gym, he always wore extra weights on his wrists and ankles, and without them, practicing at the lake shore, he felt like a lizard without a tail. Force of habit.

"Berg, may you have a light afterlife, teacher."

"Has something happened?" asked Atrael, noticing a cloud of doom on Andy's face.

"No, everything is okay. Thanks again. I will run; the "leaves" have long since gathered."

"I'll put the box in your tiv," the elf shouted in the direction of his retreating back.

"Thank you."

Andy ran a light, skipping jog towards the broad forest lake, into which ran the river that was associated with his memorable encounter with the rixes. Here was the trail creeping toward the mountain. He increased his pace. Now he would see an obstruction along the edge of the path and a fork where, he recalled each time he passed it, the village rangers had greeted him as he carried a poisoned elf on his back. The guards had rushed to the aid of their troubled fellow, who had activated the emergency magical beacon. It can not be said that the meeting was friendly. Had it not been for Lilly, he would have been struck dead by their arrows or stripped of his dull little head. He didn't know whether the violent pointy-ears would ever have figured out his mysteries: who, where, why? The dead usually keep their secrets. It was entirely possible that in order to get answers from the village "porcupine" Atrael, they would have invited the nearest necromancer. The right move, theoretically. The no man's lands (they were called that, but everyone for some reason preferred to forget about the Miur), which did not belong to any state of the world, forced the locals to treat uninvited guests with a certain degree of suspicion.

The borderlands, the frontier, a huge territory on the slopes of the great mountain Lidar; a place where various adventurers and others, sick and totally crazy, go to have a good time. Often walks of merry men ended in the stomachs of predatory, constantly hungry creatures. Quite often their lives were interrupted by other adventurers or local residents who for some reason treated the various guests negatively. Someone's head was swept off by the swords of the Miur, who considered these lands their own, but endured the rare settlements of elves and people. Settlers also believed that the nearby forests and fields around the townships belong to them, but kept their personal opinion to themselves. Why anger their warlike neighbors in vain? The dragons of the Celestial Empire and the Principality of Ora preferred to leave everything as is, because the buffer with the northern neighbor was advantageous for Ora, and the dragons had once painfully taken a beating from the Great Mother's mages, the ruler of the cat people. Since then, Miur rulers had always kept their nose to the wind, catching the slightest political hesitation. The empire grew stronger from century to century, and its rulers never suffered from lack of memory. Who knew when they would decide to punish the abusers? Realizing that their free life could someday end, the miur did not touch the elves' Mellorny groves and the border villages of humans, who created a peculiar cushion between them and their terrible neighbors and were, in fact, the first frontier of defense against ground attacks. The senior Forest Elves, perfectly aware of the situation and their status quo, played the role of border guards, meeting uninvited guests with arrows and swords. This behavior by the owners of the Mellorny groves was justified by life itself. It so happened that in the last three thousand years, only the priests of Manyfaces came to no-man's land with good intentions; the rest were hoping for rich spoils.

It was an interesting picture: the village chief Evael telling his son and granddaughter's savior about the surrounding realities, which made Andy think hard. Not everything was rosy, it turned out, in the homeland of dragons. The daily tradition of evening-time conversation between the chief and the "good guest" was a joy for both sides. Evael, who at first sight seemed to be a village "bumpkin," was an extremely intelligent and erudite person, whose aristocratic features and excellent education received in the distant past often shone through his pleasant simplicity. The grandfather and his granddaughter taught Andy Common, the language used for communication on Nelita. The chief could have deceived the newcomer by his appearance had it not been for their first meeting, at which the elf showed his true face.

The old man had many questions for the shkas who had saved his son. He did not believe that the person who had fled from the dugaria was suffering from selective memory loss. How could he forget everything, but keep his knowledge of High, the language of dragons, known to Andy as Younger Edda? What's more, the High he spoke was an old, archaic form, which was spoken in the higher circles of dragon society. Or the name? Strange name for a human; instantly recognizable as dragon's. No less interesting would be to learn about the shkas' mother, who taught him knowledge of medicinal herbs. Who was she, from what kind of tribe? He got only silence in response, shrugging of shoulders, and uncomprehending eyes. Was it funny to pretend that Evael did not see in his long double braid a hint of the Snow Elves? Only the Rauu braided using the double spike. Or his fighting skills? Simple people can't move like that. They tear their muscles, and their joints don't wield such flexibility. If he were a sorcerer, his skills would be explained by his magical nature, but the village mages checked the blue-eyed man and found no magic in him; but this too created questions. The boy was constantly covered by the cocoon of a mind shield, which he supported unconsciously. And, which was absolutely impossible for someone who was not a mage, he absorbed mana. Where did it disappear to and what was it spent on? Many questions—and almost no answers. The dugaria did not influence Kerr-Andy's mind in any way. He was only skillfully hiding behind the opportunity to keep his past a secret. It's fair to say that for Evael, Andy was a hard nut to crack.

In turn, the elf himself was a treasure chest for the were-dragon, a fount of information about the new world. In learning Common, he terrorized his mentor with tricky questions about the world order, the customs, their neighbors, and politics. The old elf often lamented that the order in the world had lessened compared with what it used to be. Once he mentioned that the once united state had collapsed into separate territories that were butting heads, turning free elves into hostages to the situation and the ruler of the empire's greed. Andy picked up on the chief's reservation and gradually extracted all the details.

And the details were both interesting and suggestive of strange parallels in the histories of the two worlds. According to the old elf, three thousand years ago, there was neither the Principality of Ora, nor the lands of the miurs, nor the Celestial Empire, nor a dozen other states, but one big country. The collapse began with the mysterious death of the ruler. Normally that would be fine: all living beings are mortal, and no one attached much importance to the death of the old dragon. But the heir disappeared, and then the brother of the deceased ascended to the throne. Then true bloods and dragons appeared out of nowhere, who came from Ilanta. What happened on their heavenly neighbor, Evael did not know, but the newcomers took up arms against the new emperor. There was a split in the country. Some of the Lords of the Sky supported the newcomers. A protracted civil war began, the result of which was the death of all the true bloods from Ilanta and the collapse of the country. The Miur did not take part in the massacre that had begun. The Great Mother did not support either side, saying that only a legitimate heir could reign over the cat people. She wasn't about to bow to the pretender who had put on a purple robe. After achieving victory over the coalition, the new emperor invaded the lands around Mount Lidar and lost half of his army, wiped out by the Miur mages. Many dragons died. Even the Emperor's true bloods could not counter the prowess of the combat mages of the mountain tribe. The defeated army retired, but the time would come when it would return. The ruler of the northern lands, Hazgar, was collecting the fragments which were once one country. In some places, he used flattery and promises, and elsewhere he used force of arms. While the three princes who fought on the side of the newcomers remained independent, both the miur and others fell under the iron fist of the Celestial Empire, which had significantly increased its borders to the east and north. There was something to think about: was it just by chance that the root of evil was growing from Nelita, where the dragons and Forest Elves of Ilanta had such a bloody conflict three thousand years ago? Why should the true bloods rush into battle against the emperor?

Andy stopped about a half a mile before the lake. The trail went right along the edge of the creek. On the left side of the trail, a broad glade of thick green grass cleared the forest giants. It was there that he met Atrael and Lilly. How long had he been living with the forest people? A month, but it felt like a lifetime. If he had his way, he would stay here, but intuition told him that the relatively peaceful time was coming to an end. Andy sat down on the log he'd jumped over four weeks ago, or six fivers, to use the local time measurement. The not-so-distant events surfaced in his memory.

* * *

Andy dug at the earth with the toe of his boot, got up from the log and walked through the clearing. The rixes he'd killed had long since been swallowed by the local scavengers, and ants cleared the remains of their skeletons to a mirror shine. A little more time and these silent reminders of a deadly skirmish would return to the ground and be covered with grass. Time. Andy looked up at the sky: how were his friends and relatives doing? The dark disk of Ilanta was wrapped in cumulus clouds. For a long time, the desire to get to Earth had subsided. Now he often thought about Jagirra and Karegar. An unclear languor and strange dreams told him that not everything was so simple now in the relations of parents. In his thoughts of home, the word "adopted" disappeared. What kind of adopted parents were they, Targ take it? From what he had learned and understood here, they were the real ones.

Dragons don't have it any other way. But that's just it: dragons. He was already guessing his mother was not the simple Snow Elf herbalist she had always claimed to be. She must have a deeper connection to the winged race. But what? What secrets was she hiding? And what secrets was he hiding? A month of "playing the fool" cost him dearly. Only the results of the game were the opposite of what he'd planned. The mages several times rushed to examine the tattoo in detail. He had to writhe like a slippery eel to come up with reasons and excuses for refusing. The mages nodded, but judging by their eyes, they would not abandon their harassment.

It seemed Evael was beginning to guess about his guest's second essence. Why else would he have given him the boiled swamp root for washing? Swamp root is used by rangers to remove their scents. What was his scent? That's just it. For the past week, Andy had begun to smell like lily of the valley, and his magic began to return. That was the hardest thing to hide. Will shields and mind shields did not guarantee the preservation of his secret, but it was hoped that the village mages would not pay too close attention to him, and Lilly would not blab about what happened at the waterfall. It happened unexpectedly....

Lilly had enticed him into a hike to the waterfall. The lumes had begun to creep into their cocoons, and Atrael sent his daughter to catch new ones. Elves preferred to use living lamps; magical lanterns somehow did not fit them. The point-ears fished large luminescent caterpillars from the banks of the reservoirs and placed them in wicker spheres woven from a thin vine, which were suspended from the ceilings and walls of the rooms. The caterpillars were fed freshly cut grass and leaves and gave off unexpectedly bright and even light. The one downside was that the living luminaries served for no more than three or four weeks; after that, they began to weave cocoons and turned into pupae, from which a huge butterfly of iridescent color hatched in a month.

Lilly handed Andy a large basket with a tight lid, whistled to Bayuk, and led the whole honest company to meet their adventures. On the way to the traps, Mimiv joined them, pretending that this path was on the way she just happened to be going. Bayuk immediately hid behind the mistress's back and began to creak plaintively with his chelicers. Mimiv snorted at the arachnid traveler, and, with her tail lifted, ran ahead.

Andy stroked the creature, which was always offended by the cat, for the hundredth time, amazed at the softness of the wool that covered the spider-like creature. The pseudo-spider's hair flowed pleasantly between his fingers and crackled from electrical discharges. Bayuk stretched out his paws and, swaying from side to side, creaked with pleasure. Who would have thought...

When Evael appeared in Andy's cottage and announced that the council had allowed him to stay in the village, he felt a heavy stone fall from his heart. Lilly jumped out from behind the old elf, grabbed her rescuer by the hand and pulled him into the street, if one could call a broad platform between the dense intertwining of the roots of the Mellornys a "street." No sooner had the girl crossed the threshold of the temporary shelter of the guest of the forest tribe, than a huge bright yellow red and brown spider-shaped creature drew near her, as tall as her knee. Lilly carelessly brushed off the six-legged creature. The spider pinched its paws, flopped onto the ground, and plaintively squeaked.

"Bayuk!" The girl's eyebrows lowered threateningly. The arachnid spread its legs limply to the side. "Bayuk, on tele tarot urrat!"

The nightly feline visitor jumped down from the roof of the prison. The spider immediately stopped pretending to be offended, jumped to its feet, and instantly climbed the nearest tree.

It turns out that the forest inhabitants specially bred the arachnoid-like creatures called naxes, receiving from them the finest silk fabric. The female naxes wove a kind of thin nest or cocoon-bag each night in the branches of trees. In the morning, the caretakers drove the spiders from their soft nests and folded the cut cocoons into baskets. The second stage was soaking the arachnoid material in special boilers, extracting it, and pressing it between rollers. The output was a thin, colorless fabric. The fabric was dried and dyed with coloring agents. The final product went to both domestic consumption and local markets, and sold like hot cakes. Male naxes were smaller than females and much more intelligent. Usually they were kept in place of dogs guarding the house and yard, but in Andy's hosts' home, the role of malicious dog was played by Mimiv.

The journey to the waterfall passed in a calm and, one might say, friendly atmosphere, not counting the fight between Bayuk and Mimiv for the fact that the pseudo-spider had scared a large rodent, somewhat resembling a short-eared rabbit, from under the cat nose. Andy caught caterpillars, and Lilly threw pebbles into a wide creek. When Andy showed her how to skip stones, the girl was impressed.

The elf girl went to the water and poked at the water with a stick, choosing flat pebbles. Mimiv disappeared somewhere, and Bayuk was basking in the sun. The blue-green crocodile snout that surfaced near the shore was a complete surprise to everyone. The huge jaws spread wide; the mouth was dotted with a fence of sharp teeth. The river monster rushed at Lilly. A shrill shriek spread over the river.

Andy feared not reaching the girl in time. She was frozen in horror. Time stopped. The basket with caterpillars hung in the air; Bayuk was frozen in place; the waterfall ceased its noise. With an outstretched hand pointed towards the crocodile-like creature, Andy let a bolt of lightning fly. The monster was thrown back. Several dozen dead fish bobbed to the surface of the creek. Following the lightning, Andy let the "ax" spell fly, cutting the beast in half. The twitching halves were picked up by the current; the water turned red.

Then there were a lot of tears and oaths about keeping silent about what had happened. Andy was in settage for a long time, checking his internal mana stores and energy channels. Killing the quork came as a surprise not only for Lilliel. The savior was as dumbfounded as the victim and the rescued elf. He had started to collect mana. He could not boast of a huge amount of energy, but the results spoke for themselves. Now he was at about the same stage as when he was sitting in the zoo of the king of Rimm.

It was no wonder that the Elven magicians saw nothing. The mana he used was, in his giant vaults, like a drop in the sea, condensate on the walls of the railway tank. If only Lilly didn't blurt out too much, no harm, no foul. The time would come when he could restore his connection with the astral.

Along with the magic, his ability to sense the world's energy relations also returned. For the last few days, he hadn't been able to find his place. It was like some string in his soul was ringing with an intense roar. Time.... It flows like water between one's fingers. Intuition and forebodings told him that the days reserved for a quiet life were expiring. Last week, messengers came from other villages with grim news. The orcs had become active at the imperial borders. There had already been several large raids into the depths of no man's land. There were no dragons with the "grays," but without the approval of the imperial astals, they would never have crossed yet another border delineated by thousands of years. The emperor was feeling out the situation.

The elves, rightfully alarmed, put a spear in the hands of every able-bodied member of their community. The convoy sent to the mountains brought back a dozen heavy gunners. The miur had decided not to skimp on magical devices for their allies. Special teams of loggers went to organize additional abatis.

"How are you at the art of assassination?" Two days ago, Evael summoned Andy to a frank conversation. The elf was blacker than a thundercloud and decided to speak without equivocation.

"It depends."

"I mean in general," the chief interrupted. "I do not ask you to fight for the village, but you can fully train the youth. And do not make a lean face. I was once a ranger. I can tell a wild rix from a domestic puppy. You do not look like a pup."

"So I look like a rix?"

"No, not like a rix either." Andy lifted his right eyebrow. "More like a rix killer. Andy, I would not ask you if it was not a dire need...."

"I will do it. All the more so since I too need to get in shape."

The elf scoffed:

"Thank you."

"No thanks needed."

"I'm grateful all the same. You could have said no and calmly left, but you have decided to stay and help."

"Who will I be training? I want to say that I cannot work

with novices."

"Will you take the Leaves candidates? The warriors and the novices from the three surrounding villages are now gathered by the lake."

"I will. But how do they feel about being trained by a shkas?"

The chief grew pensive.

"I will speak to them. And you, hm, you do not have to be shy when it comes to discipline and persuasion. Moreover, go to Atrael. He will get you a real blade, and you can hand over this manure that you call a blade to be melted down."

As per Evael's order, Andy was not shy during training. The Leaves gathered on the shore of the large lake. Wide sandy beaches were an ideal platform for mass training. The young elves greeted the blue-eyed coach with a disapproving murmur. The shkas did not inspire confidence. Of the two dozen wards, only two village acquaintances did not express their displeasure. The pointy-ears were already butting heads with the freak and got their nuts beat for it.

Andy, copying the methods of his former mentor and teacher Berg, forced everyone to do a whole bunch of gymnastic exercises, checking the stretching and their coordination. When the long-eared youth began to roar with discontent and speak in a negative way about the methods of the freak who had not been killed in the dugaria, he picked up a thick stick and called in a circle of three volunteers. A crowd gathered around the circle. The rangers left the classroom and came to watch the duel. The young boobies, playing with swords, competently stepped to the sides. Andy stood in the center of the circle, smiling contemptuously and tapping his thigh with a piece of wood. In the next moment, he tossed a handful of sand into the first opponent's face with the toe of his boot, sharply turned to one side, gently snatched the second disciple's sword out of his hands, and painfully poked him in the stomach with the butt end. The elf doubled over and fell to the sand. Quickly, in one fluid motion, Andy transitioned to a low stance, and the second student flew to the ground from a strong blow to the knees. If Andy had had a sword in his hands, the candidate for the Rangers would have been left without legs. The elf who got sand in his eyes fell down next to his companions from a blow to the forehead. The experienced fighters appreciated the man's skill and smiled approvingly. Andy rejoiced internally. He had arranged the whole show just for the experienced rangers. Young people always take their lead from their senior comrades, and very much depended on how they behaved with the mentor-shkas. The soldiers expressed their approval of the new trainer's methods. The dissatisfied rumble in the ranks of the young candidates came to naught. There were no fools among them; they didn't want to get a stick on the forehead. From that moment on, the elves took all the tutor's tricks with the serenity of elephants. Respect for the elders is highly developed among the long-eared tribe, and Andy was able to prove himself worthy of respect. All issues totally disappeared by themselves. For two days, he rode the youth into the ground. Today he was asked to work with the "old men."

"Enough indulging in memories," Andy thought, snapping back into the present. "Time's pressing. It's not good to keep yourself waiting." Andy dove into the river and carefully rubbed himself with swamp root. A few minutes later, he raced to the taiga reservoir.

The beach met him with a lively hum and new faces. *Well well, what kind of ladies are these?*

* * *

The ladies were not alone. What kind of fool would let such beauties go into the wild forest, full of dangers, without proper accompaniment? That's right, no one would.

Andy stood behind the blossoming red bushes. The flowering inflorescences perfectly concealed him, and now, unseen by the others, he could calmly assess the situation.

Judging by how the stern warriors of the forest tribe crouched before the new arrivals, they were high-flying birds. The tall golden-haired elf who was leading the delegation stopped near the sergeant Hermiel and asked him about something. The warrior bowed low and burst out with a whole speech, periodically pointing at the Leaf candidates standing to the side. The ladies and gentlemen gathered behind Goldilocks listened as well.

"Very nice," Andy thought, counting the visitors. There were nine elves, five of which were ladies, counting the gold-headed leader of the delegation, and seven humans. Among the humans, there were only three ladies. Besides a short slim elf with hair of the color of molten copper and a fine figure, all the other guests were tall. Their aristocracy and a spark of superiority over the local army flashed in their eyes. Everyone, both men and women, sported chain mail, sashes with swords, leather trousers, and high boots with lacing. The fair sex differed from the gentlemen in the green blouses and cloaks over their mail.

A pair of newcomers had wide belts with scabbards for throwing knives stretched across their chests. It was a serious company. The main elf, after listening to Hermiel, nodded and turned to the retinue. There was a lively conversation among the guests. *It's a pity I can't hear anything from the observation post. I'm dying of curiosity!*

Andy switched to true vision. He saw numerous artifacts and amulets skillfully hidden by the guests' clothing. The company which seemed interesting at first was starting to appeal to him less and less. *And who could like sorcerers who are shielded by will and mind shields? Solid dark cocoons instead of auras. You see, they have something to hide. And exactly half of them are dark spots, but who's counting? I spent a month in the forest village and all that time, I didn't see a single hidden aura, not counting myself, of course. Today is full of surprises.* His intuition, foretelling trouble, howled like a mad cat with its tail down. *How would we know if there are some lovely northern friends in this group?*

Why would Hermiel nod to the youth? That's obvious enough: the ranger is talking about a certain shkas. Yes, I'm a local celebrity. Where else can you find a freak that yields weapons better than most experienced warriors can? Andy sighed heavily: *life was so good!*

"Andy!" Pitel, a young candidate for the Leaves from Andy's settlement ran from the village to the beach. "We have been looking for you, and you are standing here!"

A curse on you! Andy thought, coming out from the bushes.

"Pitel, your tongue is your enemy."

"What?" the elf said in surprise.

"Apparently, your parents didn't teach you how to be quiet sometimes?"

The awkward question went unanswered as the visitors and Hermiel heard the elf's voice and ceased their conversation as suddenly as if someone had waved a magic wand.

A light breeze blew in. Its invisible streams ruffled the shkas' hair, which had grown below his shoulders and brought with them the smell of a flowering meadow. Stopping mid-step, he scrunched his nose. The smell served as a detonator for a mental explosion inside a box called a skull. The elves and humans who had come to the beach at such an early hour suddenly acquired other features. They did not use swamp root. That smell was slightly musky.... Yes, flowers and musk, the aqueous suspension of clouds, the thunderous freshness of ozone. It smelled like dragons. The sky. The heavens. How many of them were there? Was it the whole delegation, or just the ones covered in will shields?

"Is that him? According to your descriptions, dear Hermiel, a combat golem three yards tall should be standing before us now," the chief elf said in an alto voice.

"Good things come in small packages!" Andy spoke up for himself.

A spark of interest appeared in the elf's green eyes. The accompanying cavaliers felt threatened.

"Your tongue, shkas, will lead you to the scaffold someday," she answered.

"Usually it helps me keep away," Andy retorted. He could not understand his own behavior. The proximity of the elves, no, dragons! tore off the brakes and made him throw caution to the wind. His next escapade was not so well received. The noble did not like something in his behavior.

"Mistress, allow me to teach this fellow a few lessons in respect?" One of the gentlemen spoke up. Goldilocks' advocates piously observed the limits of what was permissible to them. No one transgressed them, except for the persons close to her, and the blue-eyed non-human did not belong to such a privileged category. "I'll teach him to bow before you." That was it, the freak had failed to bow! His free life with the Forest Elves, where no one really worried about constantly groveling in front of anyone else, had made Andy forget this custom. He was no longer used to such things.

"Don't twist your navel," snapped the disrespectful shkas. Oh, Goldilocks was right. The chopping block and the executioner's ax hovered over him. The self-styled manners teacher roared, pushed aside the short elf Andy had noticed earlier and jumped forward sharply.

The "teacher" moved quickly. He literally made a gray streak in the air. His sword flashed, reflecting a sunbeam. Remembering his sparring with Ilnyrgu, which she arranged for him on the last day of his training at Berg's school, Andy went into a trance, feeling the blood vessels in his eyes almost burst from the pressure and crazy acceleration. He jumped high up and slightly to the side, thus giving his right hand room for a short swing. The chief elf's defender flew under him; in the next moment, the guardian of good manners, having lost his target, stopped abruptly. The butt of the narrow blade bumping the elf in the forehead was a complete surprise to him. He managed to react to the danger by leaning back, but not fast enough. Everyone else present saw only that the shkas disappeared in one place and emerged in another, and the mighty warrior who had rushed into the fight, with a big bump on his forehead, swayed and fell flat on the sand. While the company was staring at the defeated fighter, Andy swiftly wiped the blood that had run out under his nose.

The defeated elf did not portray a limp amoeba for long. In one swift movement, he jumped to his feet and growled. His aura flashed with blinding light, increasing several times. Vertical pupils erupted in the pseudo-elf's eyes. *Holy moly—a dragon!*

"Thygar, do not dare! If you do, you will violate my virk," the imperative cry of the golden-haired woman made the furious dragon moderate his ardor.

The sword sang as it slid back into the sheath.

"We will meet again...," the enraged dragon said.

Suddenly some of the inadequacies of his own behavior became clear to Andy, his lack of brakes and irritation. The dragon-boy was about to molt. It was commendable he hadn't killed anyone yet. His hormones and the urge to molt were so strong that even Andy lost his self-control.

The elf, whose fragrance of field dandelions suggested she was actually a dragon beauty, turned to Andy:

"The sergeant's words turned out to be pure truth. Hermiel, I apologize." She and the Forest Elf bowed to one another simultaneously. Apologies had been given and accepted. There was no damage to their relationship. The green eyes again moved to the culprit of the scuffle. "I suggest you join the virk. What do you say?"

"No."

By the way the eyes of all those present on the beach grew wide and rounded, Andy realized that he had committed the biggest stupidity he possibly could have. Pitel's face changed various colors for a moment, betraying a whole range of emotions, the main one of which was disbelief. How could he refuse such an honor? The entourage exposed their blades. The rangers on the beach shook their heads and mentally buried the shkas. Ignorance of customs and elementary rules did not ever do anyone any good. Such little things were what gave away even experienced spies. He urgently needed to save the situation.

"I do not know who you are, what 'virk' means, or what your offer entails. I began to remember my skills six fivers ago. I am therefore not capable of agreeing to your offer due to my ignorance."

Hermiel darted over to the dragoness and hotly whispered some details from the life of the blue-eyed shkas. She listened to the elf and threw quick glances at Andy.

"Andy, show us!" The sergeant poked himself in the chest. Clearly, the guests wanted to see the mark of the dugaria. They were interested in the eight-pointed scar from the tree tentacle. He didn't mind showing them. This course of action was met "with a grand hurrah," except for one small detail—no one bothered to explain to him the meaning of a certain short word.

The forest army relaxed somewhat but continued to watch warily. They were aware of official events. Half the members of the retinue made squeamish faces, examining Andy.

"Ania, explain." The Lady of the Sky changed her wrath to pity.

"Yes, mistress!" the short person Andy had taken a liking to stepped forward.

* * *

Andy didn't end up joining the virk. Not because he did not want to, but because his impulsive refusal canceled the invitation. Still, the encounter wasn't a total loss, and he joined the princess' detachment as an independent and voluntary assistant. If he had not done that, no one would have given a broken penny for his life. Dragons of such a high position and flight do not forgive a direct insult. Period. If it had been someone else besides Ilirra, saying "no" would not have been a problem, but that was not his fate. Such individuals are not to be refused. The resounding "no" was written off to the gaps in his memory since he'd escaped from the dugaria, which was logical, considering the impact the chimera tree had on people's psyches. After Ania described the meaning of the short word, it became more difficult to refuse; to be honest, it was completely impossible.

The short word "virk," it turned out, encompassed several concepts and meanings. First, it was interpreted and had the same meanings as the ancient Irish geas and taboo.[6] Secondly, it was a test, recalling something like the grand tours of the old British aristocrats, sending their offspring to foreign lands to see the world to see and show what they could do. Third, it was a tradition that arose three thousand years ago. According to it, young Lords of the Sky who were preparing to accept service to the clan or power over it had to pass a severe test of maturity and independence, and their debt did not give them the right to refuse it. In this case, Miss Ilirra had accepted a virk, which absorbed all these concepts at the same time. She had reached the age of maturity and must show what she was capable of. The Prince Ora placed high hopes on his daughter.

The unusual exam differed from a simple trip in that it

entailed a host of restrictions and prohibitions. The dragons, if they did not possess a second hypostasis, passed the test alone. Those who could change form could be tested in a group or go as one person, but with an escort team. In any case, parents were forbidden to interfere in the affairs of their own children or to provide assistance—ey had to do it themselves, all by themselves.

The sida's words made a couple of muscles move in his brain. No one interfered with the mothers and fathers pulling some strings and introducing the right persons into their son's or daughter's retinue. Everyone knew perfectly well that hardly anyone would leave their own child completely unattended, especially dragons. Andy himself knew what it meant to love some kiddos. Tyigu, Rary, and Rury had bound him to themselves tighter than any rope could, and they weren't even his own flesh and blood.

But about the quest, that is the virk, which are practically the same thing. In the second and third cases, additional restrictive barriers began to operate. A group could not consist of more than two dozen members. During the test, dragons were forbidden to take on their true form or use magic. Who had defined these rules and how, no one remembered, but they followed them rigorously. There was, however, a tricky caveat. The rules did not say anything about magical artifacts and amulets. The group was allowed to accept no more than five friends or servants who took on your virk and the duty to follow a friend or master and strictly enforce all the written and unwritten rules of the test. The remaining members of the team could be anyone from the other intelligent races. Restrictions on race were not allowed. To receive such an invitation was considered a great honor. Humans and elves who passed the test along with the dragons usually stayed at the courts of the Lords of the Sky, became high dignitaries and enjoyed universal respect. Each new member of the group swore not to violate the agreed rules. A refusal could only be for a serious reason; otherwise, a refusal was considered an insult.

From some of what the elf said, Andy gleaned an amusing fact. The quests of dragons were actively sung by bards and minstrels. The local PR people actively promoted the topic, everywhere highlighting the difficulties of joint campaigns, erecting an impenetrable aura of masculinity around the test.

Indeed, the dragons suffered such deprivations, reducing themselves to the level of mere mortals, that their burdens simply could not be sung, and it was the duty of every reasonable person to help them overcome them.... And the people actively took such bait. Someone who was smarter might look for a hidden meaning between the lines and make his own conclusions, but no one thought about going against the system. The dragons wouldn't do anything: the other humans would kill you for it and not bat an eye.

Andy listened attentively to Ania and thought about it. Whoever invented the tradition of the "Grand Tour" in the Principality of Ora and limited it to an oath/virk/geas/taboo was a cunning and ingenious personality. What was the catch? The fact that he who used to wave his wings would now have to stamp his feet, and stamp quite far and long. The route wasn't known for being easy. The ride-on transport only added a couple hundred leagues and calluses on the rear end. The dragons in human or elf form got it just as bad as the others. Another complication collective. A third was that any violation of the virk vow by even one member of the group put an end to the whole trial, and the applicant would have to return to the starting point. Young dragons passed the exam not only to prove their maturity, strength, and endurance, which were important, but also to show their skills as leaders and administrators. The dragon manager must be able to control him or herself and his temper (a hard check for a young explosive character), make decisions in the most difficult circumstances, establish relationships in a motley team, and find the right members or performers in any society, and this is just a small part of what a future master of destinies must know and be capable of. A simple, but tricky virk tradition forced the dragons to "go out among the people," which played greatly on their authority. It was not for nothing that a whole commission of old flyers was waiting for the travelers at the finish line, scrupulously analyzing all the actions of the ata-virk (ata—has taken, ata-virk: one who has taken the responsibility upon him/herself, taken the test) and his team and decided on the success of the quest. A lot depended on their words: whether the young applicant could consider himself an adult and take his proper place, or whether in three years he was destined to go on the next campaign.

That was the fate that brought the difficult princess to the elves. Andy surreptitiously surveyed the retinue and estimated his chances of remaining incognito. The chances were slim. Her crowned parent, if he wasn't a fool, had stuffed a couple of faithful spies into his daughter's company, who were keeping track of all contacts and the princess' every step, and there was no doubt that their eyes picked up anything unusual. It was difficult to predict what they might react to.

Considering the sida, who was poking the sand with her boot, he examined the situation from all sides, but no matter how he spun it, he always butted up against the buttocks of that temperamental lady. The princess, with a piercing glance at him, waited for an answer.

"It is an honor to join your party," Andy bowed to the dragon.

"You can follow my escorts," Ilirra said, and headed for the troxes.

With a single phrase, she'd poked his face in the sand. Don't be an escort; don't go with the detachment, go behind the detachment. Be with us as it were, but don't be a bother. Andy looked at Ania and shook his head. The elf, catching the bitterness and sarcasm in the shkas' look, didn't say anything. She didn't like the mistress' decision, confined to a strange half-measure. The entourage followed the princess.

"We are leaving for the settlement, after lunch we will go to Astal Ruigara," she ordered, sitting down in the saddle. Everyone had temporarily forgotten about the shkas; the dragoness was sure he would not get lost.

Hermiel, having seen off the last trox, ran to Andy. The elf's gaze showed poorly concealed envy.

"Lucky you!" he said, sighing heavily. Among so many worthy candidates, and the dragoness chose some kind of a holy fool. Even though he handles a sword like a god, still, at first glance it's clear that there are shortcomings.

"You can say that again," the "lucky guy" said, pulling the ranger towards him by the collar. The elf jerked in the air with his feet and unsuccessfully tried to free himself from the steel grip. "Hermiel, tell me, who is so talkative and can not keep his mouth shut?"

There was no more jealousy in the gaze, only fear. Andy's face, distorted from hatred and anger, with fangs instead of teeth in his mouth and sharp claws sticking into Hermiel's neck, made the elf tremble with horror, and say goodbye to life. The shkas was not at all what they are used to seeing and who he himself pretended to be.

"Live," throwing the envious man aside, Andy spat on the sand. "If you only knew how you have set me up!" He closed his eyes and mentally counted to ten. He had to calm down; he couldn't let his emotions get the better of him. He mustn't! Feeling the foolishness inspired by Thygar's hormones subside, Andy wiped his wet hands on his trousers, glanced around at the elves, standing there in a stupor, and then helped Hermiel to rise from the ground.

"I'm sorry," he said to the ranger guiltily and, without waiting for an answer, ran to the village.

Mimiv was grieving most of all. The cat, anticipating the separation, was sitting at the threshold of the tiv and mewing plaintively with the thin voice of a small kitten. Lilly was not far from her tailed pet. The elf's nose was red and swollen, and her eyes were full of tears. Andy pressed the girl to him and wiped the tears with a hanky.

"Lilly, do not be so upset. I will come and visit you."

"You promise?"

"I will do my best."

The girl turned away. She was well versed in the subtleties of the spoken word. "Make every effort" does not mean to come or to promise. Andy would not come, he just didn't want to talk about it!

"Lilly!"

"You can just eat yourself!" Sobbing, she pushed Andy away and ran out of the living house. Mimiv rushed to her mistress, but, realizing that she was not up to dealing with her, returned to the threshold resumed her plaintive meowing.

"Andy," Atrael tossed the curtain back and stuck his head in the tiv. "Evael is calling you."

The village chief was waiting for him by the broad-leaved red fern bushes, and a hass, black as pitch, danced next to him.

"Sit down." The old elf pointed his hand at the thick root of a Mellorny protruding two feet from the ground.

Andy obeyed.

Evael took out a crystal from the folds of his clothes and activated an incomprehensible interweave. Andy thought his ears were crammed with cotton. After a few seconds, the unpleasant sensations passed.

"A circle of muteness," explained the chief. "It would be suspicious to drag you into a house, and nobody will be able to overhear us. The circle is very difficult to detect, a miur development." The elf chuckled. "The princely magicians are far from the cat people." And, squinting, the old elf got to the point:

"So which is it—Andy? Or Kerrovitarr?"

Andy shuddered. He did not expect such a sharp transition. A little later on, perhaps, but not at the very start of the conversation. The old elf wasn't stupid. He made his conclusions long ago, but for some reason he did not dare to voice them, and now, apparently, the moment has come. It would be naive for him to lose sight of such an outstanding personality as the blue-eyed shkas.

"Now it's better to call me Andy," he answered, and stared at Evael questioningly.

"Alright. As you wish." Evael said nothing, thinking about something feverishly for a moment. "Let us forget the first part of the conversation. I hope you know what you are doing. I am talking about something else...." The old elf sat down on another Mellorny root and began to broadcast how he personally, and the entire free settlement, were grateful to him for saving Atrael and Lilly, and asked Andy to accept a quiet but very frisky hass named Coal as a gift. The old elf began to count on his fingers: two saddlebags with a supply of provisions for the lizard and rider, two sets of travel clothes, a shield, two long paired swords, two wineskins with water, and two cloaks. Any bow from the workshop, Andy's choice. Fifty arrows and so on.

Andy respectfully declined the "so on." In response to his silent question the chief explained that in the forest tinder and flint are much more necessary, and there is a pair of gold coins in the city. The blades, shield, bow, and spare sets of clothes were accepted with gratitude. The soft items could be carried on his back or packed on the hass. Andy gave Evael a separate bow in thanks for the provisions.

Evael listened to Andy's arguments and nodded in agreement.

"I thought so." A tiny purse clinked in the elf's hand. "It's thirty gold pieces. Take it, I will not accept no for an answer. And this," just like an Earth magician, he took out a second purse, of a smaller size. The elf's open palm was strewn with a scattering of stones, each of which cost half the value of purse that the were-dragon received earlier. Noticing the dam in the young man's eyes, ready to break with a stream of objections, the chief removed most of the pebbles, leaving the five largest. "This is from me personally. I am sorry I can not offer anything else. Take it."

Andy reached out and took the precious stones. The old elf was right: they weighed only a little and would not be superfluous.

"Why are you helping me?"

"Do you not believe in spiritual kindness?"

"Life has taught me not to."

"Hmm, life is such a thing, sometimes it teaches, and sometimes it strips away skills and lessons already learned." Evael slapped the hass' neck a couple of times. "People no longer believe in good impulses. Everything needs a material explanation. Hm, in many respects they are right; our actions and aspirations are most often dictated by the material." Noticing that Andy slightly tilted his head to the left and lifted the corners of his lips into a slight smile, the elf finished: "We will still cross paths, it seems to me. This is not our last meeting."

"Thank you for your openness and for everything you have done for me."

"You are welcome, but next time keep yourself in hand. Viriel cannot always erase the memory of the rangers, and no one is likely to let him anywhere near the dragons or the princess' retinue anymore. Stay away from them; I do not like them. The princess does not belong here. Her dad should not have sent her to no man's land!" The elf realized that he had blurted out too much and fell silent.

"Thank you for the advice." Andy bowed his head. He caught the elf's remark. He had made a mess of things on the beach. Here the old elf outmaneuvered him.

People began to gather in the central square of the village. Residents decided to see the Princess of Ora off. A virk is a necessary thing to do, especially when a crowned person takes it upon himself, but she wanted to get as far away as possible, as soon as possible....

"It's time. Atrael will bring the bags and weapons. Go on."

Half an hour later, the princess' detachment, stretched out in a long chain, left the free settlement. Right before they left, Lilly darted over to Andy and handed him a small bag.

"Andy, you forgot the shaving kit. Grandfather found it."

"Thank you, honey, what would I do without you?" Andy, playing along with the girl, ran a hand over his chin and looked for the chief. Evael caught the were-dragon's eye and nodded briefly. In addition to a razor competing in sharpness with the famous "Gillette," the set contained an even belt, some soap root, and a fragrant essence which smelled like lily of the valley. The strong scent carried for a mile around. The grandfather had provided for what he did not think of at all. It was time to start shaving. "Goodbye!"

* * *

"Viriel, come and see me in an hour." Evael picked the mage out of the crowd.

"Alright. Is it anything urgent?"

"Yes. Saddle your trox."

Exactly an hour later, the lanky figure of the main village sorcerer appeared under the roots of the chief's family Mellorny. Viriel habitually bowed to the sacred tree, giving life and shelter to the old elf's family. He ran his hand over a thick rough root and stopped at the door. Going into the house without the old elf made for misery; he did not enjoy healing the wounds left by Mimiv's claws.

"Come in," said a cracked voice.

"What do you think?" Evael asked, pouring his guest some fragrant tea from a collection of forest grasses.

"He's a dragon, there can be no more doubt," said the magician, picking up the bowl of baked clay and sipping his drink.

"I know," the foreman said with a grin. "I have long ceased to doubt this. Tell me about something else...."

"He wasn't playing, Evael. Andy truly did not know the language. There can be no feigning how he sometimes misused elementary words and phrases. It seems to me that he was really pushed into a dugaria. Did you see his tattoo on his shoulder?"

"That's just the point, Viriel. In all my long life, I've never heard of dragons being put in a dugaria." Never! What did he do and why did the emperor decide to choose such a punishment? Why does Andy hide his second essence and hide under a cocoon of will shields? And that tattoo, too... Pack your things!"

"Where am I going?"

"You will go to the Great Mother." Evael opened a small box and took out an information crystal. "You will give THIS to the ruler of the Miur. Tell her it's from me. She knows how to activate the crystal and the access password."

"Serious business. Are you sure?"

"I am sure, as well as I'm sure of the fact that the emperor will not attack us. He needs the prince's northern mountainous provinces."

"Hmm."

"Do not snitch. More tea?"

"Perhaps. What should I say?"

"Don't say anything. This is not because I don't trust you. I worry about you. You will safer that way. If the ruler needs anything, she will clarify it herself."

"When do I leave?"

"As soon as you finish your tea. But seriously, someone should have done it a month ago...."

* * *

Andy stroked the hass around its neck:

"Don't lag behind, Coal!

The four-legged transport, black as pitch, slightly turned its head and squinted at the speaker. The rider put his hand into the saddlebag and took out a narrow strip of dried meat. A sharp movement of the head, a loud crack of the jaws, and the lizard swallowed the treat.

"Enough, be patient until we stop."

Andy reached his hand out to the animal's eyebrows, one of the most vulnerable spots of an armored scaly creature, and scratched the hass. Coal grunted and stuck its tongue out happily, just like a dog with a kind owner. The riding lizard was an amazingly good-natured creature and in no way resembled Snowball, whom he'd left in Orten. He was like a black puppy.

"Onward!" Andy lightly spurred Coal.

The hass let out its claws and set out after the main group.

After two turns of the forest trail, Ania's trox came into view, gradually moving ahead of Thygar's bird. Hearing the lizard's light steps approaching, she grabbed her crossbow more comfortably, which was glowing with a soft even light (you never know what to expect) and turned around. Upon seeing the shkas, she set her weapon across the saddle and turned away. The sida was burdened by the imposition of having to play nurse to the freak and, like the whole detachment, she hated his constant absences and falling behind. As if the virk weren't enough—now they had to worry about half-wits, too!...

Ania was a member of the branch of the elven tribe that settled in the low hills of the south of Otorn and was named after the central region of the highest elevation, "Sid." Andy had learned from Evael's explanations of the differences between elves that Sidas, or hillocks, differed from the rest of the long-eared people in their short stature and refined figures. Their skin was a delicate chocolate shade, and another difference was their eyes—they were huge and mesmerizing. Life in the twilight of caves had left its imprint.

"Do not lag," the girl said without turning around.

"Very well," Andy snorted for the hundredth time in a day.

He squeezed his lips narrowly. The bump on his forehead has long since disappeared, but the dragon Thygar had not forgotten his shame. While Andy was under Ilirra's virk, he had nothing to fear, but later on, it would be better not to turn his back….

The wind, dispersing the day's heat, brought with it the coolness of a nearby river. Sensing the moisture, the troxes went faster. Coal was in solidarity with the birds and put on speed, moving up to right behind Ania. Her trox, like a dove, was swaying its body from side to side with each step. The sida's round rear end, in tight leather pants, repeated the trajectory along with the three hundred-pound bird. Andy's eyes fixed on the sight and repeated the swaying route.

Ania sensed the shkas' interested look. The tips of her sharp ears constantly flared maroon, but every time she turned back, the insolent guy looked anywhere but at her. As soon as she turned away, everything came back to square one. The elf turned sharply.

"What are you looking at?" she attacked Andy, who didn't look away this time, but kept looking calmly at her.

"You're pretty," he said unexpectedly, bringing his hass to a halt.

Ania blushed red as a tomato. The angry words she'd prepared for him went out the window. Everything she wanted to tell the bold freak just stuck in her throat. She looked at him one more time and then turned back around.

The freak wasn't lying or kidding. After two hundred years in the prince's palace, where it was impossible to see people's real faces and feelings for magical masks and all the falsity there, she had had plenty of opportunity to hone her skills and uncovering the truths behind people's actions. Life had taught her to read every gesture, glance, tone of voice, and many other small details. In a situation where the person's aura was hidden by will shields or replaced by someone else's, she caught every gesture, listened to the beating of their heart, paid attention to their sweat and the twitching of their skin. The prince himself valued her skill. At great receptions, she followed the ruler in a quiet shadow and evaluated, evaluated, evaluated. She evaluated everyone, whispering her observations into the communicator amulet. Sometimes she could do what empaths or psionics could not do, because magic could be reliably blocked from encroachments on the will or interference in feelings, but Ania could still see through them. They didn't like her, but they accepted her, as one accepts a necessary evil.

Ania became a member of Ilirra's entourage by the order of the prince. Before that, he had had two conversations—a difficult one with his daughter, who did not like the spy, and an easy one with Ania, who accepted the will of the sovereign.

Ilirra, taking advantage of the opportunity and her power, got her petty revenge. The princess assigned her father's servant to the strange non-human, ordering her to be a chaperone until his memory was completely restored. And when would it come back? The rest of the entourage, savvy about palace intrigues, quietly giggled and wondered how the disgraced servant would manage.

But things were turning out not at all as expected. On the first day, the sida drew a few conclusions, characterizing her ward on the positive side. The shkas, like many inhabitants of princely courts, wore several layers of masks, behind which the real person was hidden. Nothing unusual about that. He was constantly closed by a cocoon of will and mind shields, but a large cat with the funny nickname Mimiv, who escorted him more than two leagues and lagged behind only at Andy's exhortations on the bank of the Ledyanka River, told Ania more than words could say. Animals can not be deceived. And the granddaughter of the elven chief and the other children waving to the departing non-human? The princess assumed they were seeing her and her retinue off. Ania said nothing; she didn't want to upset Ilirra, but the princess was cruelly mistaken. The children were not running after the entourage.

True, Andy did not cause any special trouble, and if it were not for his constant lagging behind, he would be absolutely golden. Three days ago, the lady could no longer stand it and told him what she thought about such behavior. He calmly listened to the princess, bowed, smiled guiltily, and asked about the reasons for her concern. Hadn't the princess herself told him to follow her detachment? Until now, he believed that he correctly interpreted the lady's words and never crossed the permitted boundaries, following the retinue. Neither in front, nor beside, but in the back, behind the last trox. With regards to the absences, that was his business; he had taken on the duties of rear guard and was watching out for safety, making sure no one was secretly following the accepted virk. If the princess wished, he would abandon this venture. Ilirra hesitated. There was no reason to blame the shkas; he was right on all sides. The conversation, to the great displeasure of Thygar and a couple of his friends, was hushed up.

When they got to Ruigar's dugaria, Andy said the most pleasant memories in his life didn't come from dugarias and spent the whole day in the camp, quiet as a mouse. He kept to himself and was cooking for one. In the past while, the shkas had not yet had even a short chat with any member of the detachment. The princess took a hands-off approach, watching how the others would react to the unpleasant neighbor and how the blue-eyed man would behave. He did not seem to be worried at all by the situation. As soon as they stopped to camp for the night, Andy immediately disappeared for twenty or thirty minutes, reappearing near the camp with some prey. Then he set up a fire and took care of his hass, rubbing the lizard's scales with oil and peeling small rocks and dirt out from the beast's claws and paws. After finishing his chores and setting up his tent, Andy would begin to perform his ritual; Ania couldn't put it any other way. The smells coming from his small fire made her mouth water, and she wasn't the only one. Maybe he'd lost his memory, but he knew how to cook. The blue-eyed guy was a mystery to the sida, and not only to her. Ilirra was not a fool. She inherited sharp intellect and observation from her father. With each subsequent day, looking at the ward of her father's servants, she frowned more and more.

Andy was clearly not from a peasant family. When the virk led the detachment to a second human settlement, Ania, followed by the lady, drew attention to his behavior and manners at the bar of a roadside inn. Not every highborn could use a knife and fork. Andy ate carefully, slicing pieces of juicy meat, holding his knife and fork with a light grace.

The ease of the movements showed that he was accustomed to eating just like that. After eating, he mechanically dabbed his lips with a napkin handed over by the waiter, exactly like Prince Ora in human form. He did not seem like a simpleton. Into the treasury of observations fell yet another fact. The blue-eyed man emptied his purse, buying several expensive volumes of magic from the second-hand bookseller, even though he had a puny amount of magic. Why did he need these self-instruction manuals? Once when they were riding past a musical instruments store, he sharply reined in his hass and stared at the tair. An hour later, his hass caught up to the main detachment. As per the sida's expectations, there was a cover with a musical instrument resembling a guitar attached to Coal's saddle. Where were the peasants taught to play music? The third evening of their journey, in addition to the mouth-watering smells coming from Andy's fire, they also heard the sound of the tair. And what about his combat skills? Thygar still looked at his offender like a rix.

"Pretty," thought Ania, skeptical of her appearance. No ordinary mortal ever talked to her like that.

"Do you really think I'm pretty?" stopping her trox next to Andy, the girl asked. Guga, irritated by the sharp stop, flared angrily. Ania, correcting her braid, smiled dazzlingly. "And who is more beautiful, I, Delia, or the mistress?"

Andy did not fall for the trick. He hung down from the saddle and, without stopping, picked a large field flower and presented it to the sida. Ania mechanically took the silver bloom and froze, wide-eyed, looking at the retreating man's back. *Manyfaces, is he a madman? Goddess of the All-Merciful, what have I done?*

"Ania, a silver one. Has he proposed?" A grinning Thygar appeared from behind.

"It's just a flower."

"Tell the group about it. It will be a fairy tale: 'I was given a silver bloom. I accepted the offer of a stupid shkas.' Ha ha ha!"

"Shut up!"

"What? Are you going to tear my head off?"

Ania sharply pulled the reins. The trained trox, waving his short right wing over the head of the scoundrel, instantly turned around. Thygar, fleeing from a blow that could deprive a person of his life, staggered to the side and down; his trox jumped sideways at the offending bird.

"You nasty...!" Snatching a dagger from its sheath, the dragon straightened in the saddle and then almost choked. A thin dart with a luminous magical tip rested on the buckle of his belt. One careless movement and an explosion would be inevitable.

"Why do I need your head? One move and your insides will discover the charm of the free flight."

"What are you doing??"

"Shut up! Do you need me to say it again? Your brains were never in the right place, Thygar. Now you will go to the others and pretend that nothing has happened; otherwise, the whole princedom will know that you have lost to a woman!" said Ania. There was a shadow of doubt on the were-dragon's face, but he had no choice. He didn't think for long.

"Fine. Take the dart away."

"Apologize for calling me 'nasty.' ...And whatever else you were planning to say."

"Hag!"

"Well done, that's me! I am waiting!"

The dragon apologized. Ania put the dart away.

"Do you seriously think that you will get away with it?" he asked, moving away.

"Challenge me to a duel."

"You're crazy!"

"A minute ago you said I was a hag."

"What's going on here?" Breaking through the bushes, the princess' bird came out into the clearing with its rider. "Traitor! Have you given Ania a silver one?" she asked, noticing the crumpled flower in the sida's hands, which she hadn't thrown away.

"Not me."

"Who then?"

"Ask Ania, your grace." Thygar smiled mockingly.

* * *

Once again he'd done something wrong. Andy couldn't

stop reproaching himself. *Targ, how much can I get caught by my own stupidity? I should have asked someone about the flowers. Maybe give flowers to girls just isn't something they do?* In a whole month spent among the elves, he never saw a bouquet or any elf giving flowers to women. Although, it wasn't a fact that the comparison with forest elves was applicable to hillock sidas or dragons. The forest elves have enough flowers in the settlement. The entire middle and upper layers of the Mellornys are overgrown with different colors. It's better not to climb up to the middle tier without a mosquito net; otherwise, no one could guarantee you wouldn't be stung in the hand or face a couple times.

Ania was simply smitten on the spot by my trick, and how surprised her eyes were! Andy smiled involuntarily at the recollection. *Beautiful eyes....*

Because of his thinking pleasant thoughts and not so pleasant thoughts, the rider failed to notice Coal had stopped near the bank of a mountain river. At that moment, the rider could have been taken with someone's bare hands, warm. In his pensive reflections, Andy probably would not have reacted to the signal of the "spider web." The princess' entourage came out further up the river. Among the compact crowd, Andy could see the golden hair of the mistress of the wandering caravan. The dragon was discussing something with her attendants. Usually calm, Ilirra was waving her hands like a mill for some reason. What the dispute was about, he couldn't hear. The loud murmur of the water drowned out the sound. *Who cares...?*

Andy reined in Coal. The hass, accustomed to hygienic procedures, immediately flopped to the ground, ready to get his scales rubbed with oil.

"You'll wait."

Looking at its owner, who was mowing grass on the coastal clearing with a small sickle and laying it on the place where he was going to set up his tent, the hass snarled at him in an offended manner. And what about him?

"Do not growl," the mower turned to the offended transport. "I'll set up the tent and then get started on you."

After completing his work and wiping down the lizard, Andy unpacked one of his saddlebags and took out a bundle containing a bunch of long white horse tail hairs and enchanted to prevent breaking, some fishing hooks, several bobbers of light wood resembling cork, and two thin strips of lead for sinkers. The actual fishing rods grew abundantly along the river—take your pick. After building a simple fishing rod, he walked along the river. The fisherman's bait was a whole canvas bag of larvae and worms he found under some driftwood.

"Will you have some fish?" Andy asked Coal. The lizard didn't move, but you could read the answer in its eyes. "Yes, of course, a hefty helping if you please." Andy smiled and set to his task.

* * *

With a dry click, a branch cracked. The light, cautious step told him it belonged to a woman. Andy, ignoring the sound, stayed focused on the dancing bobber. He had a bite. The bobber, pierced by a blue trox feather, dove sharply underwater. If Andy could pull sharply on the line, the fish would be hooked, and would soon be flopping about the hands of the fisherman. Planting his trout-like prey on a skewer that already contained about a dozen of its fellows, Andy turned. *Ania... were you expecting someone else?*

The sida was standing with her head down. A light breeze played with her green cloak and did not forget to ruffle her copper curls. Thin elf's thin fingers clutched the broken flower Andy had given her and trembled nervously.

"I cannot accept your silver bloom, Andy," the elf said in a cracked voice, stretching out the wilted beauty.

The flower! So that's the reason. My bad feeling was right. The silver bloom was once a bright blue flower with wide silver veins on petals, a sunny center and a completely silver stem. Now the petals had faded, resembling a dirty puddle reflecting the sky. *No wonder the elves don't give the girls flowers.... You can give your head to the chopping block that way—the flowers serve as proposals! Why would she be so nervous otherwise? She cannot....* A cold lump of regret and melancholy settled in Andy's chest. He looked at the drooping symbol of the offer and couldn't force himself to take it away from the pale girl, suddenly realizing that he did not want to at all. He liked Ania. She wasn't more beautiful than the other women in the retinue, but there was something about her that made him think about her constantly. Despite his will, Andy's hand stretched forward. For an instant, he touched the elf's narrow, hot hand with his, and the silvery bloom was transferred to him.

Flowers. In all worlds, they were a symbol of love, but here their magical beauty took on a much wider significance. Andy looked at the broken flower. It was a fitting symbol. His love was just as broken. The villain fate had brutally laughed at him, depriving him of Polana and deceiving Frida. True, the vampire didn't occupy the same place in his heart as Polana, but she was a real bright spot in his life.

Andy could see that an invisible weight was lifted from Ania's shoulders. The sida sighed in relief. The color came back to her cheeks, but the elf's green eyes remained sad. She cannot.... The weight Ania had cast off now settled on Andy. He touched the blossom and closed his eyes, only now realizing who he was and who she was. What kind of love could they have? A simple one, like many people probably do—plain old love at first sight.

"I understand," he said quietly. It was possible he had ruined her life with his little flower.

"Thank you."

Andy scoffed. Not the kind of thing you're supposed to thank people for. Although, by local custom, perhaps they do!

"Is this why the princess was flapping her arms all over the place?"

"Her lady has the right to do whatever she wishes with her arms." The sida's voice was icy.

"Alright. It's really all the same to me. Is something threatening you?"

"Yes, I might be thrown out of the royal court as someone who has put the princess' honor into question."

"Seriously, tell me why the princess wants to do that? Your fault in what happened does not exist. You took the silver flower without thinking it over." An investigator and an analyst woke up in Andy. A fragmented mosaic began to come together into a certain picture. But there were not enough facts to collect the image completely.

"It is her full right."

"No one doubts Ilirra's rights."

"The princess has a reason not to like me. I can not say anything else."

"Do you want me to say it?" asked Andy, pointing to a crooked stump with many boughs, whitewashed by the water and the sun. Ania sat down on a comfortable thick root, folding her hands on her knees.

"Ilirra was a very clever little thing, I must say. My hat is off to her." The elf knitted her brows, uncomprehending. She was hearing about the hat for the first time. "I will speak a little later on the reasons for the princess' dislike toward you, or my assumptions about the reasons for it. But for now, let us consider the fact of that scoundrel Thygar being accepted into the detachment. I'm talking about my humble self. I think I became interesting to Ilirra specifically as part of her plot against you. She deliberately invited me to the virk and sent me behind the detachment, and assigned you to watch over me. A sensible move. She created an external point of tension. It's no secret that a team is best unified by the presence of an external threat or something unpleasant for all the members. The whole retinue began to look at me as a pariah. And to make sure the half-wit Ilirra sheltered would not do anything wrong, she gave him, in essence, a personal nanny. Does not that situation lead to any thoughts?"

"Go on."

"Yes... Then a group of Thygar's friends or supporters immediately emerged. No one likes freaks; that is not surprising. They perceived my defeat of the dragon as a personal insult, but they are not intending to get involved. Thygar must resolve the matter himself and defend, as it seems to him and them, his honor. Attaching you to me, a shkas, led to their dislike automatically spreading to you as well, the involuntary chaperone. Psychologically, everything was thought out correctly. She only had to warm up the hostility occasionally. Here I made a mistake during the demonstrative showdown that was arranged for me. I should not have given her ladyship that refusal, but only the grave will correct my faulty nature." The sida, throwing a strand of hair from her eyes, smiled. "Petty insults in the following days completed the work. The detachment realized that I was an unnecessary link in the chain, and only the princess' word is restraining her from banishing the freak. The effect was achieved. And now about you. You did not take part in the silent persecution of the shkas; I will not ask why. Your rejecting the position of the rest became an opposition to the entire collective. The princess then skillfully prompted Thygar's and Delia's ambitions. Now there were two targets. The masculine members of the virk have focused their hatred on me, and the ladies have declared their objection to you, am I right?"

"You are right. The situation is exactly as you describe."

"Thank you for the kind words."

"You are welcome."

"All right, courtesy aside, moving on. Now, Ilirra just had to wait for you to make some sort of mistake, and to my great regret, I gave her a great chance to take you by the throat."

"I did it...."

"What did you do? Took a silver flower?" Andy interrupted. "Do not embarrass my hass. You just did not expect such antics from me. People do not act like that in princely chambers."

"It is what it is."

Andy picked up a fishing rod, rummaged through his bag, took out a fat larva, and planted it on the hook. "The princess reminds me of a fisherman." He cast his bait into the water. "Ilirra's patience can be envied. Once she cast the bait, she, like a true fisherman, waited for a bite. And in the meantime, she gently warmed the passions of her support team."

"Interesting comparison." Ania stood up from the broad root and sat on the shore next to Andy.

"And as soon as the fish bit, she skillfully hooked it." A smooth jerk, and another swimmer was flopping in the fisherman's hands. "Now, about her reasons for disliking you." Andy took the fish off, corrected the bait, and asked a question: "Have you known the princess long?"

"I have lived for two hundred years in the prince's court, and Ilirra has never had any friendship with anyone." The girl tilted her head to her left shoulder. "I would not say that the princess and I were very close, but we greeted one another when we met," she added cautiously.

"That is as I expected. Opa!" The large fish, not wishing to be planted on the skewer, fell off the hook and flopped back into the water. Andy planted a new worm on the hook and sent it off to fetch dinner for the hungry were-dragon. "So you can distinguish the real daughter of a prince from a double? No?" Andy looked straight into her eyes. The girl was silent, but he did not need an answer. "You do not have to say anything. There can be two reasons for dislike. Correct me if I am wrong. There is some elementary surveillance going on for the beloved daughter of the sovereign at the request of the monarch himself, and the princess was told about this openly. The other reason could be that we are not dealing with a princess. Then it becomes clear why she wants to be rid of you. The double realizes that you can expose her to the others and is trying to remove that threat by dirty yet effective methods." The elf's nostrils fluttered from frequent breathing. "It's not worth it," Andy warned Ania, who was stretching her hand towards her hip. "You can not kill me, but I am completely capable of killing you." The rod in his hands shot towards the sida, stopping a couple of millimeters from her forehead. The girl belatedly recoiled back. "If I hit lower, the bridge of your nose would break, and depending on the strength and angle of impact, I can drive the bone into the brain. Judging by your reaction, you guessed about the double long ago, and the pseudo-princess guessed that you guessed, and you guessed that she guessed: oh, what a cycle of guesses we have on our hands! But you kept your conclusions to yourself."

"Are you prepared to kill the woman you like?" Shaking off her cloak and pants, Ania asked an unexpected question. Glancing at her unperturbed conversation partner, she sat down.

"No," Andy answered honestly. "But I will not allow anyone to kill me. I have a real Virk, with a capital letter. I cannot die without finishing it!"

The girl opened her eyes wide and looked at Andy in a new way. She was unexpectedly seeing him in a new light.

"But how did you guess?"

"Eyes are given to us to see, and our heads are not only to eat with. It's no secret that war may break out any moment. During our second stop, I listened attentively to all the news from the world. There were several attacks in the principality on merchants from the empire. At the University of Darius, someone beat up the imperial bookworms. The Emperor never lets attacks on his citizens slide. It is very possible that the attacks were organized by supporters of the empire, but according to rumor, the royal security service could not catch anyone. The northern neighbor now has a reason to punish the bold offenders; he will not let them get away with these abuses. And that's the moment the prince decides to send his daughter on the virk. Which is it—stupidity or a distraction? I'm inclined to think it is the second one, but I was confused by the fact that the dragon sent her to an area where blood can start to flow at any time. Elves and humans in no man's land are building barricades, buying heavy gunners from the Miur and lining all approaches to the mountain fortresses with cutting stones. Strange solution! It does not fit in any way with what a loving parent would do. I began to look for inconsistencies and reasons. The first discrepancy emerged on the second day. According to the conversations of the retinue, Ilirra was very close to Ruigar, and then everyone witnessed their cool meeting and parting, quite unlike the parting of lovers. I was not deceived by the tears in the princess' eyes as she returned from her meeting with the governor. Actresses in the theater play much more believably. And did you see Ruigar?"

"And it was after that you took over the rearguard duties?" Ania threw a small pebble into the water; the rapid current immediately moved it along.

"Exactly."

"What conclusions did you draw after noticing the lack of surveillance?"

"Well, I cannot say that there was no surveillance at all. Birds with magical collars are constantly flying over the detachment, but yes, no one is tracing our path. Prince Ora could not confine himself to birds. Leaving his daughter with just spies would be the height of recklessness. There are a few more small observations that allow us to draw certain conclusions about the "princess." Two days ago, I read in one of the books I bought of the so-called aura replacement technique, invented two thousand years ago at the Imperial University of Magic. The book also described how to spot a replacement. There are ten features about any given aura. Three of them, when examined in detail, showed an induced or replaced aura. I checked three times. If Ilirra went on the test, why should she mask her aura? Who would she hide from? Why pile such a complex scheme? The fact that the virk is a distraction operation is clear. The detachment is a simple setup. But what it is distracting from, who is being set up and why, remains unclear.

"Can't it be any other way?"

"Who knows? I cannot read the prince's thoughts. What they really want is covered with darkness. Finding contacts with Miur is not the main task of your princess. Why are you surprised? The girl demonstratively meets with traders and smugglers who have access to the cat people. It makes anyone inevitably guess the purpose of the voyage. True, she is wasting her resources on the merchants and the dark dealers. They would never surrender the secrets of their comings and goings. The Great Mother's 'night dwellers' kill all traitors. It is easier to organize a direct envoy. I understand that the cats have not had any business for three thousand years with the dragons in power, and knocked down all the Lords of the Sky who approached their lands. They did not recognize either the emperor or the Prince of Ora, but the current situation could cause them to enter into a dialogue. If the Principality of Ora collapses, the Great Mother will be one on one with the emperor's nökürs, who have not forgotten the ancient slap in the face—helping Jagirra."

The elf said nothing, looking at Andy with a pensive gaze. Numerous sparks in her aura testified to the fact that she was thinking hard. She was analyzing his words and setting the impressions from the conversation out in order of importance. There was no doubt that Andy was being "measured" from all sides and the information she received processed in all parameters.

The bites had stopped. Small whirlpools drove the bobber across the backwaters, but there hadn't been a single bite in the last five minutes.

"Can I try?" Ania broke the silence, shooting her eyes at the bait.

"Go ahead. I'll change the bait right now."

"I'll do it." The sida took his bag and poked around in it, choosing what was from her point of view the most appetizing fish snack.

Planting a healthy red worm on the hook, she spit on the bait and cast the fishing rod. A half-minute later, the bobber drifted off underwater; the rod arched. Andy jumped to his feet.

"Bring it out, bring it out. Smoothly now, do not jerk the rod, it is not enchanted," he began to give her advice.

"Don't interfere," said the elf. "You're not gonna get away!"

The large fish stubbornly refused to give in. The rod cracked, but it held. Andy, wringing his hands, jumped along the shore. Ania was knee-deep in the river. The water stirred around her legs. The girl smoothly pulled the rod to the shore. A large, eight-pound striped fish that looked like a pike came up onto the slippery stones. The elf jumped to the shore with one leap, picked up a round cobblestone, and dropped it onto the river predator's head.

"Beginner's luck," Andy growled.

"The chupkeys you were fishing for always hide when an orsh appears," Ania said, picking up the fish by the gills, "and orshes are caught by red. A red rag, a piece of meat, a red worm—they do not care."

She'd shown him what for, no two ways about it. In one sentence and with one big fish, she'd disgraced all his fishing experience and his catch. Andy laughed. Looking at him, Ania began to laugh too. The increasing overflow of the two voices rang out over the river.

"Andy, I cannot cook fish," the sida said, wiping away a small tear from her eye.

"Well, that's the lesser of two evils. We'll think of something," Andy smiled. Ania didn't miss a trick. How cleverly she pushed his buttons and flattered him, also profiting thereby.

Coal got the chupkeys, and the orsh was gutted, stuffed with marsh onions, sprinkled with salt and rubbed with the equivalent of pepper, then wrapped in a wide river leaf and rolled into a thick layer of clay. Watching Andy's skills, Ania was surprised. What did he need all that clay for? Who would eat the fish now? He reassured the elf, saying, she will, and she'll lick her fingers, just trust him. The sida looked skeptically at the hefty clod of clay placed in the fire, but refrained from further questions. The cook knew better.

* * *

"Andy, is there a little piece left?"

"No, we ate it all. How was the fish?"

"Heavenly!"

"Imagine how they are now going to envy you in the detachment. Do you think I failed to notice your hungry looks when I cook?"

"Oh yes. Ugh." Ania, leaning back and resting her elbows on a specially set saddle, loosened the top lace of her blouse. The light of the fire cast a dark hollow between her breasts.

Andy looked away. He had seen the sida nude. The ladies did not shy away from bathing. If they announced a halt near a river or lake, they were not shy with their own bodies and did not suffer from hypocrisy with excessive modesty, but that was not what was going on now. Bathing was perceived as something natural, ordinary and did not cause any special reactions, and now the hollow was so inviting and erotic that his blood began to run through his veins at triple speed.

"Andy?"

"Yes?"

"Can I ask you something?"

"Shoot." Andy waved his hand casually. The large yummy dinner eaten in one sitting caused drowsiness and a content disposition of the spirit which the end of the world could not shake.

"Who are you?"

The good mood fell away instantly. Seemingly innocent, the question turned out to be worse than the end of the world.

"I am me, are there any doubts? Throw a stone at me if I am not me, but someone else!"

"An exhaustive answer, as the pirates of the southern seas

147

say: for someone's secrets, you pay with your teeth and life. Is that right?"

"As they say in distant countries: 'the less you know, the better you sleep!'"

The sida straightened her back. The tongues of flame reflected in her green eyes danced an otherworldly, bewitching dance. Andy admired her correct features and sensual, plump lips. Admiration was one thing, but he did not lose his caution.

"You do not look like a shkas. Freaks do not teach sword fighting. You have the habits of a noble, and the dugaria does not deprive a person of memory so selectively."

"I am me; there will be no other answer."

"Sorry if I offended you."

"It's okay. A healthy curiosity when you come into contact with someone else's mystery is natural," Andy smiled to soften the situation.

From the main camp, they heard the sounds of a tair and a natvor, an instrument similar to a harp. To the simple musical accompaniment of Renat, one of Thygar's supporters, they sang a ballad about the love of a noble knight for a certain beautiful princess. No matter what the unfortunate man did to try to gain her affection, the beauty was deaf and mute to the lover's heart's impulses. The singer's voice was clear and clean, but the tedious way he performed it killed the entertainment value.

Parting the bushes, Delia, performing the role of the princess' first maid, and Torvir, Delia's permanent boyfriend, came over to the glade lit by the fire. Andy tensed up, expecting trickery from the guests, but they behaved peacefully and invited the sida to the main camp. The cavaliers were organizing a competition for the best performer of songs and ballads. At that, the peaceful path ended. Ania was now more of a friend than a stranger for them, but the conversation with Andy went differently. Torvir said something to the effect that it would be interesting to listen to Andy (at these words, Delia twisted her lips contemptuously). Perhaps the guy who tormented his tair by day, in addition to the plucking of strings that sounded like a chicken being plucked alive, had something else, something a bit more pleasant? Was he as talented at music as he was in caring for girls? Andy didn't react to the thinly veiled insult. Torvir, smiling arrogantly, picked up his companion by the elbow and started on his way back. Somewhere in the middle of the road, Andy let out a muffled curse. May your paths be crooked, jerks.

"Are you coming?" Ania asked.

"Why not?"

"They want to shame you."

"I guessed as much. Certainly by Thygar's doing and with the tacit approval of our "princess." The girl wants to finish off her victim, and who is her victim, can you guess?"

"I can. What are you standing there for? Offer a lady your arm!"

Andy picked up the musical instrument and took Ania by the elbow. A brave girl, to appear before the others like this. The sida decided not to waste time on trifles. Spitting at enemies in the face was a beautiful gesture. It was a risky action; Andy hoped she knows what she is doing.

He hadn't played the guitar for a long time. The last time he held his darling in his hands was on the grievous day of his portal transfer from Earth to Ilanta. The three days that had passed since the purchase of the tair didn't count.

Andy was honest with himself. He played not bad. The scope of his personal skills went beyond three chords. He recalled that guy at the house, one of his sister's victims, who had a musical ear and strummed a seven-string while Andy was cooking for them. A couple of songs performed by that guy clearly showed his class. According to his sister, in role-playing games, that guy was always an elf. Music is a great force. How soon under its influence did Irina break, and how soon after did she dump him? The power of music aside, his older sister's strong temper was stronger.

Andy, carefully bypassing the stumps and warning about the roots and branches, accompanied his companion to the retinue's camp. The new participant in the music contest was greeted with deliberately friendly exclamations. The ladies batted their eyelashes; the gentlemen wished him victory. A theater of masks concealing baseness. They cast lots to see who would perform in what order. In total, six contestants were nominated to perform as forest bards.

All the performers sat down in front of the "princess," dedicating the ballads to the "queen of the forest." It should be noted that the contestants had reached a high level of musical expertise. The voices were all trained and pleasant. One contestant smoked nervously on the sidelines and warmed up, stupidly pretending to be a small music box. Andy did not expect to win; he was cooking up another plan.

When it was his turn, he broke tradition, settling in front of Ania. There was a disgruntled murmur. He didn't care! He decided to win the elf's heart; everything else was secondary.

His fingers ran along the strings. It was a little painful; he'd really chaffed them lately, but for the sake of the idea it was worth a little suffering. Memory snatched the first song from its bins, and Andy translated as he went along, performing it in Common. He reworked a few details in accordance with local realities, but the nature of love expressed in song is universal in all worlds.

"And we have a certain girl in the palace," Andy began, watching the bright lights turn on in the sida's eyes.

The moment the last chord rang out, he changed the melody and kept going:

"Enchanted, bewitched, with a wind in the field once married...."

Then there was the "Little Blue Handkerchief" and "The Dark Night."

Tears appeared in the corners of Ania's eyes; there were languid sighs from the ladies present and hateful looks from the cavaliers who had been robbed of the victory. The shkas' voice was inferior to their voices on all counts, but his songs were new, unusual, attractive, and they were filled with real feelings. The women sensed this and envied the one to whom he devoted his performance. The men ground their teeth because the attention of the beautiful half of humanity was not on them. Andy wanted to end the concert, but the amicable shouts of protest didn't let him. The choice of the fifth song was short-lived. "The Beauty Queen" was somewhat ambiguous and a little frivolous: taking into account local specifics, the line about "I'm bringing you flowers" was perceived, well, given the history of the silver bloom, uniquely and literally as a veiled proposal. Who cared what they thought? Andy didn't alter anything. If someone didn't like it, he could stick his nose in a rubber hose.

"Another one," Ania whispered.

Andy closed his eyes. He seemed to have achieved his goal; Ania wasn't noticing anyone else except him. In the eyes of some of the ladies, he read readiness to warm the simple bed in his lonely tent. Suddenly, an image and a tune emerged from a cartoon he'd seen back in those days when his presence near the TV didn't cause the screen to go fuzzy. Without opening his eyes, he sang:

"Golden ray of sunshine…."

The last chord sounded in complete silence. Andy opened his eyes. Why was everyone staring behind his back? He turned around cautiously. *Almighty Twins! Just look where my singing's gotten me!* The air was melting with an illusion—it was Ania, full size. She was depicted as he'd seen her on the river bank—sad and desperate at the same time, with a slight smile on her lips.

Now they would definitely kick him out of the group for using magic. Who would believe the image was formed involuntarily?

His magic had returned. With each passing day, Andy felt a new reconnecting with the world; his mana storehouses were steadily increasing. There was so much mana in Nelita that you could swim in it, but maniacal caution stopped him from taking such a thoughtless step. It wasn't the time or place for "bathing." While the dragons were near, that was absolutely impossible. What's more, his trial experiments with magical interweaving brought unexpected fruit. None of the entourage could see his creations. Andy was racking his brains trying to find the reason for such blindness. The answer was suggested by a magician from a human settlement when she was charging the detachment's magical artifacts and amulets. The local mage scooped up many times more mana than was required for border guard spells. The unused energy was simply thrown to the wind, and Andy observed such irrational use of resources everywhere. The world, which was full of Mellorny forests and dragons, pumping mana from the astral, never experienced any shortage of energy. The two planets were strikingly different from one another, and the magical schools developed in different ways over the past three thousand years.

Previously, the ratio was equalized by open portals, through which mana freely flowed to Ilanta, balancing the energy of the worlds. Closing the portals led to a sharp decrease in the density of the magic field in the world colonized by dragons, Ilanta. Reducing the magic field has created the need to search for new sources. On Ilanta, the schools of necromancers, who took energy from living creatures, burst into a storm of color. The technology of creating energy storage devices developed, and the mastery of artifactors reached unprecedented heights. Yes, many technologies had been forgotten or lost, but others appeared instead. No mage on Nelita had ever heard of training to increase one's internal reserve. In any magical school on Ilanta, methods of increasing one's magical reserve were taught in the first year and were included in compulsory courses. To understand the difference between the planets, imagine two people wanting to drink, but one of them is in the desert, and the other is on the shore of the widest river. The desert resident would try to use water rationally, without wasting a single drop, drinking his portion in small sips, enjoying each of them. The person living on the riverbank would scoop up a full bucket, take three gulps, spill the rest, or take off his clothes and dive into the invigorating water. In the end, both drank no more than one mug of water, but the attitude towards it was different.

The magical schools and approaches to interweaving on Ilanta differed from the local ones in their extremely economical approach to the use of mana. Each spell took exactly as much as was required to get the desired result. Unused energy was carefully, until the last drop, pumped into storage tanks. Waste not, want not. The entourage's attitude towards energy and magical interweaves corresponded. The simplest border guard spell built by Andy looked a thin web against the backdrop of sea rigging, which the dragons supplied with the help of special artifacts. Accustomed to the luminous ropes, the group of travelers did not notice the faded web. In the university textbooks Andy bought, there were incantations that, on Ilanta, were simply not applicable. There were also some real pearls. On the very first evening, lying by the fire, he came across a description of the aura replacement technique, which functioned at the junction of settage and classical magic. The technique did not require the mage to spend large amounts of energy and enabled him to disguise his aura to any creature.

Something similar, as far as Andy knew, was invented by the Forest Elves on Ilanta and was actively used; they planted the elves, changed in the womb, turned into ideal spies, in human cities and countries.

Once he memorized the instructions, Andy went away from the camp so that his winged tribesmen would not notice his manipulations and conducted a test on himself. The result was impressive: his aura shrank several times, becoming more human, and the tattoo on his shoulder grayed, eventually disappearing under his tan. Covering the altered aura with will and mind shields, he returned to his tent. Wow! It was worth parting with a dozen gold coins just for that. The surrounding mages still took no interest in him. The superimposed multi-layered disguise showed that he had a puny magical gift. He was no mage by their standards. The musical performance and his releasing the reins of control had led to a sad result.

"I think there's no point in continuing," said the "princess." Her voice was flat and expressionless, but Andy could read a death sentence in her eyes. "Andy, I demand that you come to the Circle tomorrow at noon. Since you are not an official escort, the virk is not broken, but even so, we can not leave the violation of the rules of the virk without consequences. The circle will decide your fate."

How Thygar's eyes lit up at that! Oh, he would have some fun! A whisper rustled through the retinue. A call to the Circle meant judgment. Yes, he would appear at the Circle, but he would not allow himself to be judged. It was worth immediately hinting at this; otherwise, the picturesque trial appointed by Ilirra's double could lead to the grave. No, better not hint at all; better just make some powerful arguments, solve this here and now; tomorrow it may be too late. Andy threw the tair behind his back, straightened up to his full height, and pinned his shoulders back. He put on the expression he wore in front of the Snow Elves on the day of his arrival at the Orten School of Magic. One of the retinue members, looking at him, choked on his saliva.

"Please, Your Grace, I ask you not to forget three facts. First, I am not a subject of the Prince of Ora. Second, I have not been accepted into the virk; I accompany you privately. And third, the rules of the virk, in terms of using visual magic and illusions, do not apply to me. And finally, the Circle can not decide my destiny; it can only throw me out of the detachment. It is not up to you to judge me, and all the less so for Thygar. He has not yet grown." The insult hit the bull's eye.

"Pup!" Grinning and snatching his sword from his scabbard, he jumped to his feet. "Fight!"

Andy went into a trance; the bonfire scattered in different directions from his movements. Those present recoiled from the flying logs and hot coals. The strings of the tair crashed plaintively into the dragon's head, and his sword flashed as it was knocked out of his hand. Andy gasped, having received a painful slash to the thigh. A trickle of blood flowed down his leg. Thygar, having turned the blade in his opponent's wound, pulled out his weapon. When he'd managed to retrieve it, Andy hadn't noticed. Fleeing from the second blow, he fell to the ground, punching the enemy under the knee of his left leg. The dragon lost his balance and fell to Andy's right, who grabbed the tair by the neck and pushed it into Thygar's face, cutting his left cheek and brow with the sharp end. A short roll-over and the sharp end of the musical instrument crashed into Thygar's stomach, dropping his cocoon of shields. In two seconds, he would have changed hypostasis, but Andy didn't give him the time. He ran the strings, gathered in a bundle over his enemy's head, and held them at his throat, with his knee pushing into the dragon's broad back. Thygar had lost sight of Andy because of the blood that had filled his eyes. Feeling the iron on his neck and gasping, Thygar with great difficulty stopped the incarnation by his will power.

"Come on, change hypostasis, and you'll be headless," Andy hissed, spitting blood.

"Enough! Stop at once! Tomorrow in Rollir you will both leave the detachment!" The "princess" was holding a fighting staff, the cruciform pommel of which glowed with a pale flame. The whole retinue, except for Ania, gathered behind her. "Is there anyone who disagrees with my decision?"

There were no dissenters. Andy threw off the noose, releasing Thygar, who scrambled to his feet.

Quickly and harshly, it's true, but the problem was solved. He made a rune spell interweave, breaking his connection with the spilt blood. Twins forbid some clever man would try to harm him through it. And what did he have to lose? Everyone now knew he was a mage. From the second incantation, the dark drops on the ground flared with a bright flame. *Targ! Fool!* He'd acted too rashly. He felt a horrible burning in his mouth and on his thigh; a bad burn formed where the blood had been. But he had one consolation: Thygar's back was enveloped in a blue flame too. The dragon yelled out some choice words. Apparently, a lot of blood had dripped while Andy was resting his knee on the enemy's back. *I've got to do something about Thygar. Better kill him; in Rollir, I'll to put an end to our feud. I can't leave an enemy like that alive.*

"Leave the camp." The "princess" waved the sharp end of her staff in front of their eyes.

"With great pleasure. Good night!" Andy bowed at the waist and, turning on his heels, limping, went off into the darkness.

The cold water of the mountain river cooled his head and calmed his aching leg. Washing off the remnants of someone else's blood, Andy took out of his pouch a healing "pill" donated by Evael. A funny thing about it, there was a live Mellorny seed built into it. It collected mana, allowing you to use the device at least once a day. The elves guarded the secret of making healing interweaves, of linking the seed and the artifact, better than they guarded their own eyeballs. A significant plus was that minor wounds healed instantly, leaving no traces behind. After uttering the activation key, Andy put the round piece of wood to his burned leg. A cold wave passed over his body; the burn fell from his thigh; it was instantly covered with tight young pink skin. His mouth tingled; dark spots clouded his eyes for a moment.

Andy, thinking about something, stood in the water, spit, and took a sponge and the swamp root from the pouch.

Well, how nice! After putting on a replacement set of clothes (the old one was reduced to rags), he strapped his sword on and returned to his tent. The old clothes flew into the fire. Andy picked up the silver bloom from the ground, left lying near the fire. That's it, the powers that be had laughed at him again. Happiness flashed on the horizon and disappeared.

Warning of an unplanned visitor, the border guard spell

beeped. A loose module broke away from its spot; a couple of moments later, the magical watchdog was already pouring information to its owner. Ania was walking along the path, carefully bending around the obstacles. The sida emerged from the darkness of the night and went up to Andy. The elf's eyes looked him up and down and stopped on the damp flower. The flame's reflection drew copper sparks in her hair.

"Why did you come?" he asked in a hoarse voice. "They'll punish you!"

"I do not care at all! I thought for a long time…. You can make an impression on women," she said, taking the flower from his hand and hiding it in the folds of her clothes.

"What are you doing!" he tried to stop the sida, but a thin finger touching his lips interrupted the tirade.

"Am I a fool?"

"A big one," Andy smiled, embracing the girl and burying his face in her curls.

"I have always been told that men are more eager for fools than smart women. Now I am sure of it. What were you doing, freak?" Her small sharp fist hit his chest. "Thygar could have killed you! He's a dragon!"

"He's no threat," Andy answered, kissing Ania in her pointy ear. The clasp clicked; her cloak slid smoothly to her feet.

"Andy," a narrow hand pressed against Andy's chest. "Have you had any women before me?"

"Yes," he said honestly.

"All right," she whispered, loosening the lacing of her blouse. "Andy…,"

"Yes?" picking up his beloved in his arms and heading to the tent, said Andy.

"I have not had any men yet…."

Twins almighty! A two-hundred-year-old virgin!

"How silly…."

"Silly? No—a fool!"

"Why?" Andy carefully set Ania down on an improvised cot and removed her blouse.

"Only a fool could fall in love with a shkas…."

* * *

Ania left an hour before dawn. She did not give the silver bloom back, saying that if Manyfaces brought them together again, she would accept a living flower from him, and while she was bound by duty, she could not become his wife. The virk was not finished, her mission continued. Yes, she would be punished, but their night was worth all the punishments, and the silvery blossom would remind her.

Andy sat at the dying fire until the dawn and moved the cooled coals. Ania was wrong: not *if*, *when*! He would find her, whatever it cost him. Today they would part ways. The road to the small free town of Rollir on the border of the Miurs' lands and the Celestial Empire would take less than half of the day's journey. How long their separation would be, he couldn't say, but he would do his best to make it as short as possible.

The road was nearby, and they were soon underway. Coal caught the mood of the owner and behaved as quietly as can be. The hass positioned himself at the end of the short caravan, obeying the easy movement of his rider's knees. It kept about a hundred yards from the last trox.

The looks on the "princess'" face and those of the retinue told the rider that today he had better stay away. Well, it was a small request. No problem, happy to oblige.

The sun gradually picked up higher and higher, approaching the zenith. It was no more than two hours to Rollir. Andy, no longer hiding his gift from the others, periodically set up a guard contour and checked the road. He was about to remove the last "watchdog," when on its very border flashed a threesome of large objects, each the size of a bull. A few seconds later, from the direction of the caravan, came a frightful female squeal and the sound of Thygar screaming in a hoarse voice:

"Voooogrs!"

"Coal, go on!" The hass released its claws and jerked toward the screams.

The huge beast reminiscent of an overgrown bear jumping onto the trail did not come as a surprise to Andy. He'd already prepared a fireball that hit the monster in the chest... and dissolved into small sparks without causing it any harm. The creature was immune to magic. Now that was a surprise! The monster jumped to attack the hass. A blow by its powerful paw knocked Andy out of the saddle and knocked Coal on its side. Andy flew through the air at least ten yards and crashed into a tree. The hass, who fell to the ground, fought with its front and back legs with its claws released. Coal covered the predator's side with several deep wounds, but the fight did not end well for the lizard. The vogr sunk its teeth into Coal's neck; a loud crunch sounded; the hass roared plaintively; its paws jerked for the last time; a veil of death came over its eyes. The vogr threw the dead body away and turned to Andy. It moved quickly, which seemed quite incredible for such a carcass. Going into a battle trance, Andy drew his sword from the scabbard and rushed at the enemy. His expectations did not deceive him—the predator jumped to meet him, not perceiving the man as a worthy adversary. Accelerating and falling to his knees, Andy slipped under the huge body flying over him, praying to all the gods that there was no root or cobblestone in the grass that could stop his sliding. The elven blade stretched upward split the vogr's belly, spilling its foul-smelling intestines. The vogr plaintively howled and spun like a top. At the howling, the companions of the gutted "bear" turned their attention away from the retinue and rushed towards Andy.

The first "helper," leaping towards him in long jumps, was met by the "airless bubble" interweave. Andy decided that if the animal didn't succumb to a direct magical effect, he could use indirect magic. All the air was pumped out from the bubble of its lungs. The vogr gasped and died, falling short of the human by literally ten yards. Seven-foot-tall warriors with dark-gray skins on their shoulders greeted the third predator. The rescuers appeared out of nowhere. In an instant, the vogr was pierced with a dozen spears. The animal, now resembling a porcupine, thrashed for a few seconds until the tallest warrior shattered its head with a hammer blow.

Leaving the rescuers to finish off the gutted animal, Andy ran to the side of the retinue. His heart was beating in his throat, his palms sweating from the experience. *Is Ania okay?*

Ania was alright. Thygar not so; apparently, his fate was to perish by an inglorious death. With a clawed paw, the vogr simply severed his head, thereby giving the others a chance to save themselves: the headless body changed hypostasis and blocked the path of the rest of the oncoming monsters. The first predator managed to kill Tarista, the lady's second maid, having bitten the poor girl in half, and drove Renat into the ground, breaking his spine. For magical medicine, that wound would be non-lethal. A great healing interweave and the patient would be back on his feet in a day. Then the artifacts came into play. Dragons turned out to be tough nuts; even in a deadly situation, they did not violate the sacred prohibitions, relying on themselves and on mana-loaded amulets. A fence of thorny trees grew up before the monsters; the method of indirect influence was one hundred percent justified. While Andy was inspecting Ania to make sure she was okay, the entourage was surrounded by a troop of three dozen giants encased in shiny armor. The tallest, more than eight feet tall, with a heavy hammer suspended from the waist, stepped forward and took off his helmet.

It was a Miur. The face resembled a huge, humanized cat's. The feline face had a slightly protruding nose and snout decorated with whiskers, short fur, large yellow eyes with black vertical pupils, and triangular ears with tassels on their ends protruding from the mane of reddish hair. A gold earring with a precious stone gleamed in the left ear. The warrior wiggled her mustache:

"I regret that the vogrs we chased over the border attacked your detachment. The imperial villains are constantly letting monsters created by their mages go free on our lands."

"I accept your apology," the "princess" stepped forward.

"I do not have the right to apologize, and I do not need your gratitude. I simply regret the fact of what happened," the Miur quipped. "The Great Mother will apologize if she sees fit. Bury the fallen and follow us."

"And those who do not belong to the princess' entourage?" Andy spoke up.

"As for you, I was given special instructions. You will come with a separate escort." The Miur bowed slightly, which absolutely shocked the princess and her retinue, as well as the one being bowed to.

* * *

Andy looked for Ania, but behind the tall Miur, nothing of interest was visible. The cat people immediately separated him from the retinue and led him to the side. The main warrior pointed in the direction of a small clearing:

"Wait, your things will be brought here." She gave a short command in their own language.

Three warriors separated from the main group. The commander gave them some instructions and waved her hand to the other subordinates. The retinue, surrounded by guards, disappeared into the forest.

The three cat people left with Andy went out at equal distances from each other and set about their business. He watched with interest as the huge warriors skillfully installed masking artifacts and activated them. Above the meadow there was an illusion of a tree crown. Anyone flying above would see nothing but a solid green carpet of crowns. Andy sank to the ground and crossed his legs, sitting in a "lotus" pose. The idea of making a break for it occurred to him several times, but something prompted him not to. The security guards appointed by the hefty commander were too serene. It was the serenity of the warriors that stopped him from taking rash steps. Their behavior wasn't as simple as it seemed. They were testing him, and their hidden observers were following his every move.

As if from a gust of wind, the bushes swayed. Andy flinched; he didn't observe any movement of air. Strange, but his either bodyguards or just guards didn't seem to pay any attention to the inconsistency in the laws of nature. They stood like silent statues. Then came something else. Where movement was indicated, there was an unusual haze, repeating the contours of grass, leaves, and trees. It was nearly ideal camouflage. If it hadn't been for the trampled grass, he would never have found the creature standing on the edge of the clearing. That is, creatures. Blurred half-shadows gave away three more invisible visitors.

Several shivers ran along Andy's spine. His forehead was

covered with cold beads of sweat. In an instant, he was on his feet. His sword seemed to jump out of its scabbard. At the rustle of the blade, as it was being pulled from the sheath, the masking haze disappeared, revealing yet another detachment of cats. Observers have come! His intuition saved him from trying to escape. He would have been buried there, had there been anything left to bury. Andy grunted. He noticed four of them, but a dozen warriors, clad in the same armor covering them from head to toe remained invisible to him until the very last moment. Ripples ran over them, imitating leaves and twigs. Andy remembered the Hollywood film "Predator," the effect was so similar.

Two cats were carrying his saddlebags. They carried heavy loads as if they were light. The relatively small figure of the "predator" emerged, apparently the leader of the new detachment. Andy didn't hear any spoken words; the closed helmets of the inhabitants of Mount Lidar concealed the sound. They used built-in communicator amulets to communicate with one another.

"They changed the guard," Andy thought, looking at the bodyguards hiding in the dense forest. The Miur who handed him over to the new detachment ran to catch up with the others.

"Follow us," came a voice from under the helmet. The Miur warrior, short against the background of the other heroes, indicated to him a place in the ranks.

He would follow; he had no choice. The tailed ladies knew their business, boxing him in from all sides and blocking any independent action on his part. *There's a bow of respect for you! I feel like I'm in a reinforced convoy!* The "cats'" shoulder holsters with fire-starters peeping out of them, or whatever their version of fire-starters was, neutralized any desire to behave any way but accordingly. And the bluish gunners in the hands of those jogging behind him fueled thoughts about the futility of resistance. He had no desire to turn into a pile of gray ash. They had respected him by leaving him his sword. In a situation like this, touching the sword could only lead to his slaughter. No guarantee they'd let him commit hara-kiri.

The guards were arranged deliberately. Andy observed the difference in uniforms, weapons, and probably in the class of soldiers of the first and second ranks. The Miur occupying the third rank looked like ordinary heavily equipped knights: armor, swords, spears, oval full-length shields, powerful crossbows. Given their height and physique, an ordinary Miur sword looked like a two-handed overgrown sword.

The second detachment escorting him resembled a group of special agents. In addition to swords and spears, all of its members wore masking armor. The number of magical-mechanical "machines" per person exceeded everything he'd previously seen, and the gunners made him a little proud of the importance of his person! They would not attach such a guard to an ordinary man.

What's going on here? The whisker girls know something about me that I don't! But what? Andy stopped paying attention to the road, focusing on the wide back of the Miur in front of him. *What is there about me that the others don't have? Think, Andy, think! How did the cats get the information?* Andy nearly stumbled. *Evael!*

The guess made the gears in his head spin faster. Well, old man, well! What a scoundrel! You've played us all! The chief knew that the "princess" was looking for a way to the Great Mother, but pretended to be an old moth-eaten shoe. While no one was looking, he's the one who spilled the beans! That old artful fart. He guessed that I was a dragon. He gave me that shaving kit with a whole flask of fragrant essence of swamp root to mask my real smell. He calculated everything. I tried so hard to blend in, but my ignorance of local custom didn't just stand out, it gave me away completely. And my Younger Edda, which they call High, suggested an origin far from that of mere mortals. And why did you, Andy, decide that you were the cleverest? Evael was much more perspicacious. He and Miduel are two peas in a pod. Okay, now that I figured out all that, what conclusions and assumptions can I make? Those elven mages really made a big deal over my tattoo, so I can assume it has some important meaning. So important that it made Evael share information with the main cat lady. This is serious.

Moving behind the light-trotting warriors, he couldn't shake the sensation of something amiss in the surrounding reality. It was like a speck in the corner of the eye—it didn't interfere with your vision, but the discomfort it creates was constantly annoying. Just here, something in the "cats'" outfits made him uneasy. Andy racked his brains, trying to determine the source of irritation. He almost stumbled a second time; actually, he did stumble, but the Miur at his side caught him by the elbow in time.

"Thank you," he said, but she did not honor him even with a turn of her head. Duty came first; the shkas came second.

A close inspection clarified his suspicions. The belligerent ladies' "costumes" were a high-tech product. No forge or master could repeat the details of the material so finely and faithfully. The look of the gunners and fire-starters practically screamed that they were factory assembled. The "kitties" were not as wild as he thought. What other surprises would there be? He had no doubt there would be some more.

"Stop!" the commander called.

Andy obediently stopped and shook his feet a couple of times. An hour and a half of running through the forest and uphill left a slight tremor in his thighs. Waving his aching legs, he didn't stop looking around. There was a vertical stone wall in front of them. A secret passage?

Resurrecting the tale of Ali Baba and the forty thieves, a wide gap appeared on the flat wall. Dust and small pebbles sprang up; behind the dust cloud giant gates appeared.

"Holy moly!" he thought, passing through the six-foot entrance of the slightly opened gate. The density of the concentrated magical interweaves heaped on the doors, the colors of which unambiguously indicated that they would destroy any uninvited guests, weighed heavily on Andy's consciousness. Just let them dare to come here. At least ten tracking contours were on it. Powerful gunners hidden in the walls were ready to immediately evaporate their victims. It's not nice to feel helpless. The commander of the detachment approached Andy and put a dark bandage over his eyes. The beauties were clearly taking precautions. He switched to true vision and quietly looked around. The piece of black cloth was, like everything with the Miur, not simple. It blocked the magical gaze. Dexterous hands freed him from his belt with his sword, removed the daggers from his boots, and deprived him of his hurling knives. *Now I'm in it up to my ears.* The cat woman took his hand and led him through twisting corridors, occasionally warning of steps and stairs. She gave short commands: "to the right," "to the left," and "stairs." This went on for ten minutes. Twice Andy felt the minute "diaphragms" of portals on his skin. The whole way, he could hear the breath and the footsteps of the escort beside him. At last, they passed through a passageway, and the escorts remained on the other side of the ancient door.

"Sit down," the main guard commanded, cut off the sleeves of Andy's shirt with the sharpest knife, thereby exposing his shoulders, and removing the black bandage from his head. The light was blinding; he blinked for a moment. It was a pleasant room, soft pastel colors, a mountain of cushions, amazing stucco molding on the walls and ceilings. It was lit by several magical lamps hidden in niches and shining from the bottom up, which illuminated the room without irritating the eye. The chair he was asked to sit in was the only thing that did not match.

I'm not really tired, I can stand, Andy wanted to quip. He did not like the proposed seat. His butt was telling him: "Don't sit down there, don't do it!" But instead he obediently lowered his rear end to the proposed chair, which was designed for the figure and anatomy of humans. No sooner had the organ of apprehension squeezed onto the upholstery than an enormous weight fell on his body. Invisible bonds clasped his arms, legs, and squeezed his chest. A sixth sense suggested that it was pointless to twitch. There was something unpleasant about the armchair that immediately deprived him of his wits. Finita la commedia....

"Wait." The Miur retreated behind the dastardly furnishing.

Who he was waiting for, she did not specify. Why should she? Andy didn't have very many options. The precautionary measures indicated an upcoming visit by a person with power and the authority to make decisions. He had no idea how long the wait would last, so Andy, as far as the torturous chair would allow, tried to relax. Diving into the settage, he shortened his nervous impulses to massage the muscles of his legs and hands, then for the thousandth time strengthened his body's energy channels and the connections between them.

From behind the door came the melodious ringing of bells. Andy's sharpened ear picked up the light step of bare feet. At the threshold of audibility the door, unseen behind his back, creaked.

The draft that burst into the room brought with it the smell of lavender and musk. Echoing the easy steps, the bells continued to sing, their clear sound flooding the temporary jail.

"Long years to you!" Skirting the chair, a slender Miura with short snow-white fur sat down on the ottoman in front of him.

"Straight roads," Andy didn't know how to greet the Great Mother, so he chose the usual greeting of the Forest Elves. He had no doubt he was being visited by a master of formidable soldiers. The aura of power surrounding the Miur could be felt almost on a physical level.

The Miur turned her triangular ears and shrugged her shoulders (the numerous silver bracelets with small bells let out a cheerful ringing). Andy wasn't aware that among the cat people, this gesture is equivalent to a smile. She threw several pillows under her feet and, like mercury, flowed to the floor. All this time the Miur looked intently at Andy, and he, breaking the written and unwritten norms of behavior, stared at her.

The Great Mother was about eight feet tall. Her long hair, the same color as her fur, was braided into a complex braid, which dropped almost to her knees and was marked at regular intervals by bundles of jingling rings. Her arms and legs were decorated with dozens of bracelets with the finest engraving, while the movement of her adornments created a melodic chime. The bells strung on her long tail added musicality to her person as well. The Miur's waist was encircled by a wide belt supporting a garment of the finest spider silk. Her light bloomers were white, opaque at the top and hiding something that should be hidden, but becoming transparent below the knees. Two pairs of rudimentary nipples protruded on her flat belly as dark spots among the snow-white wool; the upper, third pair looked much more appetizing, representing a beautifully developed female breast. A light muslin thrown over the Great Mother's shoulders did not hide the nipples.

The Great Mother, having given him a chance to size her up, flashed her yellow eyes with narrow vertical pupils, flowed back into a standing position, and glared at the shkas prisoner in her chair.

Feeling her powerful mental pressure, Andy immediately

shut himself off by a mental brick wall and built thousands of spiny balls in his mind that revolved around his "I." The pressure increased; it destroyed the erected wall, but came across the balls, behind which a new wall rose and dozens of thought-distracters floated. The Miur destroyed the balls and moved on, but the fragments of the wall and balls came to life, attacking her consciousness, striking from all sides. The other person's thoughts turned into clouds of small gnats, creeping into all mental gaps and interfering with concentration.

Breaking off contact, the Miur looked away. The tip of her tail twitched nervously. The bells, reflecting the hostess' mood, made a long, frustrated ringing sound.

"I respect you; I apologize," the Miur said. The rings jingling in her braid sang with the movement of her head. Andy was sure that individual rings, bells or bracelets rang for every gesture she made or word she said. It was unusual and fascinating at the same time.

"I respect you; I accept your apology," he answered in a flash.

"Show me that," she half-ordered, half-asked, touching the runes on Andy's shoulder with her polished claw, released from the pads.

He closed his eyes. A dangerous moment, but after the leader's apology, he did not sense an enemy in her. Yes, he was bound in the armchair, but there was no danger from the cat. Something suggested that the Miur just wanted to receive confirmation of her long-standing conclusions, and the mental attack was a kind of checking for fleas.

The Miur, seeing his hesitation, waited patiently. As a gesture of goodwill, the magical chains disappeared. Andy appreciated it.

"Thank you," he said, standing up and rubbing his wrists, and not forgetting to bow. The melodious ringing of the bracelets on the cat woman's right hand was his answer. He had very few options now. A demonstration was practically unavoidable. He removed the deceptive aura and took down his will shields. The tattoo showed up brightly on his shoulder. The bells on the Great Mother's tail rattled convulsively. Not noticing that she'd unleashed her claws, she grabbed Andy by the shoulder. He grimaced but bore the pain.

"Who gave you the sign of the ruling family?"

"My mother," Andy answered. There was no point in lying. The Great Mother was such a powerful mage that she could see through lies without a polygraph.

"Your mother?" the Miur was taken aback. "That's impossible. What is her name?"

Smelling the blood and feeling the moisture on her fingers, the Miur remembered and removed her claws. Her initial excitement changed to a business-like seriousness. There was no trace of her momentary confusion. An unshakable ruler was once again before Andy.

"Jagirra."

"Jagirra?"

"My mother has been called Jagirra for three thousand years. I do not know of any other name for her."

"Jagirra?" she repeated, confused. She was clearly hearing something of great importance to her. The whiskers on her face stood upright; the fur on her back rose. Shattering her mask of equanimity, her bright eyes sparkled. Her pupils became tiny stripes. A little bell rang at the end of her tail. "Are you saying that the real empress is alive? When was the last time you saw her?"

Now that's not something you hear every day!

* * *

But how? Huh? He thought the storm howling inside him was in no way expressed externally, but the Great Mother would not be the ruler if she could not read souls and catch small nuances of behavior. The cat leader noticed the confusion on the dragon's face and made the right conclusions.

"I will not leave you for long. Some state affairs require my presence." The Miur purred, turning to the door. From the motion, a pleasant ringing came from her braid in a wave from top to bottom.

An air-tight pretext. The sovereign might have a pile of affairs higher than the roof, and everything, from the first to the

167

last, of the utmost importance. But the furrow on the nape of her fur coat treacherously pointed to her extreme interest in just one of them. Andy nodded and bowed. The Miur stopped at the door, her triangular ears with tassels at the ends pressed against her head.

"At your first request, you will be escorted to me." *Prove it.* Andy saw through her cunning. Although she mentioned affairs of state, she would be running on the ceiling and gnawing on the stucco, waiting for the "client" to ripen to the present conversation. The door closed with a muffled chime.

For a few minutes no one disturbed him, then the door flew open, and several elves brought trays of fruit and drinks. As if by a magic wand, a table materialized to hold the rich assortment. Andy watched the hustle and bustle as if from afar; his mind was occupied elsewhere. *The real empress....* A picture came to life: a crystal dragoness descending to the lake shore... and a long cry of "Noooo." All his assumptions and conjectures about Jagirra's origin suddenly became reality. The world was much more vividly colored than he had imagined. Or maybe the cat woman was talking about another Jagirra? No, that one. His mother's tattoo left no doubt about the ruler's words. *It turns out that my mother is the legitimate heiress of the old emperor, deceased three thousand years ago. My head's spinning.... I need to calm down, I shouldn't think about anything for a couple of minutes....*

He occupied the ottoman the feline ruler had liked and pulled the table to him. *What are they offering me and how will they treat me? Fruits, juices, sweet water, wine. The latter will do, but very little; I need to relax, not fall into nirvana.* Andy reached for the jug of wine, held it for a few seconds, set it back down and with a determined gesture picked up the container of juice. *Wine will not do; a little later, I'll have a difficult conversation with the Great Mother. You need to keep your head sharp. One careless move and I could get my head bitten off. Right now, I'm a large fat mouse, and the Miur is a purring cat with her prey. She might devour me, but first play with me a little, and then break my spine with her paw, so to speak, using me for their own purposes. I can't believe this will be a partnership... or will it? How should I behave?*

Evael said that the cats don't recognize the emperor-impostor and refused to help the princess who argued for the decision of loyalty to the legitimate heir. In fact, they gave both dragon camps the opportunity to lather each other's spikes, while they sit on the sidelines, watching who would fail first. Perhaps I should remind the "momma" of her ancient words and step aside? What would come of that? Nothing good. In any case, the emperor, feeling the threat to his personal power, which he strengthened thoroughly for three thousand years, since no one else could get close to the throne, would go at the cat people with all his might and level Mount Lidar to the ground. Conclusion: the Miur don't need him as a banner of resistance. With a banner like that, there will be hell to pay.

Targ! It's a dirty thing, politics! No matter where you step, or if you don't take any steps, you end up in a mud puddle, or a swamp. It's a soulless machine, grinding entire peoples, wiping states off the face of the Earth. And if it can do all that, what can we say about individuals? Andy filled the glass. As it filled, the walls became transparent, showing the level of liquid inside. *Interesting and entertaining. Oh, mother, mother, why didn't you say anything? Is it because you had a really bad power trip three thousand years ago?*

Andy took a sip of ice-cold, mouth-watering juice, got up from the ottoman, and walked around the room, tapping the pillows scattered on the floor. The glass in his hand pleasantly cooled his skin; his thoughts returned to Jagirra. *What happened then, why did you renounce your power and choose life as an elf? Questions ...Who can answer them? I'll have to return to Ilanta for answers, but how can I if I've not yet recovered all my abilities? And another question: why did I lose them? It's much easier to hold conversations when you've got a few lethal interweaves ready. An extra machine gun in the house doesn't hurt. The textbooks I bought shed some light on the problem, but there was no one to ask whether it's really like that or not.* Andy finished the juice and returned to the table. *My thoughts are heading in the wrong direction. I shouldn't be thinking about why my magic disappeared; I should be thinking about how to get out of the impending doom. How can I interest and buy the cat peoples' aid; how can I bait them?* He poured a second glass of the ice cold drink and moved to the floor, blissfully stretching his legs and leaning his elbows on the pouf.

I need to look for a way of interacting with them where the political interests of the Miur and the Prince of Ora meet. Since I was stupid enough to get into a political millstone, I should try to become necessary to both political parties. You can bet your bottom dollar the Great Mother plans to use me to improve relations with the prince. Why not help her and myself at the same time? Hm, that's already a warmer and much more pleasant approach. I can't let them turn me into a faceless cog, better become a mechanic myself. If the "knots" option doesn't work out, what can I put in as an alternative? He scratched his chest; his fingers caught on the tiny scars left by the key amulet. *Hmm, is it worth taking this trump card out of your sleeve?*

The second glass had been empty for a long time. Rubbing the bridge of his nose, Andy continued to stare at a certain point on the wall. *Targ, that's it! Why shouldn't I play my own game? Will it work out and how will it be met here and at home, my murky, not yet fully formed proposal?*

Miduel stated outright that the magic on Ilanta will disappear in a few thousand years if the dragons don't return to the planet. The dragons of the Principality of Ora will not survive a full-scale invasion by the Imperial legions. "Uncle," that baddy, has the habit of destroying enemy clans down to the root. And if the prince offers resettlement? Way to kill two birds with one stone. The magic will not disappear, and the dragons will survive. Well, what about the fact that at the moment on Ilanta, no state can resist the combined power of several hundred Lords of the Sky? After all, the dragons will not be able to impose unconditional hegemony of the winged tribe on the world. The overall balance of forces will be only slightly upset. In fact, the emergence of another political pole will favorably affect the overall situation in the north of Alatar and stop the expansion of the Forest Elves. In thought, it looks great and everything goes well. What will it be like in reality? Will the prince agree to participate in the adventure? What position will the Great Mother take and will the emperor throw a wrench in the works? I should talk about this.

Andy was ready to bargain. He looked at the empty pitcher. How easy it was to turn from a victim of political games to a player. *Don't you feel a prick of conscience? You were just thinking you didn't want to be crushed by an impersonal machine, and now you're ready to throw entire states on the altar of your own interests. Two months ago you judged Miduel, and now... I really miss him. The old elf's advice would be very handy just now.*

Now I just have to figure out how I'm going to speak to my hostess. What have we? Andy drummed his fingers on the top of the table. Throwing a few berries in the mouth reminiscent of grapes, but with a pronounced mandarin flavor, he re-hashed his recent meeting with the Great Mother. *The cat ruler knew about the meaning of my tattoo. And statements of kinship with Jagirra was the last thing she expected to hear. Judging by the Miur's reaction, my mother has long been listed among the souls who left the mortal world and entered the palaces of Hel. The news that she's alive and she has a son was a shock to the Great Mother. The cat woman behaved as if she were personally acquainted with the young Empress at the time. Hmm, that doesn't make sense. From what I know, Miur live no more than five hundred years. The average life expectancy is three hundred and fifty. The lady does not look like an ancient grandma. She can't be that old, so when did she meet Jagirra? How the Great Mother is related to Jagirra remains to be seen. The question should be marked as paramount. I need all the knowledge I can get to help me maneuver the currents of the muddy sea of politics. Based on the ruler's reaction, I can make several conclusions: she didn't know that Jagirra survived the ancient showdowns and is still alive. And it's no wonder! We haven't exchanged news with our heavenly neighbors for the last three thousand years. And I didn't hide the fact that I, her son, remained ignorant of my mother's origin. So she showed tact and gave me time to recover from my shock, too. A cunning beast! She hid her shock behind politesse. Right now, the Miur's probably evaluating the situation from all sides, just like me, and figuring out what to do with the piece of cake that fell into her lap. Eat it herself or send it onwards as bait.... Just be careful, Mother, not to burst inadvertently from "overeating." This "cake" has a trick or two up his sleeve.*

Andy poured himself juice from another jug. He decided on

his priorities: from the Miur, he needed, first of all, to learn the history of his own kind, whatever her version might be. He would have time to find other options for interpreting events and comparing what various storytellers said.

"What do you wish?" A slender Miur in clothes of a dark blue color reminiscent of an Indian sari was waiting for him behind the door. The fabric further emphasized the white of her coat and the blue of her feline eyes. A wide blue ribbon was braided into her long braid.

Near the wall was a table where the weapons confiscated near the gates were laid out. Nobody prevented him from taking them back. Andy looked doubtfully at his arsenal and decided to do without it. A few thin, weightless magical interweaves prepared by him in advance would be preferable to steel. Andy looked at her carefully and grinned. The Mother knew her stuff. If his eyes weren't deceiving him, this was the younger sister or, more likely, the daughter of the ruler. The Great Mother took measures to preserve secrecy. It was unlikely she would repeat her mistake of letting the elves who served him lay eyes on him.

"Take me to the Great Mother, please," said Andy.

"Follow me," the Miur waved her hand. Countless sparks flashed on the gold threads and small precious stones sewn into the sari cloth. From the movement of her head, the dot of the magical communicator amulet on her neck was exposed for just a moment. *So, Mother's been informed....*

Following the Miur's small step, Andy mentally applauded her mother. The ruler showed herself to be an excellent psychologist. At first, she knocked him off track by presenting one psychotype with her behavior, which was more characteristic of a human woman than a member of a different race, and now she was messing with his head with the help of her daughter. Her heiress had an attractive figure, seductive even from the point of view of people and elves. Wrapped tightly in the garment, she was forced to take short steps, shaking her hips and invitingly wagging her bottom. A great way to knock the guest off guard and take his thoughts down another channel. A blatant move aimed at his youth. It didn't matter that the lady was two heads taller than him. Actually, being shorter it was more convenient to watch the tailed butt. Plus one for the cats. Only he did not fall for their trick.

They came to a mighty door which opened in front of them. Another cat came out to meet the colorful couple. She was like a copy of his escort, only her sari was a tender olive color. Andy's suspicions were confirmed as to the identity of his guide. These kitties were definitely all related.

"The Great Mother is waiting for you," the kitty in olive purred, rather than said. The sisters exchanged glances. Now, now, ladies, don't glare like that with your pupils. It's not your fault that the young shkas knows a little more about women than you expected, relying on the experience of Alo Troi, whose personality he absorbed when learning a language.

"Please," the olive-clad cat let him into the lady's office and slammed the door. Like a razor cutting his skin, the clap of the door closing activated the curtain spells. Now no sound could be overheard.

The Great Mother was sitting at a wide desk. On the polished surface lay two feather pens and three leather folders with papers. The light transparent gauze on the Miur' shoulders was replaced by a colorful cloak. The bracelets with bells on her arms and legs disappeared; the jingling rings woven into her braid were now tied with colored laces. The leader now most resembled an earthly businesswoman.

"I will not beat around the bush," Andy began, taking the initiative. "You probably realized that my mother was hiding information about her past from me. Your words about her belonging to the ruling family of the empire were a shock to me. Due to certain circumstances, it is now difficult for me to hear the truth from primary sources. I ask you to tell me your version of the ancient events. It may sound pathetic, but my family dark past caught me at the most inopportune moment, and without knowing those events, it is difficult to judge my current situation and assess the consequences of my actions. It would be extremely imprudent to somehow cast a shadow on my parents or tarnish them with improper and unworthy deeds."

The test probe was launched. The Great Mother shut the file folder she'd been examining pointedly and laid it on the edge of the table. The dark pupils in her yellow eyes turned into narrow slits. For a long time, she stared at Andy, who was now a silent statue. From under the table, the twitching tip of her tail was peeking out. She was facing a dubious choice. Refuse, and any potential cooperation could be forgotten. The blue-eyed boy's strengths would be of no use to her. Any dragon can tolerate pain and keep his secrets. She had no leverage over him. The scope of his interests was rather narrow, but telling him could be problematic. It was all simple in words, but for individuals endowed with huge power, nothing in life is simple. It would be impossible to tell him in words.

The Miur pushed back the chair and stood up from the table. Andy continued to stand motionless. He'd said his piece; it was his opponent's turn. The feline came up to him and, bending her knees, crouched. Their eyes were on the same level.

"Do you want to know the truth? I can show you." The Miur touched her temple with the released claw of her index finger. "Are you prepared to trust a cat?"

A bold move. She wasn't denying him but put before him a difficult choice: direct transmission from the brain to brain, the fusion of minds. Was he ready to reveal to someone else's essence his personal secrets, to allow her to dig into his memories? In all the books he'd read, he never heard of a dragon agreeing to the fusion of minds if he hadn't broken the other's will himself. By asking the question and setting the condition, the ruler of the cat people showed that she did not have secrets; she was completely open to him, the choice was his. The Miur knew the psychology of dragons, but in this particular case, she miscalculated....

Yes, she could look into the dark corners of his soul, but her secret storehouses would appear before his gaze as well. On the other hand, "merging" would help them better understand one another. It was better than living without a past, as he was forced to since his first notorious portal jump, and his secrets..., what secrets could he have? The medallion, the so-called "key?" His other-worldly origin? All his secrets were not worth the past, and therefore, the present. The Great Mother fell into her own trap.

"I am," he answered and looked into the eyes of the fully straightened Miur. He was looking up at her, but it was the strong look of an equal. In the Great Mother's eyes, he saw genuine respect. Checkmate. In agreeing, he had just deprived them both of any retreat path. In any case, he had one piece of work up his sleeve, already prepared and ready to be activated, which was connected to his reason and free will and designed to kill anyone who attempted to control them.

"We had better sit down." Andy looked around for a free chair. "Not here," she interrupted him. Taking him by the hand and pushing back a curtain behind the desk, she led him through an inconspicuous door. The next room resembled the apartments he'd just left—carpets, pillows, padded stools, a low table, a wide ottoman just above the floor, the subdued light of magical lanterns. A place where you could relax after a hard day's work. The Miur, dragging him along with her, sank to a mountain of pillows:

"Relax, take off your shields." Andy obediently removed the cocoons of will shields. "Clear your mind of extraneous thoughts...."

The cat woman touched his forehead with hers. Her yellow eyes turned into bottomless wells, dragging his mind into the dark depths ...

* * *

...He woke up and felt that his head was lying on something soft and springy at the same time. With difficulty focusing his vision, Andy looked up from the "pillow," which turned out to be the ruler's left breast. His right cheek bore the mark of the concentric circles of Asha's nipple. A hammer pounded in his head. He looked at the Miur, curled up like a little kitten, her mysterious feline eyes gazing back at him, and grabbed his temples....

The cunning cat had calculated all the options, not forgetting to include in the layout of the future conversation some of the most incredible possibilities, including the fusion of minds. Actually, to say she hadn't forgotten about it is an understatement. The Miur planned to gradually bring the conversation to the slippery topic of unification. His statement about Jagirra was simply incredible; the Great Mother did not believe the dragon's

175

words. She was afraid of making a mistake. In three thousand years, Jagirra had twice re-emerged out of nowhere, and once, her daughter did too. Each time, the pretenders presented irrefutable evidence of their origin, but all the empresses turned out to be agents of the secret intelligence service. Hazgar adored fishing around, finding out which clans were beginning to intrigue against him, and if he found anyone, they disappeared not only from the political scene. There hadn't yet been any stories about Jagirra having a son, or anyone having a family tattoo. The shkas did not emphasize his origin, which was strange at the least and did not match the modus operandi of the empire's secret services. A different approach, but still, doubts remained. Penetrating into the mind was just dotting the "I." The stakes were too high not to. *Tricky cat! The desire to have your fish and eat it too doesn't always come true. The dots on the "I" and other punctuation marks were a surprise to you. Is it tough getting caught in the trap of your own disbelief?*

Andy looked at the unconscious cat and squeezed his fists, gritting his teeth. He ought to strangle her. How his head ached! After all, she knew very well that unification of the minds of two different kinds of beings resulted in stunning pain, the pointy-eared jerk. On Ilanta, human and elf mages never merged with dwarfs. Silicone organisms were incompatible with humans. They had different brain structures and active magical zones. With Miur, the situation looked different. They had the same protein structure, but humans and Miur were distinguished by different biochemical processes taking place in the body, customs, social order, moral norms, etc. In other words, he and Asha were computers with different operating systems, and combining them caused irritation of nerve endings and pain.

Two fools, luring each other into traps like clinically certifiable paranoiacs. In the end, they both won and lost.

Asha was perfectly prepared, blocking her middle and deep layers of memory in advance, setting her mind's defense against breaking. At the confluence, the closed zones looked like dark patches. The ruler was right in that sense. Protection helped her stay on the brink and break off the connection with the dragon just in time. As for Andy, he didn't defend anything, just drove the Miur into a sector of his mind that was filled with a kaleidoscope of memories. Let her be occupied with other things! Asha, plunging into the cycle of events, could not tear herself away from the amazing revelations for most of the merger. She was engrossed by the world from which Andy-Kerrovitarr-Andy came to Ilanta and upset by the massacre at the school and the events at the Helrats' monastery. The moment he discovered the interplanetary portal on the lake shore was viewed several times. Much later, her attention shifted to the young dragon's mind, which was so vast and developed that the cat was confused. The Miur knew what to look at. Experience, thanks to the previous generations of rulers, was invaluable, but all her experience was somewhat useless against Andy's mind. At first, it seemed to her that nothing threatened the threads that controlled the trance, but when she realized the opposite, she was shocked. Andy absorbed her preparations faster than a flame devours dry grass. The powerful swirl of foreign will begin to dissolve and tighten her "I." The virtual killer she discovered hidden at the very edge of perception, which controlled all the processes of influencing his free will, caused a slight panic. So that's why he wasn't afraid. Fear of taking an unguarded step and being killed or absorbed and synced into someone else's mind caused the cat to break off contact.

While his counterpart was looking at the protection spell and reading his unusual biography, Andy did not waste time, leafing through the "book" that described the history of the imperial family. The painting abounded in gaps. He immediately felt doubts. He discarded some facts right away; others were accepted without too much hesitation. To Andy, the history of the reigning dragons looked biased. Hazgar, Jagirra's uncle, was unnecessarily demonized. His associates were mentioned casually, which was understandable: the Great Mother singled out the main enemy from the herd and listed his strengths and weaknesses in Andy's head, analyzed his deeds. Hazgar's companions lay on "separate shelves;" it took time to get to them. Despite the bias, Andy managed to isolate the main thing. The truth was bitter, leaving on his lips the characteristic salty taste of blood.

He recognized a secret of the Great Mothers: tribal memory. The Miur with snow-white fur had a tribal memory common to all leaders. They could freely refer to the memories of past generations, up to the tenth. Poor creatures, they had no childhood. What kind of discoveries in life could the kittens make if they remembered their mother's whole life, and the lives of a dozen generations from the very moment of their birth? They were little grandmothers. A useful gift, but a heavy burden.

Andy picked up the Great Mother under the armpits and dragged her to an ottoman. Magical contact was harder on her than on him....

He closed his eyes. Foreign memories rushed into his brain again.... How many Miur, humans, elves, and dragons perished and vanished into obscurity, gathering information about the imperial clan, analyzing and comparing all the facts and knowledge that was later deposited on the shelves of the Great Mothers' collective memory and, seven generations later, now reached him?

Humans and dragons. Dragons that had become humans....

* * *

How simple and how complex. Power, the desire to climb to the top of the pyramid and the unrestrained thirst for possession of an ephemeral thing that gives visible and invisible advantages. Power was to blame for everything....

The initial point of the fall of the dragons should be considered the opening of portals. Thousands of immigrants erupting from their depths. The arrival of people on Ilanta changed the Lords of the Sky.

The opening of portals on Ilanta and the appearance of a new race on the stage brought a fresh vigor to the life of the ancient creatures. The discovery of a way to transform humans into dragons and dragons into humans radically changed them. The fashion of a second hypostasis swept over the Lords of the Sky. The boredom that tormented many of the long-lived creatures was satiated.

The Lords of the Sky played "people" and didn't notice how or when the game turned into real life. Humanization gave them not only the positive qualities of the bipedal creatures, but also the vices inherent in that race....

The humans brought to Nelita multiplied and multiplied. A thousand years passed and their population squeezed that of the elves and the Miur, who for the time being paid no attention to the newcomers. And then it was too late. The humans developed at a frantic pace; their life was a bright fleeting flame against the background of the dim fires of long-lived ones.

In one generation, they managed to learn more than the elves. The humans were doing their very best to catch up with the ancient races. For a long time, the dragons did not pay attention to the bustle down below. They even used unfortunate humans for their experiments. By agreement with the human chiefs, the bipeds would hand over their renegades and criminals to the heavenly monsters. But life does not stand still. The human population grew; they formed governments and states and demanded recognition. The dragons, recovering from their slumber, realized that the genie released from the bottle could not be tamed. Human rulers did not recognize their authority. It was only the fear of the winged monsters' power that kept them within the boundaries outlined by the dragons, but that could not continue for long.

The first to react to the risk posed to the winged tribe by the mass of humans was Rastigar, head of the "crystal" clan. He called a council that had not been gathered for more than five hundred years, and there he outlined the prospects of a gloomy future for his fellow tribesmen. Rastigar emphasized the fact that the dragons had moved away from the sciences, giving them up to the Miur, while they themselves plunged into the passions of humans and elves.

After the explosion of an interstellar portal, which destroyed the whole city and caused the deaths of most of the scientists, nothing new came out from under the dragons' wings. What possibly could? They still hadn't restored the secret of building interplanetary portals. Society was in stagnation, or, more honestly named, degradation. Even in their home lands, the dragons felt the push from humans and elves. At the university, every other teacher was wingless. There was an urgent need to take the process into their own hands (or in this case, paws).

The Lords of the Sky seriously thought. A hot controversy broke out among the council. Once again, Rastigar came forward, proposing not to break the established world order, but to lead it. He suggested they act based on the example that had been tested on Ilanta, wherein the dragons still closely guarded the elves and the northern human state. It would be the same game for humans and elves, only now the dragons would set the rules. The Council approved Rastigar as the head of this new undertaking, and Rastigar, during all the hustle and bustle of planning, craftily snuck in a clause on direct inheritance of the important post. He was old and was taking care of his chicks: Jatigar and Hazgar.

Several decades passed during the period of intense preparatory work, after which the Lords of the Sky entered the political arena. The humans were horrified to discover that they were ruled by dragons, thousands of them lived among them and the elves. But their passions gradually subsided and the bipeds quickly became accustomed to the primacy of the dragons.

The aged Rastigar left his eldest son in control and retired. Jatigar, whose reign is now called "golden," gradually transformed the council into an advisory-legislative body, depriving himself of real power, and took the title of emperor. The elderly dragon ruled wisely. During his reign, science was again developed, and training centers were built. On Ilanta, a whole scientific complex was formed, which gathered within its walls the promising dragon youth and a large number of true bloods. He created a stable state system, balancing the interests of all sides and leaving the Lord of the Skies in the lead.

Behind Jatigar, the shadow of his younger brother always loomed. Jatigar's son perished while exploring other worlds; he never returned from a world without magic. The artifacts with mana reserves he took with him could not provide for the way back. Vatigar dissolved into the astral. Nuirra, his daughter, changed her clan and moved to Ilanta, refusing her inheritance (not without the help of her "kind" uncle). She did not want to bother with people, preferring the life of an ordinary dragoness. Hazgar, who now stood to inherit, was power-hungry. He rubbed his paws together greedily, but then the decrepit old emperor suddenly had another daughter, who was declared the official heiress and presented to the people subordinate to the emperor. The direct line must not be interrupted. So Jagirra, without knowing it, blocked her uncle's way to power. Dragons make a huge hullabaloo over all the dragonlings; the birth of a child is always a joy for them. But Hazgar, according to the Miur, had been in the human hypostasis for too long. Irreversible changes occurred in his psyche; his brother's daughter did not cause him any feelings other than disgust and hatred.

Desperate to gain the throne on legal grounds, Hazgar went a roundabout way. His plans included not only the throne of the empire. The dragon thought bigger. Power over one, albeit very large country, did not suit the ambitious and power-hungry dragon. A grandiose plan was born in his furious mind.

For more than a hundred years, Hazgar carefully warmed the ambitions of the Forest Lordships on Ilanta. Dozens of elves swore an oath on him and acted as guides to the interests of the secret puppeteer. Crashing and burning with the Rauu and the Ariates, he achieved his goal under the shadow of the Mellornys. The Forest Elves became burdened by dependence on the true bloods and dragons, who did not understand anything in their life. After all, many dragons who moved to the heavenly neighbor did not accept new trends, preferring to live the ancient way. They rejected the fashion of a second hypostasis. The true bloods could still be tolerated. Their strength was enormous, but it would be better if they continued to study science and did not meddle in the affairs of the Forest Lordships. In his home world, Hazgar successfully subjugated several clans, binding their members to himself by magical oaths.

The long line of intrigues bore fruit. The Lords of the Sky themselves did not understand how they came to be dependent on him, while the motley crew of "idiots" on Ilanta maintained loyalty to the ruling emperor and threatened to hinder the grandiose plans of the crowned ruler's brother, thereby signing their own death warrant. The true bloods, as the most dangerous enemies, had to be eliminated first.

Hazgar bought the top layer of Forest Elves, promising them the sky. His secret agents brought to the Forest Lordships information that the true bloods had found a way to bypass the ritual and painlessly turn elves into dragons. To give these words credibility, a whole performance was played out before the rulers, where a dragon agent portrayed himself as an elf over whom a new ritual was performed. The "woodies" bought it.

The next step was to help his brother meet his doom and organize an attack on his niece. The frightened girl, swallowing tears, herself flew at him in search of help and shelter....

Asha, or rather the Great Mother, who was ruling at that time and knew Jagirra, did not know the reasons for the death of the old emperor, but was very concerned about the disappearance of the heiress. The Miur could not get to the bottom of the causes of the attacks on Jagirra. She did not believe in the clues left by the criminals which pointed to the heavenly neighbor. Why would the dragons of another world want to kill the young empress? Various rumors spread throughout the country. Hazgar, appointed as the ruler of the empire, sent hundreds of agents to search for the niece who had fled from the crown, announcing a substantial reward for the finder.

On Ilanta, terrible things were happening. No one knew for sure, but according to rumors, many of the true bloods were killed there. Unbelievable, how could that possibly happen at all? The young green dragon Nedagar could have told about it. He took a blood oath and fulfilled the will of his lord. He carried poison to the feast, after which several Forest Elves who'd been brainwashed, being under the mental control of the secret puppet master, chopped off the true bloods' heads while they were asleep. The trap slammed shut. The Rauu and the Ariates, who received anonymous information, rushed to the rescue and chopped up the righteous and the guilty alike. The responsible parties fell under the swords of the dragons' followers. Many Forest Elves and their children wound up dead, for whom the blood-drenched hall was a complete shock. The real traces were swept away; all the evidence pointed to the Forest Lordships. They, led by righteous anger and a thirst for vengeance, readied their forest army for battle. They were joined by the King of Mestair, who, among others, lost a couple of sons at the feast. The second act of the terrible play was played out strictly according to the script. The various branches of the elves, humans, and dragons clashed; the survivors of the true bloods searched for the murderers, whose bones had long ago turned into ashes.

Everything went perfectly, except that the girl was able to escape from his vigilant care. Jagirra was no longer a threat; she would never again become a dragon, but the little witch managed to get to the Miur. At the very last moment, a detachment of dragons faithful to Hazgar overtook the fighting pride of the cat people as they accompanied the disgraced heiress. In the ensuing short battle, the Miur killed everyone, but the little jerk again slipped away. The thread of Jagirra's fate was lost for a long three thousand years. The Great Mother did not know that some of the pride warriors, at the cost of their own lives, gave the Empress the necessary time to get to the interplanetary portal....

News from the mother planet made its way to the surviving true bloods on Ilanta, who immediately stopped searching for the alleged killers. The dragons managed to come to the right conclusions.

Realizing that his plans could go wrong, Hazgar gave the command to implement a back-up option while it still fit into the conceived model. The self-made emperor knew the psychology of his native species, and they, as Andy now knew, were just as he expected. A large group of elves set out to visit their neighboring planet several hours ahead of the true bloods that later arrived on Nelita from Ilanta. They were a mental leash held by a pair of magicians. The dragons sent with them, who did not know the goals and tasks of the pointy-eared squad, carried them to the mountains, hiding them from Rauu patrol posts. Hazgar did not learn the results of the diversion. The "guests" from Ilanta, ruining a grandiose plan to capture the whole world, sealed the interplanetary portals.

Andy shuddered. "Grandfather" expected that the dragons who lost their families would go insane and destroy the Mellorny forests along with their inhabitants. Indeed, he himself was a…, no, Andy could not call that monster a dragon. Oh yes, Hazgar was not mistaken neither in his assessment of his fellow tribesmen, nor in his evaluation of their actions. He planned everything accurately. According to the plan, there should not have been

Mellorny forests or dragons left on Ilanta. A world without magic was a ripe apple, ready to fall into the hands of someone who possessed magic and portals. A whole world at the feet of one master! Myriad subjugated people, who could be turned into terrible fighters, would sweep away all those who did not submit on Nelita and then begin expansion into other worlds. That vile cur Jagirra, to ruin such wonderful plans!!! It remained to hope that the murderers sent on her trail found her. Pity no one could bring the glad tidings.

The discord that began after the arrival of the interplanetary guests put an end to the ancient state and grandiose plans. The former governors of the suburbs declared themselves princes and formed the Alliance. They did not care about the deceased empress; they hadn't sworn an oath to her. The princess fell victim to human vices. They tasted power and sought to keep it in their paws. Prince Ora was one of the few who questioned the goals of a new war and for a long time kept aloof, but the fiery turmoil eventually reached him. The prince believed his fellow tribesmen that Hazgar was behind the whole mess, but he dismissed all the idle stories about Jagirra. A dragon could not lift his paw against his own blood! It was impossible!!!

The new emperor, who controlled many clans, managed to retain power and defeat the armies of the Alliance. He clashed with the cat people, whom he eventually drove to the mountains. Hazgar did not forget who helped his niece. Not a single Miur remained in the territory of the empire that fell to him. All the villages were burned to the ground.

The Great Mothers of the Miur, the most secluded race of the old world, believed that the young empress remained alive, hoping that she would return someday. But centuries and millennia passed. The wars between the Celestial Empire and the other states faded and then flared up with renewed vigor. The pretender who had seized power constantly expanded the boundaries of his lands, but there was no word of Jagirra. The clan of "crystal," which bore the family coat of arms, now the imperial coat of arms, was reduced to two dragons—Hazgar and his son.

One day, at the fifth outer gates of the city, a messenger from a free elf village appeared (the very same elvish village where Evael was chief). The elf was taken to the Miur in charge of the upper lands, Gella, but he refused to speak to her, insisting on a personal meeting with the ruler. When he was pointed to the gate in a rather polite manner, he asked Gella to give the Great Mother an information crystal sealed with a secret code known only to a certain few.

Gella then detained the elf magician and took all measures to get the crystal to its destination. She realized that the information was of particular importance; otherwise, the village magician would not have made himself out to be on a death mission, trying the patience of the cats and wishing to commit suicide in such an exotic way. She surmised that the crystal could be somehow connected to the Prince of Ora's secret ambassador, who had visited the Great Mother five fivers ago. It was unheard of, but the ruler had received the ambassador. After their conversation, the guards on the Miur's southern border posts with the Principality of Ora seemed to have gone blind. Caravans of smugglers passed them without any obstacles. Gella was mistaken: the crystal was not associated with the secret ambassador from Ora. But the elf magician was immediately summoned upstairs.

Several prides of "shadows" were sent out, reinforced by magicians and the latest armor and weapons.

The information given by the chief of the free Elvish settlement excited Asha and her daughters for real. The old elf claimed to have seen the imperial coat of arms on the shoulder of a single shkas, who was actually a dragon. He then described the tattoo and said many quite incomprehensible things. Evael reported that the mysterious shkas was a fugitive from the dugaria and was not at all oriented to his surroundings, but that he remembered High. And the language of dragons in its archaic form, which only the high society of dragons spoke. The shkas learned Common quickly, and, according to the observations of experienced mages, his ability to learn was not in any way hindered by the tree-chimera. Evael told a lot more, including the coat of arms bearer's crazy reactions to things and the new methods of fencing he showed them. At the end of the recording, he added that the daughter of Prince Ora was at the settlement and was keenly interested in contacts with Miur. The shkas, who at their first meeting called himself Kerrovitarr and who absolutely did not understand what was so strange in his name and why the elf did not recommend calling himself that, joined the princess' virk as a voluntary assistant, not included in the general detachment.

What was this? It was extremely incomprehensible. It wasn't at all like the games of the prince or the emperor, but the name? What dragon would call himself that? It's directly spitting at the celestial throne. A lot of assumptions were put forward at the Great Mother's meeting with her daughters, but the most realistic one was that the shkas could be the son of someone from the Crystal clan, perhaps Nuirra, and the tattoo was drawn on him before his mother's clan was replaced.

They knew that Nuirra had two sons and a daughter. True, they did not have the right to the throne because of their mother's refusal to inherit, but Hazgar could very well have put the unwanted individuals in the dugaria. On the other hand, Nuirra moved to Ilanta. How could her son be on the mother's planet? How did he slip past the imperial and princely astals? It was necessary to check everything in detail. Maybe they were mistaken and the bearer of the coat of arms was a clever bait by the emperor. The version about Jagirra being his mother was, for some reason, not considered....

The "shadows," once they discovered the princess' virk, installed a round-the-clock surveillance with the help of birds. The results obtained gave rise to more questions than answers. Kerrovitarr's behavior did not fit into any model. He skillfully concealed the fact that he was a dragon, but still, through the numerous masks he wore, something alien, not connected with modern dragons, broke through. The songs by the fire? No one knew these songs; the music performed on the tair differed from anything they'd heard before. Judging by the conversations he overheard, Kerrovitarr guessed that Ilirra was not a real princess. The Great Mother knew about the virk. She and the ambassador discussed this topic in detail. The prince's daughter had an excellent disguise, but the shkas was not always with the detachment and therefore did not discover the real princess. But the conclusions he made based on stingy data were astonishing. Somehow, the Imperialists sniffed out the virk and launched magical creatures into the miur's lands—vogrs. The Miur decided to drive the vogrs right up to the detachment using magical controllers. The Great Mother wanted to make sure that all this was not a set up. How would the animals behave, guided by magicians through special artifacts? How would the members of the detachment behave? To the cat woman's surprise, the shkas was able to destroy two magical monsters with minimal effort.

Asha decided to meet him personally.

* * *

The Great Mother opened her eyes and looked at the dragon bending over her.

"So you've discovered the secret of the Great Mothers. What are you going to do with it?"

"Take it to my grave," Kerrovitarr replied calmly.

"I believe you."

Kerr smiled; the smile turned out ambiguous:

"Of course, we know so much about each other now...."

"And we do not know even more," Asha said cautiously, catching a ghostly threat.

"If I had known what I learned during the communication between our minds, I would have strangled you before I crossed the threshold of this office." Andy wiped the blood that was coming out of his nose with his palm. "You knew well about the danger of a merger between us."

"I did, but I decided to risk it, and I do not regret it a bit. Why did you not strangle me?" Asha's eyes and pupils narrowed at the same time. The thin strips were visible between the half-closed lids.

"For the simple reason that you too got it in full! For the same reason you are not strangling me now."

"Do you judge me?"

"How did you guess? What were you thinking when you projected emotions and your feelings towards your daughters and other Miurs on me??"

Listening to the wrathful tirade, she was silent and

187

involuntarily jerked the tip of the tail, which gave away her anxiety.

"Fine, nothing to say! You had better tell me then, what should I call you and your girls."

In some ways, Kerr was right. She did not expect such an effect from direct contact. The experience of dozens of generations did not imply emotional diffusion. Her love for Illusht and Ashlat lay on fertile soil. In the dragon's mind, the image of the daughters was transformed into an image of kids, chicks in his nest. All her sincere feelings were absorbed by him completely.

In turn, she also got a load of emotions from his draconian bounty. His one longing to return to the sky, the pain in his heart due to genuine solitude…. The worry about his relatives and friends on Ilanta and in the elf village swept over her in hot waves. His paranoid distrust towards all those around him who hadn't entered into his inner circle grated her nerves. They shared a strong desire to protect their native clans and families. Duty and responsibility were the indestructible pillars in the galaxy of vivid feelings. All the diversity of the young dragon's inner world covered her, finding its place in her soul and worldview. He was right—neither he nor she could strangle the other now…. It's not so easy to raise a hand against a being that has become a member of the pride, and they, since the experience of many generations of Great Mothers turned out to be useless, had become family, a pride.

"Call us sisters."

The dragon frowned and suddenly laughed.

"Did I say something funny?" Asha tried to get up, but he carefully held her by the shoulder.

"Lay down. And funny? I just imagined being asked who I was and replying—a Miur. I do not look like a roihe-male. There is no pouch on my stomach. Or like a rasht. That leaves only a female."

"You are wrong."

"Why?"

"You are a dragon! A real dragon!"

"By your efforts, I will soon begin to meow, although I was born a human."

"It does not matter who you were born as. The main thing

is who you became. Hazgar was born a dragon, and he became…. And you are a true blood."

"What does that give me?"

"Without that, you could not have come here." Asha pushed her "brother" aside and stood up from the ottoman.

Andy paid attention to the caveat his "sister" or "aunt" was referring to:

"I would like to know the meaning of the phrase 'true blood.' I have heard it so many times and not known what they are talking about. It gets tiring. Enlighten a 'brother,' please!" Asha stopped in the middle of her step. He caught her hand and stubbornly pulled her back: "Do not make up excuses about fatigue or some other time. You know me perfectly, well, you have found out. I will not leave it alone. I think that I deserve a little reward for refusing to break into the dark and blocked zones in your beautiful head." In fully automatic mode, Andy made a gesture inherent in Miur culture that said he would not take "no" for an answer.

The merger went a little deeper than usual; gestures and motor skills are not simply transmitted like that, he thought, noticing his own strange new behavior. The Great Mother noticed it too.

"Alright," Asha said, yielding to the pressure. "Tell me, have you ever wondered where your weight and flesh go when you change from dragon hypostasis to human? Four di[7] as opposed to two hundred or three hundred?"

"I thought about it, but what does the change of appearance have to do with the true bloods?"

"Everything. Let me explain." Asha pulled her tail under her, wrapped her arms around the pillow and looked at the short polished claws released from her fingertips. "All dragons are energomorphs. The difference between were-dragons and ordinary dragons is the latency of the energomorphism in ordinary dragons. All dragons take and pump mana from the astral; that does not depend on whether you are a latent energomorph or not. Now we

189

return to my question. During the change, the residual weight, which is the difference of the masses between the hypostases, turns into pure energy that is inextricably linked with the dragon's aura. It passes beyond the edge of the world: to the reverse side. As for what happens to the energy on the reverse side, I do not know. Sages have not yet found out. No Miur has ever been there, and the dragons turned into pure energy do not return. Maybe there were such cases, but I have never heard of one."

"Interesting...."

"Do not interrupt!"

"I am silent! You go on"

"As I was saying...." The Miur caught herself in atypical behavior and hissed angrily. Andy stretched his lips into a grin. The Great Mother reminded him most of all of Irina at that moment. Indeed—his older sister.

The cat-woman smoothed the fur on her tail, closed her eyes, and took a few deep breaths. As a result of the exercise designed to calm nerves, her large elastic breasts went up and down, and Andy noticed the circles on the nipples. Two concentric circles around the nipples meant she had suckled two kittens. She fed her daughters herself, not giving them over to a roihe-male's pouch.

"It is because of the dragon's energy transfer that people experience infernal pain during the ritual. Not everyone can endure the reorganization of the body and its connection to external energy channels. A person changes not only his blood and body; his connection with the world also changes. The solution to the fact that dragons do not eat much for their great weight lies in this. They replenish their supplies from within, not by taking on external energy through food. They unconsciously transform energy into a familiar form and send it to maintain their personal needs. Now the differences begin." The Miur again calmed her shattered nerves, weakened by the merger. "As I said, all dragons draw mana from the astral, but true bloods can enter the world of energy consciously and conduct it through themselves, acting as a channel from a river to an arid region. The stronger and more developed the system of energy channels in the body, the more mana you can pump through yourself. Also, true bloods can freely wield all the elements. To operate with elemental magic, they do not need to cast spells or build rune patterns, but this must be learned. There are uncontrolled splashes; they do not usually lead to anything good." Andy remembered a small lake of boiling magma at the school grounds. He hadn't read any incantations. Asha lifted the veil of secrecy from the nature of the phenomena. "True bloods can unite all the primary elements; other mages not more than two; some unique ones even three. And there is one more nuance. If a simple were-dragon, in human hypostasis, consumes all his stored mana, then he cannot immediately fill his stores again. A true blood, while not entering the astral, can scoop up energy from the part that has gone beyond the border."

"Hold on," Andy made a "stop" gesture. He feverishly meditated, digesting the information received. The part about him not being able to travel to another world if he were not a true blood took on meaning. Making up the rune scheme, he did not think about entering the astral. "So what you're saying is, I stole energy from myself? That is why I lost my second hypostasis?"

"Yes, you got it right. During the transfer, you used energy from the reverse side and took out almost all of it."

Andy said something in his native Russian....

"Just over half of you was left. Your unsuccessful attempt to take on your second form clearly demonstrates my correctness. The disappearance of magic is due to the fact that all mana went towards restoring the energetic forces on the reverse side. Your body has cured itself. The elven mages were surprised by your peculiarities and came up with different hypotheses as to why a non-mage absorbed so much energy and where it was spent."

"The elves do not know about this characteristic of true bloods?"

"No; studies were conducted ten thousand years ago; records of them were preserved only in the archives of the Miur keepers. The dragons themselves are not very eager to share the secrets, but we pretend that we do not remember our brothers and sisters who helped them. Your ability to create magic began to return after the restoration or regeneration of most of what you lost. Do not forget, you keep the key. Its accumulator also took a piece of the pie."

"The key, that Targ's knickknack, so that is how I got taken for a ride…."

"The key and your god are not directly related to the activation of the transition."

"What? My what?" Andy was taken aback, bewildered by the Great Mother's words.

"I returned several times to your memories and came to the conclusion that there was an invisible assistant who supplied the seventh rune, indicating the start point. The key worked after that. Someone, a true blood, rendered you a disservice…."

"There are no more true bloods on Ilanta!"

"I do not know anything about that. You have no evidence to the contrary. When you get back, you will be thorough, but for now, get rid of your hysteria and stop wringing your hands. Your valley is on another planet, and I do not intend to carry water in a leaky bucket. The images and memories in your brain prompted me to make an unambiguous conclusion: you were helped, someone intervened in the spell."

"Harder and harder with each passing hour…," whispered Andy, white as a sheet, continuing to pierce Asha with a thoughtful gaze. He did not intend to break out into hysterics; it's just the news was very out of the ordinary. Some scumbag had made him a puppet. A scumbag so experienced and strong magically that the thought of it made his skin crawl. Only an archmage among archmages can butt in to someone else's rune interweave, and he didn't remember any such characters. Based on Asha's logic, he was a puppet in the hands of an experienced puppeteer. Targ! He punched the marble floor with all his might; some lightning flashed from his fingers; a deep melted pothole formed in the solid stone.

The Miur's whiskers twitched. The fur on her back stood on end from the electric discharges running through it.

"Stop it!"

"What?" *Take a deep breath, once again, arms at your sides, calm down.*

"Stop it," repeated the Miur. "Nobody controlled you, calm down. With the true bloods, this is simply impossible. Any impact on the psyche, no matter how subtle, leaves long-lasting marks, you do not have them."

Andy shook his head sadly. On Earth, without any magic at

all, they'd learned to influence people through various methods, and here they had an instrument like that readily accessible.

"Believe me, the fusion of minds allows the outside observer to identify any influence at any level. In your case, we have a point, a single, one-time intervention in the course of events. Someone was watching you that day and was very happy with the misdeed of the inexperienced dragon who sent himself here." Asha held out her hand and touched him on the shoulder consolingly. "Even an energetic being can not constantly watch you. There is a reason why worlds are separated from each other by a border. Crossing it requires expenditure of mana on both sides. It is entirely possible that from there it is much more difficult to get into the materialized world, because here most of the energy has a strict fixed form and is subject to other laws."

"I am calm," he said and put a mask of indifference on his face. The light sparks in his aura, once again under control, disappeared. Let his "sister" say whatever she likes in an attempt to console him. Maybe she's right. It wasn't possible to put control nodes on a true blood, except for marriage nodes. But it was very possible to influence the other people around them. A man does not live in a vacuum. Any actions or steps he takes are created under the influence of other beings and the circumstances imposed by them. Everything would be fine; he would return home, find the cur, and cut off his head. Just give him time.

"Then answer me this: why can I still not take on my true form?" Andy returned to the initial topic of the conversation.

"The answer lies in you, here," the cat touched his forehead. "An internal ban, a taboo, fear of the astral. You are wary of being noticed. Our minds work in such a way that we put up insurmountable barriers for ourselves and we tear them down ourselves. This condition depends on will and belief."

"And desire?"

"Desire, yes," Asha replied complaisantly. "You can overcome yourself. You will do it again."

"What a nice conversation we are having, especially for me. I got much more than I bargained for."

"And yet we have both gained invaluable experience,"

Asha concluded tactfully.

"Oh, well...." Andy sneered skeptically. "Besides experience, you have gained a real trump in terms of politics. You will beat all the emperor's and princes' aces."

"Politics." The miur sighed. Her whiskers drooped. "Targ take politics. It is because of politics that we have become hostages of ancient vows and have been driven into the mountains. The miur are on the brink; our population is growing, but where can we live? The cities under the mountains are getting crowded. Soon the forests of Lidar will not be able to feed all the hungry mouths."

Aha! While remaining outwardly indifferent, Andy pricked up his ears. The ruler would not have been a ruler, had she not conceived a move that would trigger some bargaining. *A ruler without politics is like borsch without sour cream. I've had it, to Targ with it!* He lay down on the couch and stared at the ceiling.

"Asha, please, do not skirt around the matter. I do not want to play these games. I am quite fed up. Let us skip the Targ-loving manipulation. And really, after a merger like that, what manipulation can there be between us? Let us decide once and for all. If I can help, then I will help; if not, then I will tell you so directly, and you should not expect help from me. I am tired of politics and politicians. I want normal relations even in a narrow family circle. Since you allowed me to call you sister, let us act like it." Having finished his tirade, Andy suddenly moved to the edge of the ottoman and looked Asha in the eyes. The miur shuddered involuntarily at the sight of the yellow vertical pupils that erupted in Andy's blue eyes. Through the human face, the dragon was looking at her. "Tell me, how did this happen?"

"It was a magical vow given carelessly by the Great Mother Irrshart to Rastigar. There were not many Miur then, and she was not taking a risk to swear that we would live where there are villages and cities of our people. Rastigar wanted to separate the races from one another and thereby prevent inter-racial wars. We had a lot of land. The Scarlet Mountains were all ours."

"What is so bad about an ancient vow? The conditions have changed, and Great Mother Irrshart is long gone."

"She is gone, but I am here, and her memory, which contains the blood oath, is transferred through the generations. I cannot break the vow, even though I did not make it. Apparently,

Rastigar knew of the secret of the Great Mothers, or he guessed, and deliberately caught us in a trap. The old dragon was worried that we would become the strongest race, and he took forward-thinking measures to prevent the growth of the powerful Miur."

"The war Hazgar started took the Scarlet Mountains and the foothill regions from you. He destroyed all settlements, and the vow does not allow you to return. The Miur did not live there anymore, so going back would be 'resettling.' Think about what you are saying! And undoing the vow? A magical vow can be removed by a direct descendant of the one to whom it was made. Can I rid you of this burden?"

"It is not that simple. According to all the laws, you are a direct descendant, but you do not wear the crown. Only Jagirra, the real empress, can do that. That is why Hazgar is a pretender. No one conferred the magical crown to him. He has no connection to the throne."

Interesting situation. I completely understand Asha, and I really do sympathize. The Great Mother has had to do an insane balancing act so as not to pull the Miur into some conflict and to try to keep a lid on their population.

The caste system and raising of the rulers to the rank of goddesses (for many thousand years the Great Mothers had the opportunity to adjust the social order to suit themselves) kept the people from unrest, but how long would the slopes of Mount Lidar contain the demographic growth? The number of Miurs was steadily increasing, and the demographic problem had come to the fore. Universal worship, of course, is good, but no more bread would come from it. When people are full, they make fewer demands.

Andy got up and walked around the room. For some time now, he'd noticed that it was easier to think on his feet. Asha did not interfere. The cat felt the direction of the dragon's mental flow and hoped for a positive result of their brainstorming. Grabbing the pillow and pulling her knees up to her, she watched the two-legged pendulum pace back and forth.

With his hands behind his back, he measured the room with wide strides. The task was before him. If you think about it, Asha wants to offer me help in returning Jagirra to Nelita, but I'm against it with all my heart. She no longer belongs on the dragons' native planet. What can I suggest as a way out and how can we solve this puzzle? Or maybe... you wanted to play your own game. Why not make the first move right now? Judging by the Miur's reaction, she hadn't guessed his thoughts about resettling their race to Ilanta, so....

"Asha, two clarifying questions if you please." The cat nodded. "First: does the scope of the oath encompass both worlds or only Nelita? Second: is there a fundamental difference as to who exactly can liberate the Miur from this vow?"

"What are you up to?"

"In the world I come from originally, it is not polite to answer a question with a question."

The Miur snorted and thought.

"The oath concerns Nelita," she answered, her eyes flashing. "Any one of my daughters can break it; it does not necessarily have to be me."

"Very well," Andy said through his teeth and returned to the ottoman. Crouching at the very edge, he leaned toward the Great Mother.

Asha, sensing that the conversation had taken on a serious tone, set the pillow aside and straightened her back. Before Andy, there was no longer a "sister," not a relaxed cat, but the leader of the very old race, full of will and dignity. Her glance, her body language, everything about her radiated royalty.

"I will not drag the cat by the tail," Andy said and proposed his idea to the Great Mother. There was more than enough space on the planet, enough for all. The southern Rocky Ridge was completely empty, the northern Rocky Ridge was half empty; even so, both were bigger than Mount Lidar and its foothills. If Prince Ora supported the idea of resettlement, then there would be no problems making a deal with the Rauu, and they, in turn, would press on Tantre. Gil distributes arable land along with the right to autonomy; he would gladly give away a piece of the mountains. If push comes to shove, you can capture the mountains bordering the Great Desert. The borders there are so fuzzy that no one would put up a fight. The huge territory does not obey any sovereign; there will be enough space for both the Miur and the dragons. Andy addressed all possible arguments and counter-arguments. The threat of a full-scale invasion by the imperial forces really lit a fire under the Great Mother to make a decision.

The time came for the Great Mother to think. Asha withdrew into herself. Even the tip of her tail, always living a life of its own, fell to the floor like a piece of thick rope. Only her triangular ears spun forward and backward from time to time.

"Let us go to the office," said the Great Mother, smoothly getting to her feet. Her tone made it clear that the games were over, now every word should be closely watched. There are no relatives in politics; there are partners, allies, enemies, and, as it were, neutrals, who are always asked to take a side, because there are never real neutrals. Every player pursues his own interests.

"There is a grain of soundness in your proposal for resettlement, very sensible. You can open portals, or one portal. The 'key' obeys you. I will teach you how to use it," the Miur said, sitting at her desk. He didn't ask Asha how she knew how to use the ancient artifact. "Now the main thing is, I need guarantees. Can you guarantee the inviolability of the settlers, at least for the first three to five years? I do not demand vows; I do not ask the impossible. But we do need time to strengthen ourselves in the mountains."

"I can not make a promise that I will not fulfill, but I will do my best to ensure peace in the new lands. That sounds more honest and correct. And the Great Mother cannot demand anything from me," Andy besieged the cat, clearly embodying the postulate about there being no relatives in the world of politics.

"Well, let us stop on that point." The Miur didn't like the "prick," but she had made the rule herself and couldn't blame Andy for playing by it. Her tribal memory was a great help, but often situations arose that would have been impossible a thousand years ago. What's more, a thousand years of experience doesn't always aid one in communicating with people, since a person's worldview, the diplomatic etiquette, and the ruling dynasties change many times during that time. "Second, I ask you to arrange the meeting of the Empress and the Great Mother as soon as possible." At first, Andy didn't understand what Asha was talking about, but then it came to him. "One of my daughters will go with the settlers and become another Great Mother. The new family must have a ruler."

"I can not decide for the empress, but I think that she will concede to your request if it is voiced through me," Andy answered diplomatically, shifting the responsibility of the Miur's request to someone else. Once his grandfather, a Soviet politician, had taught him not to take anything on himself, to answer evasively and always leave a loophole for a couple of steps back and two steps forward.

They hashed out their positions and outlined ways to solve future problems for another twenty minutes. Discussion of urgent tasks was interrupted by the question of dragons. Would the Great Mother help in negotiations with the prince?

"Why do you think the prince organized the princess' virk?"

"Why?"

"In the principality, two large parties of dragons are actively intriguing against one another. Reformists and conservatives. The conservative party consists of old people remembering the old emperor. The dragons who fled from the principalities seized by the emperor also belong to them. The reformists actively promote integration into the empire. It would be more appropriate to call it an imperial or pro-imperial party. Your portal jump here and activation of the portal key have upset the outer perimeters of the interplanetary portals. The magical seals have been attached to external circuits."

"So the portals are no longer actually sealed?"

"That is correct, but it is impossible to open the gates without the key and the password. The conservatives would be happy to stay as far as possible away from the empire. They are mostly refugees from the lands conquered by the Celestial Throne. They perfectly understand the threat looming over the Principality, but there is nothing to be done. They have nowhere else to run. The prince has to constantly maneuver between the interests of the opposing parties inside the country, although he himself tends towards the conservatives. The virk was organized to strike at the reformers, not at the whole party, but at the leadership."

"Ilirra is a figurehead. There was no princess in the virk."

"There was and there is." The Miur's face reflected the pleasure she took in doing a good job. "Most of the campaign, consisting of constant shuffling in different directions, was designed for clever people, like you. They had to identify the substitution, and they did. Thus, the prince opened himself up to a strike from his opponents, and they hastened to take advantage of this opportunity, releasing all the dogs on the ruler. Not all, of course, but some odious persons blew their cover completely. The parent of the well-known to you Thygar is in hysterics. One of the tasks of the virk was to discredit political opponents through their children, and the princess managed that successfully. Her double did a great job leading, and you got the role of the general agitator. The cleverly heated passions bore fruit. As far as I understand, Thygar was about to molt but was stuck in human form. Upon entering the virk, he accepted its rules. Ilirra played on his irritability. The prince managed a clever combination. Through the virk he brought himself under fire, forced his opponents to reveal themselves, and at the very end, he will indicate to them the success of the campaign and will present the ambassador of the Great Mother, who will come to the capital with Ilirra's detachment. The trap will slam shut. The prince's political opponents will be shattered by the false accusations that they threw at the prince and they will quit the game. They will not be able to prevent mobilization."

"So, Ilirra was in the detachment all along?" Andy thought for a moment.

"Undoubtedly."

"Her servant Ania!" he guessed. The inconspicuous, quiet errand girl of the detachment. The double was under her control all the time, and she spread rumors and gossip, egging the dragons on in the name of her pseudo-self. "Okay, so we have figured the virk out. Let us go back to the conservatives. Why are you betting on them?"

"Many of them remember the old emperor and took part in the past war on the side of the coalition. Hazgar has only the scaffold in mind for them. The option of moving to another world will be welcomed, but they will require guarantees. Let us think, brother," the Great Mother tilted her head to one side, "what you can offer the prince and those who will agree to follow you on behalf of Empress Jagirra."

* * *

What could he offer? Targ knows what guarantees the dragons would ask for. He couldn't offer them anything except love, peace, and harmony. The loyalty of the Rauu? No, the Lords of the Sky couldn't care less about some Snow Elves. If they have two hundred volunteer dragons, no armies could possibly drive them from the mountains. The Miur, if needed, would act as the first ground echelon of defense.

Andy looked at the spirited Asha and was dejected. Promises, promises. The situation was tight. What could he offer?

Cutting off his thin chain of reflections, the crystal chime of an invisible bell sounded in the office. The finest whiskers on the Great Mother's nose stood upright, reflecting her extreme discontent. The tip of the tail twitched several times.

"I asked you not to disturb me," she said into the emptiness.

Instead of an answer, the front door opened, revealing her daughters, dressed in thin robes and translucent shalwars. Illyusht's and Ashlat's arms and legs were adorned with numerous bracelets. Small bells were sewn onto the wide belts supporting the shalwars. Across the twins' waists hung sheaths with ritual rashag[8] knives. The cats' long braids were part of elaborate hairstyles.

The sisters' knives were tied with gold ribbons that informed people who were "in the know" that they also belonged to the priestesses of the Temple dwellers. Andy was in the know due to what he'd learned from Asha at the confluence of minds. He looked at the Miur, feeling a warm, paternal feeling for the unexpected sisters gush up in his chest. Apparently, they noticed the changes in his aura. The sisters exchanged glances and simultaneously turned their gaze towards their mother.

"Rimas,[9] have you decided?" The sisters bowed respectfully.

"Yes." Asha rose from the table. "The fusion of minds was

worth the risk." Rapid shots of two pairs of eyes in Andy's direction, and again a look full of reverence toward their mother. The ruler looked sternly at her daughters, then went on: "Before you is Kerrovitarr Jagirrat, the son of the real empress."

Andy immediately felt discomfort from the sisters' penetrating gaze. *"Jagirrat." That must mean the son of Jagirra. Almost like a Russian patronymic, but from the mother's name.*

"Why are you dressed for a reception?" Asha asked, and, remembering something, hissed irritably. "The princess! How much time has passed? Oh, what awful timing."

Five hours, Andy said to himself, his inner chronometer continuing to tick regularly and measure the invisible stretches between the past and the future. With everything that was going on, the melding of minds and the incredible news that the empress was alive, the Great Mother had forgotten about some of her duties. But the duties had not forgotten about her. It was clear that talking about guarantees was postponed for an indefinite period. *Maybe it's for the better; there will be time to think about the current situation and provide a logical basis for non-existent guarantees.*

"The sun has bent towards the Horned Fault. The appointment shall take place in two hours in the large hall," Ashlat replied, bowing low. "You asked me to remind you."

"Illusht, take Kerro...," the Miur stopped mid-sentence and turned to Andy, who was shaking his head. It would be better not to use a title. If one of the cat people blabbed, all their plans could collapse overnight. Let him be a simple guest.

Asha understood without words. "...Take our guest and pick up a suitable vestment for him. He is invited to the reception. Ashlat, call the maidservants and help me get ready."

Andy tore his butt from the comfortable chair and went with the "sister." Illusht's behavior portrayed complete equanimity, but the yellow stripes that flashed in her aura gave away her annoyance at being assigned the role of the guide and assistant. She was utterly unmoved by the unwilling patron's origin.

201

"Will my invitation be an insult to the princess? She might regard that as a provocation: the clan-less shkas turning out to be an equal and at the same table as her," Andy asked the agonized question. "Perhaps I should do this?" He closed his eyes and imagined himself in elven hypostasis. His body seemed to be poked with a thousand needles. "There are plenty of elves in the city. No one will be surprised if another elf attends the official part of the reception."

The three cat women stared at him wide-eyed. *What? Okay, I get it if it's just Illusht and Ashlat, but Asha? Did she miss the part about my third hypostasis during the confluence?*

"You look just like her," the Great Mother said, shocked. No need to explain who she was talking about. The ruler's daughters, who kept the same information in their heads as her mother, received visible confirmation of her words about the "guest's" kinship with the empress.

"A bad idea." Illusht walked closer to Andy. "Sometimes among the dragons from the princess' retinue, there are experts in family heritage or specialists in clanship. The history of the imperial family was studied by many, and an elf who resembles the empress might cause unnecessary and premature suspicions. Better we will declare you a disciple of Rimas who disappeared six months ago and went out into the foothill human city on the border with the empire. It is unlikely that the Principality has ideas about such subtleties. Maybe the ruler took on the whim of taking a disciple of the human race. Nobody needs to explain anything to anyone—this is our internal business."

"No it is, then." There was a new acupuncture session, accompanied by a range of unpleasant sensations, and the familiar face returned to its place.

Just in time. Under the merry jingle of bells, no less than a dozen Miur and female elves entered the office. The newcomers were carrying trunks bound with copper strips. Andy realized that this was his queue to leave; he was only attracting attention to himself. He lightly tugged Illusht by the cloak, bowed low to the Great Mother, turned towards the door, and... came face to face with a tall cat woman. The gaze resembled an "X-ray machine" or Tsar Ivan the Terrible, who saw his boyars through and through. He wanted to run as far as possible from the green fire of the eyes, to hide under the earth, just to not feel their consuming flame. She was dressed in a white hooded cloak with a deep hood covering her face. The Miur's right hand clasped a carved wooden staff with an onyx pommel.

"Eldest," Illusht greeted her, bending to one knee. *Got it, the Senior Priestess of Manyfaces deigned to visit the ruler.* She was the head of the ecclesiastical hierarchy of the Miur. She radiated an unshakable power. Her magical essence was so rich and felt so strongly that Andy felt a shiver down his spine. The Miur was not a true blood, but he was ready to bet that with all his strength he would not stand against her for more than ten seconds, and even that might be flattering himself. Behind the cat's shoulders, he could sense a force that in another place would be called divine. Andy, still not taking his eyes off the Eldest, struggled with steel in her eyes and the treacherous trembling in his own knees. Something inside him kept saying that he mustn't look away first. If he did, he would lose, and there would be no way back. No one needs a broken dragon. Another voice told him not to let his guard down. The Great Mother hadn't used all the aces up her sleeves—there were cards in her pile, there were! And he, the dolt, fell for it, believed that the felines were lying low. What if they suddenly disintegrated him into molecules, right this minute? The cunning cats showed him a carrot and put him in their harness. Pull, dear. The "momma" was a hundred steps ahead of him. She could have eaten the dragon for breakfast during the confluence, as easy as snapping one's fingers…. What could a humble guy from a Russian town do against a den of cobras like these?

"Who are you?" The Eldest, without taking her eyes off Andy, walked around the kneeling heiress to the throne and approached him closely. The Miur's green eyes flashed especially brightly. Andy instinctively erected another cocoon of protection around himself. The light in the priestess' eyes faded; all the sounds in the office disappeared. A dead, deafening silence reigned. The priestess threw off her hood. A piece of gray hair fell from under the cloth. The Miur's face bore numerous wrinkles. A few thin, lifeless cobwebs hung on her whiskers. The skin on the neck, overgrown with brown and gray fur, was gathered in folds.

By the way the servant of the goddess behaved, it was clear: she wielded considerable power and represented the second branch of power in the cat people's state, the spiritual one. Of all those present in the study, the Great Mother, the Eldest Priestess, and Andy remained standing. The others were kneeling and bowed their heads for a while, looking at the small patterns on the stone tile.

Oops. It was too late to get down on his knees now. The staring contest created a storm. Only at that moment, did he realize that by his behavior, he had placed himself on the same level as the supreme authority of Mount Lidar. The priestess waved her hand. The massive doors of the office slammed shut with a roar. A strange numbness attacked Andy; he seemed to have fallen into a viscous jelly. He'd obviously gotten off on the wrong foot with the old hag, but why wasn't the Great Mother saying anything? How could he get out of this situation now?

"Who are you, bearing the seal of a Guardian?" repeated the old woman. Her left hand swiftly shot forward; the black painted claw on the forefinger ripped open the thin fabric of his shirt. "Eight rays of the sun." The priestess' lips broke into a satisfied smile, exposing her strong fangs. Anger arose from the depths of his soul. His blood boiled from the adrenaline. Who did she think she was?! Without taking any account of his actions, Andy freed himself from the viscous substance holding his hands and feet. The priestess took one step back.

"I see." The Miur was the first to break eye contact and turned her head toward the Great Mother.

Darn. He did not win, but he did not lose. Andy felt that he was standing in a pool of molten stone, but for some strange reason, he did not feel the heat. Short lightning strikes shot from the tips of his fingers to the floor, and in the office, there was a heavy smell of ozone. What, Targ's tail, what in the world was with him?

"But you did not answer my question."

"And I will not answer...." He heard the shocked breaths of those ones their knees. *I know, I'm a fool, and there's nothing to be done about it.* "The Great Mother will answer, Eldest. If she deems it necessary," Andy added. The tip of the ruler's tail jerked nervously. Well, he had made a mess for his new "kin," and he felt better in his heart for it. Let Asha handle this matriarch, he'd had enough staring contests to last a lifetime. A lemon after the juicer looks better than he did now, after two phrases of conversation with the Eldest. *Targ take your internal "disassembly!" Being a mouse between two hungry cats is not a very enjoyable pastime. Theater of the absurd!* "I gave my word to keep quiet. I have never broken my own vows in my life and do not see any reason to now. I apologize." He clicked his heels and bowed his head. The high double-leafed door swung open without any interference from the crooked old woman. *Wow! Life, it turns out, is so beautiful!*

What Asha would do with the involuntary witnesses of the "friendly" conversation was none of his business. In the cell, there is a prohibition, tongues cut, do not care. She would come up with something. She had enough imagination and would sort it out somehow. He too would have to figure out which way to go. The portal frames had been taken down as unnecessary.

"Follow me...." *Illusht's fur seems to have faded, poor thing. Actually, I can see it's shedding in droves. Have I offended her?*

"Who was that?"

"Someone who could send you to the fire!"

"Would the Great Mother not have intervened?"

"Pray to Manyfaces that she would have, but be careful. We do not need squabbles with Temple dwellers. They have become too powerful over the last few years, too powerful." *So pathetic! She'll make an awful priestess.* "Remember, do not ever embark on Arshag's path. She is a fearsome enemy."

Andy practically ran behind the Miur, who was taking long strides down the corridor and pondered her last words. The rapids of the inner world of the militant race of felines proved to be very dangerous; the boat of a lone rower could be smashed to bits and no one would notice. He was between a rock and a hard place. Gradually, the stream of his thoughts calmed down. The multicolored stone frescos that lined the hall formed a harmonious picture.

Not only had the Great Mother noticed the threat hanging over the feline race. The Matriarchy of the Temple dwellers and the Senior Priestess also kept abreast of things. But if the ruler's hands were tied by ancient vows, they could not hold the priestesses back at all. Gradually a kind of opposition formed among the higher clergy, which posed real competition to the Great Mother in the struggle for power. Andy paused for a second, but he was not mistaken in his conclusions! As often happened on Earth in the past, secular and spiritual powers were sharpening each other's teeth. The Temple dwellers could act more efficiently. Asha's talks with the Prince of Ora's ambassador and the sale to the Principality of the latest developments in the Miur weapons workshops were a response to internal threats. The Great Mother was frantically seeking allies. Asha had a good reason for blocking whole sections of her memory from free access. She was afraid that he would sort out the palace intrigues and would switch to the side of the servants of Manyfaces. There was no doubt that the ruler skillfully arranged the sudden arrival of the Eldest in her office and pushed him to butt heads with her. The cunning cat! Now he could not escape from her boat.

Guards stood at attention as they passed by. Andy stopped abruptly. Because of the turn of the corridor to the right, he heard familiar voices.

"Come on," Illusht grabbed his hand.

"Wait, are there dragons here?"

"Yes. Come on."

Andy tore his hand away and ran to the turn; the voices got louder. He formed a virtual mirror and looked around the corner. Two princesses were walking down the hall. The real one differed from the double in the rich decoration of her clothes. Behind Ilirra was her dilapidated retinue. They weren't dragons—parrots, honestly. Ania's copper hair could be seen in the middle of the line that accompanied the royal.

A foul hiss came right in his ear:

"Do you not have enough trouble with the church? Do you want to add the dragons to them as well?"

Andy grabbed Illusht by the cape and pulled her to him; he was tired of being pestered:

"Shut up, or should I tell you how you created the problem with the Temple dwellers for me?" The cat bore her teeth. "I have not trusted anyone for a long time and do not believe in the coincidence of such meetings. Thank the merger for the fact that I now treat you like family, but do not think of pushing me. Is that clear? Yet I am ready to be a good child if you detain Ania."

"Who?" Illusht retreated.

"The elf with copper hair."

"Oh, your female." The Miur pressed her ears to her head.

"Do not dare!" Andy hissed.

"Well, you gave your word. Hide in the second niche."

Before the "little sister," who had caught him in the trap of promising to be a good child, could change her mind, he slipped into the second niche from the portal frame and covered himself with all possible curtains.

Illyusht fulfilled her promise and managed to separate the elf from the retinue. The detachment, led by a dozen Miur, after passing Andy, who was hidden in his dark corner, disappeared into the arch of the spatial transition.

"Ania!" he grabbed the elf by the hand. She was hurrying to catch up with the others, and he only barely managed to block a knee to the groin with his leg. Illyusht wisely remained behind the turn. "Ania, it is me!" he shouted, intercepting a narrow knife with his hand.

"Andy?! Andy, do not." The sida closed her eyes and stopped struggling.

"Ania," Andy said in a wheezy voice and buried his face in her hair. "Why have you closed your eyes?" he asked, glancing at his beloved's face.

"I did what was forbidden, and I have been punished. I am no longer allowed to see you."

"What nonsense is that?"

"It is not nonsense. The princess punished me as one who has brought shame upon them by my relation…."

"You are foolish," Andy interrupted her. "You have not brought any shame to anyone, believe me."

"Ilirra thinks otherwise. It is not my place to judge her. I should obey. Andy, I have to go."

"Your Ilirra is a total idiot. She played the role of a servant and thought that no one would find her out. I do not care about her punishments or bans. Do you hear me?" He embraced Ania and kissed her on the lips passionately. The sida did not respond to the kiss. Salty tears streamed down her cheeks. "Go. I will find you, no matter where you are. My silver bloom blossoms only for you."

He let the elf go. Ania took three steps, sobbed, and turned around, never opening her eyes.

"I love you," she said and ran to the portal.

"You dragons really complicate things," Illusht said from around the corner. "You hide behind guises and create unnecessary problems. If you would tell her that you are a dragon, all would be simple."

"Ania is not a dragon."

"Who told you?"

"Dragons smell like flowers. Everyone has a unique scent."

"Yes, but sida who have undergone the Ritual do not smell. That is a strange characteristic, unique to them. Come on!" She pushed Andy, who was frozen in a stupor. "You did not know?"

"I did not know. I did not know, Targ!"

Illusht grabbed his hand and dragged him along. A few minutes later, they came to some room, where she handed him over to the hands of two roihe males with the order to pick up his clothes for the official reception, and then she evaporated, promising to return for the dressed guest in half an hour. Finally, the Miur added that a squire would come bearing his sword.

The male, who called himself Richt and sported fur of an attractive brindle color, led the guest through a whole suite of rooms in which hundreds of costumes for members of different races were neatly hung, in various sizes and for all occasions.

Suddenly, Richt stopped and started talking, as Andy thought at first, to himself, but then everything was made clear. A small kitten with fawn-colored fur came out from the pouch on his belly half-way and looked around curiously.

"Hello," Andy told the girl (it was a girl). She squeaked and dove back into the safe fold of skin. She did not hide for long. After about ten seconds, a small hand moved the edge of the pouch and stared at him with the dark beads of her eyes.

"Rio, sit still." Richt stroked the girl on the head. She lost interest in the strange creature and pressed her lips to the nipple concealed under the fold of skin and sweetly smacked. The male, holding the baby, waved to Andy as if to say "follow me." Andy stomped after Richt and compared the anatomy of females and males.

Roihe on average were shorter than females by about a head, much narrower in the shoulders and looked more slender. At the same time, the males had powerful leg muscles and a broad waist. This was because they had a pouch of skin on their stomachs like a kangaroo in which they carried kittens. During the merger, Andy obtained a lot of interesting information. It would seem useless cargo settled in his brain, but it helped out at the right moment.

The Miur were interesting in the very structure of their social order. The males did not dispute the matriarchy that had developed at the dawn of civilization. The females were larger and stronger; they played the role of hunters, warriors, and defenders of family, in their case prides. The slender and more delicate males, unable to fight on equal footing with even with the weakest representative of the fair sex, acted as educators of the younger generation. Why and how such conditions developed was a mystery covered in darkness and the harsh conditions of deep antiquity, but nature played a trick with the miur, rewarding them with the most complex biochemistry and the resulting relations between the sexes.

Unlike human women, whose possible sex was interrupted for natural reasons for several days a month, Miur females menstruated once every three months for three or four days. On these same days, with a sexual partner of the opposite sex, they could conceive and get pregnant. As for sex, he had seen some of the females wearing a pronounced pink color because the males only reacted to the females during the indicated three or four days a quarter. It would seem that was it, the role of the male was fulfilled, but then the cunning trick played by nature began. If during the coition the male partner was a roihe male, at the moment of conception, a biochemical mechanism triggered the growth of two lower pairs of mammary glands in the offspring, whether it was male or female. The glands in the males were hidden by a fold of skin. The hips and pelvis grew wider, and the fold of skin on the belly over thirty weeks of pregnancy turned into a real pouch. The male acquired characteristic "female" features.

Kittens, relative to the mother, were born small, from four and a half to about five and a half pounds in weight. Usually, one to four kittens were born per litter, with one male for every five or six females. Then the mothers had to decide whether to feed the offspring by themselves or to give them to the male's pouch. In females, the two lower pairs of nipples, as in the male upper pair, remained in a rudimentary state. Most often, the choice was a refusal to feed the young and to transfer the kittens to the father. Released from her squeaking load, the females immediately rushed to take advantage of another gift of Mother Nature and licked the white drops from the nipples of the roihe, thus freeing themselves from such a painful stage as the burning of milk in their own breasts. So nature divided them into female hunters and rare males. To say that the roihe were completely defenseless would be wrong. They ran so that cheetahs could only eat their dust, but this was the sole upside of their strong leg muscles.

Rasht males were also born among the Miur, who had no skin pouches on their bellies. One rasht was born for every ten or twelve roihe. The rasht were called "big brains" for good reason—these big-headed males kept all the cats' science. Big brains differed from females in their slightly reduced dimensions and physical strength, but larger skull size. They did not like fighting, but they were more flexible than females and on occasion, rasht became dangerous fighters. The commander of the detachment who accompanied Andy to the city was a rasht. Each big brain was valued at his weight in gold, and if the makings of a mage were discovered in him, he was truly prized. The boys were given the most first-class education by the Miur standards. The cats took full advantage of the big brains' natural tendency towards critical thinking and system analysis. They loved solving complex problems and searching for new discoveries. One time, the rasht, with a few females, had worked in the same laboratories as dragons, but those times were long passed. During this period they gained ground in scientific and technical fields over the other races of Nelita. To the good fortune of all the others, there were not as many big brains among the Miur as they themselves wanted.

If you look at the feline society through the prism of a simplified social structure, it looked like a bee swarm or an ant colony. The Great Mother took the queen's place, the simple females were politicians, soldiers, and workers, the roihe male played the role of the educators of the younger generation, and the rasht males were a separate superstructure that did not allow the nest to regress to a more primitive level. Often some of them got tied up in the field of politics, acting as advisers and reaching great heights. Great Mothers and females from high society took only rasht as husbands.

"Come," Richt bowed. "Allow me to choose a ceremonial sarun for you."

Why not? Go on, choose one. Richt bowed once more, snatched an information crystal from his pocket, inserted it into a groove in the wall, and led Andy to a white circle.

"Sir, please do not move, let the spell tie your size to the info-crystal database."

Wow! They have almost a computer system on the magic analyzers. Andy froze. An illusion emerged over the floor showing suitable suits hanging in rows and shoes lined up beneath them. Less than ten minutes later, dressed in a new outfit, he stomped back, stepping on the stone tiles in soft boots up to his knees. A sarun turned out to be a costume remotely reminiscent of Cossack clothing: a white shirt with a deep v-neck exposing his chest, loose trousers made of weightless spider silk and tucked into the boots, and a wide belt wrapped around the waist seven times. The belt was fastened with a scabbard for the rashag.

Next, he had to be fitted with the proper props. Richt spent a long time choosing a knife and a scabbard. He mustn't make a mistake; everyone paid attention to the rashag first of all! He must show the status of the owner and his position in society. The guest in the state "dressing room" was led there by Illusht herself, which meant a lot. Ordinary people don't drive an heiress to the throne by the handle. What did that imply? He must belong to the upper class, therefore, the scabbard should be blue, a heavenly color. And for closeness to the Great Mother, he must attach a red ribbon to the knife handle.

Richt dug for a long time. The result of his work would be a multi-colored sheath and a bouquet of ribbons. Andy was tired of the roihe's penchant for fashion and reminded him of the time. He limited himself to the blue scabbard and two thin ribbons of red and green on the handle of the knife.

Illusht was already waiting for them. She slapped Richt on the shoulder approvingly, appreciating his work. Having earned the gratitude of the daughter of the ruler, he literally shone with happiness.

"Why are there only two ribbons on the rashag?" she asked her one question. "Enough!" Andy cut her off.

The Miur looked him over again, pulled up the belt, straightened the knife and asked him to follow her. A young cat positioned herself behind Andy, carrying his sword on a special cushion.

* * *

The sounds of dozens of drums, large and small, some reminiscent of traditional Japanese taiko, filled the vaults of the large reception room. The roihe and the females, standing in rows, played a reassuring musical rhythm with lots of ligatures. Their glossy fur, aloof expressions and expressive movements complemented the drum sticks flickering in their hands. The wide, thin, silky sleeves of the roihes' dressing gowns danced with the colored ribbons tied to the females' forearms. The drums would sputter, then fall silent. The silence would immediately be broken by the sounds of the small drums from the first row. The music expressed the pitter-patter of rain, the noise of the wind, and the rustling of leaves. The pounding of hooves as a herd ran across the forest came from the second row. Heavenly thunder crashed; lightning bolts seemed to flash before their eyes; they rang giant tambourines, five feet in diameter.

Andy never would have thought that ancient musical instruments could capture the murmur of a creek and the sound of the wind, thunder, and thousands of familiar sounds. Leaning his elbows on the pillow, for the first time in a long time he really relaxed and enjoyed the virtuosic skill of the musicians. Using special brushes, some Miur voiced the waving of the wings of birds. The sticks touched the wide surface of the biggest drums weightlessly; the hum from the light touches made one's blood run faster. It seemed that rather than a drumbeat, he heard the pulse of his heart, beating in time to the rhythm.

The young Miur sitting behind him with a pillow on which his sword lay in the scabbard, throwing off her mask of equanimity, swung her head from side to side and bounced up and down in her spot.

The last fractional chord sounded and the drumming ceased. Dancers sailed slowly into the center of the hall as if hovering above the floor. Three dozen slender and flexible Miur with fur of a gentle blue color moved with a strange intermittent step. Each movement corresponded to the crystal chime of various tambourines or bells. A wave of right hand and the bracelets tinkled harmoniously; a turn with a slight wiggle of their hips and the merry chime of the bells tied to their belts intertwined itself into the dance. It was unbelievable. Andy did not sense any magic, but moving one's body in such a way, with such extreme control, was akin to real sorcery. It seemed incredible and inconceivable that they could ring exactly the intended bell, bracelet, or tambourine, and not some other one. Andy glanced to the right with just his eyeballs: he wasn't the only one taken away by the performance. The princess' retinue seated ten paces from him was also up to their ears in the music and dance pattern, the young squires with swords on their knees even more so.

According to an unwritten ancient tradition, guests were allowed to bring their personal swords with them, but were forbidden to touch them. The simple solution was that a young Miur squire was attached to each guest, who kept the invitee's sword on a special pillow. The guardian's place was behind the weapon's owner. It was a pity that Ania wasn't around; she was sitting next to the princess and the Great Mother on a high pedestal directly behind the princess' entourage. Ilirra was speaking about something with Asha, who periodically leaned towards the dragoness. Etiquette dictated that neither he nor the entourage was allowed to be near the crowned heads during official negotiations. Ania was seated on the pedestal as a translator and first advisor. As it turned out, she was completely fluent in the native language of the Miur. Ilirra insisted on her presence.

He managed once to exchange glances with the copper-haired sida and blow her a kiss when, accompanied by Illusht and Irissa, who bore his sword, he entered the hall. Who cared about etiquette? Illusht didn't see anything; she didn't have eyes in the back of her head. Irissa, whom he called Iris, snorted in her whiskers, but Ilirra did not like the air kisses. The dragoness' face stiffened. She said something to the girl and looked at the shkas angrily. Ania guiltily lowered her head and stared at the floor. She didn't look at Andy anymore. The pointy tips of the elf's ears glowed crimson. The princess pointed at a spot on the floor on her left. Ania bowed and moved to the new spot, her back to her boyfriend. The retinue pretended he didn't exist. The short rashag on his stomach did not impress them, which could not be said about Ilirra. She appreciated the knife and the color of the scabbard, but Ania stayed in her new spot.

While he was looking out for his sweetheart, the dancers with the bells flew off the dance stage. A holy place is never empty. Instead of the tailed girls fluttering over the floor, a new batch of cat people came out, clattering on the stone tiles with special metal claws on their toes. The light in the hall faded; the dance floor fell down five feet. Andy turned to Iris.

"Fire fever," the sword bearer tossed at him, smiling, her eyes flashing with excitement. Andy smiled. The cat was mentally among the dancers.

"Hey!" The impact of metal claws on the floor caused sheaves of bright sparks. A minute later, his former skepticism was gone without a trace. It really was an extravaganza with a capital "E." If it weren't for the alien surroundings and the absence of any ties with the Earth for the cats, it could be assumed that they are dancing an Irish jig, performing complicated geometric steps to the fervent music, but also knocking out sparks from their feet and periodically shouting "hey." The incredible movements of the dance were supplemented by the different colors of sparkling flame that burst from under the Miur's feet.

The platform gradually rose upward. New characters appeared from the darkened aisles. Iris squeaked enthusiastically.

"What?"

"Spellcasters of the elements! The sword dance!" The ecstatic brilliance of the Miur's eyes was replaced by a fanatical fire.

An unpleasant premonition tugged painfully at his heart....

* * *

"Are there supposed to be elementals now?" Ashlat asked her sister.

"Yes," answered Illusht.

"I know, but look, half of the dancers are from the Temple dwellers. There they go doing their own thing again."

"It is not good. Tell the guard and warn mother. I will go to the guard, then move closer to the dragons."

"To the dragons or to the dragon?"

A new action unfolded on the stage. The dark stone of the floor grew scalding hot....

What the sword-wielding Miur did on stage was indescribable. The only accompaniment to the dance was the enthusiastic screams of spectators and the clinking of colliding deadly steel.

The intricate swordplay between groups of dancers caused various elements to come to life. During the first theatrical duel, two huge Miur with red belts called upon the element of fire. The stone of the stage was heated; it glowed with unbearable heat, but the artists did not notice the elements, continuing to tread on the floor with bare heels. Then there was air. The swords' sweeping caused small whirlwinds. Sharp gusts of wind knocked over tall crystal glasses and waved the spectators' clothes. Earth and water followed air.

Then the cat people lined up around and led a bristling steel dance. It seemed impossible to survive among the blades, but none of the dancers was even wounded.

The dragons did not hold back their feelings and hooted at the top of their voices. Andy tried not to succumb to the general frenzy but more and more often caught himself thinking that he wanted to be there, on stage, with a sword in his hand, so fascinated he was by the skill of the spellcasters.

Suddenly, one of the fire spellcasters left the dueling and

stopped right in front of him. The tips of her twin swords rested against his throat. Iris said something inarticulate. Andy felt the handle of his blade slip into his hand.

"Take your sword, you are being summoned into the dance!" the squire ardently whispered. He drew the elven blade from its scabbard and followed the topless giant.

The fatal circle dance drew him into its depth. In the center of the circle, a sea of strength splashed. Andy was seized by real euphoria. He was intoxicated by the energies poured into him by the Miur. He did a strange dance, attacked, retreated, and again attacked. But he was sure of one thing: the steel in his hand would not hurt, hit, or wound anyone today, just as the swords of the others could not harm him. If they did, it would be the greatest blasphemy. The dancers wielded the elements; he was the element!

The Miur increased the tempo. Ha, he could go faster! The cat people turned to their own familiar tribal elements. *What, they don't sense that I absorb them all, Fire, Earth, Water, and Air? I live in and through them. I am the fire!* Lightness filled his body; it was flying away, a full retreat! It was a circle dance of steel, a dance of Death, a dance of Life, a dance dedicated to Manyfaces and the Twins. In the wave of excitement, Andy did not understand how he slid into the astral. From the floor rose fifteen-foot high flames and covered him head to toe. The world exploded with a kaleidoscope of colors. With his entrance to the astral, there was a sense of integrity which he had not experienced for nearly two months, and then a sense of danger cut through his nerves. He did not take off his shields. Constant control kept the body from an uncontrolled change in hypostasis, but energy poured into the world.

At some point, the insanity stopped; the huge flames fell, and he locked eyes with the Eldest priestess sitting at the very end of the hall. Triumph fluttered in the old cat woman's eyes. She had achieved her goal. The dance was a trap! No. By an effort of will, Andy was able to shield himself from the ocean of energy, but at that moment, he had to remove some of the shields; it was impossible to control all the many parameters at once. The celebration in the priestess' gaze was replaced by anger and confusion. A dull pain cut his left shoulder....

Guards with full-length shields filled the hall. They fell

upon Andy. He lost consciousness….

Nelita. Celestial Empire. The Celestial palace...

"She is here." Hazgar grabbed his left shoulder. "The foul creature…."

"Who is, father?"

But the dragon paid no heed to the question. He rubbed his left shoulder and looked at his son pensively.

"You did not feel anything?"

"A slight prick in my left shoulder."

"Pup, how can you call yourself my son if you cannot put two and two together? That slight prick means that she is here, alive and unharmed!"

"Who are you talking about, father?"

"Your cousin, Jagirra." Hazgar was thinking about something. His son did not want to interrupt his train of thought. "I know where she is. Go, get ready to take the troops. She will not escape from me again."

Part 3. Three Wars.

Russia. N-ville.

"Mehdi, wake up!" shouted Chuiko. "Carefully now. Apply the load with short impulses; otherwise, we might get kicked out again. God forbid that the load be dumped."

"You're preachin' to the choir," the Indian replied without an accent, bit a pencil between her teeth, and lightly touched the joystick. "Vitya, smoothly raise the pressure on the exterior. Countdown!"

"Ten, nine, eight... one, we have a visual! Oh, great. The orcs raised the dead into zombies again! Those freaks," the voice of the invisible Vitya sounded in the earpiece.

The camera captured the burning city suburbs, besieged by the huge army of green orcs. Thousands and thousands of living dead raised by the orc mages and shamans stepped awkwardly, resembling a destructive mudslide. They moved through the ruins of houses towards the city walls. An endless column of undead marched along a pontoon bridge across a wide river. On their backs, the zombies carried bags and baskets of sand and ladders. The last rows of ghouls were hugging sealed pots and gleaming light-colored cobblestones. The wave of living dead didn't seem to notice the fire directed at it from the city walls. No fireballs, arrows, moats, or explosions of magical mines, nor dozens of other gadgets and spells tearing the bodies into pieces, turning them into black fried pieces of flesh, could not stop the dead army. The earth was covered with greasy ash and lined with a foul carpet of rotting flesh left from past unsuccessful assaults. The pits and moats that appeared before the dead could not stop the offensive onslaught. The bodies fell down and filled the moats; the next wave treaded on them, continuing with unrelenting force approaching the brick walls. The bodies of the corpses torn to pieces twitched and convulsed for a long time; only those who lost their heads fell dead. Carts with the shamans on them moved behind the army of zombies. The green-faced and gray-skinned orcs from the besieging camp could afford not to be stingy when it came to zombies. They brought tens of thousands of captured humans and their gray-skinned tribesmen with them.

Many scientists couldn't sleep for several days afterwards, having witnessed the bloody ritual of turning the living into the undead. The most terrible thing was, the orcs were helped by human mages....

Defenders of the city stood on the walls, tired and exhausted by the continuous assault. The city was also subject to massive magical bombardment. But the shields the mages constructed still held up against the fiery ramparts, blurring with bright flashes of beautiful but deadly fireworks. Teams of weapons bearers dexterously manned magical machines. In addition to them, numerous lifting mechanisms were assembling devices resembling satellite dishes that shot something like lasers. The city's combat mages conjured upwind and dispersed the smoke. The released hundreds of griffons and ride-on winged lizards into the sky, reminiscent of dragons. The bombing of the besiegers' camp began. In response, a magical "zenith" cover was activated. Over the camp, luminous domes popped up all around. Fire flashed in the sky as the power traps went off, turning the griffons and their riders into bloody stuffing.

* * *

Leaning back against the wall, Iliya looked at the Indian scientist and pondered. Someone once told him that the intellectual center of America is located in Delhi. After working with the Indian for two months, Kerimov was ready to agree with this statement. If there were more than a dozen people in India like her, the other countries would soon be helpless to do anything but look sadly at the red lights of the locomotive of Indian science heading off into the future.

Mehdi Shrestha got into the closed scientific center thanks

to the patronage of Iliya's old acquaintance and school friend, the linguist.

Kopilov, who followed the advice of the "authorities" and gave his consent to cooperation, received a spacious office on the negative-seventh level of the underground complex and a dozen subordinates, simply could not come up with a result that would satisfy the scientists and the military. Faced with the difficulties of mastering a foreign language with no dictionaries or primary sources, he remembered a young woman he met a couple of years ago at a symposium in Rome. According to Kopilov, if anyone could find the key to the language of the inhabitants of the other world without any computer programs, it would be this linguist-polyglot. Command, which was against attracting foreign experts to secret research, scratched their heads and decided to take a chance. So, Kopilov and a couple of his young "referents" went on a business trip to the southern countries.

Mehdi agreed to work under the guidance of her Russian colleague. Perhaps, it was because he showed her photos of ancient books with an unknown writing system, "found," so they said, by Kopilov's colleagues in the remote taiga of snow-covered Siberia. Or perhaps, it was a handsome secretary, who enchanted the Indian with his sky-blue eyes, child-like smile, and charming dimples. The fact that the inhabitant of the Hindustan Peninsula put a lot of effort into getting Valentin's attention said a lot in favor of the second version. The psychologists participating in the operation who compiled the new member's psychological portrait were rubbing their hands in satisfaction: Valentin did not disappoint.

So, a foreign visitor came to Russia when spring streams were running through the streets of the snow-covered state. And a woman no less, who agreed to work in a mostly male environment in the very patriarchal country. The thirty-year-old Indian, who spoke seven languages, including Russian, beautifully, was very surprised by the rapid flight from Moscow to the Siberia. It seemed to her that the distances in the northern state were much greater. Imagine her surprise when Kopilov, who had invited the guest to a bite, in a very private conversation accompanying a light breakfast, introduced her to the director of the closed scientific institution.

Iliya liked Mehdi at first sight. There was something about the young woman that made him believe what Kopilov said about her. Medium height, pudgy, with long, blue-black hair hanging in a braid down her back, the Hindu's black eyes had a piercing gaze in which one could easily read a powerful intellect. She dressed in saris and shalwar suits while the weather permitted. She instantly linked the name Kerimov with the publications that were appearing in the press and the incessant conversations about the Russians opening a passage into a parallel world. Developing a cover operation, the state "office," under whose patronage Iliya now had to work, had made him a public figure.

The Russian "guarantor's" negotiations with the premier ministers of India, China, and Japan were successful. The foreign rulers were impressed by what they saw, and all expressed a desire to start a construction by Russian engineers of portals on their territory as soon as possible. Funding would not be a problem.

Mehdi immediately understood that there were several worlds, not just one, as they wrote in the foreign press and as the culprits themselves claimed. If Russian colleagues had invited her by such roundabout paths, that meant there was a lot of work to be done, and it was not intended for just anyone's eyes and ears. She also realized that anyone who agreed to such a tempting offer should understand that there would be no way back. Since they didn't ask her permission, but rather simply chocked it up to the fact, she understood she had little choice. The real bosses of the group headed by Kerimov were pragmatic people and wouldn't take no for an answer. If there was a need for her humble person, okay then…. To put it plainly, anyone who refused the tempting offer after learning what it was all about would return home feet-first, and she felt a strong desire to live. Summarizing all of the above, she agreed, but with one small condition. The "condition," sipping coffee at a neighboring table, was not against working as an assistant to a foreign scientist, all the more so since the authorities wanted it that way. Fast forward a little: a month and a half later, the third group, the one developing the foreign "virgin territory," celebrated a merry wedding, which was not at all messed up by the restrictions in the form of the complex walls and secrecy.

It should be said that Shrestha turned out to be the straw

that broke the camel's back. The collective of philologists and linguists she led did the impossible. The scientists worked day and night. Mountains of materials and videotapes were analyzed. Four weeks later, a translator program was presented to the scientific council. They proposed attempting to decipher the speech and writing of the main language of Ilanta, called Alat.

Once she completed the main work on the magical world, the Hindu immediately re-directed the team to work with the block of high-tech worlds, but Ilanta remained her main love after Valentin, who, by the way, proved to be an excellent technical expert on power plants. Mehdi never acquired a love of the worlds with advanced technology. She was given strictly metered information and was allowed to preside during the opening of the "windows" in rare cases only, unlike when they were opened onto Ilanta. Mehdi understood that the Russians, while remaining behind an invisible border, were brazenly stealing other people's achievements. She had free access to television, and it seemed strange to her that a pair of news channels flashed a message about the imminent start of construction in the Nizhny Novgorod, Ivanovo, and Amur regions of factories focused on the production of high-tech household appliances and computer components. The Russians had never bothered with that nonsense, and all of a sudden they were popping up everywhere. The deadline for the completion and launch of the factories was just eighteen months from now. It was clear as day that they'd gotten their hands on other-worldly technology, which was allowing them to become leaders in many fields. They had successfully extorted money from Japan and China for their backlog and were preparing to connect the milking machine to the "Indian sacred cow." All her conclusions were based on information lying on the surface, but how many gigabytes and terabytes were hidden on the bottom of the sea?

From the very first day, the Hindu literally lived and breathed the world of Ilanta. Her eyes lit up with fanatical splendor every time they opened the "window." For less than a month, despite her position and foreign origin, she had already several times sent requests to command to be included in a group of training "parallel astronauts." The papers remained unanswered; the leadership did not hurry to let one of the best personnel go.

However, it made certain concessions, and by their carelessness inadvertently did Paul Chuiko a bad turn. Once she received permission and a pass for access to the group three operator's room, Mehdi often came to the "launches" into the magical world, into which the son of the deeply respected Iliya Kerimov had the misfortune of transferring. But simple contemplation was not enough for her. Her restless nature longed for action. For a long time, Shrestha carpeted the floor of Chuiko's office with requests to entrust her with the second operator's chair, arguing that she needed something to do besides correct errors in computer translation. Paul's response that management was required to pass a certification and without the approval of the higher-ups, he couldn't allow the outsider to manage complex equipment went in one Indian ear and out the other. She demanded an examination, during which she showed excellent knowledge in the fields of nuclear physics and chemistry. She'd been on a first-name basis with computers for fifteen years. Soon the fortress of command, with the sweeping signatures of a long line of officials and custodians of state secrets, surrendered and put up the white flag: Mehdi received the coveted chair and a control panel. Along with the panel, she received full admission to the third group's work and signed a pile of papers, in which she was informed in bold print and no uncertain terms what would happen in case of violation of the requirements specified therein. The newly-baked operator then learned that everything was not so rosy in the magical world.

All Chuiko's doubts about whether he'd done the right thing were dispelled by Iliya. Kerimov felt inwardly that the new operator was capable of surprising the leadership more than once and hastened to reassure his former subordinate. His feelings did not deceive him. During her third launch in the role of the second operator, Mehdi discovered an anomalous zone in the mountains known as the southern Rocky Ridge. Approaching it, even in observation mode, caused a load dumping. She suggested that the "zone" was a man-made formation. Further studies confirmed this. The "zone" was a shield, an obstacle preventing the building of subspace portals.

To study the phenomenon in the mountains, they opened a

gate and released several long-range drones, which headed south. The drones, packed with scientific equipment, filmed and photographed dozens of characteristics and returned. The data obtained allowed the second group, which dealt with direct hyperspace transitions, to create effective barriers against unauthorized portal openings. Mehdi earned her second thank you.

The restless member of the third group proposed organizing a permanent tracking point on some educational institution of magical orientation. There were no objections, and a week later, a thin black folder and an 8-gigabyte flash drive containing information on the so-called reference points on the planetary surfaces in which the most favorable conditions for creating stationary portals are present was laid on Kerimov's desk. In addition to the dry formulas, figures and conclusions that emerged from the "Bandar-log stomping grounds" of the second and third scientific groups, several educational lectures were recorded on a digital medium, which were given by researchers in the magical school of a foreign city called Orten. The video was accompanied by subtitles with a translation.

The resulting materials produced the effect of a bomb. On their basis, Alex compiled and provided mathematical proof that the directions of the opening of a subspace portal could be tracked. Remezov poured gasoline onto the fire. He defended the hypothesis that the residual radiation or track could be determined when a particular portal was opened.

Passions in the academic environment ran high. Half the staff almost lost their heads. If the regime had been slightly more lenient, the thing could have escalated to fist fights, but for now it included only screaming, swearing, name-calling, and a headache for the main boss. The major general did not show up to meetings of the scientific council without a bottle of aspirin. To test all the crazy hypotheses, several express expeditions were formed to the Atlantic, the Mediterranean, and the north of Russia. The results of the fieldwork stunned many. All the old sailors' tales about dog-headed people no longer seemed like fiction or a fairy tale. Homer's immortal "Iliad" was painted with new colors, and the tale of Atlantis was perceived in a completely different way. Many conclusions were drawn from the results, the main one being that several thousand years ago, inter-world portals were open on Earth. What caused their opening and closing remained to be seen, but the information fascinated all and alarmed many, first of all, the military. The third group was ordered to reorient towards studying military conflicts with the use of magic. The generals decided to study the experience of others in detail.

Iliya Evgenevich was quietly rejoicing at the decision, hoping that the researchers would be able to get on Andy's trail. Olga, who, after the memorable "launch" fell into a strange prostration and apathy, gradually came to her senses. His daughter did not talk in her sleep for more than two weeks, was pale and ate practically nothing. A week ago, getting up in the middle of the night to go to the bathroom, he heard a whisper coming from Olga's room in an unknown language. Iliya went to the kitchen and sat down and rubbed his eyes, relieved. Funny thing, life: the conversations that scared him earlier were now perceived as a sign of some kind of normalization and recovery. The next morning, Olga was eating an omelet prepared by her mother and went to school in high spirits.

Without delaying the matter, that morning Kerimov phoned the major general and asked to meet. Leonid Vladimirovich was very surprised at the scientist's actions and asked first of all for an explanation. He did not like ambiguities. The box holding the secret was opened simply: the scientist demanded to be shown the latest data of the group that was watching his daughter. Kerimov did not believe that the state security had removed surveillance. And he was right: the remote observations did not stop day or night. After the initial meeting, the general asked for a timeout until 17:00.

By five o'clock in the afternoon, a short report with a dozen photos attached was ready. The specialists' general estimation on the supernatural was that the younger Kerimov was cut off from certain energy sources. The photographs of the strongly faded aura indirectly confirmed this hypothesis. Recently the dynamics had reversed. The girl's aura was gradually recovering. Five of the photos clearly demonstrated improvements. Meanwhile, the psychics involved in the project noted the child's growth potential.

225

If before, she had been "drinking" energy indirectly, now Olga was replenishing her losses herself. Two color photos with circles and arrows indicating characteristic changes in the girl's external energy field were attached. It could be said that a sharp break in the external power-up initiated a certain qualitative leap, and the renewed connection spurred the recent changes. Iliya Evgenevich, after reading through the rubbish on the paper, asked for oral explanations. The psychic invited by the general looked at Kerimov, shrugged his shoulders, and explained his conclusions in plain Russian.

First, the psychic reminded him that he and his colleagues assume a certain connection between Olga with Andy. Kerimov nodded; he had not forgotten the major general's revelations. So, for a while, the relationship had become thinned out or disappeared. The chief of state security and the chief of science exchanged glances. Both gray-haired men recalled the memorable opening of the "window" and the short assertion: "there," with the child's finger pointing at the planet emerging from behind the clouds. The disconnection had a negative impact on the, um, child's health... (The psychic cast a quick glance at the general's guest.) ...And Olga had to look for ways to fill the loss, because.... Here the supernatural "charlatan" hesitated, twirled his fingers in the air, and said that it was impossible to explain the phenomenon in simple words and that the guesses and conjecture that were spinning in his head were simply inexpressible. In short, Olga had found a different way to restore her energy. How did the experts determine that the daughter was once again connected with Andy? The "specialist" took the photos of the auras and outlined a certain area in pencil as if to say, the color scale in this area corresponds to the observation data up to the sad moment the external connection broke off, which allowed them to draw the appropriate conclusions. With no more questions, Iliya thanked his colleague. The psychic quickly said goodbye and left the office.

The conversation left an unpleasant aftertaste. The invited "miracle-worker" clearly feared Kerimov and hardly concealed his feelings. Iliya folded the photos into a folder and set it on the general's desk.

"Iliya, do you have any other questions?" the major general asked sympathetically.

"No, Leonid Vladimirovich, no questions. Perhaps, a couple of thoughts are running around in my brain, but I couldn't rightly call them questions."

"What thoughts?"

Kerimov put his broad palm on the folder with the documents, held it for a couple of seconds, then pushed the papers forward to the general.

"Do you think I believe this lie?" The general smiled sadly. "No, no, there is truth in it, but not the whole truth, and not just the truth. And your psychic, the 'soul conjurer,' only called up doubts about Olga and in a strange way about myself. I could feel his fear physically. What the hell is going on?"

"I assumed something like that," replied the general, turning to the window. "I will be frank with you. They, psychics, are afraid of the changes taking place in your daughter and in you."

"What?!"

"You heard me, and you understand me. Dammit, Kerimov, don't play the fool. Olga is affecting you somehow."

"You said something about changes?"

"Alright," the almighty general's shoulders drooped. "You asked for it. The photographs you've just seen are fake. Olga's real aura, according to the 'soul conjurer,' is not human. Do you understand now? I reinforced the group; now there's 24-hour surveillance on your daughter. In case of unforeseen excess, I will have to isolate her, but I sincerely hope it won't come to that. Now for your unforgettable person. According to recent observations, on your aura there's an intense glow that allegedly speaks to the discovery of extrasensory abilities. You felt someone else's fear and separated the truth from the lies. Do you understand, Iliya, that you're becoming a dangerous person? I can keep the secret for now, but as soon as it gets out, they'll come after you for real. I'm not kidding."

"Is that an offer?" Kerimov asked, after a moment's reflection. "My loyalty and obedience for your silence?"

"Oh God, Iliya! What do I need your loyalty and obedience for?! Can you even hear me? Please put two and two together, finally, will you? Last time we talked, I told you about the influence of the other world. Let me say it again: the other world has penetrated into our dimension, and your family has become the vehicle for the changes it initiates. What do you think, what actions should I take?"

"I see; thank you for your frankness. I have a lot to think about."

"Please, if it's not too difficult, let me in on your enlightening thoughts. If you come up with something, let me know. That's not an order. It's a simple human request. Maybe our thoughts will converge, or your decision will allow us to solve the problem. No matter the benefits it might promise, it's still a problem."

After their conversation a week ago, Iliya spent the whole day feeling frustrated. He was mostly upset by what the general left unsaid. His son was influencing his younger sister. What then was the youngest Kerimov? If Olga wasn't human, what was Andy? Was Olga turning into a mage? Didn't the general himself say they were fantastically lucky that Andy is a mage and was able to integrate into the local society beautifully? And now there was a note of panic in his voice, and he was throwing up his hands helplessly. He seemed deliberately obscure. If only he could find out what kind of game the secret services were playing, what buttons they were pressing in his soul and what they were trying to achieve. After a while, the conversation with the general seemed more and more like a theatrical performance. All the world's a stage....

Iliya looked at Mehdi and reflected on the vicissitudes of fate. The Hindu had said more than once that she would gladly leave this old Earth and move to a secluded world, and that only Valentine was keeping her from such a rash step. Or she might even take Valentine with her. Mehdi was not afraid of the war that broke out in the north and east of the largest continent of Ilanta. Full of optimism, she firmly believed in the existence of calm, quiet, peaceful corners with untouched nature and a lack of civilization. Kerimov wanted to believe, but the madness on the screen made his heart sink. Scientists could not get to the bottom of the causes of the war. They got the impression that everyone took up arms against one another and staged mass slaughter with the use of magic. In the north of the continent, humans fought against the green orcs and the gray-skinned orcs that joined them. The same humans, having overcome the steppes and mountains, besieged the fortresses of white-haired elves and short people with luminous hair. A huge army of northerners fought their way inland. The green orcs, fleeing from the north, destroyed everything in their path. They left only dead, scorched earth behind them, and every settlement they crossed was wiped out down to the last cat. In the east of the continent, the white orc armies were loaded onto ships and sent to capture large islands two hundred miles from their shores. During one of the last "launches," scientists recorded on the cameras a real amphibious operation with the use of carrier-based aircraft consisting of large griffons. Hundreds of griffons with riders on their backs soared into the sky and headed west. Strange pieces of wood were tied to the magical creatures' saddles, which turned out to be magical torpedoes. The universe can joke: in the fairy-tale world, a battle was unfolding, an analog of Earth's Pearl Harbor. The "torpedoes" thrown by the griffons successfully reached the huge rowing vessels standing in rows in the vast harbor. In only twenty minutes, all that was left of the navy fleet, caught unawares, were the tops of masts protruding from the water and a bunch of wooden debris floating on the surface of the sea. The landing troops that came with the half-birds finished the job.

If not for the war, Iliya would have found his son and handed Olga over to him. No matter how scary it was for him to admit it to himself, his daughter did not belong on Earth. He could indulge in self-deception and illusions about a peaceful life, but the circle of political war closing in on his discovery was invisible only to the blind. The two world wars that raged in the last century served as a reminder, by their millions of victims, of the fact that one wrong political decision or word was the difference between political battles and combat. How long could those in power continue to balance on the brink? From the realization that Pandora's box was open to him too, things became even more terrible. The secret service put him on the front line and actively turned him into a public figure, presenting him to the world as a genius, looking beyond the horizon. But beyond the horizon was the emptiness that settled in the soul.

Mehdi was right. She was absolutely correct in her efforts to be sent into the unexplored world.... If Olga could help him find Andy, then Iliya would send her to him. The problems she was going through needed solving. That would be the best way....

Nelita. Miur territory on the border with the Principality of Ora.

"Where are we going?" Ania asked the tall, well-built Miur.

The cat laid aside her sword, which she was polishing with a special stone, and looked at the elf of the princess' retinue with the piercing gaze of her green eyes.

"The shortest road to your prince lies through the gorge of Singing Waters."

The cat woman wanted to add something else, but changed her mind. Turning away from the retinue, she continued polishing. What, Ania wondered, did the Miur use blades for in their skirmishes with the orcs? They wanted to show daring and strength? Stupid. Every feline who accompanied the small caravan of the princess and the Great Mother's ambassador had magic holsters attached to her thigh for fire-starters. Two mighty Miurs carried heavy gunners, one shot of which left a deep funnel in the ground up to fifteen feet in diameter. In a short battle with the imperial mercenaries that appeared on the path, not one warrior took advantage of the technical superiority of the weapons. Their masking armor was more than enough. The orcs, who did not expect a scanty bunch of elves and humans to be covered by a dozen "ghosts" of the ruler of the Miur's personal guard, paid dearly for disrespecting the borders. The "ghosts" seized the three dozen fanged creatures from both sides and immediately chopped the enemies into cabbage. It's tough to fight with a blurred spot that is not detected by true vision and against which search amulets refuse to work. After a twenty seconds or so, the sound of clanging metal ceased; the Miur removed the camouflage and finished the wounded robbers who inadvertently decided they could cash in on what might be going on in the borderlands. Two cats dragged the deafened orc commander into the bushes. Loud cries that made the birds fly from the branches and get as far as possible from the terrible place testified to the prisoner's cruel interrogation. The warrior who covered the dragons pricked her ears and listened to what was happening fifty yards from the camp. Her tail twitched from side to side, but the stone that stroked the blue steel did not stop. The cries soon fell silent. The sudden silence led to two possible scenarios: the prisoner could no longer tolerate the torture and the breaking of his will by the cat mages and went to Manyfaces' palaces, or his tongue was untied and, having gained the necessary information, the felines bashed his brains in. The second was more plausible.

"He started singing, my blue-winged dove." The Miur resumed grinding her sword. Ania said nothing. She did not want to fall into the claws of the "kitties." They could make even dragons talk. They would soon find out why in the world there were mercenaries roaming about the foothills.

They did not have to wait long. The bushes swayed. Parting the thorny branches with her hand, the warrior who had interrogated the orc stepped onto the field.

"Let us go, quickly!" She said and ran towards the way out of the gorge.

"What is happening?" Ania rushed after the Miur.

"In half an hour, an orc regiment will be here. I reported it to the external guard. The general alarm has been declared in the cities."

"What regiment? That is…," Ania was dumbfounded.

"War." The cat woman stopped. "The emperor gave the command to attack. The mobile orc divisions have invaded the far Border and are attempting to cover the roads and caravan trails. All the air platforms and griffons are lost. We ran into the scouts they sent ahead. Pray to Manyfaces that our shields will not allow Hazgar to build portals. Otherwise, his legions would have already attacked the Principality, but even so, we do not have long to wait. Before I cut his throat, the orc told of the huge camouflaged military camps that have been destroyed in the last twenty four

231

hours on the border. The imperial generals will strike at any moment." The Miur stopped speaking suddenly and listened to the quiet whisper coming from the communicator amulet in her helmet. She turned towards her partner, who had already put the stone away and began rubbing the blade with a velvet cloth. "Anrisha, your three will remain to cover the virk."

"I understand," Anrisha said, throwing her sword into her scabbard. The feline took a piece of wood of unknown purpose from her backpack and attached it to the fire-starter. The resulting device most closely resembled a thick fire iron with two handles, but it strangely looked much more deadly than before. "You have got it coming to you, white-furred fool, for starting trouble with the priestess," the re-armed captain of the three warriors muttered quietly, under her breath, and with thinly concealed spite and a strong taste of despair and regret in her voice. But the elf heard the foul words. "Hazgar found me immediately. Not one day passed after he sensed that tattoo, and already we're in for it."

Ania was afraid to miss a single word of the guard's muttering. This Miur probably knew the reason for the commotion during the reception. Perhaps, it was connected to the emperor's reasons for his recent actions?

"Wake up, listen up." The shout interrupted the elf's train of thought. "Tell your kinsfolk to drop all their luggage and get to the stationary portal as soon as possible. We will travel light. Like a fly!" Anrisha's yellow eyes flashed with an angry fire.

Ania, as if she'd gotten a kick in the butt, dashed towards the princess' entourage, which was resting in the shade of the Mellornys. The commander of the military threesome of "ghosts" ran after her. War. The cat woman was telling the truth. It was not a subject people generally lied about. Oh, Manyfaces, why now? Why?

Nelita. Lidar Mountain. The miur city under the mountain. One day earlier…

His eyes did not want to open. The colors of the awakened elements still danced in them. Andy could hardly restrain the whirlwind raging inside, consisting of a fierce flame, a roaring wind that turned into sharp knives of ice water, and grains of sand that tore at his skin. Returning from nothingness, the golden dragon actively absorbed surplus energy, redirecting it to the astral.

Andy did not understand how he fell into the clever trap. The spellcaster infested his mana and somehow tore off the outer shields. Immersed in the euphoria of the warlike dance, maneuvering between the flames, he didn't notice the red-hot stone beneath his feet or the manipulation of the Temple dwellers near him. A single glance from the old hag sobered him up in an instant, just like a tub of cold water. The ruler's personal guards rushed into the hall, instantly lined up around the "dance floor" and separated him with high full-length shields from the perplexed guests. Two dozen Miur armed with gunners cut the Eldest priestess off from the blocked exits. The "jammers," which were turned up to their highest power level, coupled with the mana absorbers, hit his nerves—hard. It was too late to do anything about it. With the impression made on him by the return of the virtual golden dragon and the entirety of his self-awareness, Andy temporarily relinquished control and immediately received a painful injection into his left shoulder. A whole bunch of other people's feelings fell on him, including surprise, mean-spirited rejoicing, contempt, and disgust, as if someone saw a cockroach in front of him. The scariest and strangest thing was, Andy felt a family tie to the creature that hated him. The contact lasted no more than a couple of seconds, but, realizing that the relative posed a serious danger, he broke off the connection, all the more so because he needed to calm the raging storm of energy. The destructive power of the elements and the boundless power of the astral did not escape from him, but the struggle with himself took its toll. Unable to withstand the heavy weight, his legs buckled. Andy collapsed on his back; someone's hands immediately picked him up and took him somewhere. He didn't care, as long as he could pacify the whirlwind inside himself and not allow his shields to be shattered.

"How is he?" A familiar silky voice sounded louder than a tambourine. It caused hundreds of bright flashes in his head, which tinged his head and temples with pain.

"He is waking up," a second, unfamiliar voice answered.

"As soon as he is himself, call me. Illusht, you stay with Andy. I am going to the ballroom."

Asha... the Great Mother.

From the depths of his memory emerged one of the last images captured at the reception: dressed in a cloak sewn from real gold threads, the Miur with snow-white hair looked triumphantly behind him, and behind him the guard surrounded the Eldest priestess. The rest of the Temple dwellers were pressed to the walls by oblong shields. The guard.... The elite fighters could not have broken into the reception hall unless they were given appropriate orders in advance and placed in hidden rooms, shielded from the magical scan.

"Why?" His wayward lips uttered of their own accord. Andy opened his eyes.

The Miur leader, who had taken a few steps toward the door, returned and walked up to him.

"Leave us," Asha ordered her subordinates.

There was the rustle of clothes, the ringing of bracelets, and the soft feline footsteps. The room was instantly empty. The slammed door and a powerful canopy of silence prevented any eavesdropping. There were three of them in the room; the order to get out did not apply to Illusht.

"What did you tell the old woman?" Andy asked, barely managing to use his swollen tongue.

"That is a strange question. Do you really need to know?"
That darn cat has a way of conducting conversations!

"That is what I thought," Andy uttered. His headache subsided, clearing up room for rational thoughts. "I should have guessed about your trickery earlier. There are no coincidences. You purposely arranged the Temple dwellers to come in to your office during our meeting, and then gave her some wrong information, thereby forcing her to act imprudently. Tell me I am wrong." Andy turned away from his "sister." He felt dreary; once again he'd become a political pawn. With his unwitting help, they cleaned out an unwanted, dangerous competitor. It was disgusting that he was the one who gave the "sisters" a deck of trumps. The old priestess recognized him as the bearer of the "key." Asha had only to push the competitor towards the decision she needed, and she did not miss her chance.

"I had to." Her voice was made of steel.

"What would have happened if I had not been able to restrain myself? Do you think you have won? It is an empty victory, I declare."

"I believed in you. The Eldest had been preparing a dirty trick for a long time now. The reception was the perfect opportunity for her to strike. The priestesses needed war. They thought that if they got rid of the ruler and her daughter, ancient oaths would no longer be binding. They accumulated a great power under Mount Lidar, which will enable us to bring down the empire."

Andy, overcoming his headache, stood up from the cot. The mother and the daughter carefully watched his every move.

"Did the priestesses have a reason to think so?"

"They had and have a reason. But toppling the empire is not within our power. What did you mean about an empty victory?"

Andy briefly told them about an ancient Earth king who beat the Roman army. The king won the battle but lost the war. The victory bled him dry, and the Romans still had more than one legion they could pit against him. While he was telling the Earthly story, his brain was laying out the information received in the course of the short conversation. He realized the cat people had a destructive weapon. Apparently, knowing they had the deadly power in their corner, a pride of the highest nobility and Manyfaces' matriarchs decided to act contrary to the will of the Great Mother. "They needed war." Apparently, that was her political party's goal. Well, they had achieved their goal. The old hag's true motivation was now clear: she took aim at the ruling family and strange guest, who smelled like a dragon from a mile away. The high priestess wanted to unmask Andy, revealing his essence, to trigger the start of the war, if not from their side, then to provoke an attack from the empire. The Miur would have no choice but to defend themselves against a full-scale invasion. The wrinkled feline came to certain conclusions and played all-in, the clever cat, calculated the opposite side's actions and one-upped the ruler. Asha, confident of victory, wholeheartedly trying to discredit the spiritual leader, admitted the spellcasters to the hall. Her faith in Jaga's son, however cavalier, was justified. He was able to withstand the awakened elements and the astral, but, despite her arrest, the other Miur won.

"Apparently, the Eldest thought otherwise. The old cat got what she wanted. The emperor will march on Mount Lidar and the Principality of Ora."

"I do not think so," Illusht entered the conversation. "What…"

"You should have thought first!" Andy rudely interrupted his "sister." "By failing to think of the evil that could be done, you handed your tailed rear ends to the emperor. Now think about the good you have done and be satisfied. I have been discovered!"

"No one noticed anything. You were covered with a fire that masks auras. Then the 'jammers' kicked in," Illusht said calmly. Asha glared at her daughter and touched her ritual knife with her right hand. The Great Mother got seriously upset. She began to feverishly piece together the recent events.

Andy opened his shirt and showed them his left shoulder, where there was a golden dragon and the runes were flashing bright red.

"The blood seal…." Asha breathed in amazement. Illusht covered her face with her hands. "The empress hid a seal with a bond to the family blood under the coat of arms! Do you mean…."

"I already told you. I have been discovered," Andy answered sadly. "At that moment, it seemed like a hot needle stabbed me in the shoulder. Along with the needle, I got a bunch of foreign thoughts and feelings in my mind. I have never felt such hatred towards myself."

"Hazgar," the mother and daughter said simultaneously.

The ruler of the miur zoned out of reality for a moment. She was standing up straight; her frosty look bored into the wall, and only the bright flashes in her aura revealed her intense mental processing.

"Andy is right," she said, after returning to reality. "We

have very little time. The emperor can begin transferring troops at any moment. It seems to me that he took you for Jagirra, and Hazgar will not tolerate a threat to his own power. Today we send the ambassador and the princess' virk back to the prince! Prepare, you will be my Voice." The Great Mother took Andy by the shoulder. "You will tell the prince the truth about the 'key.'"

"Yes, and what about using the key? I do not know how."

"Illusht, go to our guests and announce the end of the reception. Let the princess immediately get ready to embark on the way back. Tell her that a detachment of 'ghosts' and my ambassador will go with the virk. The reason for haste I will explain to her in a couple of hours." The daughter bowed low and ran out of the room. "And we, 'brother,' will have yet another merger. Are you ready?"

"Where will I go from the top of the Mellornys," Andy muttered.

* * *

His head ached wildly. The second confluence of minds in one day also left its mark. No spells cured the headache; settage threw up the white flag in front of the misfortune too. The ax would have helped, but such radical treatment was not included in Andy's plans. For the last hour, his to-do list was empty. The Great Mother and her heirs planned this time for him.

The city was in a state of turmoil. Despite the strict measures taken to preserve secrecy, rumors of the arrest of the Eldest priestess and her assistants seeped into the city. What happened in the palace with every hour took on a new dimension; a whole lump of incredible details was added, culminating in the appearance of dozens of corpses.

The border guard posts reported on the Imperials' sudden activation. Hazgar's strategists released hundreds of griffons into the sky; dozens of combat dragon threesomes were flying along the border perimeter, but no dragon or rideable griffon had entered the neighboring lands yet. Bird spies spotted an active bustle near three punches in the space shields. The emperor was preparing an invasion. The case smelled of kerosene; Andy's idea to fly on griffons was a flop; the half-birds couldn't stand the smell of the Lords of the Sky. The dragons, following their Targ-loving virk traditions, refused to change hypostasis. The stubborn fools. "The virk will end on the territory of Ora!" Ilirra announced. Dumb lizard!

Andy's head hurt even worse from the anger boiling inside him. He wanted to kill someone, starting with his older "sister," who had made a whole horrible mess of things, but she, fearing for her hide, avoided the annoyed dragon. She maintained her communication with Andy through the communicator amulet and her daughter. Illusht did not like this new duty her mother had put on her shoulders. In the absence of a "whipping girl," the new-found relative could have torn her tail off, but the ruler's orders were not open to discussion. She resigned herself to it, especially since the "brother" gradually calmed down.

"This is what I was thinking about," Andy addressed the heiress.

"What?"

"How will the dragons treat me as ambassador? Will not this be an insult to them? Ilirra does not tolerate me—that is one. Could a servant of Manyfaces leak information on the side? Before the reception, grandma had a lot of time—that is two."

"It will not be perceived as an insult," replied Illusht. "We smart kitties have already taken care of everything. Officially, you will not be with the embassy. An ordinary Miur will appear before the prince of Ora."

"What do you mean?"

"Analysts suggest that the borderlands of the Principality and the land of the Miur are now, even without the Eldest, teeming with imperial spies. They have been issued a tip to look for the blood seal."

"The Great Mother thinks Hazgar will be searching for his niece, not her prodigal son."

"It is possible. But we decided not to take any chances. You will go as a Miur. No dragon or mage would ever think of looking for you in that form."

"TARG, are you suggesting I take on a fourth hypostasis

and get a sex change? Over my dead body."

"I said nothing about a fourth hypostasis. We will prepare a puppet spell for you. In thirty minutes, let us measure the bodies. If you have a better idea, I am prepared to listen. If not, get ready to pee sitting down for a couple of days. You will not fit in a small male puppet. Female Miurs are larger, more your size. So, shall we? Remember, you will need a few hours to get used to the body, and time is precious."

"Let us go... what are these puppets like, anyway?"

* * *

The puppets gave the impression of being cat people, only gutted and sliced from crotch to throat. The powerful, tall Miur lay in translucent cocoons which reminded him in a very unpleasant way of the dugaria. The big brain who greeted Andy reassured him that they were grown inorganically and had no connection whatsoever to the actual Miur or the insane transformation tree. "Hope not," Andy thought.

"Shall we go to the fitting room?" the learned cat said cheerfully. "I suggest we go straight to the peasant women."

He jumped to one of the largest cocoons and ran his hand over it. It opened, revealing a mighty female Miur body.

"So, let me see," the big brain jumped behind Andy. "In my opinion, this is the right one. Take your clothes off and climb into the puppet through the incision on the abdominal cavity. Lie on your back, hands along your sides, legs thrust into the puppet legs. There is free space. You should have enough room to fit from neck to crotch, with your legs reaching to my 'girl's' knees. I hope your protégé has not yet eaten?" the laboratory manager asked Illusht. "Some elves have trouble with nausea."

Andy slid into the "suit." Overcoming his uneasiness and disgust, he went up to the slimy puppet and climbed inside as if climbing into a sleeping bag. First, he thrust his legs, then the rest of the body disappeared into the "bag."

"Very well," the owner of the puppet theater rejoiced. "Now I will activate it. This will be a little unpleasant."

Andy lay inside the warm body and watched as the opening closed up from bottom to top. Suddenly millions of tiny but sharp needles shot from the inside surface of the pseudo-Miur and dug into his skin. "Unpleasant" wasn't the word for it. He felt like a red-hot rod had been inserted into his spine; his head, arms and legs were covered with invisible fetters.

"It will be disgusting right now, but still, open your mouth," Andy heard through the red mist.

"What?" he wanted to ask, but onto his face, covering his eyes, mouth, and nose, something like a mask fell from which a whole bunch of live tentacles instantly penetrated into his mouth, down his esophagus and into his lungs. At the same time, Andy felt some substance being pumped into his blood which made him "swim" and immediately pass out.

"Is that it?" Illusht asked, surprised.

"I will check." A slap to the cheek brought Andy back to life. Roaring like a wounded dragon, he jumped up from the sheet and grabbed the male by the throat.

"I'll kill you, creature!"

"Let him go, you will strangle him!" Illusht cried. In his rage, Andy dropped the big brain and picked his "sister" by the neck. The male ran under a table and let out a frightened yelp. Andy tossed the heiress to the throne away and chased after the quick scientist, but apparently, this wasn't the first time he'd run away from frenzied customers. He employed his super speed and disappeared behind a thick iron door. The slaughter spell sent after him knocked helplessly against it and dissolved. The clever cats had thought of everything....

"Magnificent synchronization and excellent response. The dragon aura is completely camouflaged; it is no different than a Miur mage's aura," the voice of the big brain was heard from inside the box near the wall. "I, perhaps, will refrain from the rest of the tests, but I will warn you. Since the puppeteer is a dragon, do not expect more than five days. The puppet is not designed for dragon's blood. In five days, it will be deactivated and wither. The lady will tell you about the ways of quick release from the outer shell and self-deactivation."

In the box, something clicked; the instruction was completed. The last thing Andy heard from him was muffled cursing at the stupid dragon who decided to treat him to an unplanned jogging session, from which a brutal appetite always awakened.

"Have you calmed down?" Illusht asked, looking sadly at the bent bracelets on her right wrist, victims of the small skirmish.

"I am calm," Andy answered, forgetting to use the female grammatical form in his speech. Illusht corrected him.

"You will have to forget that you are a male for a few days and carefully watch your tongue. Is that clear?" She stood on her tiptoes and looked into the "cat's" green eyes.

"I will try."

"Do not try—do! Let us go to my apartment. I will teach you what you need to know, how to act. We will talk for a long while. You do not know any of the local customs. I will have to explain all the nuances and make sure you remember them well, as well as all the information the Great Mother gave you. Yes," she stopped near a low table on which lay some sort of suit, neatly folded. Illusht handed the outfit to her new tribeswoman. "Put this on."

"Oh, now what?" Andy swore: the outfit included something like a corset and a D-cup size bra. "I will not put that on."

"As you wish."

"What do you need puppets for? Why do you have this lab?" Andy asked, pulling on the string of a wide shalwar.

"Shall I ignore you or lie to you?" the cat answered, annoyed.

"I see."

"Let us go. We have little time. We will make sure you 'see.'"

Andy picked up the giant bra with the tips of his feline claws. What that heiress wasn't telling him to do! But, oh well, he did not have long to endure. An ugly grin stretched across the face of the puppet. The whiskers on her snout fluttered belligerently. The real Miur leaned back a little, suddenly realizing that beneath the whiskered shell, paws, and tail was hiding a far from harmless individual and angering him was not worth it if she valued her own safety.

Nelita. Miur territory on the border with the Principality of Ora.

Andy, urging the dragons on with shouts, touched the communicator amulet with his hand. He could not shake the feeling, more like the confidence, even, that Irran had not said everything. The experienced Miur would not have created an unreasonable rush, a crazy hurry for no reason, especially not because of some regiment of steppe orcs that were more helpless in the forest than a blind kitten. A hundred and fifty border guards reinforced with gunners or fifty "ghosts" would have dealt nicely with the orcs, but the commander ordered them to retreat at the pace of a race car. Something was fishy. The situation was clearly worse and more complicated than previously stated.

"Irran, what is really happening?" he put on his helmet and asked through the amulet.

"If we do not leave here in ten minutes, we will have nowhere to hurry to," Irran answered. "The dead do not run."

"Okaaay, apparently, the orcs feel the same way about the scouts as I do about yellow-winged butterflies."

The dragons' troxes suddenly twitched in place and flapped their short wings. Something was troubling the birds. Andy listened to the roar from the opposite entrance to the gorge.

"On the ground, activate protection!" was heard in the communicator amulet.

"Get down!" he yelled at the top of his puppet lungs, knocked Ania from the saddle, and covered her with his body. The rest of the retinue did not wait to be thrown down in such a rude manner. They quit their saddles in a hurry. A low rumble abruptly passed and turned into a piercing whistle. A deafening clap sounded. The air became stuffy, and the troxes and those who disobeyed the command and remained standing were knocked down.

"Stay down," Irran's magically enhanced voice cooled the fervor of some hasty men who decided that the danger had passed.

There was a whistle, a second clap... and the treetops cut off by an unseen force fell on the detachment. A boom. In the hustle and bustle, no one bothered to lay the troxes down on the ground and cover them with protective domes; now half of them lay torn to shreds. Hell was going on in the gorge. One boom followed another. The air was filled with the whistling of stone fragments flying in all directions; the trees surrounding the meadow turned into chips. Ignoring the instructions, Andy formed a communication channel with the protective perimeter and pumped mana into it. The defense he built covered the entire detachment. A cloud of dust hung over the ground that mingled with the woody juice and bloody sludge from the dead birds. The brown-gray-green waste flowed down the arch of the tangible protective dome. The princess' virk and Miur were saved by their magical artifacts and armor. Without them, many, not holding out for Andy's improvisation, would have repeated the fate of the feathered transport.

"Run out of the canyon until they hit us with an 'acoustic fan' a second time," Irran commanded.

"Where's the cover?" asked one of the Miur, dirty as a chimney sweep.

Irran's response was untranslatable.

An incomprehensible anxiety and a sense of discomfort piled on Andy. Understanding nothing, he looked around for the cause of the anxiety. Targ! Burning with unbearable heat and making the hair curl over his head, several giant fireballs flew over the gorge.

"WE RUUUUN!" Irran shouted, throwing the elf who had remained without a means of transportation over her shoulder, and taking ten-foot strides, rushed to the exit from the mountain trap. Behind them were the troxes and the other "ghosts" who instantly picked up the "horseless." None of the dragons sneezed at that method of movement, not a peep of protest. They very much wanted to live.

They were almost there. Most of the detachment crossed

the low crest that separated the gorge from the exit to the plain, but Andy, his three and a couple of the princess' entourage members were hit by a shock wave. The earth trembled violently under their feet. The sounds behind them were deafening. At the far end of the gorge, where the orc regiment was supposed to be, hundred-yard-high tongues of flame rose to the sky. The roaring fire flooded the narrow stone sack between the mountains. An air mass, hardened from the explosions of red "balls," which absorbed a myriad of broken stones and chips of broken trees, struck the backs of the escaping riders and Miur. Andy caught a glimpse of the outlined contours of individual magical protection around his companions and the dragons. As chips and stones hit him in the back, an unprecedented force picked up the remnants of the detachment and carried it through the air, shooting them from the narrow mouth like a cork from a bottle of champagne. Stuck in the body of the puppet, Andy's feline instinct to land on four limbs played a cruel joke. No matter how he controlled himself, the events of the last few minutes and the involuntary tumbling flight deprived him of his orientation for a while. The landing was hard; a "cushion" formed in time which extinguished the speed, but not enough. The wide breastplates of the puppet's armor were squeezed inward from the impact on the sharp stones. The defense amulets planted during the attack of the orc shamans were completely out of power; there was no time to recharge them. Convulsively opening his mouth and trying to breathe the air knocked out of his lungs, Andy rolled over on his back....

"Targ...," he wheezed, diving into the astral and erecting a multi-layered dome around himself, but a several-ton piece of rock struck his unfinished defense and hit him in the left shoulder, throwing the puppet body back a dozen feet, then rolled on. "Aaah!" Only the ability to control and suppress the pain, honed by the multi-month incarnation, saved him from losing consciousness and allowed him to retain his reason. The magical construction did not crumble, which saved its owner from the rest of the avalanche, in which, praise the Twins, there were no more giant boulders.

The collapse completely covered the way out of the gorge. If any of the orcs in the regiment were left alive, following their own two legs would be pointless, and the Imperialists had no griffons.

Andy's internal chronometer stopped. There was not a single crazy thought in his head. He did not feel the passage of time. It was nice and pleasant for him to lie on the bare stones and look unblinking at the sky as it cleared of the dust and at the white clouds huddling near the horizon. But all good things come to an end. The shuffling of steps on his right and the dirty head of Irran that appeared in his field of vision interrupted the thoughtless contemplation.

"Was that a cover?"

"Indeed it was," said the commander, leaning forward and picking up something from the ground.

"With a cover like that, we do not need any orcs with imperial dragons. If we had delayed only a little, we would have been smeared on the rocks. By the way, what is going on?" Andy asked for the second time. Theoretically, the situation was understandable without unnecessary words, but he wanted to receive confirmation of his conclusions from another source.

"The invasion," replied the Miur, squatting down in front of him. "Lie down," she stopped him trying to get up. "Milla! Here! Hurry!" cried the feline, and again turned to Andy. "Lie down, now Milla will help you, sorry, your arm cannot be saved."

At first, he did not understand what she was talking about. A dull pain awakened in his left shoulder, and a bloody stump in Irran's hands put everything in its place. The boulder that struck his shoulder tore off the puppet's left arm. Pain flared again; a red fog fell over his eyes. Illusht had not warned him that between the puppeteer and the artificial body there was such dense communication. Or was this a feature of his own organism, previously unknown and not taken into consideration?

"Milla!" he heard from somewhere far away.

Andy dove into settage. His inspection of the body revealed an unsightly picture. If his body was more or less normal, not counting the bruises on his back and injuries to his left shoulder, the shell of the puppet began to change, and not for the better. The five days the feline declared were now reduced to a maximum of three. Black and gray areas of dying tissues and a crimson blot around the shoulder spoke for themselves. The big-headed cat was right about one thing: these puppets were not designed for dragons.

"I am alright," Andy said, coming out of his trance and pushing Milla's hands away. He didn't want the healer figuring out who Anrisha really was. The Miur in the detachment were informed that the new girl was a secret ambassador, but they did not need to know that she was a Russian nesting doll. "I am a mage. I will make do. Are there any fatalities?"

Irrand showed two fingers. If she was surprised by the behavior of the wounded, she didn't show it. The feline guessed that armless cat had incredible power. To herself, she thanked Manyfaces for the restraint and wisdom of the ambassador, who did not get into a dangerous situation with unnecessary advice and did not try to show off her power.

"Who?"

"Vishmarna from the second group and Maruel from the princess' retinue. Covered with boulders. Maruel is not a dragon, Ilirra confirmed, so she has no chance."

They urgently needed to contact the Great Mother. The situation had changed radically. A light walk turned into an exhausting march. It was necessary to coordinate their actions. Andy leaned his right hand on the ground and sat down. The strap of his fire-starter slid off his shoulder. He couldn't feel his backpack on his back, and he did not remember losing it. Targ only knew where and when it left its owner. And this was not good. Apparently, the amulet of direct communication got fried along with the backpack. Why couldn't they have just sent a communicator amulet in a spatial pocket?

Andy composed the "fiery palm" interweave and burnt the wound on his left shoulder. He did not know and had never tried to find out if the Twins really existed, but virtual games with Hel never ended well. Today the goddesses had smiled on him again, and two souls went to their halls, where the souls of the orcs went, too. Andy realized it was time to take the initiative, not just passively swim with the current and obey circumstances. It was high time....

"Irran!"

"Yes, Milady!" The cat woman caught the change in the ambassador's voice and felt the change of power. *Wow, quick. The girl will go far, if she survives, of course. Let's hope Death will not look at her.*

"Invite the princess to me. Also, as we descend into Mellorny Forest, do whatever it takes, but provide communication with the Great Mother."

"Yes, ma'am. What is the password?"

Well done, she immediately grabbed the gist. Glancing at Milla, Andy leaned over Irran, whispered the code they'd set up in advance and one of the passwords in her ear. He had already realized that life throws all kinds of crazy scams and scenarios at you, including those that you do not expect at all. And the loss of the family communication amulet could be one, so they immediately stipulated reserve communication methods with Illusht. After hearing the ambassador, the cat woman banged her fist on her chest and ran off. Andy, whose puppet suffered a great loss of blood, beckoned to Milla. Leaning on her shoulder and supported by the healer, he hobbled off. Halfway down the road to the natural bivouac, they were met by Ilirra, accompanied by Torvir and Renat.

"So, boys," said Andy, "step aside, I need to talk with your lady. Without you."

"How dare you," Ilirra began to boil.

"I dare." Andy snapped his fingers. The two male dragons were instantly covered with invisible chains and curtains of silence. Torvir and Renat's arms and legs were bound. They resembled fish, soundlessly opened their mouths and rolling their eyes, but the bonds held. If the "boys" were in their true hypostases, they would have been able to free themselves... And they would be free in about twenty minutes. "Your Grace, listen to me carefully, I will not repeat myself. I am the Voice of the Great Mother." Ilirra gasped. "I hope you understand that my words have the power of the miur ruler's words?" The dragon nodded. "Very well. You can guess many different things about the latest developments, but the true cause is war!"

"And you know the reason?" Ilirra blurted out, accidentally using the informal form of "you." She tilted her head to her shoulder. Her aura blazed with all the colors of the rainbow, among which anger, irritation, and fear were particularly prominent. The princess tried to hide her trembling for her defiant "you." The "acoustic fan" had left an indelible mark in the soul of the young dragoness. For the first time in her life, she was so close to death that powerful adrenaline fluids and the smell of wildflowers literally beat Andy in the nose.

"You," he corrected her, using the formal address. "Be so kind as to observe etiquette," he snapped at the nervous beauty. "I know. Both the reason and the purpose I will tell your father. Prince Ora should learn about them as soon as possible. Now, about how to achieve this. We are now going down to Mellorny Forest where I will contact the Great Mother and where your virk ends."

"The virk ends in Ora!" Ilirra said, somehow not sounding too confident. Andy's and the puppet's blood, which contained a healthy portion of adrenaline, surged through his veins. *Now there's an idiot for you!*

He hissed like a steam locomotive, put on his defense, grabbed the princess by the dress, and pulled her to him. The dragons accompanying the mistress writhed like flies in a spider web. Young people, what can you expect?

"The virk will end in the forest at the foot of a stone scree. There you will change hypostasis, grab the Miur in your paws, and fly to the nearest stationary portal. From there, we will be transferred to the prince's palace. Building a portal near the mountain does not make sense; the spatial shields will not allow you to make a coordinate reference. The emperor's attack on the Miur is a distraction maneuver. Hazgar's real goal is the Principality's territory. You can cling as much as you like to your traditions, but I do not give a shushug for them," Andy said rudely. "If we do not hurry, the deaths of Vishmarna and Maruel will be in vain. And the future deaths of thousands of Miurs, dragons, and subjects of the prince will be an indelible stain on you, Your Grace. Decide, can you take on such a burden?"

"Mistress!" Irran ran towards them from the camp. "The Great Mother is in contact! She immediately demands to speak to you and Her Ladyship!"

Andy dismissed the princess. With a flick of his fingers, he freed Renat and Torvir from their bonds.

"Do not jerk," he said to the dragons.

* * *

"The emperor received permission to march his troops unimpeded through the Principalities of Wirr and Archen. While we were waiting for his legions in the north and east, imperial diplomats were secretly negotiating with the southern princes. Hazgar deceived both me and the prince. He managed to enlist the support of Lord Archen, who has been promised one-third of your father's land in exchange for his support, princess."

"And will Wirr," the ruler grinned, "get my foothills too? Hazgar is very generous."

"The imperial army is on the march?" Ilirra asked, going pale.

The Great Mother shook her head sadly:

"They are already on the border of the principality. Hazgar gave command over to his son. An hour ago, the emperor's dragons burned Sardat."

"Sardat is a trade town. It has never had large garrisons! What was the purpose of destroying a defenseless population?!" Ania cried, sobs in her throat.

"Intimidation…. Hazgar used Sardat as a deterrent, a hint that there will be no mercy," Andy said quietly. He felt worse. He could barely keep on his feet. The union with another body left an imprint. His head was dizzy from the loss of blood; he saw little spots swimming before his eyes. The illusiogram rippled. The image turned into a thin strip and disappeared. "What happened?" Andy turned to Irran.

"The imperial mages are jamming us. They are somewhere nearby."

"The virk is completed," the dragoness said firmly, glancing at Andy. She took a few steps back, changed hypostasis, grabbed the ambassador in her front paws, and took off into the sky.

* * *

"It's a shame I can't see Ania," Andy thought, hugged as he was against Ilirra's wide breastplates of a rich emerald color. "I wonder what color her scales are?"

The small herd of dragons, making their way with synchronous flaps of their wings, flew westward. Rare observers, far below, were amazed at the strange load in the paws and on the backs of the ancient monsters. It wasn't every day you could see the Lords of the Sky carrying people, or, what was previously considered impossible, Miur.

Rivers and rare settlements or outposts rushed under Ilirra's light green belly. The continuous carpet of the forest spread out over the entire visible area. Carefully spinning in the tight grip of her clawed paws, Andy settled himself more comfortably and, for lack of anything better to do, undertook to analyze the events of the last few minutes.

The picture was interesting. The princess' action was unexpected. Her impulsiveness and behavior screamed youth. Ilirra was young, very young, by dragon standards, not far from kindergarten. Her second hypostasis and age of only three hundred years gave her a pass for some rash steps. But Gray would have thought twice, maybe even three times before picking someone up in his paws. Andy would never take any load in his front paws. The burden would become an insurmountable hindrance if he needed to use magic. Some spells required free hands; without them, throwing a fireball and activating many other weaves were impossible, as the direction of magical movement of the structure was determined by the hands or paws. Flying over obviously dangerous territory, Ilirra deprived herself of the ability to enact a rapid attack and limited her own defense. The landing was a problem too. Now the dragon would have to land using a long run on her hind legs; the front ones were occupied by the Miur. They say cats have nine lives, but he would have to wait and see how she did during the very tricky maneuver. Hopefully, this was not the first time she carried a passenger in her paws.

The passenger, lulled by the measured swinging of the wings, built a guard cocoon around himself and plunged into settage. While there was free time, he had to bring his body into relative order. Andy examined himself, adjusted some energy channels, and then turned to the outer shell. A few seconds was enough to realize the gravity of the situation: the puppet's time left alive was rapidly decreasing. An attentive examination revealed the cause of weakness and generally poor condition.

Andy opened his eyes and looked down at the winged shadows running along the green crowns. Somewhere among the group was the creature who spoiled his health. The parasite interweave found in the puppet's blood was distinguished by its jewelry-like work and the gracefulness of execution. Not long ago, thinking about magic and analyzing the work of local magicians, he came to the conclusion that thin weaving was not popular here. The spell cast on him proved the opposite. Someone in the dragon company was able to weave a weightless lace, so imperceptible that he did not feel its initial impact, and now it was too late to do anything. If he were a real Miur, it would not be difficult to cope with the magic infection, but the body of the were-dragon inside the puppet did not leave a single chance for the artificial shell. The dragon's natural immunity, like a mirror, deflected all attacks of the curse from itself, returning the cocoons that budded from the parasite to the external shell body, which was already weakened by the wound and the effect of the foreign hypostasis hidden inside. The result was a double blow, killing the "Miur" Anrisha better than any sword. The unknown assassin had planned for her to die in three or four days, but in real life, it was less than half a day. Dark gray spots appeared on the site where the left arm used to be. Swiftly spread out in all directions like a cancerous tumor, the necrosis that began at the tip of the stump was spurring the process on like a charioteer. Basically, it really sucked. Somewhere alongside him an enemy was hiding, striking at one of the key figures of the envoy. The Great Mother said that the virk was initiated with several goals, and achieving at least one of them justified the campaign. The princess' detachment was a hodge-podge team. He couldn't exclude the possibility that there could be a secret agent of the forces working under Hazgar's wing. And so it was. The Miur ruler's ambassador did not fit into the political alignment; Hazgar's henchmen couldn't allow the rapprochement of the parties and union of Prince Ora and the Great Mother. The unfortunate puppet was collateral damage.

Ilirra started flying lower. Andy, as far as possible, twisted his neck and glanced at the approaching small town. The road flashed by, blocked with carts and levitated cargo platforms. Thousands of people were moving along the slopes and trails. Many human figures were burdened with trunks and bales; women carried babies. In the gaps between the trees, horse-drawn hasses and troxes galloped. According to the characteristic coloring of the riders' clothing, the experienced gaze recognized Forest Elves. The mass of people was heading towards the city. A military march was moving towards it. Hundreds of small figures swarmed on the peaks cleared from vegetation surrounding the settlement. Without switching to true vision, he could see the strongest haze of interweaves of magical constructions. The city was preparing for defense.

Upon seeing the dragons, people and elves left the carts and rushed in all directions, trying to hide under the crowns of trees. The soldiers in the army line acted differently. They gathered in a circle and put up shields. A couple dozen mages were located in the center of the circle. On the outer perimeter, several weapons bearers instantly installed heavy gunners on special racks. Apparently, the parade of refugees and the city had already undergone an enemy raid. The reaction to the air-borne danger spoke for itself.

Ilirra was beating her wings fast and hovered in the air. She unclasped her front paws. Andy did not have time to be frightened, as he was caught by a black male. The image of the emblem of the principality flashed brightly before the princess. The warriors, who were standing in a defensive construction, lowered their shields. Several dozen people separated from the detachment of troops, who cleared a decent section of the road from the carts and platforms in a couple of minutes. The dragoness went to land.

* * *

"What do you mean it does not work?!" the princess cried.

"When will it be working?"

"In five or six hours."

"What were you looking at?"

"At the sky," a small wrinkled old man answered the dragoness. "When five imperial 'vultures' are circling over the city and firing at the houses from gunners, you look at the sky and fire back with whatever you can." Ilirra frowned. She was insulted by the comparison. "If that would make any difference," the mage finished quietly. Despite his bodily dryness, the old man sported a bright aura which testified to his powerful magical potential. "The dragons flew upon us suddenly. They came out of nowhere, and in the next moment, the northern barracks of guards shot up, but the Imperials killed the griffons in three minutes. It's good that we were warned about possible provocations and managed to put up a shield over the center of the city. The raid could have had more devastating consequences, and then the legionaries arrived in time... We extinguished the fires quickly, but we could not save the portal."

"But how could the Imperialists have gotten to the portal? It is in a fortress!" The princess would not calm down.

"They did not. In order to destroy the suspension towers along the perimeter, all they had to do was throw a couple of discharge arrestors at the edge of the city. They blew up and released so much mana that the portal contours began to lose their coordination, and the towers fell," a lieutenant spoke up in place of the mage. He was the commander of the regiment that met them at the city gates. "We do have extra tower components on hand, but it will take time to install and check them."

"Alright," Ilirra said, "we will wait."

Andy, holding Milla's arm, listened to the princess' squabbles with the leaders of the free city of Libr. The news was bad. Little was left of the stationary portal. They would not be able to make a quick exit from the borderlands or contact the Great Mother. Imperial raiders had thrown a lot of "jammers" into the surrounding forests—artifacts that create insurmountable obstacles for magical communication. The city council sent a dozen detachments to search for and neutralize the annoying "guests," but no one could guarantee that the Imperialists would not repeat the raid and fill the neighborhood with a new portion of "gifts." And time was flowing like water. He called Irran over.

"Irran, please rent a room in a hotel."

"I do not think we will find even a single place with vacancy. Milady, you saw the refugees flooding the city with your own eyes. Where have they all come from?"

"I do not know, but I think the Great Mother could shed light on the subject." Irran looked at the ambassador with a surprised expression. "Most of the refugees are Forest Elves, and where did they live?"

"In the Mellorny groves in the foothills," Irran answered. Andy nodded.

"Now imagine what will happen to the groves if the Imperials and our external guard start magical combat. How many fireballs were launched against the orc regiment? The gorge of Singing Waters has been burned up like dry hay in an oven, and what will happen when they start firing at the settlements? The elves do not have the necessary number of magicians to build protective domes of the required power. With massive bombardment, no artifacts or accumulators will help."

"If it is as you say, how were the 'vultures' able to fly over Miur territory?" the princess turned to him. "Why were they not shot down?"

"That is just it. I am not sure…," Andy said, almost using the male form of grammar, but then correcting himself, "…that the attackers were indeed Imperials. It is entirely possible that similar attacks were carried out on all nearby cities that have stationary portal sites. The prince has enough internal enemies and pro-imperialists in Ora. Now they had a fine reason to curry favor and trap a certain careless dragoness. They could have put on anything they liked and painted it to look like the 'vultures'' armor, then retreated under the cover of a curtain of invisibility to hide which way they came from. Fear and panic after the bombing are provided."

"What made you think that the attackers were not Imperials, Milady?" the lieutenant asked Andy.

"It was because I counted over two dozen patrol circuits over the city, and none of them, according to your story, worked.

How is that possible? Or do not your mages change the frequency of the control interweave, so that it can be faked in five to ten minutes?"

"They change it four times a day. Are you saying that there is a traitor in the magistrate?"

"Yes, that is what I am saying. Someone gave the attackers the 'keys' to the guarded perimeter. Counting the time it took to hand them over, activate them and get out, we can safely conclude that the attackers were from the inside and had no relation to the imperial army."

Ilirra was a scary sight at that moment. Although her calm face and ironic expression did not betray her emotions, the colored sparks of her aura that made their way through the shields left no doubt that she was in the utmost confusion. The virk started out swimmingly and ended up a disaster. Andy did not throw out the information about the magical parasites to the princess, or the assumption of an "ill-wisher" in her retinue. That conversation would require careful treatment and a private atmosphere, but having a tête-à-tête with the dragoness would not be easy to arrange. Announce the traitor's presence in public, and he would hide, and the chances of finding him out later were null. For now, the cretin did not suspect that the lethal interweave had been detected and a cast made from it which allowed them to discover the identity of the scoundrel. It was possible by using a simple spell, triggered by the blood of the "parent" of the curse. But if you scare the enemy, he will put some protection on or change his blood for a short time—then all efforts would be dashed.

"I must tell my father everything, immediately," the princess said. "How can we aid you in rebuilding the portal?"

"You cannot," the old mage said. "New towers are already being erected. Then they will have to be tuned; that will take no less than five hours. With all due respect to you, Your Grace, please just rest and regain your strength. I ordered ten rooms in the hotel of the magistrate to be released for you and the honorable Miur."

The old man bowed politely yet with dignity. The lieutenant saluted them. Ilirra bowed her head in response. The corners of her lips twitched. She was not used to this sort of address. Libr was located on the territory of Ora, but considered a free city. Its inhabitants rarely saw dragons and did not have any special reverence for the creatures. The princess' entourage felt the lack of reverence fully.

The princess did not go to the hotel. Instead, she went to the portal site, followed by the entire retinue. Glancing at the dragons and pausing on the slender figure of Ania, Andy shook his head. According to the cats, the sida had not changed hypostasis and flew on Renat's back along with Milla, Irran, and Simiba. He waved his hand and pointed towards the magistrate. The old man struck him as a sane person who did not lack experience in magical affairs. If he said five hours from now, that meant it would be so, well, or nearly so. Moreover, Andy was getting worse with every minute, and rest was just necessary.

"Milady, are you alright?" Milla asked sympathetically, looking him in the eyes.

Alright? Do I look alright?? I need to get out of this puppet. It won't last, well, maybe it'll last another twelve hours or so, but I sure won't! The necrosis was affecting the respiratory tubes; the infection had also spread to the eye nerves. He would make a good ambassador—deaf and blind.

Three hours later, the puppet was blind in one eye and deaf in the left ear...

"Irran, Milla, gather the 'ghosts' in my room," Andy ordered.

"Yes, ma'am!" Irran replied and ran off to carry out the order. A few minutes later, all the Miur were gathered in the spacious room.

Counting the cats present, Andy activated some spells and closed the apartments off from peeping and eavesdropping. He formed an impenetrable smoky shroud along the walls and a hung a curtain of silence which cut off all the noise from the inside, but still allowed them to hear what was going on outside.

"Mistress, why such precautions?" asked the healer.

"Because I am not a mistress but a master, and they call me Andy," Andy answered. The Miur gasped simultaneously. Anrisha's ribs trembled violently in her chest cavity. A deep tear appeared by itself and spread downward. The ribs split apart with a loud crack and out stepped Andy, in all his naked glory. "Now listen to me carefully." Several of the "ghosts" recognized him as the mage that had danced with the spellcasters of the elements. The puppet's ribs snapped back into place. The bloody scar sealed itself up, bottom to top, and the puppet fell lifelessly to the floor. "As you have guessed, I am the real envoy. I will be commanding you starting now."

The felines said nothing. Milla kept looking at the body on the floor and then at Andy and back.

Someone banged on the door.

"Milady Anrisha, her grace summons you," Renat's voice said. "The mages have fixed the portal!"

Andy looked at the ceiling....

* * *

"Irran, tell him we will be there in five minutes," Andy said. The Miur made a doubtful face but did not object. Renat paced outside the door for a few minutes, waiting, but when they took too long he decided to leave.

"I hope you are going to explain to us what in Tma's name is going on here," Irran said, turning back from the door.

"Yes, briefly and clearly." Andy did not feel like getting into all the messy details. Instead of words, he grabbed a thin golden plate from his special pocket which looked like a credit card. He handed it over to the feline. "If you have any questions, I will answer."

Irran, taking the magical card, ran her claw along the edge of the rectangle. An illusion of the Great Mother appeared over it. All the "ghosts" present in the room crowded behind the commander. While the detachment listened to the ruler and read the text that was magically bound to the card, Andy pulled a uniform and a light mail vest from his "pocket" and quickly put the armor on.

In the cat race, obedience to higher ranks had been hammered since childhood. The magical "backstage pass"

257

presented by Andy, in which the ruler ordered all citizens without exception to render the necessary support to the owner of the device, made an indelible impression on the tailed ladies. The line about the shkas having full access to any army unit put any last doubts to rest.

No one had any questions. If the warriors were interested in the lifeless body on the floor, how the man came to be inside it, and for what merit he was given the full confidence of the over-cautious ruler, they did not express them. Outwardly, the cats remained unperturbed, thus showing remarkable restraint. Not even one lady twitched the tip of her tail. They could languish with curiosity, but it was unlikely they would be satisfied with detailed answers. As the saying goes, curiosity killed the cat. The change of body had gone very smoothly with the miur. Now he had to persuade the princess of his authority. The dragons were unlikely to accept the disappearance of Anrisha and the appearance of the new ambassador as calmly.

"We're heading out," he said, fastening the buckle of his sling with two swords behind him and heading to the door. Irran shouted a guttural command. The cat people activated their protective amulets and the communicator amulets in their helmets.

Unceremoniously pushing the ambassador aside, one of the Miur opened the door to the corridor. The once-cat-woman, now man shrugged indifferently. "The girls" decided to play at security. He didn't mind, as long as they did not interfere with his plans or stand on the front lines of a magical attack or defense, if necessary. Having thrown a deliberately lazy look at the doorway, already half-obstructed by the zealous bodyguard, Andy felt the hair stand on the scruff of his neck. All the space behind the thin haze of the curtain of silence was filled with a complex magical pattern. The fine interweave resembled the work of a knitting master; it was weightless lace, just as airy and filled with numerous curls, its designs often alternating, gathering in intricate patterns. The work of the unknown master could have been admired for a long time, if not for one thing—the curls were full of serious danger. The beautiful patterns were filled with deadly poison, and the power points of geometric structures served to secure the capture of the victims.

Time slowed down and contracted like a spring. Feeling the

red mist of a trance cover his eyes and a lethal dose of adrenaline splash into his blood, Andy composed a spell and directed it towards the cat that had stepped her right foot over the threshold. He had to make it in time—one more moment and the Miur would be caught in the "lace" like a fly in a spider web, and death would pour through the threshold. The warrior who pushed him was swept aside by a magical "ram."

"Stop!" Andy screamed, throwing a static double-sided shield over the opening. The magical assassin gravitated towards the living flesh but ran into an insuperable barrier. The collision of the "shield" and "sword" lasted for a brief instant, but during that time the curls managed to turn into long thorns and shoot thousands of needles which got stuck in the protective energy field. The shield faded but held. "The creature!" Andy roared, he did not doubt for a second that the magician who had put a parasite curse on the puppet and left a "surprise" in the corridor of the magistrate's hotel was the same person. He had no doubts about the identity of the piece of filth that had wormed his way into the princess' entourage. "Milla, Riur," he called a second mage as well. "A window... follow me, we'll intercept them. Quickly!"

"What... what??" Irran's unfinished question hung in the air.

One cry came from the hall, heartbreaking, on one note. A man ran through a section of the hall that was lit by an open door. The poor man, stuck in a trap placed in someone else's game, decomposed right before their eyes. The shreds of hair and pieces of skin fell on the wide floorboards; smelly slime dripped from the man's mouth, nose, and ears. Before reaching the second turn, he fell on the planks of the floor and grew into a shapeless puddle. A terrible death.... The stranger acted as a minesweeper, giving his own life to de-mine the hall. His death rattle had not yet faded when the magical lace crumbled into small fractions, which immediately evaporated with spectacular trickles of saturated steam. There was not a trace of the magical trap left. Andy mentally applauded the failed killer, who proved himself a top-notch professional. The self-destruction of the interweave destroyed absolutely all the energy fingerprints. Now no magician ding the energy traces would be able to determine who was present in the corridor a minute ago, let alone an hour or two, which means that they would never catch the ill-wisher.

The commander of the "ghosts" was the first to come out of the brief stupor that had seized the detachment. With one movement, she tore the gunner off her shoulder and shot several times at the window wall, taking out a decent piece of the third floor along with it. Andy jumped through the smoking opening. Next, wailing with righteous anger and wishing to punish the traitor, the others followed.

"Three follow me, the rest go down below," Andy instructed the felines, pointing to the tile-covered rooftops and the pavement. He then used a levitation spell to rise to the roof of the magistrate. "Do not get involved in the fight, I authorize the use of gunners. Press Renat to the fortress. I'll try to take him alive if he changes hypostasis—knock him down, cut the freak!" He shouted the last order and jumped over to the roof of the next house. Smashing shingles with their feet, Milla, Riur and a third, unknown Miur ran beside him. "Milla, Riur, go to the neighboring streets. I'll just drop back, I do not have any armor." The felines, who took off their invisibility for a moment, synchronously nodded, and, wrapped in magic curtain, jumped onto the roofs of the houses in the parallel streets. Andy slightly slowed down. A chase is a good thing, but don't forget about the astral. Renat proved visibly and without a doubt that in a magical duel, he would be extremely difficult to beat. Difficult, but not impossible. The dragon was a mage, but his opponent possessed an unlimited reserve of mana. Dismissing such a trump card would be a reckless decision. Andy was more confident in himself than ever. Merging with the world of energy came instantly. The image of the golden dragon flared in his mind brighter than a thousand suns. The astral double sparkled with force and, as if reprovingly, shook his head on his elegant neck, sending his master an endless stream of questions: "Where have you been? Why did you leave me alone?"

The tattoo on his left shoulder started to itch. The flow of strength somewhat weakened the induced shields. Andy looked at the cavalcade of elves sweeping through the streets below on troxes and carefully touched the family coat of arms.

"No one can have two deaths, and no one gets to refuse

one," he thought.

Suddenly the troxes cawed loudly. An invisible force carried two birds off the road; the riders flew out of the saddles and rolled onto the pavement. The pride of combat Miur appeared from around the corner. A dense box of warriors, covered by full-length shields, swept along the narrow street like an icebreaker on jet propulsion. From the roofs of the houses, one could see how the tailed Amazons split the crowd like pack ice, causing the townspeople to cling to the walls of the buildings. Several oncoming wagons with drivers who imagined themselves to be masters of the roadway were thrown back by two Miur mages. No one else tried to get in the way of the "ghosts" after that.

One thing he liked about the tailed "girls" was the fact that they didn't hesitate for an instant. Once they received the order from their ruler, they no longer doubted for a second the authority of the blue-eyed non-human, who turned out to be especially close to the monarch. Discipline was priority number one for the cats. They were ideal warriors and assassins. With his last word, they turned into inexorable arrows moving in the direction of the designated target, and only death could stop their flight.

"I see him," the communicator amulet came to life. One of the Miur, galloping fifty yards ahead of Andy, stopped on the roof of the last house before the central city square. The masking mode they'd turned on made her invisible to the outside observer; the fact that shingles scattered and cracked under the kitty's feet did not bother anyone. People are not accustomed to looking up, and the many-voiced hubbub of the crowd was as effective as any canopy of silence to ensure the privacy of their communication.

"Where?" Andy asked, leaping onto the next ramp and "suspending" another runic scheme of killer character in his mind.

"Behind the second fountain in the central square."

"Got it!" He sent three free sentry modules, converted into scouts, in the direction of the city square. "Yes, the label worked! The module is leading it! Irrand, bypass the square. You have to come from the market side; I'll block the road to the fortress."

"Yes, sir!" Irrand answered in a frenzied voice through the magic radio. Andy grit his teeth: all she cares about is having fun.

She should be chasing balls in a house rather than commanding a detachment.

"Irran! Be careful, do not go near him. Strike from a distance; Renat is not the half-wit he pretended to be. You cannot be too cautious...."

"I got it. Irran out," the cat stood up. "Do not try to teach me what I already know," she said under her breath.

"Break up into threes. Block the streets leading to the square. If this lizard even thinks of taking off, shoot at his wings. Let us see how he does at repelling fire from different directions."

Andy hid behind a wide chimney. He did not have magic armor, and making a grand show-off gesture would not be in his best interest. If everything went as planned, the pride would drive the prey to him. But for now, the important thing was to prepare as many combat rune schemes as possible.

Remembering the lessons Gray taught him, he hammered out fatal interweaves one after another: "firestorm," "air knives," "battering ram," "ax." He slightly energized the nodal runes and set his work aside, ready for use. Small lightning interweaves composed a parallel flow. Now that's know-how! After their training fights, the ancient dragon always arranged a debriefing, during which Andy seemed to turn into a bug.

"If you're up against a more experienced and sophisticated enemy," the old dragon Gray once told him, "then you should not try to defeat him, contrasting sophisticated skills with complex schemes. It will be much more effective to use several elementary but energy-saturated structures. Always keep with you a dozen different pre-made spells; your connection with the astral allows you to easily bring their number to hundreds or more. Remember: simple interweaves are easy to combine and alternate the sequence of their application. Four or five sample patterns allow you to make a multitude of bundles with completely unexpected properties, and while your opponent makes up and imbues a complex combat scheme, you bring down on him a real killer hail of dozens of spells. The enemy will take a beating and go on the defense. As soon as the dome or shield appears, he lost. How many strikes can a passive or active shield withstand if you hit it with all your might? In a real battle, there is absolutely no time to put up a stationary defense. Five or six direct hits, a maximum of a dozen, and then he's yours...."

Thank you, Gray. You had a good student, even if you're not the one to examine me right now. It's for the best. A battle with an unfamiliar opponent will show whether or not your ward is prepared to fight independently. Andy, completing the "ax" interweave, decided to diversify the menu. In addition to a hundred ready-made spells, he compiled a scheme of "earth knives" and a "fiery rain" scheme. A "press" and a "sledgehammer" were added to the magical arsenal, the runes of which were pumped up with energy. As soon as he pronounced the activation key in his mind, the lethal power of the spells would break out.

"Careful, he's noticed us!"

Silence... It seemed to last forever. Andy fell into a trance in the blink of an eye and looked out from behind the pipe. He did not know how Renat was able to spot one of the Miur triplets, but he drew his conclusions instantly: the cats had come for his head.

For the observer in the combat trance, the events on the square unfolded as if in slow motion. A sound like nails on a chalkboard grated his eardrums. Renat sent a dark "harness," visible to the naked eye, in the direction of the warriors he'd discovered. The humans and elves who fell under the influence of the spell gathered into a huge bunch and threw themselves at the Miur. The film of the shield flashed brightly. The amulets did not disappoint, but this did not save the people. The bodies reflected by the static barrier were magically accelerated and flew in all directions at a speed of one hundred miles per hour. The living "shells" knocked down and maimed the city residents and refugees who were in their path. Many of the "harnessed" ones ended their lives upon crashing into the stone walls of the surrounding buildings. A din of many voices rose above the square, but this was only the beginning...

Renat was just getting warmed up. A crowd of frightened people rushed to seek salvation in the side streets, but many did not have time to make three steps. The traitor stood in the center of a fountain, in the center of which was a tall stone statue of a bearded man. It collapsed, crashed into the Miur's defensive field, and shattered, sending shrapnel flying in all directions, killing the righteous and the guilty alike. After the stone shower, a spell unknown to Andy struck at the center of the miur's defensive barrier. The protection couldn't withstand it. The dim glow faded completely. A fireball that burst at the feet of the feline, who was armed with a gunner, put an end to her career. The warrior was thrown twenty feet up in the air. Renat seized the opportunity to finish off the opponent, throwing some complicated crap at her. A red-brown puddle spread out from under the fallen body onto the pavement. With that, the dragon's tactical successes were over; the pride mages coming up violently attacked him with a dozen different interweaves. The cats, unlike their opponent, could not go at him at full strength. The magicians feared one of their spells would accidentally kill a fellow clan member on the opposite side of the square, so they attacked often, but with weak spells. The dragon went into a deep defense mode and decided that there were a lot of them, but only one of him, and that today was not his day. Thoughts about the unsuccessful day resulted in a change of hypostasis. By Renat's thinking, in his true form, he could take advantage of stronger and more destructible interweaves, or at the very least fly away, but... Andy's partners were fully rehabilitated from their brief stupor in the hotel. The dragon, in his haste, failed to take into account the small nuance that for one or two seconds at the time of the change of appearance, he would not have protection. The energy spent on defense would change for a brief moment in order to change his form. Irran did not disappoint. The gunner in her hands spat out a few fireballs; the third shell-spell didn't encounter any obstacles, if you don't count the webbing of Renat's right wing. He could forget about escaping by flight; no one had taught him how to fly on an honest word and one wing.

The wounded monster's thunderous roar rang out over the square. He was not even thinking of moving his legs to flee. The dragon answered Irras's third shot with a long tongue of flame from his angry open mouth. The commander and one of her companions managed to dive into the fountain. The third cat was burned up faster than a match. Neither armor nor protective amulets saved her from the dragon's wrath. With his somehow detached perception, Andy noted that the hot flame turned a dozen townspeople to ashes. The wounded humans and elves simply did not have time to get out of the way. Meanwhile, Renat observed that only one opponent was blocking the way to the fortress. The Miur from the second detachment gave herself away by shooting from a gunner, which did not do any damage to the black-scaled monster. He had put up a shield that was feeding from a strong magical accumulator amulet on his left paw.

Retribution was not long in coming. The dragon proved capable of unexpected attacks. A second later, the cat and a third of the roof disappeared in a bright flash, and her killer quickly moved his paws in the direction of the street leading to the fortress with a stationary portal, where at that moment the princess and her virk were.

The time had come! Andy jumped off the roof, sending a bundle of five interweaves in a short flight to the vis-a-vis. A landing, a roll, and five more blanks shot at the black truck moving at full speed. Five gifts from the Miur mages hit the rear hemisphere of the dragon's protective dome. Bam! The shield burst. A weakened shield usually disappears with an explosion like that. Renat, once again using the accumulator, built a new dome around himself. Andy grinned carnivorously. His mentor turned out to be right. The spells pumped with astral energy after a dozen hits drained the black dragon's protection and drained his amulet. *It's time for surprises! Do you like the "earth knives?"* Slapping his hands on the pavement, Andy continued shooting at the enemy. The composite interweave worked with a slight delay, but for now, he could beat the stuffing out of him with a simple "battering ram."

The black spikes of the "earth knives" interweave, once it was ready, skewering the dragon like a butterfly on a needle, punched through the stones of the pavement and his strong scales.

Before the enemy could come to his senses, Andy caressed him with several lightning bolts and kicked the crap out of him with a "sledgehammer." The opponent, who lost his sense of reality, was imprisoned in a power trap.

"Renat, Renat, I did not expect such baseness from you!" Andy said, standing a bit to the side of the defeated adversary's snout. His enemy was not dead and was fully capable of spitting fire.

"Andy," Renat growled, jerking his hind legs frantically.

"So you...."

"I will ask the questions," said Andy. "Keep your eloquent speech for the answers."

"Do not hope. You are too late. Your ragged cats will soon be finished... kugh, kugh!" The dragon coughed, coughing up dark clots of blood. "You can not expect any answers from me, stinking shkas."

Renat was right about that. Andy could indeed remain without the answers to his questions about the "butterfly's" masters' identities, their goals, and tasks. His soul yearned for satisfaction, but apparently, the dragon spitting blood from his punctured lungs thought otherwise. He didn't give his employers away. Perhaps he had taken a blood oath. In that case, torture him to death if you like; you still wouldn't get anything from him but nonsense. The situation required some sort of extraordinary solution.

Renat went on, "What is it, shushug dung? Funny, I am in the grips of your spell, but you are the one who is stuck. Dragons can endure pain, and I am not afraid of death. Ha, you will not get to the capital...."

"Are you not afraid of death? Oh! For you, I prepared something worse than death," Andy answered.

"I wonder what it could be?" the dragon tried to brave, but, upon seeing yellow pupils erupting in his tormentor's eyes and catching the smell of lily of the valley, he slammed his mouth shut.

A small bolt of lightning struck Renat in the side. And another, and another, and another. The dragon, squealing with pain, struggled in his fetters. Andy fired another and another. The smell of burnt meat filled the square. Andy almost vomited. He was torturing someone for the first time in his life, but he continued to increase the tempo. The whine turned into an ultrasonic squeal, lightning struck the neck and head, and when the tortured beast did not have the strength to squeal, an attempt was made to crack the barriers to his mind. The mind-cracker's reward was several bright images, including the sovereign and the prisoner's employer, the same person. Realizing that the secret could not be saved, Renat, using a magical interweave, threw off his fetters and collapsed onto the pavement....

Andy, spattered from head to foot with dragon's blood,

looked at Irran, who shot the zealous prisoner in the head.

"What did you do that for? I would have managed."

"He could have killed you. You saw how he broke free from the bonds."

"Everything was under control. Although,... thank you."

"Of course," Irran crinkled her nose amusingly. "Did you learn anything?" A typical cat—curious.

"There is a little something. I remembered the employer's face well; it remains to find out his name. I do not like to stop halfway, but some people do not even know how to hold a weapon. We need to arrange a training session."

"Another time. For now, be prepared to answer before the princess."

"Ilirra.... You are right. Gather the detachment; we are late already. Go to the portal site."

"And that?" the feline waved at the decapitated body planted on the stone spikes.

"The city cleaners will take care of the garbage."

A minute later, after throwing the dragon's body into the care of the magistrate, the small detachment, bristling with gunners, moved towards the portal site.

A hundred yards from the coveted gate, Andy heard cheers. Why would people be joyful? Everything pointed to the fact that the magicians had restored the portal and were welcoming high-ranking guests into the city.

Strange... Weren't the guests and hosts bothered by the explosions in the central square? And not a single guard went to the fortress with a report? War had knocked on their front door, and they were living like pigs in the backyard—no grunting until they were brought to the slaughterhouse. Someone in a fawning voice was speaking animatedly before a certain Ruigar. Andy looked inquiringly at Irran.

"It is Ruigar, the governor of the astal of the northern borderlands," the cat answered, correctly understanding his questioning gesture. "There are rumors that he and the princess... They, umm...." The commander of the "ghosts" struggled to finish the sentence in her embarrassment. Andy could hardly restrain himself from laughing. "And judging by the rumble, I'd guess Milla put up a canopy over the whole area, and the guards were taken out in the first seconds."

When their destination was no more than fifty yards away, the gates to the portal site flung open.

"Targ on a shushug!" Andy gasped. "Fire at the guards!" He activated a power trap which slammed over the princess' retinue. Ilirra herself and her cavalier, who Andy recognized as Renat's employer, rolled on the ground from a powerful "battering ram." Andy struck at the elf, but a static shield flashed over the pair and knocked them both to the ground. Ruigar immediately jumped to his feet but flopped back again—heavy fire from a gunner did not allow him and the princess to rise. Andy calmly activated the "press" interweave, pressing the dragon to the pavement like an asphalt paver squishing a frog. Ilirra was immobilized with fetters.

The Miur, in the fever of the fleeting battle, did a number on not only the guards, but a good portion of the magicians from the portal staff. A third of them now lay like limp dolls on blood-stained stones. The rest shook at the sight of the two heavy gunners aimed at them. They did not think about resistance. The attack was completely unexpected for them. They realized that if dragons caught unawares could not counter the fighting pride of the Miur, what could be said about them—ordinary residents? Milla walked among the captives and confiscated their protective amulets. One old goat-looking man tried to say something but was immediately pulled up with a muscular arm above the pavement. Milla, slapping the grandfather on his long robe, fished a flat disc on a long chain from his pocket. The old man flopped to the ground. Twelve people, Andy counted up the shaking group. Not a single warrior. It was no wonder the warriors took them in five seconds.

"The portal key activator," said the cat, passing the disc to him.

"Well," Andy grumbled after catching the key, which was completely uncomfortable under the hateful looks of the princess, Ruigar, and the restrained retinue.

He looked for Ania and stumbled upon a look of contempt. Though there wasn't any hatred in the eyes of his beloved, regret that she had carelessly associated herself with a dirty shkas was read clearly. And what did he expect? To all the prisoners, he and his "cats" looked like the aggressors. It was unlikely that the governor disclosed the details of his business to the prince's daughter.... No, he did not feel guilty, on the contrary, after dealing with the snake-filled gang, he was going to walk along the tails of the poisonous reptiles. Intuition and his rear end, which are so sensitive to trouble, shouted that he should drop everything and make a run for it, but common sense crushed his panicky objections with an iron fist. It was too late to retreat anyway, and he had nowhere to go. It wasn't by chance that Ruigar came to visit this out-of-the-way town—he was probably informed of the coming arrival of Ilirra and her retinue. Taking into account the presence of powerful jammers scattered throughout the forests, the question of a protected channel came to the forefront. Here the logical chain acquired yet another thick link about the imperious jerk at least knowing of the events taking place, and if he made certain allowances, about his involvement in them as well. Andy did not believe that someone could contact the representative of the prince and quickly set up the portal without proper preparation. The strangeness of the masked dragons' attack on the city left no doubt about Ruigar's game on two fronts. The stream of heavy thoughts practically made him dizzy, but Andy kept looking at Ania. Apparently, the elf read something in his face; she lost her nerve. The girl's gaze lost its sharpness; now it displayed only confusion and a lack of understanding.

"You are wrong," he mentally replied to the sida, and turned away.

"Let me go, or else...." the governor said.

"Or else what?" Andy hissed, squatting on his haunches before the dignitary. "What else?" Rage and anger began to boil inside him. Obeying a light movement of the hand, the power cocoon became denser. The governor grunted. "You are not in a position to threaten," the pressure of the cocoon weakened. "Think about it: do not aggravate me. I have many questions for you, this may take a while...."

"Andy," Irran stepped forward. She was spinning a thick ledger in her hands and patting the tip of her nose pensively.

"Yes?" He knocked his knees, stood up, and left Ruigar to consider the whims of fate. His back burned with a look of hatred from the princess. Irran was right. The governor and the princess...

"We have a problem," the cat said and handed the ambassador the ledger, her claw leaving a clear mark on the last page, covered with sweeping handwriting.

"Amazing," Andy snorted, "and I thought we were just dancing a jig."

"We will be," the commander of the "ghosts" answered confidently. "If you believe the records of the local pen pushers that serve the portal station, and there are no grounds for doubting them, three dozen mages arrived with the governor. Twenty of them are on rideable troxes. The delegation was announced an hour ago. The mages had only just rebuilt the coordinate link."

"You are not mistaken?"

"No, I learned to read at six years old. Here all the arriving persons and opening times of the portal are described in black and white. If anyone is wrong, then it is the clerks Milla offended, the goat-bearded manager, which is hardly possible. Stationery rats are accustomed to keeping strict accountability."

"Somehow I do not see here any mages, or troxes."

"Nor do I. If the mages are not here, then they are somewhere else, but at any moment they can come to the party, then it will be time for dancing."

"I understand what you are getting at. Order ten of the 'ghosts' to see to defense on the wall, and I will continue the fascinating conversation with the distinguished governor." Andy imperceptibly beckoned Irran with his finger. The Miur casually bent down to correct the shield on her right leg. "Make it so the princess and the entourage will hear our private conversation," he whispered, then already louder, in a full voice: "Perform!"

"Yes, sir! Irran turned around famously but did not have time to fulfill the order. An incomprehensible doomsday began outside the city walls. "I am on the wall!" In four huge jumps, the commander reached the wall; two more leaps and she was up the flight of stairs. Underfoot, the ground trembled noticeably. The peaks of the country hills, cleared of vegetation, which were visible from the front of the portal site, were enveloped in a multicolored radiance. With each second the radiance grew brighter and brighter. High in the sky, trampling on the laws of nature, the real northern lights glowed and shone with miraculous beauty. Measured vibrations of the soil turned into slight shaking. A blustery, hot wind blew from the hills. Andy turned to the governor. A triumphant flame in the eyes of the captive dragon made it clear that the very worst thing had happened. "Rejoice," Andy thought grimly. "You do not have long left." If his assumptions were correct, it was worth looking for the lost mages in the same area. It was about ten or fifteen minutes of a light jog on trox-back to the hills.

Suddenly the trembling ceased; the unearthly light went out, but the keen sight of the were-dragon and the no less keen cat-vision allowed them to see the red glow far to the east, where the Miur Mountains were.

"What the...." Andy looked at one of the fighting mages, but Riur fled to him of her own accord.

"Resonator! They launched a resonator!"

"Stop! What resonator? What for?"

"If powerful high-frequency oscillations are created from the field side of the spatial shield, then the devices that generate the field get out of sync. The resonator left the borderlands with no shields."

"A sucker punch," Andy nodded. Now nothing was stopping the emperor's legions starting the invasion. *Oh, Ruigar, Oh, you son of a.... Under the Great Mother's nose you managed to roll out large-scale construction, disguising it as a defensive complex, and to give proper credibility and the need to strengthen the defense. You arranged a theatrical performance with those imperial "vultures," didn't you? Hmm, and did the mages know what they were getting into?* A wide field for assumptions and various hypotheses, but there was no time for plowing it. Although, what prevented the governor from taking blood oaths from his subordinates or getting tough on them with deadly sins or applying a combination of both methods...

Grabbing an empty box, Andy placed it near the governor. Riur strengthened the fetter interweave on the retinue, but "forgot" to energize the sound curtain. While the thoughtful shkas paced in circles around the captive lying on the ground, the curtain was completely depleted. Not noticing that the interrogation had ceased to be of a private nature, the shkas sat down on the box and turned to Ruigar with a lifeless voice that did not express any emotion:

"Now I understand why you ordered Renat to kill the Great Mother's ambassador, but I am much more interested in knowing what causes and circumstances forced you to betray the prince?"

Andy did not see how Ilirra flinched and opened her eyes wide and how deep disbelief and despair covered her face. He did not see the slight smile touching Ania's lips. He stopped noticing everything around; the whole world was for him just the interrogation of the prisoner. "I do not advise you to keep quiet. I would not want you to repeat Renat's fate. He did not live long with his cracked mind."

Andy built the conversation from the very beginning in such a way as to maximize the exposure of the truth. Dragons possessed magic and could distinguish truth and falsehood, but who prevented him from replacing concepts or not telling the whole truth? The truth was a terrible weapon in skillful hands. It was necessary to use it properly. He aimed the interrogation at Ilirra.

In any case, he couldn't avoid meeting the prince sooner or later, and it would be better if the heiress were, if not an ally, which was most unrealistic after today's events, then at least not an enemy. The neutral position of the ruler's daughter would be enough. Ilirra, despite her youth and love interest, was an intelligent woman and would forgive him the forced captivity. In the end, she would understand the reasons for his actions and would not take revenge.

"What did you do to him?" The governor asked flatly.

"I killed him," he said as if he were used to killing dragons. Ruigar looked into the shkas' face and froze inwardly. The freak's eyes seemed empty, but the sepulchral cold coming from their depths did not allow him to doubt the veracity of what he said. The commander of the cats really had killed dragons more than once.

"And me...."

"Do you think I will kill you? No, I will do my best to deliver your carcass sound—I will not say safe—to the prince's palace. It is not my prerogative to judge you. The prince himself will decide your fate. If you were hoping that the emperor would reward you for your betrayal, then I must disappoint you. Hazgar hates traitors. Once a traitor, always a traitor. Like any ruler, he uses their services and then quietly sends the used 'material' to the palaces of Manyfaces. Why would he want those who lost their honor and went back on their word? But anyway we seem to have gotten off topic. Back to the question: I want to know the reasons. I do not recommend being silent or lying. Do not make me use torture. Renat did not believe me, and he died."

"Renat was scum…."

"You should not talk that way. You must say something nice about the dead, or nothing at all," Andy said and struck Ruigar with lightning. The air smelled of ozone. Having received the shock, the governor swallowed air. He hadn't heard of magic like that. The tortuous interweave hit the nervous centers and gave a strong pain. It was almost impossible to tolerate. "The boy was devoted to you like a faithful dog. Unlike you, he deserves respect." A second bolt touched the governor's head. The stink of burning hair was added to the smell of ozone. "You can die with honor; you can die without honor. Death can come quickly and graciously, but it can delay. If you prefer silence, it will stay for a long time and take you in its arms like a limp vegetable. After ten minutes of my exercises, you will not have the strength for anything. And, breaking your mind, I will not particularly worry about preserving your sanity."

Here Andy was bluffing, and in order to prevent the governor from feeling the lie, he hit him with a third bolt. "Shall I continue?" He bent over the breathless dragon.

"No, I will tell you…."

"Wonderful. Was it worth getting tortured?"

"Hazgar promised not to hurt Ilirra and to let her go overseas if I helped remove the Miur shields. If I refused or told the prince about the conversation, he threatened to execute her before my very eyes with the most excruciating execution, I could not…. I wanted to send her to another continent…."

"And you believed him?"

"Yes, the emperor was not lying; I would have sensed a

lie."

"Naive," thought Andy.

"How did you meet?"

"Two fivers ago, his messenger arrived; he arranged a direct communication channel."

"You lovesick fool," Andy said, turning to the quieted retinue. The princess was sitting on the ground, embracing her knees with her hands and gazing stupidly at the ground. "I believe you love the prince's daughter. The rest is 'iffy,' do not make me continue...." He raised his right hand. A few electrical charges slipped between his fingers.

"Do not dare!" Ilirra snapped out of her trance. "Do not you dare, you cur!"

"And she loves you. The ancients were right: love deprives the mind. Targ, a melodrama from the theater!" Andy switched to Alat. "Now I will cry, a villain and two lovers. No, two villains, the rest are white and fluffy. My uncle is a fine fellow. He found the key to controlling this moron. I respect him; he knows how to achieve his goal."

"Uncle?" Ruigar's eyes widened.

How about that! The governor fluttering on in Alat?

"Is Hazgar your uncle?" repeated Ruigar in Alat.

That's it... I'll have to kill the fool personally, although I'm no better....

* * *

Ruigar looked at his captor with half-veiled eyelids. He did not expect that a strange shkas would suddenly speak in one of the languages that was spoken among the southern peoples of the neighboring planet three thousand years ago, or that he would blurt out such shocking news. He did not risk anything, giving away his knowledge of the language from another planet. Death at the hand of the prince's executioners or death from a shot by the Miurs' gunners were no different. Both lead to Manyfaces' palace. The terrible torture, which disconnecting the sensitivity of his nerve fibers did not soothe, left no doubt about his own destiny. They would send him straight to the other side. The dragon saw the strange magical fetters of Ilirra and Ania shift as they moved, as Ilirra tried to break free. The emperor's name, pronounced in an unfamiliar language, made them stand like a row of hunting rixes. Ania was thinking about something. The way she looked at the tormentor, he could tell the sida had come to some conclusions, but she did not rush to voice them. The tormentor himself stared at the governor with his unblinking blue eyes and was silent. The cold spilling around him became uncomfortable. Uncomfortable—that's putting it lightly.

In another place and under other circumstances, Ruigar would have enjoyed talking with the blue-eyed impostor. He had already used an incredibly interesting magical interweave to capture the retinue and the governor. The concise, extremely cost-effective in terms of mana spell, which was exactly down to the last nodal point, was not consistent with any known magical school, which in itself was strange. The magic shackles held a surprise, hidden within the rune scheme. Any attempt to free oneself from the invisible fetters made them stronger and stronger. An energy source scheme embedded in the structure of the interweave drained mana from counter-spells, redirecting it to reinforce the spell. Ruigar, trying to break the magical chains with a direct impulse, nearly choked from the tightened cocoon, which squeezed him until his ribs crunched. No more attempts were made to free himself. The princess' retinue faced the same difficulties. The dragons jerked for a few minutes behind the villain sitting on the wooden box, but, once they realized that the fetters only grew stronger, they quit their useless struggles.

The governor turned cautiously to his left side. The shackles did not interfere, which was good. His chest was already numb from lying on the hard stone. From the moment he was captured, it took quite a long time for him to overcome the shock and try to somehow turn the situation in his favor. He needed to find the connection between the shkas and the cat people. Their unquestioning obedience to the non-human was no less strange than his magic. At first, Ruigar thought the Miurs were bewitched and under a submission spell, but an examination with true vision did not reveal any magic clamp or leash on the warriors that would control their minds. The version about live puppets did not materialize, which means that there was something else. Logic dictated the only correct conclusion: the pride was transferred under the command of the freak by the order of the Great Mother. The "ghosts" did not obey anyone else. Even the ruler's daughters could not give orders to the formidable soldiers. Immediately, there was a blatant trampling of the felines' ancient traditions: carrying out the orders of a scoundrel. The phrase about the emperor put everything in its place. The white cat got out of her funk and started a big game, but she was sadly mistaken: the emperor would never allow an unplanned grafting of a branch onto the family tree. All the emperor's nephews and nieces were accounted for, right up to the seventh tribe. Where would another one come from? The old fool had decided to release another "liberator" into the world, even found a suicidal dolt for the role of the nephew. She should have come up with a "granddaughter," too, for all the good it would do her! Interesting: did she tell the new "relative" the story of the last self-styled Jagirra, or did she omit the details? Hazgar was a master of coming up with painful executions. The dragon was dying for a long, long time....

"How do you know Alat?" the shkas said, finally reviving. Ruigar wanted to say something smart, but, assessing the look on the shkas' face, thought the better of it. The "nephew' was not as simple as he seemed. He very well could have convinced the Great Mother of his claims; maybe it was not worth hurrying with the disclosure of the linguistic map. "It seems. I. Asked. A question?" the shkas repeated, separating each word.

Ruigar, carefully rolling on his back, glanced at the executioner and froze motionless. Narrow yellow pupils erupted in the freak's blue eyes. A series of scales broke through on the right cheek, and the pads of the fingers became decorated with sharp black claws half a finger long. With some sixth sense, the governor realized that lying was inappropriate; Death itself was looking at him. A few seconds ago, he was dealing with a magical mutant who was too big for his britches. Now, he was a dangerous, angry dragon, who had thrown off the mask of a simpleton. Perhaps, the Great Mother was right after all. There was something in the dragon, who stood up from the box, which made him treat him with all due respect and piety. Ruigar felt his back freeze to the icy stones. The "nephew" leaned over him and whispered ominously:

"I do not advise lying or keeping silent. You will regret it."

The governor, who had lived more than one thousand years, felt the sticky tentacles of fear growing out of the unknown depths of his subconsciousness, taking possession of him. The terror that seized him was akin to the horror he experienced two fivers ago. The emperor was so persuasive in his words that it was impossible not to believe the threats. It seemed that no one could be more convincing, but life proved that this was incorrect. The impostor could turn out to be a real nephew because he could instill fear do no worse, if no better, than his crowned relative. A family trait, so to speak.

"I was born on Ilanta." Ruigar barely pushed the words through his squeezed throat.

"Go on, I am listening carefully."

"My father and mother lived far to the south. My parents were studying the Alatites. I was with them, the language of the savages was not difficult to learn...."

"What wind brought you to Nelita?"

"Thirty years before the war, my father was invited to work at the capital's university...."

* * *

The devil was not as scary as he was being portrayed. The governor could be called a fellow countryman. To some extent, the situation had become clear. It was just that circumstances pitted Andy against the connoisseur of the languages of another planet. He should remember this and say nothing for now. How many of these "countrymen" were fluttering around Nelita, and who was counting them? He found one—there might be others.

Stopping the mental impact on the high-ranking prisoner, he leaned his elbows on his knees, put his chin on his hands, and thought hard. Thoughts, thoughts.... Andy massaged his temples. He was in up to his eyeballs now. How sick he was of spy games! The Great Mother, the Eldest, the Emperor, the princess, the governor, Ania—they were all weaving their personal webs.

Navigating the sea of political intrigues had zapped his energy. He was fed up!

"Maybe you will melt the ice?" Ruigar coughed, frozen to the pavement.

"You will suffer," Andy answered, glancing sideways at Irran, rushing from the wide portal site. "What now?" he asked the cat.

"Milla says someone is entering the settings of an exit point for the beacon signal of our portal. Whoever they are, they are opening a spatial passage!"

"Get away from the portal, everyone, now! Shelter the prisoners! Take up defense at the outer walls!" The warriors immediately moved the retinue behind the five-foot-thick stone parapet near the south wall. "To battle!"

At the same time as he gave the last order, he covered the prisoners with several shields. The Miur got down from the walls and occupied the sheltered positions they'd determined in advance. Irran had assumed there could be a situation where the enemy breaks through the portal, so she in advance determined the boundaries of defense. They should have killed the governor....

The space between the two portal frames turned into a ripple. It filled with a bright light and seemed to burst. Ahead of the humans, a detachment of dozens of metal golems with the coats of arms of the Principality of Ora on their chest jumped out onto the portal platform. Andy raised his left hand, gesturing to cancel the order to immediately open fire. Following the golems, people began to come out from the open throat of the portal; dragons appeared after the people.

"Targ! It is a good thing we did not start firing," he said to Irran, looking at the dragons emerging from the portal. The tribesmen were dressed in a sort of armor that covered their wide breastplates, but this was not the main thing. A protective block was inserted into each metal plate of the dragon armor. In magical vision, the armor sparkled like a cut diamond crystal. It was completely impossible to break such armor, except maybe by a shot from one of the fortress chuckers, and even so, no guarantee. The new characters, taking up the defense, competently distributed themselves around the palace square. The golems put up a multi-layered protective field.

"Shawars!"[10] cursed Irran.

"Shawars," Andy repeated, following the cat's lead.

Tearing through the thin film of space compressed by magic, fifty "ghosts" stepped onto the pavement in heavy armor that covered their entire bodies. Watching the incoming troops, he almost missed two characteristic claps from the newly opened portals. One passage opened in the center of the city, the second behind the city walls.

"I do not understand," said Irran, looking at the second squadron of cats appearing in the square, rolling out magomechanical constructions that most resembled artillery guns and anti-aircraft devices.

"What is not to understand?" Andy went out into the open space, levitated the wooden box over to himself, and sat down on it. "Have you ever heard the saying about eggs and baskets? The rule that forbids storing all one's eggs in one basket?"

"No."

"Well, now you have heard it," he answered the kitty cat, with a wave of his hand removing the shields from the princess' retinue and deactivating their bonds. Only Ruigar remained bound hand and foot.

"One word and you are a rotting corpse!" The governor nodded. "And here are the distinguished guests!" said Andy, feeling incredible fatigue descend upon him. The busy day had drunk up all his strength; he could hear his heart pumping blood through his veins.

Illusht appeared on the site, surrounded by bodyguards. Beside her, a mighty emerald dragon stepped cautiously.

"Father!" Ilirra jumped to her feet.

"What did you say about eggs?" Ania approached Andy. She had taken advantage of the commotion and running around.

"There is a rule that says do not store all one's eggs in one basket. The Great Mother wisely followed it, sending two embassy detachments to the prince, one of which from the very beginning played the role of bait. Can you guess which? And why are you all of a sudden switching back to the formal address with me?"

"I do not know who you are really," Ania quipped.

"Even so," Andy said, standing up from his makeshift seat. "I thought you guessed everything."

"I can arbitrarily build various assumptions about your person, but will my guesses be correct?"

Andy could not comprehend what the conversation was or what Ania was trying to achieve. His head refused to think at all. He had to sleep. An hour would be good, but two would be better. Otherwise, he would collapse in the middle of the city and fall asleep on the pavement.

"No respect," came a booming bass behind his back.

"Oh!" squeaked Ania.

"You have not earned it!" Andy snapped, turning to the prince. The dragon released two streams of thick smoke from his nostrils in surprise. "Irran, follow me."

"Where are you going?" Illusht was taken aback.

"To sleep!!!"

"What do you mean, sleep?" The prince and the princess could have competed in a variety show with a synchronous speech duet act.

"It is when you lie down, close your eyes, and stay motionless and quiet for a while!"

Andy turned sharply on his heels, clicked his boots with his heels and headed toward the fortress gates. Ahead of him and behind him, Irran's "ghosts" instantly lined up in rows. The cats went with activated protective amulets and weapons ready to fight. The prince twisted his neck inquiringly and turned towards the Miur princess. She jerked her tail and showed the commander of her "ghosts" an open palm, with a brief gesture stopping the detachment which was ready to punish the impudent man. The emerald dragon, restraining his fury, released a second stream of smoke from his nostrils. The guard dragons, armed with hefty fire-starters, remained standing motionless. For the prince's subjects and bodyguards, it remained a mystery why he didn't fire a long tongue of flame at the person who had crossed the line. Ora threw a questioning glance at Ania, who watched the detachment retreat behind the gates with unconcealed sadness on her face.

"I beg your pardon, Your Grace," Illusht bowed ceremoniously, "for the conduct and manner of Her Majesty's ambassador."

"Yes," the dragon struck the ground with his tail. "The Great Mother could teach him a couple of lessons in how to treat the crowned heads…. What did you, your highness, mean by calling that impudent boy an ambassador?"

Illyusht nervously twitched her triangular ears:

"The Great Mother gave this impudent man her Voice."

"A human?!" The prince of Ora choked with surprise.

"It is not that simple," Ania approached the ruler.

"He is a dragon, Your Grace." Ora stared at Illusht. The miur nodded, confirming the sida's words.

"So, what else do I need to know?" the ruler asked, waving his wings, not addressing anyone in particular. "And who will tell me what happened here?" he asked, bending over Ruigar in his impenetrable magical cocoon. "Daughter, you do not want to tell me anything?"

* * *

"Spread yourselves out," Andy shouted at the warriors as soon as the detachment left the gates of the fortress. "In a dense formation, you are a very good target. Three in the avant-garde, three in cover, watch the flanks and roofs of the houses. You never know when someone might catch us, as we caught Renat."

The city, when viewed from the height of a small hill on which the fortress with the portal was located, resembled a ravaged anthill. From the bright archway of the portal illuminating the outskirts, live rivers of troops flowed toward the central gates of the city wall. Dragons flew out one by one. Covered in dark visual curtains, platforms with heavy weapons swam out of the arc, around which fortifications were immediately built. Soldiers pressed refugees and city residents to the walls of the houses, who had come to gaze at the prince's army. Like a flock of crows, dozens of dragons circled above the second portal, which opened between the hills on which the lieutenant's assistant mounted the resonator. There was no way to see what was happening there.

281

After the artificial earthquake, a dusty haze hung in the air.

"Sir," after giving the necessary instructions, Irran went to Andy, "where are we going?"

"To the hotel. I really do need a couple of hours of sleep. That dying puppet really exhausted me."

"?!" The cat woman tilted her head to her right shoulder.

"I was one with her," he explained to the warrior, who nodded understandingly.

"Why did you not stay with the prince?" Irran decided on a third question.

Andy stopped. The rest of the cats stood beside him as mute statues. The "ghosts" did not show their interest in the question with a single gesture or glance, but the auras that blazed in different colors gave them away. Until the very last moment, the elite soldiers did not believe they would leave the fortress alive. They were prepared to defend their commander to the last drop of blood, cursing his language and manners in their souls...

"No reason to. Nothing would have changed. The emperor outplayed the prince and the Great Mother."

"Hmm," the feline said incredulously in reaction to his last sentence. "So that is why you did not kill the governor?"

Andy looked attentively at the commander of the "ghosts." She was very keen. Smart girl, but too many questions...

"Irran, do not you think you are asking a few irrelevant questions?"

"No." The girl was not at all embarrassed. "In following you, we made our choice." Now it was Andy's turn to wonder. "In the presence of Her Highness, we have listened to you. Now none of us has a way back, and that is not because the Great Mother called you her Voice. We owe you for saving our lives—twice. Rimas entrusted you with her honor, we have trusted you with our lives."

The "kitties" had taken upon themselves a debt of blood. Cool... and stupid. A thoughtless decision. From now on, they were connected to him until his death, and he could not change the cats' decision with any words. When did they find the time, by the way? Andy blushed to the very tips of his ears. *Well done, Irran, you really poked my face in the mud. Sobering, however! Honor and life, Targ take them. That's not a lot of responsibility for me or anything*.... But the commander's words left a pleasant warm trace somewhere deep in his soul. These girls would never betray him.

"I am a dragon," he said. Milla and Riur exchanged glances. *Just wait, more surprises in store for you.* "In addition, I am the keeper of the key to the interplanetary portals." All the Miurs' ears stood upright—surprise! "The prince fell for the emperor's trick, played out with the help of the governor. Look there," Andy pointed towards the mountains. The warriors synchronously followed his index finger. "What do you see there?"

"The mountains," said Irran.

"I had no doubts—the mountains. If the Imperial legions had begun an invasion, what would have happened over the mountains?" The cats thought for a moment and, as if on command, turned to Andy. "I see you got it. There would have been a magical light show over the mountains. Besides the shield, the borders are covered by defensive complexes. Why are they silent?"

"Why?" one of the "ghosts" couldn't contain herself.

"The legions have not crossed the border," Irran said. "What about the army camps the orc told us about?"

Andy sighed heavily and leaned against the cat's gunner.

"Both the camps and the portal arcs are real. I am inclined to believe the orc. According to him, the army team arrived at the points of temporary permission in one night, so it was probably a transfer of troops with the help of a large number of magicians. The story about the magical portals is true. The emperor's army was like a loaded gunner; I have no doubt that he fired. The prince missed the last chance to travel on an interplanetary portal. It is only my personal opinion, but I am ready to bet my head and tail on it: the imperial thugs have already crushed the last defender and entrenched themselves around the former princely property. The interplanetary portal is not so far from the border. I think that in order to capture it, the mages have built dozens of stationary gates."

"Sir, when did you guess that?" asked Irran.

"When I interrogated the governor. I remembered the map of the area and laid down the facts."

"Why do we need an interplanetary portal?" again the "ghost" spoke up. The warrior was hushed from all present.

"For resettlement to Ilanta," Andy answered shortly.

Irran released and retracted her claws several times. She had understood the situation:

"Her Highness Illusht knew about your mission, sir?"

"Yes."

"Now your reaction is understandable. She was supposed to keep the prince in the capital and persuade them to send the army to cover the interplanetary portal, or at the very least, to convince them to install a space shield around the portal. Why did she not do it?"

"I do not know. I can only assume that Illusht arrived in the capital of the principality right when they were sending the prince to the border, and she had no choice but to follow the ruler. Probably, she came to the same conclusions that we did, and therefore, let the disrespectful attitude to the prince go unpunished. Something like that. Ruigar did a great job. I do not know what the emperor promised him, and I do not want to know more. Let Ilirra kick the truth out of him. Besides, it was getting dangerous to keep agitating the jerk. The governor could have thrown out a pair of dirty little facts defaming the ruler. I do not need such knowledge. Oh, how those in power despise those who bear their secrets. I would not put it past Ruigar to do away with me and you in that very conniving, sophisticated way. So I learned the big picture but did not climb into the dark jungle."

"What are you going to do?"

"I already told you—sleep!" Irran's eyes widened. "Sleep. I can afford to fall out of reality for an hour or two. Two hours of banging my head against the wall now will not solve anything. Later, I will think about how to get out of this mess. Think and think again. I have some ideas; I will run them in my head from all sides, then go to the prince. Running around in circles without an action plan does not make sense. Andy, stumbling from the gunner, straightened his sling with swords and sniffed sullenly at his own, now his very own warriors. "What are you just standing there for? March to the hotel!"

* * *

His internal alarm clock measured an hour and a half from the moment his right cheek touched the pillow. He slept soundly for about forty minutes. Actually, he fell asleep instantly, but the cries and curses that were heard outside the door drove away his dreams. An important princely official came to the hotel and demanded they free up the room. The Miur guard in the hallway pointed out to the gentleman which way was up, and advised him to leave the premises; otherwise, he will be helped to overcome the space separating the second floor and the front door of the establishment, by kicks. The official left himself but promised to return. Andy tossed and turned for about twenty minutes on the soft featherbed. His interrupted sleep waved goodbye. He did not want to get up, but, saying goodbye to Morpheus, Andy overpowered himself, rolled off the bed, and rinsed himself in a barrel of ice water installed in the small bathroom. The room was not deluxe. The downy featherbed was the only thing that distinguished this number from a room in a roadside inn. He felt better already. His brains started working faster. He ran his hand over the sun scars on his chest. Something clicked in his head. "What if?" Jumping out of the barrel like a bullet, he rubbed himself with a towel and quickly dressed in clean clothes and armor. Securing his swords, Andy jumped out into the corridor.

"Irran!" he shouted. A couple of seconds later, the door of the next room burst open, revealing a wet, disheveled cat woman dressed like Eve, but with a gunner in her hands. Apparently, the Miur had decided to take a bath, but was interrupted by her boss' cry. For a moment, Andy froze like his father's computer when he got closer than six feet away. The cat had an excellent, proportional figure, and there was absolutely no hair on the body. The furry covering, not counting the tail, was only on her arms and face. Much later, Andy learned that the warriors removed the fur on their bodies with a special ointment since while wearing the magical armor, the thermo-regulation regime was not always observed (something the designers did not work out), especially in stressful and combat situations. The fur got soaked in sweat; in about two or three hours, the cat would begin to smell. A radical way to get rid of the problem was complete depilation.

"Yes, sir!' The Miur's voice functioned like a "reset" button for the frozen operating system.

"I need a detailed map of the southern lands of the empire. Send someone to search, and you can finish bathing."

"Yes, sir!" The cat disappeared into a large room set aside for the warriors with ten beds. Andy remembered how the magistrate's representative screamed when they came to settle a second time. The miserable-looking man squealed and spat so much that Milla suggested the poor man had a red-hot awl up his backside. It was no skin off her nose. She stood there calmly and quietly while the ambassador listened to another stream of "delights" about himself and pondered particularly brutal ways of killing an official. The magistrate could not give two craps about different ambassadors. The people of the free city did not bow to anyone. And who, Mr. Ambassador, will repair the building? The flow of words went uninterrupted. The conflict was resolved by a tight and rather heavy bag with coins of a dull yellow metal. The little man, with a predatory glint in his eyes, quickly counted the coins and personally led the detachment to the allocated rooms.

"There are no other apartments. Everything is occupied. If you destroy a wall here too, you will have to go sleep in the street," he grumbled upon leaving. Andy watched the greedy man leave. "War is hell... to some. Others line their pockets from it."

His train of thought was derailed by the sound of the "spider web" signaling and the trampling of numerous feet on a staircase. The pair of miur standing guard lazily stood up from the walls. The warriors drew their swords. Only an idiot would shoot from a gunner in a small crowded room. The corridor was not an outside wall. The damage would collapse the floors under them as well. A burly man in an expensive coat appeared in the hall. The visitor was followed by three mages and over two dozen princely guardsmen. Behind the military, he saw a whole delegation of human pencil pushers from the offices of those in power. The troops' faces reflected the determination to deal with the insolent people who did not blossom with due respect for the princely pencil pushers. But, upon seeing the Miur, they immediately lost all fervor and began to glare angrily at the main pencil pusher. The mages mentally shared the troops' opinion.

"In the name of Prince Ora, evacuate the premises," the lover of expensive clothes bellowed, waving a scroll with a wax seal. "I have orders from His Lordship."

"Is he insane, or what?" thought Andy. The looks on the Miur guards' faces had the same question.

"Give it to me!"

The paper rat held out the scroll.

"Clear out!"

Andy read the text, fondled the wax seal with his finger, almost tasted the document. Then he calmly pronounced:

"Sir, I do not wish to offend you, but please be so kind as to seek habitation somewhere else." He tucked the scroll into his belt. The bureaucrat almost choked. His face flushed purple, making him resemble a boar.

"Do you know who I am?!" he exploded. A certain organ came to mind. "If you do not get away this instant, I have the right to give orders to the guards and mages. They will free the numbers by force."

"Really?" Andy's will shields dropped for ten seconds, allowing the mages to see his aura in full detail. Their pale faces and the glances that ran from side to side suggested that the trio wanted to be as far away from the hotel as possible. Then the guards began to grow pale. When a fully equipped combat pride comes out of the room, one involuntarily turns pale. "Go away!"

"What?!" the fat man began to boil with indignation. "I..."

"Accompany your master out of here," Andy said to the mages, turning the raging official into a living statue with an immobilizing spell. "With that, we will assume that the conflict is over. I will not complain to Prince Ora about your behavior, but you will explain to master...," he took out the scroll and read the name, "... Porvo Durrie, that next time I will tear his 'durrie' limb from limb, and I will put his head on a stake, and the prince will be stomping on his remains for having to hush up the scandal."

The mages nodded feverishly and picked up the frozen body. The "evictors" departed much faster than they came.

"Sir, the map of the empire." Irran came out of the room.

"Good. Let us have a look."

Andy waved his hand to Milla and Ramita, who, according to Irran, often went beyond their borders on raids while on duty. The commander of the "ghosts" did not need an invitation. Having changed into her guard's outfit, she went to the master's room.

"Sir, why do you need a map of the imperial lands?" Milla was burning with curiosity.

Andy wanted to get annoyed that they kept calling him "sir," but, glancing at the mage, he realized that his indignation would be enjoyed with pleasure. The cats would not depart from their traditions by one iota and would continue addressing him according to etiquette.

"Why do I need a map, you ask?" Andy lightly touched the right lower corner of the map three times. It activated a magical illusion. The map became 3D. The cats watched as Andy noted a couple of points in the imperial lands, tying them to the illusion. "Ramita, what can you tell me about the area closest to the borderlands, located around this spot?"

The scout gathered her thoughts for about ten seconds, then gave out detailed information about the small settlements located near the indicated place, which were not marked on the map.

"I see. Milla, what can you tell me about the possibility of building a portal for these coordinates? Will there be any difficulties?"

"No," answered the Miur. "In the valley where you propose to move, there are many characteristic visual landmarks, and portals can be built 'by sight,' that is, attached to the image. The only difficulty may be the spatial shield, but in this case, you can open the portals somewhat in the distance. There is no large border shield there, and a small circular shield can be pierced if there is a sufficient source of mana."

The questioning lasted about twenty minutes. Andy went "hmm," revised and refined his plans and wrote something down on the back of the map.

"Why a map, you ask?" He folded the paper up neatly into his pocket. "The nearest point to us is the cargo interplanetary portal. It seems to me that it is not the army that is guarding it, but something smaller, perhaps a regiment. In reality, there are a hundred guards and a couple dozen magicians."

"Sir, do you want...,"

"Oh, yes, Milla, I do! I really want to." Andy's gaze became sharp and malicious. His lips formed an unkind grin. "The Emperor will be very surprised if someone takes a portal on his land. I bet your head he does not expect such impudence!"

"And why mine?"

"I rather like my own; I am accustomed to it." Irran laughed; Ramita looked at her and giggled. "Enough laughing. In fifteen minutes, all 'ghosts' will be ready, and we set out towards the prince. Irran, there will be a special task for you: convince Illusht to create a direct channel of communication with the Great Mother. I saw her 'ghosts' leading a platform with accumulators on it towards a large communicator artifact the size of which, compared to a jammer, would be like you compared to a mosquito. Milla, prepare a ceremonial outfit for me, so I can change right before we get to the fortress. Walking around the city in official rags is not too comfortable. Alright, it is time."

* * *

Exactly fifteen minutes later, the envoy, reserving the rooms behind it, left the magistrate's hotel. The cat warriors lined up in the usual order, covering Andy from all sides. Halfway to the prince's fortress, which turned into his headquarters, had passed without incident. The detachment began to climb the hill. The warriors, clad in armor, relaxed a little and missed a large cat that jumped down on to the pavement in front of the master from one of the rooftops. And thanks be to the Twins that they did miss her!

"Mimiv?"

"Mrrow." The local beauty showed in an unambiguous gesture that she wanted to be picked up.

"Mimiv, where are your owners?" Andy asked, picking up the cat.

"Here!" Andy turned at the sound. Under the low peak of the front entrance to the house from which Mimiv had jumped off stood Evael and Lilly.

"Andy!" the girl rushed to him.

"Let her through." In a couple of moments, the little elf was in the arms of her father's rescuer.

Mimiv meowed meekly, but it was not in her power to compete with her owner. She had to run to the ground. "Hey, Lilly. Easy trails, Evael."

"Straight roads," said the old elf, who looked around at the Miur with an attentive glance. "'Ghosts, hm? It is nice to realize that I was not wrong."

"What are you doing in the city?"

"We have been here more than a fiver already, the whole clan. We even brought the saplings of our ancestral Mellornys with us."

"You evacuated?"

"You can put it that way."

"Are the warriors and mages with you?"

"Or course. How can it be otherwise?"

"Very well," Andy thought for a moment. "Let us go, we will talk on the way. It will be a serious conversation."

"And where are you off to?"

"To the prince."

"Sir, look!" Ramita shouted, pointing at the mountains.

Andy narrowed his eyes. The real northern lights were blazing over the mountains.

"A distraction maneuver," he said, and explained: "Too big a time gap between the disappearance of the shield and the attack. Hazgar simply wants to keep the Great Mother and the prince on their toes, threatening from that direction."

"'Sir,'" the old elf whispered softly. "I sense the conversation will indeed be quite serious."

* * *

Ania, with half-closed eyes, watched Andy. A large mirror took up an entire wall of the cabinet the prince had chosen for the official reception of the Great Mother's ambassadors. She observed the reflections of the hosts and guests present in the room. It was a handy thing: it helped hide the interest that the guests might feel from a direct look. This way, they only guessed what the elf was thinking, standing frozen behind the Prince and Princess' chairs. The sida gently touched her tight corset. Behind the bone plates, near her heart, lay a silver bloom wrapped in a silk kerchief.

The prince slightly moved his head, listening to the rustle of clothes behind him. The elf exhaled inaudibly. The crown on the ruler's head gave off a scattering of rainbow sunbeams. The girl did not know what the sovereign was thinking about. She was hoping he would fulfill his promise to release her from the vassal oath after the important reception.

Andy had come to the fortress three hours ago and immediately asked for an audience. Ora at first wanted to refuse the impudent beggar, but the Miur princess presented the same request. The prince took a small time-out to decide his next course of action and summoned Ilirra. The conversation between father and daughter behind impenetrable sound curtains lasted over an hour. Ania was not summoned. The sida could guess why he decided what he did and could not disagree with certain reasons in favor of granting an audience. But the princess could not be an unbiased advisor, and the ruler wanted to formulate his next few moves, given the situation. The dragons couldn't understand who was playing first violin in the Illusht-Andy duet. On the one hand, Illusht was the daughter of the Great Mother, endowed with the power to conclude military and civil unions. Ora wanted to take full advantage of that. On the other hand, the ruler had chosen Andy to be her Voice. Why, they wondered? What proposal was the Great Mother going to make, that to voice it, she would choose a dragon not known to anyone? And why exactly this dragon? What was special about him, besides the suspicion that the ambassador might be a true blood? After talking with his daughter, the prince decided to ask Ruigar, who spoke with the mysterious diplomat in a language unknown to a wide range of people. During the interrogation, Andy had mentioned Hazgar, and what he said was very surprising to the former governor. The information was so important and shocking that the captive dragon's aura shone for several minutes with all colors of the rainbow. What did Andy say to him? The girl was very sorry that she did not understand a word. She caught the general tone, but without words, the mosaic did not want to take shape. Ruigar smiled with bloodied lips and told the prince where he could go. Fear flashed in his eyes....

Andy was a complete mystery and did not hurry to give away clues to solving his secrets, but Ania was not a deaf-mute. During the entire virk, the shkas kept making the others think, and his deductions pushed the sida to the brink of killing the clever fellow traveler, but he immediately warned her of the fallacy of that rash step. Ania then reasonably decided that it would be undesirable to rush things, and she was not mistaken. The meeting with the "ghosts" and the reception arranged by the Great Mother confirmed the correctness of the main line of conduct and added questions. It wasn't a secret to anyone in the retinue that the high priestess's arrest during the reception was somehow connected with the dance of the elements and the familiar shkas. No one had ever seen a splash of spontaneous magic like that before, ever. Only Manyfaces knew how the Miur (or not the Miur?) managed to retain control over the destructive energy. All the elements at the same time... No matter how skillful the spellcaster may be, all the elements simultaneously were subject only to dragons. Then Ilirra asked her father's spy: "Are you thinking what I am thinking?" Ania did not know what the princess was thinking, but all the lady's thoughts were generally easy to read on her face. The young dragoness could think and analyze. She did not at all like being led by the nose like a little puppy. Ilirra cautiously asked about the silver bloom and met a wrathful look... The sida was not planning on letting anyone in on her inmost feelings, and Ilirra was the last person she would have wanted to see in her inner world. But Andy had firmly established himself there, and not only there.... By the time the virk/envoy was on its way back, the woman knew for certain that the blue-eyed shkas who had given her this flower of love was a real dragon. But to share that with the princess...

Ania once again directed her gaze towards the mirror's surface, glancing at the straight face of the Great Mother's ambassador. Surprisingly, during the negotiations, not a single muscle moved on his face. It seemed the dragon was presenting himself as a stone monolith, imperturbable from outside factors. Even his aura, which Andy did not hide, did not flash with colors of anger or annoyance even once. He had himself completely under control. She didn't believe that this was the same man who had once given her a silver bloom, or that the statue sitting in the "lotus" pose on the sofa could actually have feelings.

"No," said the prince, rising from the table. "Are you asking me to run away? What kind of prince would I be if I give the people who trusted me, the elves and the dragons, up to the clawed paws of the usurper? My answer is no!"

The prince did not accept the offer, which was his right. Andy easily jumped to his feet, now face to face with the aged ruler. For several seconds, he looked at the prince, summing him up as if he had just seen him for the first time. External curiosity in no way affected the color scheme of the aura. Internally, the ambassador remained a piece of ice, but... under icy shells, hot hearts are hidden. Ania again touched her corset. The prince had promised her freedom.

"Allow me to demonstrate?" said Andy, undoing the belt of his ceremonial attire.

* * *

This time, His Lordship met the ambassador in human form: he was a tall, gray-haired old man, with wide curved shoulders, an angry look in his sky-blue eyes, and an aristocratic face with a fine mesh of wrinkles. He reminded Andy of a dense oak, widely sprouting branches. The oak had deep roots and up to now had successfully survived the storms of life. This latest hurricane did not frighten the wise politician, who for three thousand years managed to dance on the blade of a hot knife.

Andy corrected the ceremonial rashag, to the hilt of which more than a dozen colored ribbons were attached. Illusht personally tied a whole bunch of ribbons on it; the look of it made jaws drop in the prince's entourage. For those in the know, the ribbons said more than any words.

For over an hour, Andy portrayed himself as a silent idol.

According to protocol, Princess Illusht and His Lordship settled the main issues of military cooperation. Each of them brought a whole staff of clerks from diplomatic services. War was going on; the rulers had no time to settle every petty fact. That's what their bureaucrats were for. To solve small current issues. When the prince and the princess had talked over the main points, it came time for Andy's proposals, which crossed out all the agreements that had just been reached. They themselves were to blame: he asked to be given the first word, but the old dragon said no.

"Are you asking me to move to another planet?!" The prince said in shock.

"Yes," Andy did not beat around the bush. "No sweet life on Ilanta is foreseen. There, war is raging as well, but it is a way for you to avoid total destruction."

"Two hours ago, I was informed of the loss of the interplanetary portal. The emperor seized it and has already organized defense. How do you plan to make the transition?"

"You can win the portal back.... There are other ways too." Andy did not show his cards. Inwardly, he sensed that he had not been taken seriously, and the ruler of the besieged lands would not build upon his initiative to resettle the people.

"No," the old dragon replied after a long hesitation, rising from the table. "Do you propose I flee, abandon my land, honor, and dignity? My answer is no!"

"*Stubborn old fool*," Andy thought, not allowing his thoughts to reflect on the external energy shell. "He's drowning and pulling others down with him. A good answer, though. The prince is worthy of respect for self-sacrifice, but what should I do? Without dragons, we won't get any portals. Checkmate. The time for trumps has come."

Andy stood opposite the prince, removed his belt, bared his chest, plunged into the settage. Following the instructions of the Great Mother, he mentally merged with the gold disc that had settled inside him and began pumping energy from his internal reserves to the key accumulator. The ruby lit up like a red lantern; a light ripple ran over the surface of the amulet from the stone; the runes on the amulet flashed. Breaking the skin, the key burst out of him.

"I am the keeper of the key," he wheezed, glancing at Ania.

He handed the key to his neighbor, who passed it to the prince. All present took a moment to examine it in all its glory and then handed it back to Andy, who put it back in its "place." The wounds so similar to the mark left by the central concress of the dugaria cocoon closed up. A wave of flame swept over his body, burning up the blood that had spilled out.

"My answer is no!"

"That is a pity."

"The audience and the negotiations are finished. We can return to your question tomorrow or the day after tomorrow when intelligence will estimate the number and combat capability of the emperor's troops who seized our portal. How long did the Great Mother give you the right of Voice?"

"Just for the negotiations."

"That is fine; we can solve the issue privately."

It was a fiasco. Before the negotiations, Andy hoped that the prince, trapped by the Imperial legions on both sides, would seize the opportunity of relocating to another planet with all four paws. But life and Lady Luck ordered otherwise. *Stupid protocol drafters, Targ-loving Illusht. Why did she have to give the old dragon hope? That awful cat. She destroyed the whole game. Has she completely gone off her rocker, promising military support on behalf of the Great Mother? Targ, Targ! The old fart beat the Miur—he got her signature on the document; now he'll play differently.*

Andy bowed low to the prince, accepting his decision.

"I ask everyone except Her Highness to leave the office. We need to talk privately," said the prince. "Daughter, you know what to do."

Andy's sixth sense, which had saved him more than once, alerted him that the old flyer's words were about him personally. *Sooo, his Lordship has contrived his game and given the go-ahead to start it. I'm so SICK of them all!!*

"Irran!" quietly called Andy, coming out of the negotiation room.

"I am here, sir!"

"How is the channel coming along?"

"All is ready. In fifteen minutes, the mages will launch the sound-muffling amulets."

"Go quietly as a fly to the mages. I need to speak to the Great Mother!"

"Yes, sir!"

"...The old goat... Twins almighty, why am I so unlucky?!" said Andy in Alat.

"Have you been refused?"

Andy turned around and locked eyes with Ruigar, who was crucified between two power posts. The magical poles, shimmering with greenish light, pulled mana out of the prisoner. The governor was in human form. All bruised and bloodied, in tattered clothes, he no longer resembled the imposing macho he was a few hours ago. Tomorrow he would be executed.

Andy was wrong: Ilirra loved power much more than she did the governor of the northern lands, if she even loved him at all. History abounds in thousands of examples of unbending men breaking down because of their love for noble maidens. There were reverse cases too, where women fell because of their loves, but not now. Ruigar, who was in it up to his horns, mistook what he wished for reality, and now he was slurping boiled soup with a ladle. Hazgar bent him, Andy broke him, and Ilirra finished him off completely. The girl did not forgive betrayal. When she got over the initial shock, the princess did not say a word to her father in defense of her former lover. One admirer less, no big deal. How many more would there be? The dragon had become too human, too...

"Yes, he refused."

"I can give you some advice." Ruigar spit a bloody loogie.

"Hm, that would be interesting to hear...."

The dragon flashed his eyes at the guards on the perimeter of the site.

The hint was understood. Andy fenced himself and the prisoner in with a sound curtain, which had to be constantly fed. The columns greatly weakened the structure of the interweave.

"I know what you want; the Miur of your squad blabbed. No, no, it is not what you think. Two or three unrelated words, but I can draw pictures and draw conclusions. Here in the borderlands, you have to. Are you from there?" Ruigar pointed his chin at the luminous sickle of Ilanta and coughed. A new bloody spot of spittle decorated the pavement. The prince's executioners really did a number on him. "You do not have to answer. I was at the portal complex three fivers ago. I personally studied the remaining seals. The true bloods of Ilanta knew how to impose magical obstructions. Nobody could break them in three thousand years, but now only a key is needed to open the portal. I realized something was wrong with you when I looked at you with true vision. I saw threads of scars on your chest and a dense energy cluster in the center of your aura, besides your perfect knowledge of an unnecessary and forgotten language from a foreign planet. Then there are your magical interweaves that are not taught in any school. I put the facts together and came to an interesting conclusion. So you are from there?"

"What can I say…."

"So I am correct." Ruigar swung on the invisible chains. "A-huh, HUH." He coughed. "Did you ask the prince for help returning?"

"No, why?"

"What did you ask?"

"I suggested relocation."

"You told him about yourself and…,"

"Do not take me for a complete fool." The conversation was starting to bore him. He was supposed to be giving advice.

"Alright, be an intelligent fool." Ruigar stretched his cracked lips into a smile. "The prince will not let you go. He will do everything in his power to keep you beside himself, then give you up to Hazgar. Ora knows very well that the emperor dreams of getting his hands on the interplanetary portals. Now you are a pawn in a grand political game. A valuable pawn, truly."

"More valuable than you?" Andy lifted one eyebrow.

"I am trunk change," the dragon said bitterly.

"You said something about advice…."

"Today in the capital the conclave of clans is meeting. Not all the prince's subjects support his policy of staying and fighting. Many forced migrants would gladly be removed as far as possible from the emperor. The prince plans to visit the conclave; the mages have set up a portal. I am in chains, and people are not shy about talking about state secrets. In their eyes, I am a dead man. What can the dead tell?"

"A lot if you raise him in time and the brain has not begun to rot. For some reason no one on Nelita practices necromancy; that field is not plowed…"

Andy looked at the former great state official and thought about how Ruigar's words converged with his personal thoughts. He had already begun to take steps in that direction. Evael had begun turning the gears among the elves and especially trusted humans. It was plan "B" in case of failure of the main mission, which now could safely be called failed. The old man had assigned him one clan magician for communication and coordinating their actions. As it turned out, the point-ears were even craftier than they seemed. They found a way to bypass the jammers but preferred to keep the secret from friends and enemies alike. Kerrovitarr was a happy exception.

"Do you want to live?" Andy said, igniting sparks of hope in the prisoner's eyes with his unexpected question. "Well?"

"Yes." Ruigar stared into his eyes.

"You will take a blood oath of fidelity to me, an immutable pledge."

The dragon did not think it over long.

"I agree."

"Terrific." Andy felt like a Sith Lord from Star Wars, but what else could he do? The prince left him no choice. What do stubborn people do when you don't let them in the door? Climb in the window!

"Wait," Andy said, grabbing Ruigar by the chin and removing the sound curtain. "You brute!" He stuck a strong, deliberate, ostensible blow to the jaw. The captive jerked on the invisible chains. The kick in the stomach made Ruigar moan. "You wanted to play me, you cur!"

The dragons guarding the site grinned. They would not have made merry if they could see the smile on the prisoner's lips and his hopeful eyes.

* * *

"Sir, we can not get through the interference," one of Illusht's telephone workers leaned in front of him.

Should have seen it coming. Ilirra took action while daddy was distracting the feline princess. The connection would not be restored until the ambassador was separated from the Great Mother's heiress. Andy hoped Illusht would not enlighten the prince on the details of the Great Mother's work on the resettlement of the Miur. Nothing was threatening the white cat, but he was a different story: his status after the unsuccessful negotiations looked very doubtful. The ruler gave him the right to be her Voice only for this meeting with the prince. Now he had turned into nothing, and he had to strike while the iron was hot, before they noticed the change. Ruigar pointed out the direction where to look.

"Irran."

"Yes, sir."

"The general meeting. Where is Nariel, the elf mage?"

"Everyone is here, sir. Is something happening?"

"I lost the status of the Voice. I need to high-tail it."

"Where to?" asked Irran, always ready for action. Andy narrowed his eyes.

"Would you like to walk to the capital of the principality?"

"I have always dreamed of visiting Raygor."

"We will do this…. Capture the teleport platform…. The second dozen Miur should tie up the portal mages. You have five minutes to prepare. We are on!"

No one expected an attack from the inside. The dragons that were conveniently located on the heated stones of the site with the convict were blinded and deafened by the bright flashes from the tricky blinding and deafening interweaves that went off before their snouts. A dozen cat people, peacefully marching to the fortress gates through the portal platform, dramatically changed many mages' plans for the evening. The teleport operators did not expect the attack or the charged gunners in their faces. The second group of Miur appeared in front of the arc in five seconds. The

Miur smelled like alchemical potions and blood. It was not possible to blind everyone, so there was a case for the use of gunners. Three cats and Andy, slipping past the blinded dragons of the guard, freed the prisoner. Andy cut the governor over his forearm.

"Your oath!"

Ruigar quickly whispered the words of the magical oath. They were not able to get away without some adventures. When Andy and the three miur, one of whom was dragging a huge bag hidden by a small magical curtain, crossed a small courtyard between two barracks while moving towards the portal site, Ania and several dragons of the princess' retinue came out of the nearest building to the dungeon. Ilirra's servants, stunned by the meeting, fell to the ground and became prisoners of force for the second time in a day.

"Ania!" Andy cried.

"On it!" Milla dashed towards the swearing dragons and threw the elf over her shoulder.

"To the portal, quickly!" A mild "press" spell hit the dragons, silencing their cries. Next, a strong curtain of silence fell on the fettered dragons.

* * *

"Activate it!" Irran towered over the goat-bearded boss of the portal mages.

"I do not...," the old man stumbled.

"My dear sir, we have absolutely no time to bicker with you," Andy said in a voice full of doom. "In a minute, the prince's guard will fly here and kill us all, but if you do not activate the portal now, then you will feel terribly sorry that you lived this minute. Irran!" The cat stretched out her arm, grabbed one of the portal mages without looking and tore off his head. "Riur!| A second clerk was in an iron grip. "I am going to count to three. On 'three,' she will tear your colleague's head off. Two. Riur!" The man's head remained in place; he never said "three." A siren howled over the fortress; powerful magic lamps lit up the sky.

"Curse you! I will open the portal!" squealed the goat-bearded man.

"Hold your tongue; otherwise, we will cut it off. Well, quickly!

The old man tore a chain from his neck with a key-portal plate, inserted it into the groove on the right stela, and began to drum out short spells that were also passwords. A few winged shadows flew into the sky with the huge flap of wings. The dragons were too late by just a little bit. The portal opened up and absorbed the detachments of Miur and four people. The cutting stone attached to the left stela left Prince Ora without a fixed teleport for five hours. There were spare blocks in the warehouse, but they had to be installed and adjusted. Illusht received an official note of protest but managed to get out of it, saying that Andy had ceased to be the Voice, since the prince himself stopped negotiations, and that she would pay decent compensation to the families of the victims.

"Welcome to Raygor! Where to now?" Andy asked Ruigar.

"To the main city square. I would advise the ladies to use mimicry."

"Lead the way...."

Ruigar waved for them to follow him and stepped off the teleport site. Andy took Ania by the elbow and followed. The Miur lined up in two ranks, but they did not hurry to activate their mimicry armor. Instead, the cat women took colored scarves out of their pouches and tied them around their necks. The sida scoffed knowingly. Andy glanced at the elf, then at the cats. Something clicked in his brain. Indeed, that would be better—the handkerchiefs of mercenaries would divert attention more reliably than unseen armor. Detachments of Miur often moonlighted as mercenaries in the far south. The warriors needed combat practice, and where could they get it if not in a war zone? The appearance in the city of mercenaries guarding an important gentleman would attract interest, but not enough to attract the close attention of law enforcement agencies. War was going on; many aristocrats had ceased to appear in public without protection, especially aristocrats such as the governor of the northern lands. No wonder he invited the best soldiers into his service.

"My friends," the former governor stopped at the gate, Andy turned to the sound, "we need to hurry."

Surprisingly, the dragon held up well. No one, even the most attentive and searching glance, could determine that under the charms of the city dandy's magically induced image lay scraps of once elegant clothes and numerous wounds.

"We are ready," Irran reported.

On Andy's command, the kitties hung their gunners behind their backs and drew their swords.

"Let us go," the Great Mother's Voice said, the voice of reason the prince refused to listen to. He could only hope that he would be luckier at the conclave. Prince Ora left him no choice. He would have to fight dirty; there was no time left for politesse. "Ania, I hope you will not do anything stupid."

The girl silently shook her head. What could she do? The greatest folly had already been committed. The master would never believe that the kidnapping was not partially her fault. It was an accident, an incredible combination of circumstances, fate, karma, anything, but not her will. Ilirra told her father about the sida's escapade during the virk and the flower she had accepted. She herself had undermined the princess' confidence in her by succumbing to her feelings. Rulers like Ilirra do not forgive mistakes. The closer you are to the throne, the colder the stone in your chest. No feelings, no attachments that interfere with the fulfillment of the master's will, NOTHING. Ania had spent more than two centuries already behind the prince, like ice, an impregnable fortress, a secret weapon that reads strangers' faces and thoughts like an open book. She had never complained to anyone, ever, preferring to keep everything to herself. But life in the palace was killing her slowly and surely. True, she survived the Ritual at ten years old. But had she known then what she would have to face, Ania might have preferred death. When she was a child, she had been exploring a tunnel when she became the victim of an avalanche. The mages threw up their hands, but her father knew there was another way to possibly save her—the Ritual. Persuading the dragons who lived nearby to try was not difficult. He believed she could endure the pain of the incarnation. That was the last day she saw her father. The prince flew in from the capital and took her to live with him. He did not give blood and had no right to do with her life as he would, but he was the ruler, and he took their daughter from two old dragons and one elf. Ora was interested in the rare phenomenon. Usually ritual children over five or six years do not tolerate the pain. They perish. She was raised in the palace, inspiring loyalty to the ruling clan. They gave her the best education, but could not give her a family or a home. For two hundred years there was an emptiness around her. Ania secretly dreamed of a house—a small cozy cave far away in the mountains, the strong wings of her beloved dragon, under which it was so warm on cold nights, and of children. Palace life, with all its vices, passed by her. Ora kept a close eye on his "ice" and held her on a short leash, like a rix. The prince was well aware that if the young dragoness formed any attachment, it would instantly affect the quality of her work, and did not allow her unnecessary contacts. Outwardly, Ania resigned herself, hiding a rebellion in her soul, subconsciously wishing to escape from the vicious circle and finally live her life. The sida did not like the prince's court, where lies and hypocrisy were ubiquitous. It corroded the very essence of human nature. The woman was afraid of eventually turning into one of the poisonous creatures at the master's throne. Maybe that's why she so recklessly rushed into the abyss of passion for Andy? On the other hand, that action was not so reckless in the light of the desires deep in her soul. The blue-eyed man, enveloped in a halo of mystery, nevertheless seemed an island of reliability amid the raging sea of empty passions and politics around her. He did not care about the dragons, the virk, or lofty goals. He lived and let others live. He was the first to pay attention to her as a woman and was not afraid to reveal his feelings. "What will be, will be!" she said to herself, succumbing to an internal rebellion and the heat of passion. She made up her mind right then and had never regretted what she did. She decided she did not give a crap about all the gossip and obstruction. She did not betray the master. Although Andy did not confess to his second hypostasis, she did not need him to. She would have to be blind not to see the wings on his back. She did not need the strange eyes to alert her to what he really was.

Their fleeting connection left an indelible mark. The prince understood her motivations, both lying on the surface and hidden. The result of an unpleasant conversation was a promise to let her go her own way after the end of the negotiations. Negotiations ended; the master did not keep his word. She left of her own accord, albeit with someone's help.

Ania looked at Andy. Her beloved was leaning on the parapet and seemed to be examining the city, but the look in his eyes told her that he was hovering somewhere else. There was a deep fold between his eyebrows, which testified to the weightiness of his thoughts. The elf was not mistaken. Andy was going over options for what he would say at the conclave and trying to systematize information about the principality and the war.

Something strange was happening in the country. The war, which began according to the classical canons, had flowed into some other phase. Illusht, who managed to visit the capital, shared news and observations. According to the feline princess, it appeared that the emperor deliberately held the army led by his son back from the lightning strike deep inside the country. Hazgar gave the spring of popular discontent time to unwind, reasonably hoping that the pro-imperial forces would begin subversive work and would face opposition from the Prince's loyal subjects and numerous refugees from recently captured princedoms in the east of the continent. Civil unrest was useful to the invaders: the weaker the stubborn elderly emerald dragon's power, the easier it would be to remove the pieces of pie that fell from his claws. The union of the Great Mother and the prince to the emperor and his hangers-on was like a bone in the throat.

The Miur watched and waited; the Miur feared. His "older sister" once said she had something with which to meet the hordes of her northern neighbor. The feline race far outdid their likely associates and opponents in the fields of tech and armaments—that was no secret. But not one crowned neighbor suspected the giant megalith-accumulators resting in the lower caves and deep-sea underground lakes, the bottom of which were lined with tiles made of rock crystal and malachite. It wasn't out of the goodness of their hearts that the cats did not touch the Mellorny forests and allowed the elves to live on the surface. Thousands of special lenses buried near the surface collected the mana produced by the "trees of life" and transferred it to distribution centers, where real magician dispatchers decided where to direct the energy flow—to put it into action or disperse over Mount Lidar. The Great Mother had her reasons for masking certain areas of the brain before the confluence. Had Andy seen the main underground storehouse of mana, he could have become ill. During the virk he learned that every self-respecting monarch has mobile sources of mana. Ten-ton blocks were used for this purpose, consisting entirely of artificially grown crystals or rock crystal. The prince had fifteen or twenty such megaliths; the emperor owned two hundred. Ilirra did not say anything about the military "treasury" to the Great Mother; the dragon simply did not know that the white-haired cat had about two thousand "batteries" on hand. A large lake located at a depth of one mile from the surface served as the main "battery." Hundreds of rectangular megaliths stood in slender rows on its leveled bottom. The tension of the magic field made one's hair literally stand on end, one's clothes light up and the water boil. It was hotter in the giant cave than in a Russian banya. Dozens of pipes led steam and water to the surface; an equal amount of pipes were used to supply cold water. Most of the springs that gave hot healing water and originated on the slopes and ravines of the great mountain were of artificial origin. Outsiders and the curious were told a fairy tale about volcanic activity. Their neighbors did not know about yet another mystery that Andy had to face, that is, to encounter: he spent several days in this "mystery's" shoes. Thousands of puppet cocoons were awaiting their time. Evael, in conversation with him, left aside an important detail in failing to mention that right before the evacuation, the miur ruler's volunteers went through the human and elven settlements on the surface of the mountain with a fine-tooth comb. The warriors were interested in recruiting tall young men and women as "puppeteers." The Great Mother announced the mandatory mobilization…

"Raygor!" Ruigar said breathlessly, leaping across the parapet and stopping at the edge of the observation platform. "The pearl of the Black Cliffs!" A wide wave of his hand outlined the white stone city lying below.

Raygor was somewhat like Orten: wide streets and avenues, numerous islands of greenery, sparkling ponds, bright illumination.

Complementing the street lighting, three powerful magical lights hung over the city. From the few small suns or moons, all buildings and people cast three or four dull shadows.

An unaided look could distinguish the areas where dragons lived from human quarters. Hundreds of different palaces had one thing in common: broad landing areas. The higher the dragon was on the social hierarchy, the higher his or her house was. Many buildings seemed to float out of the thick forests of the mountains surrounding the city and hung on steep slopes hundreds of feet above the ground. Only having wings could allow you to reach those dwellings. Despite the war, the city continued to live a bustling, unbridled life. From the height of the portal site, it was clear that the streets were full of idle public. Dozens of dragons constantly flew up and down on wide takeoff patches among the streets. "Please, follow me," Ruigar's voice forced him to look away from the beautiful landscape. "In order to get to the square where the conclave is meeting,...."

"Wait," Andy interrupted him. He scratched his right leg and side. "First, we need to find some sort of merchant selling ready-made clothing and change. I do not deny you are wearing exquisite garb, but any mediocre mage could see through the illusion and your cheeks will become a spectacle for all to see... not those ones," he said, pointing to his face. "And I could use some floral oils."

Ania stepped away from him a couple of steps, sniffed and, recognizing the scent as that of a dragon, tilted her head to one side, saying:

"Are you molting? Since when?"

"It is the second day."

"For some reason, when I am standing next to you, my mood falls, and I feel like, well, killing someone. How are you holding it in? You did not look flustered at all during negotiations with the prince."

"Well, yes. Not at all?" Andy roared. He shouldn't have scratched himself. Now he was itching all over, especially his rear end. The tail that did not exist at the time reminded him of itself with thousands of light jabs. He immediately wanted to smash his head against a wall.

"It is strange. Molting season is over," Ruigar interjected

into the conversation. He could not smell odors yet; it took several hours for the tortured nose to recover.

"For some reason, my molt does not fit in with the spring cycles of Nelita. I hold it in using willpower and a cocoon of impenetrability."

"The key," Ania said softly. "You showed the key to the prince…."

"I should not have done that. He should not have found out about my little secret."

"You cannot change the past."

"Exactly! It can be repeated, though. Human stupidity is inexhaustible. I will repeat the trick with the key at the conclave, but I will put it number one during that circus performance. I do not need everyone, but I need some volunteers. They will consciously take risks in order to get out of sight of the emperor's servants."

Andy caught himself in a strange pathetic gesture, pointing to the horizon and trying to capture the uncapturable. "Seems molting is ticking me off. You guys, please, just in case, be ready to remind me that today is not the most suitable day for verbal battles. The main thing is not to overexert myself. I will kill someone, and then I will be upset."

* * *

They made it to the store and the conclave on time. The meeting, or "flying" of the representatives of the dragon families, had not yet begun when Ruigar, taking advantage of the fact that news of his duplicity had not yet reached the capital, pressed on the authorities and made sure that they were first in line to speak. A wide platform was erected in the center of the square for the dragons who would be speaking.

Andy stood at the entrance and looked at the arriving dragons. Yep: the first rows were for the rich and famous, the second for those who supported the first, and the rest were for the

307

crowd. At last, wings stopped flapping in the sky; a tense silence settled on the crowd. Everyone had arrived, they could start. Andy felt a hand on his shoulder and turned around:

"Ania?"

"Give it to them good." The sida glanced towards the square full of dragons. "It is a shame I do not know what your real name is."

"I came, I saw, I conquered!" Andy smiled. "It is time. You will hear my real name in a few minutes."

Ania followed him with her gaze and returned to the detachment.

"I am curious: why did you follow him?" Ruigar asked quietly, so as not to attract the attention of the Miur.

"Why did you?"

"I did not have any other choices."

"I understand. It was either the executioner's ax or life and an uncertain future which might end with that very executioner's ax. Did you give an immutable pledge?"

"Yes, and a blood oath. We are now connected."

Ania glanced at the platform and shook her head. She was making up her mind about something. She then stared at the former governor and said:

"If you even think of double-crossing him, I will kill you myself."

"To what do I owe the honor? Do you know who he is? No?"

Ania said nothing. It was enough for her that he was Andy, the future father of her children. The rest didn't matter.

"Most honored guests," a loud voice said from the platform. "I would like to inform you of the true reasons for the war and make you an offer. Unfortunately, Prince Ora refused to listen to me and said "no" to what I am about to suggest."

A quiet concerned hum of voices rang out among the crowd.

"Quiet!" the chosen administrator of the conclave barked. "Go on."

"Thank you," Andy ceremoniously bowed to the old dragon. "The emperor is trying to take control of the interplanetary portals and seize the key. I am the guardian of the key."

"Liar!" One of the scaly beasts couldn't hold back. Andy closed his eyes.

"I suggest relocating to Ilanta."

"The boy is lying and wasting our time. In whose name can he suggest relocation? Where is the key? Let him show us, or stop this nonsense!" the same doubter went on.

His itch had become unbearable; he so wanted to kill the loud-mouth. The flower oil was not as effective as expected. Some dragons supported the loud-mouth and joined him in demanding that Andy show them the key. Like wolves at their counsel in Kipling, only instead of Shere Khan, they were pulling Hazgar by the tail.

"Silence!" the administrator shut them up.

"On behalf of my mother," Andy went all-in. He realized that competing with them with his narrow experience of intrigue and verbal battles was useless. To achieve victory, he had to drive the opponents into a state of shock and deprive them of the upper hand, but many dragons' eyes had glazed over already. You do not have to be a genius of logical deduction to understand that the winged race is actively calculating the situation and preparing logical traps for the subsequent conversation. "My name is Kerrovitarr Gurd; I am the son of Empress Jagirra," he cried out, changing his hypostasis and summoning the key.

The hum of the crowd hushed like as if someone had waved a magic wand. The crystal dragon, dropping his old scales, turned to Ania:

"How do you like me now?" he asked, scratching his right side with his hind paw.

Celestial Empire. The emperor's southern high command...

A bright sunbeam, reflecting off a black marble column that was so polished you could see your reflection in it, fell on the

309

face of the old dragon lying on the very edge of a wide rocky platform. The sun was gradually rising higher and higher. Following the luminary, the ray slid along the dull golden scales on the nose of the ancient monster. The dragon, resembling a stone statue, did not seem to notice the hot touch of the sunny ray. The living mass of the dragon's body still did not move, not noticing the gusts of wind as they rose the slightest swirl of dust, nor the obsidian floor, the same color as the columns, nor the tile remnants of last year's grass on the ground below. The sunbeams, reflecting off the bodyguards' polished armor as they stood, frozen and silent like statues, periodically turned into company for a large bright spot that had fallen from the column and touched the eyes of the Lord of the Sky. But he only closed his eyelids momentarily, not making one movement to turn away. Despite the master's periodic glance in their direction, the bodyguards stayed still; they knew that in such moments, the master should not be bothered about trifles or about anything at all: behind the mask of imperturbability lay carefully hidden vexation, which could turn out to be something particularly unpleasant for any madman who dared to interrupt the Lord's meditation or to cast an unguarded look at him.

The oppressive silence was disturbed by the sound of footsteps coming from the direction of a high arc located near the rock wall and covered by the shining haze of a subspace passageway. The emperor closed his eyes and listened. Sometimes he loved, as now, determining the state of a guest purely by sound. A firm step and the resounding clatter of riding boots spoke of the visitor's confidence, but the creak of thick leather gloves clenched in a fist, and the slight whistling of the air drawn in through the nose destroyed the original impression. The subtle smell of sweat was indicative of the excitement and touch of fear that the tall young man was experiencing as he stood ten feet from the massive head of the old crystal dragon.

"Sit down, son." The resonant bass, echoing among the columns, made the heir shiver nervously. The emperor secretly laughed to himself, although he did not show it. Obeying the unobtrusive gesture of his clawed paw, two comfortable chairs and a small table arose between him and the frozen young man. Two graceful elves emerged from the arc with trays in their hands. Without looking up from the floor tiles, they momentarily set the table, after which, bowing low and backing away, they disappeared into the silvery haze. "What are you standing there for?" asked the dragon sympathetically and immediately roared: "Sit in the armchair! Very good. Tell me, son."

The young man, who could have passed equally well for twenty-five or thirty-five (sometimes there are people who are "frozen" on the threshold of some age line), nervously swished his hand over his head, pushing down his short spiky hair.

"What is it you want to know, Your Majesty?"

The emperor immediately changed hypostasis, took a step forward and slapped the heir across the face, hard.

"Why is that puppy still alive?" he asked, watching as the red contours of the monarch's hand appeared on his son's cheek. After standing for a few seconds, the emperor took a step back and sank into the second chair. "You do not have to answer. I am aware of your excuses."

"Your Majesty, he is closely guarded. My agents have made four attempts; none of the killers came back. The scum killed the last pair personally, using an unknown kind of magic," the heir swallowed, "all that was left of the dragons was a pair of dried mummies."

"That is not an excuse. Do you understand that every day we lose our political foothold?"

"Yes, sire!"

"You understand that, and you're not doing anything about it?!" the emperor asked quietly. The heir went pale. The bodyguards tried to blend in to the shadows. A shock wave shot from the monarch in all directions. Hazgar took a deep breath and calmed down. "You decided to play soldiers, son. I hoped that I brought you up as a manager, but every day I am more and more convinced that my heir has become a stubborn warrior, unable to get out of his boots and assess the situation as a future ruler, rather than as a general. I am disappointed."

"Your majesty, I acknowledge my guilt fully and am prepared to undergo the necessary punishment." The heir hung his head.

"Undergo it you will." Hazgar smiled carnivorously. "You

are my son. You are given much, but much is expected from you."

The emperor took a bottle of effervescent wine from an ice bucket and filled two wine glasses with the burgundy liquid. He sipped the wine and thought for a long time. His son, trying not to disturb his parent, froze with the glass in his hand.

Hazgar was used to setting the conditions for others and imposing the rules of the game, but the appearance of a dragon in Raygor who called himself the son of the empress threw him for a loop. The boy stated that he was the keeper of the key to the interplanetary portals and could organize resettlement, for which they would need to win back the southern complex, which was occupied by Imperial legions. He backed up his words with evidence, the key, and the coat of arms—an unexpected move which violated the usual ideas about the rules of political games. Hmm, what rules are there in big politics, besides survival of the fittest? The conclave nearly ended in a mass brawl. Arriving in the capital, the prince found a real tangle of his subjects and titled individuals from other principalities snarling at one another. The boy was not there; the administrator sent him to his own fortress. There was a split in the country....

The Emperor himself had several times put on a spectacle involving an impostor with a supposed claim to the throne and had cleaned out the dissatisfied parties well, but now the situation had gotten out of control. The Great Mother unexpectedly supported the pretender. Earlier, the ruler of the Miur tried to keep aloof from worldly games. Now the dam of voluntary seclusion had burst. The blasted cat! What horrible timing. She suddenly decided to stick her nose into the situation he was planning to resolve with Prince Ora alone. In one move, he could end the war and turn the prince from an enemy into an ally. However, not all was lost. He had not yet abandoned his plans, because Ora had not refused him, only asked for time to think. In any case, the prince's options were win-win, but could he keep dancing on the edge of a knife? He hoped the cute cats and their "mother" would not take the emerald dragon by the throat. No, they shouldn't be able to. They ruined relations with him by betting on the new candidate for the imperial throne, or was "mother" sure of victory? What was she trying to achieve and what goals was she pursuing? Manyfaces, how tangled it all was! Where could he find a foothold? He sorely lacked reliable information. A whole fiver had passed since the conclave, but he still did not know what was going on around the new leader of the resistance, what forces he had on his side or what actions he intended to take. And it was no wonder: those who have experience in the art of being invisible had gathered around the jerk. Some of them had been organizing personal security for over a hundred years and some old farts for over a thousand. One thing was certain: the boy was coordinating his steps with the Miur ruler. The channel was maintained through the elves, but how? How, Manyfaces?! The emperor reached out his hand to the bottle and poured himself another glass. His son was not offered wine. The thorn in his side had the support of the clans of dragons who fought against the Celestial Empire three thousand years ago. Not every one, but enough to ensure that in one day, an independent power pole was formed in the principality, independent of the prince. Sources on the other side of the front informed him that the elves were acting not only as "signalers," but the refugees had, in just a couple of days, formed a fully combat-ready militia, strengthened by a supply of a large batch of modern weapons. The impostor concluded an agreement with the ruler of the miur and the head of the council of forest elves. The treaty with the miur was so wide-reaching that the prince, who had met with the daughter of the Great Mother a day before, was dumbfounded by the cats' impudence and treachery. The "son" and his entourage did not bother with politesse or etiquette, but he acted with all the grace of a wolf, breaking all the traditions. Which was understandable: time was working against them. The shabby ruler did not care at all for her reputation: several portals were opened on the ancestral lands of the old lunatic Turgar, who was the administrator of the conclave. His spies were not able to find out how many. But he knew that they spilled prides of combat cats out of their arcs like locusts. An hour later, the clan lands were covered with protective domes and shields. Attempts by the prince's internal guards to disarm the uninvited guests were met with fierce resistance, which ended in the defeat of the legitimate ruler's forces. The prince was again left on the sidelines, but some old dragons, remembering the old emperor, Jagirra's father, who had previously held neutral positions, decided to side with Jagirra's so-called son, along with their clans. Ora was between a rock and a hard place, one on one with the imperial army advancing on the capital of the principality. Hazgar rubbed his forearm. The family coat of arms burned like fire. The magical drawing did not lie; the young Kerrovitarr belonged to the ruling clan. It turned out that his niece had found a mate and produced offspring. How wise.... The girl had matured. Now if only he knew how many children she had and how she managed to give birth to a dragon while in elf hypostasis. Had she thrown off the "snare" spell? Should not have been able to. It was not within her power to break such a curse, especially when tied by her own family's blood. Or did the miur mages manage to affect the fetus, and it developed in human form? If the assumption was true, then the "beloved niece" could produce more than one small heir, and Hazgar had no desire to catch another "flea." He wanted to do away with Jagirra's nest once and for all. After all, she had been hiding for about three thousand years. And could she have hidden anywhere else but with the miur? Perhaps, that was why the Great Mothers never supported any of the impostors. They knew where the real empress lived, and when the time came, took the side of her offspring. The beasts!

Hazgar again rubbed his shoulder and suddenly pounded his fist on the table, cursing in his soul the prince, the son who had played at war, the old cat that had emerged from her burrow, and himself, who had fallen for the child-like gambit. The pugnacious miur proved to be a dangerous and cunning opponent. She had played both prince and emperor like cornered mice. Hazgar grit his teeth. Three days ago, along the borders, all the spatial shields were restored in an unexpected way. His attempt to break through again ended in failure. The cat people easily burnt his assault legion and the thousands of mages he had allotted them. The vile scum—they did not mess around. In the borderlands, an ideal wasteland appeared with a diameter of ten leagues, an even circle, sprinkled with a thick layer of black ash. How much mana would a blow like that take? The cats do not have any true bloods. Where did they get power like that? The emperor did not dare send his superweapon into battle; he remembered well the slaughter in the mountains that took place three thousand years ago when his dragons, arranged in attacking formations, burned up like birds in a forest fire. They meant to isolate the miur from the rest of the world and starve them out. Without food supplies from the outside, they would either quickly become kind and complaisant or die from dystrophy. Hazgar was not planning to go meet them in the underground caverns; the "moms" had turned Mount Lidar into a real fortress, which was too tough for him. The presence of three dozen true bloods in reserve was not the decisive factor in a future battle.

"Your Majesty!"

The emperor turned to the voice. Near the arc, a man was bent in a low bow, in the uniform of a messenger. Hazgar grinned knowingly. The old palace lizards were afraid to butt in during his conversation with his son, but they found a decent way to do what needed to be done: they sent a human. The emperor would kill him in anger, and who cares; there are a lot of humans.... "A message for you from Prince Ora!" he said a cheerful voice and bowed even lower.

"Give it to me," Hazgar extended his hand. After handing the packet over, the messenger turned on his heels and left calmly. Neither the father nor the son caught a whiff of fear. Hazgar drummed his fingers on the table several times: an interesting human. He ought to instruct the head of security to collect a small detailed file on him. If there was nothing defamatory, he should promote the biped and bring him closer to himself.

"Your Highness, may I know what it says?" his son spoke up.

"You may. All the more so since this message concerns my heir directly." Hazgar attached his personal seal to Prince Ora's print that was on the letter, thus removing one cunning interweave. If any tried to open the letter other than the person to whom it was addressed, he would lose his hands. "Interesting," Hazgar said, looking at the thin infoplast, "what revelations does Ora want to tell? A simple letter is not enough for him."

The Emperor became absorbed in reading. At first, his face brightened, but the state of satisfaction did not last long; the third page contained a description of something unpleasant. Hazgar read the message and put it aside:

"The prince has accepted my offer, hmm, and is ready to join the campaign against the pretender."

"So easily, your majesty? Old man Ora is not so simple; he can benefit from any situation."

"How right you are. For some reason, the old man knows how to calculate the odds and agrees to become related...."

"WHAT?!"

"Ora agrees to give his daughter in marriage to the heir to the empire. I suggested forgetting the enmity and said that I will not destroy those dragons and humans faithful to His Lordship.

"But how, why? The girl just turned three hundred years old."

"Age is not a drawback to be paid attention to. Unlike you, she is able to think in the interests of the state and consciously step over the idolaters fallen at her feet. Ilirra is smart and, what is most important to you, beautiful. Her dowry is good, but it seems to me that after my death, she will rule the country, not you. The girl has a real managerial talent, far beyond yours. It is really an excellent match. Now, let us see what my crowned fellow wants to show us."

The emperor ran his finger along the lateral rib of the infoplast. A three-dimensional illusion of a huge military camp from a bird's-eye view unfolded above the serving table.

The emperor took the letter, read it again, glanced into the distance and began to listen carefully to the speech of the ghostly prince.

Principality of Ora. Turgar's ancestral lands. Andy, T minus six hours...

Andy sank in exhaustion onto the hard narrow cot. Only a little time was left; he had to sleep, had to.... Mimiv immediately appeared beside him. The cat twisted around herself a couple of times, opened her jaws, and sniffed the hide of the animal, which smelled of sweat, moth, and lily of the valley, which at the same time served as a cloak and veil, and, turning her tail, lay down next to the were-dragon. A minute later, only two sounds were left inside the curtain of silence Andy put up: Andy's rhythmic breathing (he fell asleep instantly) and Mimiv's happy purring.

Principality of Ora. Raygor. T minus six days...

Even in his worst nightmares, Andy could not have imagined the real avalanche of events that would follow his openness at the conclave. He felt as if he had served as the trigger for the ensuing political explosion. And he was not far from the truth. The heads of tribes and old clans who had fought against the self-proclaimed emperor three thousand years ago instantly evaluated the situation and accepted him as the son of the legal empress.

Turgar was the first to come to his senses. The ancient dragon looked in disbelief for a few seconds at the crystal dragon that had appeared instead of the boy, going over the disparate facts and events of the last five or six centuries in his head. The picture of the world that did not want to evolve before had now acquired a finished form and clarity. The dragon cautiously touched the key with his claw and pulled his paw away—the strong electric discharge that slipped between the artifact and the curious Lord of the Sky testified that the young strong crystal dragon was the keeper of the key, and that the key was not a fake.

Very interesting... If the boy were telling the truth, the imperial troops' unexpected intervention and the emperor's desire to take the portal became clear. Activation of the key undid part of the seals put on by the true bloods of Ilanta. But how did the key get to Nelita? Turgar was aware of the historical fact that the keys were left on the heavenly neighbor. That meant.... The old dragon looked at Kerrovitarr and the artifact hanging on his chest with a blood-red stone in the center. It can not be.... The interplanetary portals were sealed, and none of them worked, which meant the boy was a true blood and somehow able to move from planet to planet. Only true bloods possessed a practically unlimited mana reserve. Turgar looked at the square covered in dragons and locked eyes with a couple of them just as old and crazy as himself. Apparently, the same thoughts came to their minds as well. The old people nodded at his silent question and, ignoring the uproar and hubbub, began to actively make their way to the dais. Several perceptive younger heads of clans followed in the ancient dragons' wake. The wedge cut through the crowd and settled directly at the dais. The young people immediately began building a protective dome. Turgar grinned approvingly. The young male and female dragons were much more intelligent than he thought. They quickly calculated the chances of survival of their families and clans in the besieged country and decided to join the guardian of the key. The possibility of avoiding inevitable death was paltry; the hope of a successful outcome was much preferred. Even if some dragons perished while attacking the captured portal, the death of several members of the clan does not mean the disappearance of the whole clan. It was a chance, a real chance to survive. They were the first who seized by its elusive tail. None of them had illusions, they knew that the emperor would somehow or another eventually suppress the principality, and with it all those who were opposed to his will. Hazgar's policy of complete and total destruction of opponents pushed them towards a natural alliance with the heavenly guest....

The sida stood on the platform:

"I am with you," said the elf.

The four words broke into a string of silent glances and nods.

"Please accept my service." Turgar turned gracefully to Jagirra's son, spread his wings and inclined his neck to the ground. "I remained true to your mother."

The other dragons gathered under the protective dome repeated Turgar's bow of fidelity. Andy smiled internally—the cunning, slippery lizards. The old people, through him, had pronounced a vow of service to the empress. Not to him; what was he to them? He had no regalia; no one confirmed his dignity, but there was a universal catch-all no matter how things turned out. Serving the legitimate ruler, the empress, was an honorable and noble occupation. And not bad either that the vow was pronounced in the presence and testimony of the young offspring of the royal family. The son would bring the right words to his mother. In the dragons' eyes, he now acted as a vehicle for the interests of the legitimate ruler, who, because of the intrigues of her uncle, was holed up on another planet. Andy did not know how to read thoughts, but his sixth or seventh sense guessed at the hidden fears and hopes of the tribesmen gathered at the platform.

"It will be difficult," he said. "But with your help, WE will overcome all difficulties."

He emphasized the word "we," which did not go unnoticed. Everyone understood the underlying statement. The keeper of the key was not going to storm the imperial fortifications alone. He would require everyone to make every possible effort to successfully complete the evacuation from the planet. The boy was no fool. Well, they were willing to take a chance; life left them no other choice.

"I suggest we gather in another place." Turgar looked at Andy with an expressive look, "it is not safe in the capital. With your appearance, Hazgar's agents may become active, probably already have."

"I support that," Andy answered. Brevity, as is well known, is the sister of talent, and the grandfather should be supported. In addition, intuition was advising Andy to keep him closer, and what better moment than now, right away, to nominate the manager for one of the main roles. Not only would it be nice for Turgar, Andy could take some of the heat off himself by doing so. The ancient dragon had been brewed for thousands of years in a cauldron of intrigues and could teach him a lot. A small gesture of trust can be more useful than a chest of gold. "Do you have any suggestions?"

"I ask you to honor my ancestral nest with your presence. There, no one can stop us." Just as Andy suspected—Turgar was positioning himself in the role of his right wing, blessed is he who believes.

"Alright." Andy quickly glanced at the others. The dragons silently agreed with Turgar; no one objected, so the position was chosen. Apparently, the old man enjoyed great authority.

"I think no one will be offended if I voluntarily withdraw from myself the duties of administrator. We need to fly to the eastern portal site and from there teleport to my nest."

"I agree," Andy answered, "but I have one obstacle."

"What obstacle?" Turgar raised his wing. He spoke for all Jagirra's supporters.

"Irran!" The feline warriors walked up onto the platform. "The miur cannot fly."

Behind the warriors, one of Evael's mages coughed:

"Elves too are more or less earthbound."

Turgar twitched his wings.

"Uh...."

"The 'ghosts' do not serve my sister. These warriors swore an oath to me," Andy interrupted, not revealing the details of the oath. He laid one more trump card on the table. He had to see how the philosophers would take his calling the Great Mother "sister." In fact, he had almost admitted kinship with the miur. Much depended on the reaction of the Lords of the Sky surrounding him. This was a test of their attitude towards extensive cooperation between dragons and miur. There were no other options for him. Andy was not accustomed to throwing words around, promising Asha he would relocate some of the cats to Ilanta and assist in the removal of the ancient vow, and then not doing it. He was not going to give up obligations, not even for the sake of the dragons.

"Sister?" one of the shocked tribesmen asked. The news knocked the ground out from under them. The ruler of the threatening miur had allowed him to call her "sister." It was incredible. If anyone was tormented by lingering doubts about Kerrovitarr's belonging to the ruling family, they were disbanded definitively. The miur would never support a pretender.

"There is enough room on our backs," Turgar smirked. "Whoever wants to join me, you know where to find me. Let us fly...."

The dragons withstood the test.

* * *

And then things got real. The political and military whirlpools merged into one terrible funnel and dragged their unlucky victim down. The fiver swept by in an instant, marked in his memory by a torn line of events. Over the incomplete week, he further distanced himself from his human side, moving to the next stage of perception of the world. It's hard to be yourself when you're watching the familiar world of thousands of humans, elves, Miur, and dragons collapse due to your decisions. If it weren't for Ania and Lilly, who arrived in the camp the next day with an army of elves and humans from the border, Andy would certainly have failed. The people close to him served as an anchor, restraining him from reckless actions. Ania was always there, and Lilly... Evael laughed that he now had two sons and did not care who was the restless girl's real father. Andy did not know that Turgar had sort of cornered the old elf and seriously questioned him about trust. The elf looked into the dragon's eyes, asked him to lie down and answered that children and cats do not mistake these sorts of things. Pure souls, like moths, are drawn to the light. Back at home he already noticed Kerrovitarr's unambiguous attitude towards children and his desire to take the girl under his wing, to protect her from dangers. Dragons have many negative features, but their remarkable paternal instinct outweighed everything. And yes, he completely trusted Kerr-Andy. To the question "why," Evael cleared his throat and demanded an oath of silence from Turgar. The dragon hesitated for a few minutes, but curiosity got the better of him. The elf maintained a theatrical pause and then told the ally a rumor about the merger of minds of Kerr and the Great Mother. The dragon was impressed to the tip of his tail. While he was digesting this information, Evael imperceptibly faded away.

Ruigar blossomed unexpectedly. The former governor turned out to be a real organizer. Three days later, he occupied the third place in the secret table of ranks. He took on the responsibility of building and maintaining order in the temporary camp. It was hellish work. Hundreds of dragons and thousands of people, who were fleeing their lands in whole villages and driving their flocks of cattle and other domestic animals with them, joined daily. When leaving, people burned their houses and crops; detachments of liquidators destroyed teleportation arches. The emperor's army was left only scorched earth and poisoned wells.

The old dragons really pulled out all the stops. In less than twelve hours, real headquarters and security forces were formed; a group of fifty dragons was assigned to Irran, which was responsible for the safety of the leader of the resistance. The winged race accepted being subordinate to the miur normally and did not grumble. On the first day together, they prevented two assassination attempts. Prince Ora, who had bounced back, tried to control the insurgents. But when his agents took a beating on the nose from the self-defense units consisting of dragons, elves and the hundred-fold assault forces sent by the Great Mother, all on a parity basis, he stopped attempting the use of force.

A lot of events happened during the five-day period, but it's better to go in order....

* * *

Upon arrival in this high-mountain fortress called a nest, Andy asked Nariel to contact the former village chief.

"Evael," he said to the illusion after all the ritual greetings and blah blah blah, "I will not beat around the bush. To the point: I have two requests for you. First: could you send a couple of mages to the Great Mother for communication? And second, it would be phenomenal if everyone wishing to join our cause... would come to Turgar's lands."

The old elf moved his brows and for a few seconds and disappeared from the conjured circle.

"We need a portal," he said, emerging from the hazy fog. Andy turned to Turgar. The dragon nodded and moved his head towards the two high steles located a hundred meters from the take-off platform:

"You can try to open the portal from the other side."

"Fine," Evael said. "Nariel knows our coordinates. Our mages will need yours. I have a couple of options in terms of the connection...."

Andy shook his wings, changed to his human form and, wearing only his birthday suit, walked right up to the illusory elf:

"Perhaps you want to say that you have... a channel that allows communication with Asha?"

"Yes," Evael wasn't perturbed by the suggestion. "Do you remember our old town mage, Viriel? He is still in the Miur city.... You could cover yourself, Andy, although you will not frighten

Lilly with the sight of a naked man." The old elf slowly smiled. "In an hour," he said, the smile instantly disappearing. The illusion went out.

"What do you need to speak to the Great Mother for now?" Turgar leaned over Andy.

"We need to agree on and coordinate our actions. The ruler can allocate weapons and help with the construction of portals, or do you think that without help from outside we can capture the portal?"

The dragon pondered.

"Maybe we were wrong and reckless to follow you without thinking, but there is no turning back. Do you want to add anything?"

"She is on board," Andy answered. "Ancient vows," he said into the fog.

The winged old dragons nodded unanimously. Whether they believed or pretended to believe, in any case, everyone would check and recheck the information through their own channels. Many vows were given in ancient times; Andy did not doubt that the persistent dragons would unearth an abyss of interesting facts which Asha failed to mention. Let them. The more clues he had, the easier it would be to keep the ally in check. He needed an equal or slightly dependent partner, rather than a puppeteer dictating the conditions to him. While the miur and the dragons who decided to leave were directly dependent on him, they could do nothing but follow in his wake: they had bets on him in a gamble, where the stakes were life itself. In fact, before moving, they would obey him, not unquestioningly, but not openly contradicting him. No one was safe from the intrigues and scandals that could be uncovered, especially in such a motley company as was supposed to gather in Turgar's ancestral lands. After the "move," all would be peace, love, and friendship at first, but then they would start to tear the blanket apart. He had to stock up on as many pressure levers as possible and use them accordingly in time if necessary.

He chuckled to himself. Jagirra would throw a fit and have more than one thing to say about it.

Andy scratched his buttocks furiously, blushed, and

changed hypostasis.

"We have time before the magical communication session with the Great Mother. I propose distributing responsibilities. Any suggestions?"

Those present began to think about it. That's right, let them think in the right direction. Turgar's, Ruigar's, Ania's, and a couple of old dragons' eyes glistened. They saw Kerrovitarr's game through and through. Yes, they would definitely think in the right direction. Andy shivered. What had he gotten himself into this time?

* * *

"Attention! Countdown! Ten... nine...." Several young dragons had congregated behind Nariel and activated spatial beacons. Ten minutes ago, Evael got on the "phone" and told Andy about his conversation a half an hour earlier with the Great Mother. (He was fast. Andy got the impression Viriel didn't leave the miur's side for one second, and she was actually just waiting for the signal to speak and act.) The ruler expressed her wish to personally negotiate with Andy and the heads of the clans who supported him. In order to configure the communication channel, they needed to set the beacons in action, which is what the "signalers" were now working on, under Evael's supervision. "...One! Go!"

"Manyfaces, what is happening?" Ruigar voiced the question on everyone's mind, stepping back from the large glowing ball that arose in the middle of the communication circle.

The ball, emitting a blinding raspberry glow, quickly grew in size. The delegation of negotiators headed by Andy, who was in human form this time, slowly backed off and built protective shields. Irran's Miur and the arms bearers of the fortress gunners immediately brought the weapon into combat position and aimed it at the communication platform. The magicians activated their defensive amulets. In a second, the fortress bristled with all sorts of weapons; the soldiers prepared combat spells. The crimson ball momentarily faded, after which it sharply increased in size and turned into a luminous arc.

"A portal!" Turgar gasped.

For a few seconds, nothing happened. Dozens of pairs of eyes stared silently at the silvery haze. Right when the expectation reached its climax, the haze broke and revealed two tall miur in ritual blue saris, which signaled the purity of the visitors' thoughts. The cats held white shields with the inside facing the others, another indication that the guests came in peace.

The first to snap out of it was Turgar.

"Lower your weapons," he cried, realizing what was about to happen. "Clear the platform!"

The Miur in the saris majestically moved away from the arch and fell to their knees; the "ghosts" of the Great Mother's personal guard, encased in mimicry armor, descended onto the pavement. Following the guard came standard bearers, holding the state standards and the ruler's personal standards. Andy made a sign to Ania and Turgar to remain in place and shot a glance in Irran's direction. The warrior shouted something guttural, took her gunner, and in three seconds, arranged her detachment behind Andy. A dozen dragons in combat armor with the emblems of the Turgar clan joined the miur. The guard of honor was ready.

Andy mentally thanked Asha from the bottom of his heart for being delayed with the exit and not letting those meeting her fall in the dirt. True, in along with gratitude, he was furious at her for the trick with the portal. A drama queen, Targ take her!

"Let the way be pure!" Andy and the Great Mother bowed low to one another at the same time. He had somehow picked up on the strange ritual greeting while he was in the Miur city and could not understand its meaning until he asked Illusht to explain the sacred significance. Without boasting, his "sister" explained that in this way the contracting parties greet each other and demonstrate the purity of their thoughts and intentions, and that they will make every effort for mutual understanding, as well as for the speedy development of a solution that is to the negotiators' liking. The phrase also means that in the negotiations there are no insurmountable obstacles for the parties.

Before he could straighten his back, he heard hard hurried steps behind him. Acting strictly according to protocol, Turgar and the heads of the families came up to them. As a result, the ritual of mutual greetings lasted fifteen minutes. It was a state visit, Targ take it. The old dragons had not foregone one iota of prescribed rituals and diplomatic protocols for centuries, hiding their initial confusion behind the formalism. Andy got angry, and the Miur ruler cast a sidelong glance at him and enjoyed the situation, Targ it all!

* * *

The negotiations dragged on until morning. Andy just could not imagine that in a few hours so many questions would be raised. The whole time he modestly kept aloof, occasionally nodding in the right places and giving the reins of government to Turgar's capable paws. The old dragon and the ruler deserved each other. It was obvious that both derived real pleasure from conducting joint negotiations, the stupid formalists. The third party was the elusive Evael, elected at the elves' emergency meeting as the temporary head of all the clans. For two hours, Andy suffered stoically, grit his teeth, and tugged at his hands, and then apologized, and left the huge meeting room, which could freely accommodate three dozen dragons.

"What happened? asked the Great Mother.

"Molting time," Turgar answered for him. "Shall we continue?"

And they continued, while Andy changed hypostasis and for a good hour, scattering the old scales away, rubbed himself against the fortress walls.

The ways of the negotiators turned out to be pure. The question was whether the topics under discussion obstructed the agreements reached between Prince Ora and the Great Mother. Asha showed him the final communique, in which it was stated that the Great Mother undertook to protect the northeastern borders, to provide a certain amount of weapons (the list was attached) and, upon agreement with the prince, to strike at the provisions bases of the emperor's southern army. That was it. The cautious ruler of the principality was afraid to bind himself with obligations, and she did not insist. The reigning Miur demonstrated clearly how in reality one could have one's fish and eat it too. On the one hand, she would abide by the letter of her contract with Ora, remaining, as it were, uninvolved. On the other hand, in sending Andy to do her dirty work, she was widening the divide in the principality among the dragons. Asha believed that Kerrovitarr would find support among the dragons. Closer to noon, agreements were reached on all points of interest to the parties, and Asha departed, but the arc of the induced portal did not close.

An hour before the final point in the negotiations, Asha, Turgar, Andy, the illusory-ghost Evael and Nariel, providing communication, remained in the hall. Andy took from his pocket an information crystal with a map and pointed at the interplanetary cargo portal three hundred leagues north of the Celestial Empire's southern border. The attack was scheduled for the sixth day; delaying any further was ill-advised....

No sooner had the ruler's tail disappeared into the silvery haze than from it emerged platforms loaded with supplies. Armaments, tents, armor fitted for humans and elves, building blocks for portals and, last but not least, a real royal gift—five charged megaliths. At three o'clock in the afternoon, the magicians built another portal, through which Evael's elves and humans began to arrive at the wide valley below the fortress. Andy took Ania with him and personally met the cunning old elf, but before he could hug the gray-haired elf, Lilly hung on his neck, and Mimiv drew up at his feet with a plaintive meow. Embarrassed, red as a lobster, Andy stroked the girl's hair, not noticing the wide smiles of the soldiers and refugees emerging from the arc and of Ruigar, who was nearby, who saw the ruthless killer in a whole new light. For the former governor, a busy workday was just beginning. He needed to accommodate thousands of people, provide shelter, food and water, build pens for cattle, and that was only the beginning.... Ania, having lost her mask of cold estrangement, was standing on the sidelines and flapping her eyelashes in amazement. She obviously did not expect such a manifestation of emotion. The river of people, meanwhile, did not stop flowing from the archway....

In the evening the builders arrived. A thousand miurs, under the leadership of a dozen big brains, began erecting ten portal arches: three huge dragon-intended ones and seven smaller ones for humans. On the anti-gravity platforms, a dozen megaliths were disguised among the building blocks. Real anti-aircraft devices arrived with the builders. The cats brought strange, luminous structures resembling satellite dishes and installed them at all the highest points around the valley where the portals were. The Great Mother took her obligations as an ally seriously. It was terrible to imagine what preparations were being made in the foothill cities.

Day by day the camp grew. By the evening of the fifth day, there were about one hundred and fifty thousand humans and elves and about two thousand dragons in the valley.

On the morning of the fifth day, Andy was attacked by Targ knows what kind of assassination attempt, during which Lilly was slightly wounded and Yurish, a miur from Irran's second division (she had two, consisting originally of ten warriors each), was killed. The security services were twiddling their thumbs. The dragons who attacked Andy were met with a "moss" spell. When he saw the girl falling to the ground, he was furious and completely lost his mind, in an instant building an interweave of the blackest necromancy, which was completely unknown on Nelita. The "moss" dug into the attackers' skin and in thirty seconds drank the strength and life from them. Andy almost kicked the bucket from the amount of life energy and mana obtained in this way.... That day he realized that he was feared. The people around him were afraid of his anger and ability to quickly dry a being full of strength into an empty drum.

T minus three hours and counting....

In the camp that night, except for the crystal dragon, no one slept. The soldiers of the assault detachments were checking their weapons and cleaning their armor, gunnery and swords. The elves tested their bows. Hundreds of dragons, to the light of the magical lanterns suspended high in the sky, went over their attacking and defensive constructions for the last time, arranging V-formation while in flight, and multi-layer defensive circles. Special units of Lords of the Sky honed the settings of air traps and mine spells. Thousands of refugees packed their belongings and loaded them on carts and levitating platforms. Mile-long lines formed in front of the portals built by the miur; there was chaos all around them. Noise, hubbub, crying children, rixes yelping, and cattle mooing in protest. The animals could sense their fate and did not want to go to the slaughter. Hundreds of mages, illuminated by the neon light of the megaliths, which were charged to bursting, spun around the giant arches. Andy slept. Soon he would need all the strength he could get. Asha warned that the key would suck up his entire reserve.

The end

The Dragon Inside:

Becoming the Dragon

Wings on My Back

A Cruel Tale

Crown of Horns

Home at Last

GLOSSARY

Geography

Alatar—the largest continent on the planet of *Ilanta.*

Aria—a continent located north of Alatar.

Astal Ruigara—the north-eastern province of the Principality of Ora, borders with the Freelands and the miurs' territory.

The Scarlet Mountains—a vast mountain range located on the territory of the Celestial Empire north of the Freelands; once belonged to the miur, but three thousand years ago, all the settlements of the cat people in the Scarlet Mountains were destroyed by the Emperor Hazgar.

Ilanta—a planet.

Ilite sultanate—a state located to the east of Rimm; shares borders with the Patskoi Empire and the Steppe.

Empire of Alatar—a state existing two thousand years ago that pursued an aggressive policy of conquest. Approximately sixty percent of the total area of the continent of Alatar was subject to the Empire. The continent itself was named in honor of the Empire. Northern kingdoms such as Tantre, Mesaniya, Meriya, and Rimm were at one time secluded barbarian provinces of the Empire. As a result of civil war, the Empire of Alatar was broken into separate states and ceased to exist.

Kingdom of Mestair—a legendary human kingdom located on the territory of modern-day Taiir and the Great Principality of Mesaniya, which existed three thousand years ago during the age of the dragons. As an independent state, it was destroyed by the dragons and their allies during the war with the Forest Elves and few human states that had joined them.

Mellorny campground—the settlement of the last Forest Elves in the Freelands.

Mesaniya—A Great Principality located north of the kingdom of Tantre.

The Marble Mountains—a large mountain range crossing the northern part of Alatar from north to south. From the north, the range is bordered by the North Sea. From the south, by the Southern Rocky Ridge and the Long sea.

Nelita—The second planet in a triple solar system: Ilanta, Nelita, and Helita. Nelita is considered the dragons' native land; it was named in honor of the goddess of life, Nel. The literal translation is "eye of the goddess of life."

Ora—the principality of the dragons on the planet Nelita, formed three thousand years ago as a result of a break from the Celestial Empire; was named after the prince.

Ort—the largest river in the north of Alatar, flows across the territory of the kingdom of Tantre.

Patskoi Empire—a human state with the capital at the city of Pat. The Emperors of Pat consider themselves the heirs of the Empire of Alatar.

Celestial Empire—the largest state in Nelita, formed by the dragons over ten thousand years ago.

Rimm—a human kingdom located east of the Marble Mountains.

The Light Forest—the state of the Forest Elves, limited to the growth area of the Mellornys.

The Freelands—the foothills of the Lidar mountains, adjoins the

331

Celestial Empire, the Principality of Ora, and other principalities. De-jure does not belong to any state. It is de-facto controlled by the miurs, who consider this land theirs.

Steppe—the self-designation of the kingdom of the white orcs. Located in the east of Alatar.

Tantre—a large kingdom, second largest after the Patskoi Empire, located in the central part of north-western Alatar. Geographically limited by the Marble Mountains and the Northern and Southern Rocky Ridges. Has access to the Eastern Ocean and the Long Sea. Its capital is the city of **Kion**.

Taiir—a dukedom.

Miscellaneous

Alat, High (also known as Younger Edda), *Common*—the languages spoken on the planet Nelita.

Alert-dert—a military rank corresponding to that of captain.

Astal—a word that includes several concepts: both lord and ownership. The most accurate translation will read: "One who has taken responsibility upon him/herself. A domain, for which they answer with their honor and conscience." One of the meanings is vicegerency.

Ata-virk (**ata**—having taken, **virk**—trial)—someone who has accepted trials

Berk—a large poisonous omnivorous animal resembling an armadillo.

Chucker—a magical artifact that allows its user to throw balls of capsulized spells.

Circle of the Twelve—the ruling caste.

Concress—from the word "**concrescence.**" A bundle that attaches to a person, causing changes in people in the cocoons of the converte —the magically transformed chimera tree. Through the main bundle that joins to the person in the center of the thorax, and the bundles produced by it, there is a connection with the nervous system and an intravenous "feeding" of the person being changed, and also the departure of natural waste.

Drag—a rideable flying lizard.

Dugar—literally "mute." A magically and biologically altered person with an erased memory, the dugars possess great physical strength and extremely low intelligence, they easily obey. Used for dirty and heavy work.

Dugaria 1. The mage-derived chimera tree that enacts the magical and biological transformation of intelligent beings into dugars. 2. A prison in which people are transformed.

"Fangs"—personal bodyguards of the Emperor of the Celestial Empire.

Feather—a junior military group of twelve to fifteen rideable animals.

Fiver—a week in Nelita (five days). Month—six fivers. Every fifth day is considered a holiday.

"Ghosts"—miur intelligence agents, possessing special mimicry magic equipment that allows them to completely merge with the surrounding terrain.

The Goddesses' Eyes are what people call the planets Nelita and Helita. Helita, Nelita, and Ilanta make up the system of planets that revolve around their sun.

The Gray Horde—the collective name for all the "gray" orcs residing in the northern coastal steppes; the strongest khanate of the "gray" orcs was also called the Gray Horde.

Gross-dert (**gross-** leading, **dert-** wing)—a military rank in the air units of Tantre's army, corresponding to that of colonel.

Guardians—dragons (true blood mages), who stayed on Ilanta to guard to portals. At the time the events described herein took place, all guardians are thought to be deceased.

Gunner—a hand-held weapon, functions like a magical chucker in that it fires magic, but much more powerful. Works from a crystal accumulator, unlike a chucker, which fires spells in capsule form.

Hel—mistress of the world of the dead.

Khirud—the main god in the pantheon of the "white" orcs. Khirud the lightning-armed is the god of warriors and daredevils.

"Leaves"—elf rangers.

Manyfaces—the goddess of everything that exists.

Miurs — an intelligent magical race. In appearance much like humanized cats. Average height over eight feet tall. A matriarchal society divided into castes. Females are larger than males and play the dominant role.

The Northern Alliance—an alliance of Tantre, the Rauu Principalities, and the dwarf kingdoms.

Odin—a Norse deity.

Pound, jang—the currency of the kingdom of Tantre. Pounds come in silver and gold; jangs are small copper coins.

Quork—a large amphibian, a predator, akin to a crocodile.

Rasht—miur males who do not have pouches. They are only slightly smaller than females. Besides their lack of pouches, rasht differ from the females in their skull capacity. Females sarcastically call males "big brains" when out of earshot.

Rauu—Snow Elves. The first artificial race created by the dragons for battles against the orcs.

Rix—an animal akin to a wolverine

Roi-dert—a junior officer's rank, corresponds to that of lieutenant.

Roihe or *roihe-male*—males with pouches on their bellies for carrying the young.

Rune Keys—used for opening portals.

Sarun—male ceremonial dress.

Secret Chancellery—the state security organ in the kingdom of Tantre. It deals with political investigations, searches and torture, internal and external intelligence, counter-intelligence.

Servants of Death—helrats, priests of a cult forbidden in all countries which perverts the very name of the goddess Hel. Hunted dragons and actively promoted human sacrifice.

"Shadows"—the collective name for the warriors and operatives of the secret services in Nelita.

Shanyu — the high khan of the Gray Horde.

Shkas—degenerates, geeks, magical mutants, etc.

Sida—elves who prefer to settle in the hills.

Targ—the dwarf god whose name took on a negative connotation in almost all countries, often used as a curse word. Occupies the niche of mischief-maker and prankster, analogous to *Loki* in some sense.

Teg—the polite form of address of a nobleman; *grall*—to a mage. *Teg grall*—form of address of a noble mage. *Tain, taina*—titles for high-borns, male and female, respectively. Professor/master/mistress [first name] Teg grall (tain/taina) [last name].

Temple dwellers—the priest caste in miur society.

Tiv—a small dome-shaped house which can be grown from magically altered plants.

Trox—a large non-flying bird. Can grow up to thirteen feet high. Used as horses and hasses, as a transport animal.

True blood—a mage who, unlike others, can work directly with the astral and consciously take mana from it. Other mages can extract mana only from the planet's magical field.

Vogr—a predatory animal created by the mages of the Celestial Empire, the size of a bull, resembles a bear.

Book Recommendations:

Please remember you can download a sample of our books from our website.

Fayroll by Andrey Vasilyev is an exciting adventure story about Harriton Nikiforov, a journalist forced to write a story about the newest online craze 'Fayroll'. Along the way he meets a variety of interesting characters and finds a life changing epic quest that will change his life forever. Fayroll is available now.

About us

Litworld is an innovative global digital publishing house. Born in the minds of literature enthusiasts, Litworld's main focus is the new generation of literature.

Our mission at Litworld is to find the gems of the modern entertaining literature and bring them to English-language readers. We believe that good books should not exist in isolation, so we want to make the best fantasy novels available to all in the easiest, most accessible way, while providing our readers with the highest quality stories.

Our vision is to create a new, comprehensive publishing ecosystem where the borders of literature and culture are easier to overcome. We are happy to be part of this cause by matching the most talented and creative local authors with the latest technology and top professionals from all areas of publishing. In this way, we connect writers with their global audience.

However, let our books speak for themselves! Check out our selection, which offers series selections for all tastes—from epic or romantic fantasy to LitRPG. You decide which world to discover next!

[1] The OBKhSS was the Soviet financial police. They were responsible for regulating economic laws in the fight against theft of socialist property.

[2] The most common nickname for the KGB, the Soviet Committee for State Security, when it existed.

[3] The main task of the laboratory, a part of the US Department of Energy, is the development and maintenance of nuclear weapons systems. It also conducts a variety of studies on issues related to national security, non-proliferation of nuclear weapons, energy and environmental protection.

[4] A reference to the slogan of the Pioneers, a mass youth organization of the Soviet Union for children of age 10–15 that existed between 1922 and 1991.

[5] A reference to the Orwellian concept of "thought police," also to Stalin's Great Purge.

[6] In Irish, a geas is an idiosyncratic taboo, whether of obligation or prohibition, similar to being under a vow.

[7] Fifty pounds.

[8] A double-edged knife up to one and a half feet long and two inches wide, symbolizes belonging to the ruling clan and warrior caste.

[9] Literally, "illuminated." The official title of the Great Mother.

[10] Foul language in miur, literally means "shabby tail."

98804189R00199

Made in the USA
Lexington, KY
09 September 2018